AN EXECUTIVE
DECISION

AN EXECUTIVE DECISION

Book One in the Executive Decisions trilogy

GRACE MARSHALL

Published by Xcite Books Ltd – 2012

ISBN 9781908917805

Printed and bound in the UK

Cover design by
The Design House

An Executive Decision is dedicated to that wild and wonderful and supremely unpredictable organ which keeps us alive, and keeps us in love, and keeps us in hope – the human heart.
Thank you, with all of my human heart!

A special thanks to Melanie and Helen, who were with me way back at the beginning of *An Executive Decision* and have encouraged me and cheered me on through the long journey.

Thank you, Renee and Jo and all of the lovely Ladiez at Sh! You've been a bright spot in my writing journey almost from the beginning. Not only are you a fount of information, fun, and encouragement, but you're an endless source of inspiration to me. Hugs and kisses and my deepest gratitude.

Thanks to the indomitable Hazel Cushion, and all the fabulous people at Xcite Books for making my dream of the *Executive Decision Trilogy* a reality.

Thank you, Lucy Felthouse, for cracking the PR whip, when necessary, and for staving off more than a few panic attacks for this neurotic writer. Thanks for all that you do. I couldn't have done it without you, EP!

Thank you, Kay Jaybee, for always being there and for just being your fabulous self. The journey has been so much more fun because we've shared it. You're amazing!

Thank you, Raymond, for putting up with me when I'm not my charming self and loving me anyway. Thank you for believing in me and being proud of me and easing the journey. There's no one my human heart would rather have by my side. Volim te mnogo!

Chapter One

DEE GAVE HERSELF ONE last inspection in the mirrored walls of the elevator. No tell-tale trembling or sweating; the stage fright was all hidden beneath a well-polished exterior. How could she be this tense? She'd been in business with the big boys long enough to have nerves of steel. But this was Ellison Thorne she was meeting. The man was in a league of his own. She'd waited three years for this opportunity, and she was determined he wouldn't see the mass of quavering jelly beneath the calm.

But when she reached the executive suites of the Pneuma Building, Beverly Neumann beckoned Dee into her office. 'Ellis is stuck in traffic. He figures it'll be at least another half hour.'

'That's too bad.' Dee tried her best to mask her disappointment. She had a meeting with a potential head of marketing for Sportwide Extreme Adventure right after this, so there'd be no lingering if Ellis didn't arrive before her hour was up.

'I know he'll do his best to get here,' Beverly said. 'He's dying to meet the woman who threw a drink in Terrance Jamison's face at Jasper and McDowell's big New Year bash last year.'

Dee blushed. 'Not funny, Beverly. I nearly lost my job over that.' She still couldn't figure why Jamison hadn't sued her ass off or had henchmen break the legs of her family and close friends. Even now it made her nervous that he'd taken it so graciously.

'And if you had, there'd have been ten companies in line to hire you, including Pneuma Inc.,' Beverly said. 'It was so

1

worth it. If only I'd had the presence of mind to record it all on my iPhone, you'd have been the queen of YouTube. You seldom get that calibre of entertainment at a corporate New Year's party.'

Dee glanced at the front page of *The Oregonian* lying on Beverly's desk. There was a photo of Ellis shaking hands with the governor. The caption read *Ellison Thorne, a force of nature working for nature.* She studied the image, one of many she'd seen of him. Though there was a warmth about him in photos, it was never blatant, always slightly distant. She was familiar with that distance. She'd been accused of it herself by colleagues who just didn't understand her sense of focus.

She lingered over the photo, admiring again the strong geography of his face laid bare by short brown hair with its patina of bronze. The well-defined jaw and firm brow created a fortress of sorts, keeping his emotions and thoughts from the prying hordes. From it, he looked out on the world through dark amber eyes that never missed anything and never gave anything away. Heroes were like that, she thought, and she had idolised him and his company for a long time.

It was through Beverly that Dee occasionally caught more intimate glimpses of Ellison Thorne. That was a part of their meetings Dee looked forward to.

Beverly nodded to the seat in front of her desk. 'Might as well relax. He'll get here when he gets here.' She turned her attention to the forest of plants behind her desk and began misting the broad leaves of something that must have come straight from *The Little Shop of Horrors*. Thanks to Beverly's insistence that a green workplace actually be green, the whole ten-storey, cantilevered edifice of the Pneuma Building was one colossal hanging garden. It was healthier that way, she'd said.

Dee sat down a safe distance from the sinister-looking foliage. 'Is Ellis still giving you a hard time about your trip to Brazil?'

'Yep,' Beverly said. 'One minute he's treating me like an old lady, saying it's too dangerous for someone my age to go trekking through the jungle, and the next he's telling me I'm too young to retire and he absolutely can't run the place without me for at least five more years.' She brushed pollen from the jacket of her power suit. 'Five more years! Do you have any idea how much life a person can miss out on in five years?'

'So what will you do?' Dee asked.

'Well –' Beverly rearranged the leaves of a large fern as though it was her favourite child '– first I'm going to Brazil. I haven't had a real vacation in longer than I care to remember. And when I get back, if he doesn't find someone to replace me while I'm still here to help train them, that's just too damned bad, because in exactly one year, I'm out of here.'

'Good for you,' Dee said. 'Life's too short not to go for it when you get the chance.'

'Yes it is, isn't it? And speaking of going for it –' Beverly sat down in her chair and leaned conspiratorially across her desk '– I hear there's an accountant over at Ab Con – what's his name, the one with the dark hair that always looks like someone's been running their fingers through it? I hear he sent you flowers.'

'I recruited the best finance manager in the history of finance managers for Ab Con, Beverly. I earned every one of those flowers.'

'Earned the flowers?' Beverly frowned at her and clucked her tongue. 'What part of the man being hot for you did you not understand, sweetie?' Before Dee could cut her off at the pass, Beverly was on a roll. 'Honestly, you're hopeless, Dee Henning. I understand your focus, your drive to succeed, really I do, but I gotta wonder how you can even call it success when you're so wrapped up in your work that the only way you'll ever get laid is if they put it in the job description. And frankly, if I had my way and I was running the business world, sex would be a contract requirement.'

Dee rolled her eyes, but Beverly clasped her hands on top of her desk, doing a fair imitation of a psychoanalyst. 'I worry about you, Dee. I really do. Not having time for sex just isn't healthy.'

'You're probably right, it probably isn't –' Shoving half a

dozen files across the desk at Beverly, Dee changed the subject. 'But it's also not healthy for Ellis not to have a replacement for his retiring executive assistant.' The title "executive assistant" was entirely misleading. Dee knew that Beverly, not Ellis, had chosen it. And though technically she was his equal in the business the two of them, along with Wade Crittenden, had begun 13 years ago, Beverly preferred to work quietly with no pompous moniker to live up to. She wore the title proudly and carried the incredible burden it entailed with panache and enthusiasm. Dee was certain that whoever took up Beverly's weighty mantle would inherit the humble title as well as its prodigious responsibilities.

Just then Beverly's BlackBerry buzzed. 'Damn!' She punched in a quick reply. 'Ellis says the traffic's at a standstill. I was really hoping the two of you would finally meet before I head off to Brazil.'

Dee buried her disappointment. Meeting Thorne was not the real reason she was here, she reminded herself. She still had work to do. She nodded down at the files of resumes of Beverly's prospective replacements. 'Best get to it then, hadn't we?'

But Beverly pushed the files to one side and picked up right where she'd left off. God, the woman was tenacious! 'Seems to me the obvious solution is to include sex in certain job descriptions, like for an executive assistant, or a secretary, or any position where two people work closely. That'd be a good start, don't you think?'

'Great idea. Maybe I'll find a nice male secretary for myself.' Dee gave the door a quick glance, certain she'd heard someone approaching. There was no one, but even if there had been, she was sure that wouldn't have stopped Beverly.

'I think that would be a wise decision for any busy executive,' Beverly said. 'And I doubt you'd have any shortage of applicants. Ellis wouldn't either, and the benefits to both of you – well, I think you'd be amazed. I've given it a lot of thought, and I personally can't see a downside.' Beverly continued her speculations. 'Just think of how much more relaxed the two of you would be if you and Ellis had a reliable source of stress-free sex available when you needed it. Imagine how much more focused you'd both be if your junk wasn't interfering with your brain.'

Dee straightened in her chair. 'My – junk does not interfere with my brain.'

Beverly leaned over the desk like an accusing lawyer. 'Ah, but how do you really know that, since you're not getting any?'

'Beverly –'

'The Executive Sex Clause could reduce sick days.'

'I'm never sick.'

Beverly came around the desk and laid an unsolicited hand on her forehead. 'I've been thinking you look a little pale, and you feel a bit warm to me.'

Dee brushed her hand aside. 'I'm fine. I don't need the sick days I've got, and I bet Ellis doesn't either.'

'A good thing, since you wouldn't have time to take them if you did. Forget sick days, think of the increase in productivity, the boost to creativity. Think of the serenity in the workplace. That alone's gotta be worth something.'

'My productivity's fine and I'm very creative. Plus I work at Jasper and McDowell. Serenity isn't part of the package.' This conversation had gone far enough, farther than Dee wanted, and she really didn't have time to wait any longer for Ellis. It looked like the long-awaited meeting with the force of nature would have to wait for yet another time. Dee nodded to the folders on Beverly's desk. 'As interesting as the idea of a Sex Clause might be, if you insist on deserting Ellis, I need to do my job and find someone who can take your place, which won't be an easy task.'

When the meeting finished, Beverly walked Dee to the door, glancing down at her watch. 'Sorry you missed Ellis. But you know how it is with busy executives; it's catch as catch can, isn't it?'

Dee had the distinct feeling the woman wasn't talking about work. She said her goodbyes, promising they'd get together over drinks when Beverly returned from Brazil.

'I missed her again, didn't I? She's going to think I'm avoiding her.' Ellis dropped into the chair in front of Beverly's desk and flipped absently through the files Dee Henning had just left. 'It's not her I'm avoiding, it's your silly retirement plans.'

'You won't be laughing when you come in here some morning and find my desk empty. You'll be SOL big time, boy.'

Ellis pulled one of the files from the stack and handed it to her. 'Here. Here's my choice. Why not Tally Barnes? She's about as qualified as anyone, I guess.'

She shoved the folder back at him. 'You know why not Tally Barnes, now stop being a smartass.'

He offered her an amused chuckle. 'Who are you kidding, Beverly? You love this place, and you know it. You're not going to retire. How many false alarms have there been now, three? Four? I've lost count. Face it; you'll work here until you drop dead.'

'Believe what you want, but don't say I didn't warn you.' She pulled a manila envelope from the top drawer of her desk and handed it to him.

'What's this?'

'My replacement. Since you won't help, I've taken matters into my own hands. She's been right under our noses all along.' She rubbed her hands together with a shiver of anticipation. 'Come on, humour me.'

Still holding her in a disapproving gaze, he took the envelope as though half expecting it to be booby-trapped. He opened the clasp, then slid the contents from inside and gave it a glance. 'Wait a minute. This is a file on Dee Henning. You can't be serious. You want a headhunter to take over running half of Pneuma Inc.?'

'Don't be such a snob, Ellis. It's not like she'll be taking over tomorrow. I'll be here to train her up to suit your persnickety standards.'

'Then why not promote Tally Barnes? I don't see what you have against her. She always seems fine to me.' He nodded to the top file in the stack Dee had brought in. 'She already works for Pneuma Inc., and she's a lot more qualified. You could train her up.'

'Oh, she's already convinced she's a shoo-in. Hell, she's already planning to redecorate my office. Wouldn't be too surprised if she has plans for you too. Don't give me that snooty smirk. She's a trouble-maker, Ellis. She's great at ass-kissing, and that's why Tally Barnes always seems fine to you. I don't like her and I don't trust her, and you know I'm a good judge of character. Trust me on this; she's not right for my job, no matter what her resume says.'

'Suit yourself.' He returned his attention to Dee Henning's details. 'How did you get this information anyway?' The file was too thick for a simple resume, and some of the pages looked like handwritten notes that had been photocopied. Others were odd sizes, some were written on Post-it notes, and the whole package smacked of Beverly's scheming.

'Portland's a small city.' Suddenly Beverly seemed particularly interested in the leaves of a Christmas cactus sitting on the edge of her desk.

'Beverly?'

'I'm friends with Irv McDowell, OK? At least I think we're still friends.' The look of driven-snow innocence gave way to something just slightly this side of devious.

'You've been headhunting from the head headhunter? Dee Henning's Jasper and McDowell's star recruiter. Surely Irv didn't give you this willingly.'

Beverly ignored the question and nodded at the photo he now held in his hand. Short, dark hair framed blue eyes, a straight Roman nose, and a full-lipped smile that suggested competence, with a touch of mischief. So this was what Dee Henning looked like. He'd often wondered.

'She's exactly what you need on all counts. Though it's true she's only a few years out of grad school, what impresses me is her accomplishments during that time. She reminds me of you back in the early days – young, hungry, dedicated … And pretty too. Don't give me that look, Ellis, you'd blush if you heard some of the juicy conversations about you I overhear in the ladies' room.'

He put the photo of Dee aside and flipped through the file. 'What all do you have in here anyway?' He read out loud from

7

one of the photocopied pages. 'Classically trained, voice and piano? Oh, that'll come in really handy at Pneuma Inc. In fact, I was just thinking of requiring it for all new employees.'

'Stop being an asshole. It's background information, just stuff that's good to know.'

A handwritten note stated that both of Dee's parents were musicians. Her father had sung in the chorus for the Paris Opera. Her mother was a soprano, who went to Paris on some summer programme; nine months later, Dee came along. Ellis suddenly felt like a voyeur. 'This is none of our business.' He tried to shove the file back at Beverly, but she refused it.

'For chrissake, Ellis, there's nothing in there I haven't already wheedled out of the girl over coffee or drinks. Don't be such a wuss.'

'I'm sure she didn't give you the copy of her finances over coffee and drinks.'

'Oh that. Just tells us that we can't appeal to her with money alone.'

'Clearly she doesn't need it,' he said. He was surprised to find someone so young had such a good portfolio. She obviously knew how to make money work for her. She wasn't exactly rich, but give her a few more years, and she would be.

'My point exactly. Musicians tend to be poor, and I think our Dee has taken it upon herself not to follow in her parents' footsteps.'

'If the need ever actually arises for me to interview her, what makes you think she's even interested in working for me? She's got a growing career with Jasper and McDowell making very good money.'

Beverly frowned. 'Jasper and McDowell is a means to an end. Surely you don't expect someone with her talent to settle in there permanently, do you? It's the experience of working here with you that'll appeal to her. She's a perfectionist, never does anything half-assed. She's always striving to be the best. She's driven, just like you are. Remember that when you interview her.'

He shuffled pages. 'What did you have to do to get this stuff; tie Irv to a chair and beat him with a tyre iron?'

'It's amazing what a man will tell you over a couple of drinks.'

'You got him drunk.'

'It wasn't that hard. He never could hold his booze. I can't believe I didn't figure it out sooner. She's perfect for my job.'

Ellis looked down at the resume. 'She's not perfect for your job, Beverly. She's too young, too inexperienced, and this is not even her area of expertise.'

'The woman's a headhunter, Ellis. She has to be competent in lots of areas. Besides, we've always been risk-takers at Pneuma Inc., and those risks have always paid off. I'll train her myself, and you'll see, within a few months she'll be able to run this place on her own.'

'An opportunity she'll never get because you'll never retire.'

'Forget about my retirement, Ellis. It's time. You know it is. We need someone in training for when the inevitable happens.'

He gave up pretending to ignore the photo, which was definitely the nicest thing he'd looked at all day.

'Hire her, Ellis. It's not just that I'm retiring, but I'm old. Hell, I could drop dead anytime. Then what?'

'Oh for chrissakes, Beverly, we both know you're too damned ornery to die. You'll outlive me. But I tell you what, if and when you do drop dead, I'll hire her. Hell, when you drop dead, I'll give her your job on a silver platter and train her myself, I promise. Now, can we get back to running the business here?'

Chapter Two

THERE WAS NO ONE at reception in the executive suites when Dee arrived at the Pneuma Building. Even stranger, there was no sign of either of the two secretaries. The door to Ellis's office was closed, as it always was, but Beverly's office was open. Dee knew the woman well enough that she was comfortable going on in. She pulled the three new files from her bag and laid them on the desk, then paced in front of the open door.

The office seemed strangely empty. There was no sign of the usual misting bottle or any of the plant care implements that usually littered Beverly's desk, no laptop shoved to one corner, none of the usual haphazard piles of papers, no gardening gloves draped forgotten over any of the bigger planters, none of the usual detritus that indicated the big woman was in residence. Dee checked her BlackBerry to make sure she had the right date. Even though she wasn't early, she was certainly not late. Beverly had deliberately planned for Dee's to be the last appointment of the day. She had invited her for drinks after. Once Dee had rechecked the time, she peeked out the door to the open reception area. Still no one.

She was relieved that she wasn't late. She'd come straight from the airport with only a brief stop at Jasper and McDowell to pick up the files she needed. That hadn't been her plan, but it had become necessary when the missed flight in Rio had caused a domino effect with her other flights. She gave one last glance through each of the folders, which wasn't necessary, but it was something to do, then moved behind the desk to admire Beverly's private jungle. She ran her fingertips over smooth, waxy leaves that felt cool to the touch. Nothing looked any different than it had when she saw Beverly just before she left for Brazil. But she was sure Beverly would recognise each new bud and each new leaf that had grown in her absence.

It wasn't like Beverly to be late. Dee was just contemplating going in search of her when suddenly there were voices in the hall.

'What the hell are you doing in Beverly's office?'

A hard hand on her arm spun her around none too gently, and she found herself face to face with Ellison Thorne, who was clearly not pleased to see her. In fact, the powerful grip on her arm, the storm cloud look on his face made her knees weak and her voice difficult to find.

Just then, Beverly's secretary burst in. 'Ellis! That's Dee Henning.' She laid a gentle hand on the man's arm. 'Ellis, it's all right. Dee had an appointment with Beverly. She doesn't know.'

'Doesn't know what?'

The knot growing in her stomach suddenly tightened like a fist as the secretary turned her attention to Dee, her face drawn, her always square shoulders tight. 'I'm sorry, Dee. I would have let you know, but we couldn't get hold of you.'

'Let me know what? I was out of the country. I told Beverly. What's going on? Where is she?' It was then she noticed Ellis was in khaki walking trousers and a rumpled matching shirt. The man, who had never looked anything other than pristine in his photos, wore several days' growth of beard, and even from behind his glasses, she could tell he hadn't slept. He still didn't release her arm.

He held her gaze as though he were searching for something in her face, then he drew a breath that sounded like he'd just come up from the depths. 'Beverly's gone missing.'

The room spun slightly, and the buzzing in her ears made everything sound far off, even her own voice. She jerked her arm away, nearly toppling back into Beverly's plants. 'What do you mean she's gone missing? How can she have? She was with the best. She assured me the people she was with were the best in their field. She said she'd be safe. She promised me she'd be safe.'

This time Ellis took her by the shoulders and gave a gentle shake. 'She's missing, Dee. That's all. We've lost contact. That's all. We'll find her.'

She stepped back and ran a hand through her hair, a little embarrassed by her outburst, but it was Beverly they were talking about. 'What happened?'

'There was a tropical storm. Unseasonal. The outfitters lost contact with the expedition.' He looked down at the clothes he wore. 'The storm was supposed to break. I went down to look for her, but the weather got worse, and I had to come back.'

'You went to look for her?' Dee said. 'Are you out of your mind?'

The secretary fidgeted uncomfortably, but Ellis offered her what might have almost been half a smile. 'Probably, but I went anyway.' Then he heaved a sigh. 'Look I really need a shower. Sandra's ordered Chinese. I need to eat, she says, and I know better than to argue with Sandra. I'm sure she'll have ordered enough for a family of six.' He nodded to the door. 'If you'd like to join me, I'll tell you everything.'

Ellis's office was nothing like she expected. It was much more like an apartment than the lair of one of the most progressive businessmen in the US. He led her away from the big oak desk that sat, with its full complement of office furnishings and necessities, in front of a wall of glass looking out on to Mount Hood. He led her down a short hallway into a lounge that could have easily passed for a library in an Edwardian manor house. The blue leather furnishings were dwarfed by bookcases full to capacity, and the coffee table in front of it was strewn with an eclectic disarray of books from poetry of the English Romantics to modern theories of cosmology to Stephen King and everything in between.

It didn't take him long to shower. He returned in jeans and blue cotton shirt open at the neck, sleeves rolled carelessly halfway up his forearms. He was once again clean shaven and his short hair was still damp. As Sandra arrived with the Chinese food, he shoved the books off onto the floor and made room for dinner. The secretary left for the day, and Dee silently helped him spread the meal, feeling shy and almost embarrassed to have seen beyond the man's façade, to be sharing such an intimate view of him, the man who, in her mind's eye, was always so much larger than life. When the meal was spread, he smiled up at her, his glasses slipping down the bridge of his nose, and her stomach did a little somersault at the sight of him like this. She blushed. It embarrassed her that she did so, but she did.

She was taller than he had expected. In the black heels she almost stood nose to nose with him. And her eyes, her eyes were even bluer than they were in the photo. The contrast with her nearly black hair and her pale skin was stunning. And the way she talked; it wasn't the antiseptic elocution he had grown used to hearing from women in the business world. There was something interesting about her barely perceptible accent. He wondered if she owed that to her French father. The last thing he wanted was to entertain. The last thing he wanted was to make nicey-nice, and yet he had invited her to join him, and when his arm brushed hers, when the silence between them seemed strangely comfortable, he wasn't sorry for her company.

When at last they were seated, Dee spoke without preamble. 'What happened?' she said around a mouthful of spring roll, covering her lips daintily with one hand. Ellis could instantly see why Beverly was impressed. There was no nonsense about this woman. No subterfuge. But then to have earned such high praise and respect from Beverly, he would have expected nothing less. Even more importantly, she was Beverly's friend. She must feel as gutted as he did right now.

'The guides had taken her into the rainforest,' he said by way of explanation. 'Some really remote area, where there was a nest of harpy eagles.'

Dee nodded. 'She told me she had her heart set on seeing harpy eagles.'

Ellis continued. 'I knew they'd be out of contact while they were there. And she promised me it was no big deal, that this was a regular expedition for the outfitters. She promised that she was in the best possible hands. Then the storm came in. They were supposed to have been back before it hit. Damn it!' He tossed down his chopsticks and stood to pace. 'Why the hell couldn't she just go to the zoo to see harpy eagles, or watch them on YouTube like everyone else does?'

'You know why not.' Dee nodded to his plate. 'Sit down and eat.'

'Jesus –' he grumped '– you're damn near as bossy as Beverly.'

She blushed – a beautiful pink blush – and fidgeted in her seat, no doubt remembering that this was his domain, and she was still trying to decide if she were here on business or not. When she squared her shoulders and nodded to the sofa, he figured she'd decided she wasn't. He was glad.

He dropped down beside her, picked up the chopsticks, and stuffed his mouth full of Singapore noodles, more because he could tell it pleased her than because he had anything resembling an appetite right now.

He swallowed his noodles without chewing, and continued. 'I waited until I got word that there was a lull in the storm, and I could actually fly in. I barely got there before things picked up again.'

Her full lips were a tight line, as though she were making every effort to keep her mouth shut, to keep her disapproval to herself. But she failed. 'What did you expect you could do down there on your own besides put your life at risk along with Beverly's?'

'I wasn't alone. And my team's at least as good as Beverly's. They know the area like the back of their hand. If anyone could have gone in and found her, they could.'

She raised an eyebrow. 'And all that with the added responsibility of keeping the CEO of Pneuma Inc. safe. Nice.'

'I happen to know a good bit about trekking in the rain forests, Dee. I would have been just fine.'

'I know what an outdoorsman you are, Mr Thorne. Everyone in the Northwest knows that.'

'It's Ellis,' he interrupted her.

She bit at a prawn as though it had somehow offended her.

'The point is, Ellis, your team would have gone in level-headed and calm. They would have gone in without any personal feelings one way or the other. I doubt you'd have been able to do that. I know I wouldn't have.'

He shrugged. 'Anyway, it doesn't matter because no one was going anywhere, and in the end I was lucky to get a flight out before the airport shut down again. I would have stayed, but Beverly has an important meeting tomorrow. She'll tear me a new one if it gets cancelled.' He felt helpless anger bubble up into his chest as though it would strangle him. 'Damn it, I don't have time to do her job and mine. The woman's 63 years old. She shouldn't be traipsing around in the rainforest out of contact with everyone like some stupid teenager.'

Dee studied him over the top of her chopsticks. 'She deserved a vacation. Besides, she was doing what she wanted.'

'I know that, but I need her here, and I need her safe. In spite of the woman's bossy, crazy wackiness, I need her. I need her.'

'I know,' Dee said. 'I need her too. My visits with her keep me sane, and the nuttier she is, the more sense everything makes.' She laid down her chopsticks, folded her arms across her chest, and held herself as though she were suddenly cold. 'I'm sorry, I didn't mean to sound so airy-fairy. Beverly would laugh her ass off. She's far more concerned with getting me laid than keeping me sane.' She cocked her head to one side, her lips curving upward in a little quirk of a smile. 'Though I suppose she probably wouldn't see much difference in the two, really.'

'Her Executive Sex Clause?' he asked.

She nodded, and he thought he saw a whisper of a blush cross her cheeks. 'Not likely to happen at Jasper and McDowell, though. In fact, the thought makes me a little queasy. But still, I won't deny that it's an intriguing idea under the right circumstances.'

He chuckled. 'Believe me, I hear about it ad nauseam, along with all her other hair-brained schemes, and I won't complain again about any of them once she's back here safe and sound.'

'Yes you will,' Dee said. 'It wouldn't be nearly so much fun for either of you if you didn't.'

Before he could agree with her, his BlackBerry rang and he grabbed it from the book shelf behind the sofa. 'It's from Brazil,' he said, feeling the muscles in his shoulders tighten and his stomach clench. She was on the edge of the sofa next to him in an instant, her eyes locked on him. The call took less than ten seconds. It jump-started his brain back into the hyper-alert state it had been in since Beverly's disappearance, the state it had only just come down from in Dee Henning's comforting presence.

'Storm's breaking.' He mouthed the words to her. She moved still closer, trying to overhear the conversation. He placed a finger to his lips and strained to hear. 'All right,' he said. 'I'm on my way.' He disconnected and all but catapulted off the sofa. 'That's the outfitters. I made them promise to call me the minute they knew anything.'

She was off the sofa too, following him to where his backpack leaned against a wing-backed chair. He'd had Harold prepare it and deliver it to the office just in case.

'And?'

'I'm going back. Jeffries is on standby with the limo. The plane is fuelled and ready. I figure we can be at PDX in 30 minutes, if traffic's not too bad.'

She grabbed his arm and pulled him to a stop. 'You can't go back without at least a night's rest, Ellis. You're exhausted, and what about Beverly's important meeting?'

He jerked away from her and hefted the pack onto one shoulder. 'Fuck her meeting. I just want her safe.'

'Ellis, be reasonable. As soon as things settle, you could get a phone call from Beverly laughing the whole thing off. Do you know how upset she'd be if she knew you'd put yourself in danger traipsing down there when there was no need? Please.' She grabbed the backpack and wrestled it off his shoulder. 'You know I'm right. Just rest. Just for tonight, and then tomorrow …' She stepped into his personal space and placed a hand on his biceps. 'Tomorrow I'll go with you.'

'Are you crazy?' He jerked his arm away. 'You can't go with me, Dee. It's awful down there, flooding, wind damage …

It was bad where I was and I wasn't anywhere near the worst of it.'

'I've just spent a week in the Andes working for Sportwide Extreme Adventure. I can handle it if you can.'

He held her gaze. 'And were there bodies floating in the streets where you were?'

She caught her breath, grabbed for the back of the chair, and nearly stumbled. All the beautiful colour went out of her face, and he was sorry he'd said anything.

'Bodies, you didn't say anything about bodies, Ellis. Why the hell didn't you tell me there were bodies? Jesus!' She ran a hand through her hair and looked around the room wildly. 'Why the fuck didn't you tell me?'

He took both her arms and steadied her, looking down into those deep, serious eyes. 'I didn't tell you because I didn't want to worry you. Christ, it's bad enough for those pictures to be going through one of our brains, let alone both.'

She straightened her shoulders, nodded, and stepped back. 'All right, but that's in the towns, isn't it? I mean we're talking the rain forest; trees, tall trees, lots of them. That's where Beverly'll be. It'll be better there, surely it will be. And no people. No bodies.'

'I didn't get that far. I don't know what to expect, and we don't know where Beverly was when the outfitters lost contact. I don't want you there, Dee. And neither would she. Don't you understand?'

But of course she didn't understand, and he really didn't expect her to. God, she was as stubborn and pig-headed as Beverly. She held him in a hard blue gaze. 'She wouldn't want you there either, damn it.'

'Don't tell me what she would want. I don't care what she would want. I'm going, you're staying. That's final.'

Dee shoved both her hands onto her hips and glared at him, her eyes suddenly like raw heat. 'You're not my boss, and I do what I want, and right now I'm telling you you're being an idiot.'

It came as a total shock when he grabbed her. He didn't see it coming. He didn't see any of it coming. Before she could do more than utter a gasp of surprise, he pulled her to him so hard that he feared he'd given her whiplash, then he did the unthinkable. He kissed her. He kissed her hard. His mouth was bruising and tyrannical against hers, like he'd forgotten how to be gentle, like he'd forgotten how to be civilised. He swallowed her breath even as she fought to swallow his. At first she pushed him, pushed him as hard as she could, and he thought she was pushing him away, but her mouth sparred with his for still more contact. He only yielded enough to step back, pulling her with him, kissing her harder, holding her tighter, tight enough to crush her breasts against his chest. She bit and nipped at him like an angry wolf, with him yanking and shoving her jacket off her shoulders and going to work on her buttons while she pushed and shoved and clawed.

There was ripping and tearing. At least one button went flying. He wasn't sure whose. He didn't care. He'd fucking buy her a new suit if he had to.

With one hand he tugged and yanked her skirt up over her hips, with the other he shoved down the straps of her bra and kneaded and cupped until his thumb raked her nipples into heavy, responsive peaks.

She managed to force his trousers down over his hips as he figured out how to release the front catch on her bra. 'Wait, wait,' he said, struggling to breathe in the charged atmosphere, trying to keep his head clear. He nearly elbowed her as he tugged his wallet from his pocket.

In his distracted efforts, he stumbled backward over the backpack, pulling her down on top of him, forcing the breath from his lungs with a grunt.

'Oh my God!' she cried out. They landed in a heap sprawled across the soft carpet. With her sitting astraddle him, he yanked and tugged at his wallet, money, credit cards, and receipts falling like confetti until he found the silver foil packet, which he ripped open, launching the condom into the air in his frenzied efforts.

'Shit,' they both cursed at the same time. She was already tugging at his boxers as he grabbed up the rogue condom, rolled it down over his arcing erection, and thrust up into it, nearly bucking her off his thighs with the effort. He tugged the crotch of her panties aside. For a second he glimpsed the warm depths of her before they clawed and shifted and positioned to get what, until now, neither of them had known they needed so desperately.

Once he pushed into her, it was his turn to cry out. 'Oh God, Dee! I can't stand it!' He grabbed her hips and held her tight. 'Hold still. Don't move. Give me a second.'

It had been a long time since he'd had any sex other than with his own fist, and his sensitivity was astounding, embarrassing actually. His chest rose and fell like bellows. Dee sat impaled, eyes closed, hands cupping her breasts, breathing like there was fire in her chest. She felt stretched exquisitely tight and warm and tetchy around his girth, and the few seconds he held her there seemed an eternity, suspended in the delicious agony of needing to thrust, but knowing to wait. Just a few more seconds until he felt in better control

When he was certain he wouldn't embarrass himself, he gathered her to him, feeling the carpet abrade his elbows as he rolled on top of her, still buried to the hilt. And he began to thrust. She tightened her legs around his hips and rose in rhythm to meet his efforts, growling at him as he growled back, balling her fists against his back, straining upward onto her impaler, meeting strength with strength. And her strength was impressive. She was all muscle and sinew, rounded and softened with delicious curves engulfing him in the feel and the power and the scent of femaleness, the tidal scent of steamy summer, the scent of lust tightly controlled. No doubt some of that was his own. And the blending of the two was intoxicating.

It was all over in a few minutes. They exploded into release like glass shattering on concrete. He came with a heavy groan and collapsed on top of her while she convulsed in orgasm. Surely he was dreaming. Surely he was asleep, and his psyche had fabricated the whole experience in an effort to relieve stress. Surely it couldn't be real. He'd wake up soon.

They lay panting on the floor in a tangle of discarded clothing and trembling limbs, as his brain gradually regained control. In his fantasies, he always made it last, lingering to tease and pleasure Dee their first time together. And it was true; he actually had fantasised about her, about the woman he'd never met, the woman whose photo was in the dossier Beverly had put together. He'd fantasised about her from his first glance at Beverly's wild concoction of a resume. And he had no doubt that had been a part of Beverly's scheme.

But he was always a good lover in his fantasies; no awkward moments, no clumsy efforts. In his fantasies he always pleasured her like she'd never been pleasured before. He never imagined he'd take her with such force. He never imagined he'd take her at all, at least not in the real world. God, what must she think? He found himself remembering Beverly's Executive Sex Clause. No doubt this situation would meet with her approval, but at the moment, he wasn't sure what he felt, other than dismayed that he'd lost control.

Finally he found the breath to speak. 'Dee, are you all right? I'm so sorry. I don't know what came over me; I don't know what I was thinking. I didn't mean to be such an animal.'

'I like animals.' She spoke around laboured breath.

The sting her nails had left across his shoulders and back convinced him she might be a bit of an animal herself, a thought that brought with it a new wave of arousal, which he tried to suppress. 'Nothing like this has ever happened to me before. I want you to know that I never, that I wouldn't –'

'I know. Me neither,' she said.

Neither of them made any effort to get up or to move out of each other's arms. In fact, the feel of her so close was worth hanging on to. He'd rest for a little while with her so nicely wrapped around him. Just for a few minutes, then he'd call Jeffries to take him to the airport. Just a little while longer, close to her warmth. That was all he needed. Just a few more delicious minutes.

Chapter Three

'HE'LL BE WITH YOU in just a minute,' Ellis's secretary said. She left Dee seated uncomfortably in Beverly's empty office. As soon as she was gone, Dee stood and began to pace.

It hadn't been her intention to see Ellis. It had been her intention to sneak back into Pneuma Inc., claim the files she'd left on Beverly's desk, and leave quietly. Then, when Beverly got back, she'd give them to her in person. There had been no need to bother anyone, no need to bother Ellis. She intended to leave undetected, just like she had done last night.

She couldn't even think about last night without a full-fledged infestation of butterflies rising in her stomach and chest. She'd had sex with Ellison Thorne, for fuck's sake! Just like that; no planning, scheming nor contemplating. They had humped each other's brains out. And it had been amazing, if all too brief. But that wasn't the point. The point was that it shouldn't have happened. He was her client. Well, Beverly was; Pneuma Inc. was. It was so unprofessional. What the hell must he think of her? She knew it had been only for comfort, but he was Ellison Thorne, and she was a nobody. And she had always been a professional with a good reputation at Pneuma Inc. And now this.

Last night they had dozed together in each other's arms after they'd had sex. It was wonderfully intimate until guilt got the best of her. She had extricated herself from his arms without waking him, which was a testament to just how exhausted the man was. She'd covered him gently with the blanket from the back of the sofa, then she had hurriedly dressed and left, forgetting the files on Beverly's desk.

When she'd called Sandra this morning, thinking just to

sneak in and get them, Sandra told her Ellis wanted to see her. Though she was relieved that he hadn't carried through with his crazy plan to return to Brazil last night, she was not looking forward to their encounter. She paced the floor in Beverly's office nervously.

'You have my staff wrapped around your little finger.'

She jumped at the sound of Ellis's voice. Unlike last night, unlike their first encounter, his tone was cheerful, his smile welcoming. He stood dressed in a charcoal suit with a silver blue tie over a crisp white shirt, once again looking like the Ellison Thorne she had grown used to seeing on the covers of magazines and on the evening news. He held a coffee in one hand and a glass of iced tea in the other. 'Sandra informed me that this is for you.' He handed her the tea and offered her a smile that made the butterfly dance move lower in her abdomen. Much lower. 'It's your personal glass, she tells me. Reserved for the only person in the history of Pneuma Inc., as far as I know, that Sandra would deign to even bring coffee to, let alone make a special drink for. She's an executive secretary, and a damn good one. She's not a housewife, a fact she reminds us all of periodically.' He pushed the door shut behind him and the butterfly dance got wilder.

She took the tea. 'Any more news?'

He shook his head. 'Storm's abating more slowly than expected, so I'm still here. But it is abating. Beverly's meeting went as well as could be expected under the circumstances.' He held her gaze. 'We're keeping her absence a secret until we know for sure what's going on, so I had to lie to Alan Marston. Not an easy task.'

She knew Alan Marston, or at least by reputation. He was a client of Jasper and McDowell's from time to time, but even as good as she was at her job, he would work with no one but Fred Jasper.

'Beverly owes me big time for dealing with Marston,' he said. He moved behind the desk and pulled a key from a side drawer. 'Sandra told me she locked the files in the top drawer this morning when she got here. She figured you'd forgotten them after everything that had happened.' His gaze seemed heavier with the last words, and she felt it like a weight, like the weight of his body. She struggled to pull her mind back to the business at hand.

Ellis unlocked the drawer and gave it a tug, but it wouldn't open. 'Feels like something's stuck,' he said, jerking it hard. His hand slipped, banging his knuckle and abrading the tip of his finger in the process. He caught his breath and bit back a curse.

'Are you all right?' Forgetting herself, Dee was at his side in an instant, taking his hand in hers.

'Fine.' He forced a throaty laugh. 'No blood, no loss of limbs. I'm fine.' The nearness of him radiated over her skin. He smelled like outside. There was no distance between them, and dear God, he smelled like outside. She wanted to take him in her arms. She wanted to bury her face against his chest and breathe in the scent of him. Christ, what was the matter with her? How could she even think such things under the circumstances? It took them a second to realise that his fingers were curled around hers.

They both stepped back. Ellis offered a nervous laugh. 'Right, let's rescue these file folders for you then.' He slid open the side drawer, and found a ruler, which he inserted into the breach then gently pried. 'Who knows what the woman has tucked away in here?' he said, offering her a sideways glance with a spark of mischief she'd never seen in any of the photos of Ellison Thorne. It made her insides feel like warm honey. 'Wouldn't be surprised to find a packet of some exotic fertiliser or a trowel, garden gloves. With Beverly nothing would surprise –' The drawer gave and he caught the arm of the chair for balance as the whole thing nearly dislodged onto the floor.

Dee gave a little gasp, swallowing back the breathless laugh that had resulted from their shared moment of awkwardness.

Sure enough, the three file folders were on top. Ellis carefully extricated them. 'Here are the rescued files, property of Jasper and McDowell.' He read the black label across the top folder, as he handed them to her. Then he returned his attention to the open drawer. 'And here's the problem.' Ellis pulled out the newspaper that had wedged itself in the drawer.

It was the same one that had been on top of Beverly's desk the last time Dee had seen her. On the front page Ellis and the governor of the great state of Oregon still smiled and shook hands as though nothing had happened, as though nothing had changed since the last time Dee had seen it.

Ellis chuckled softly. 'You wouldn't know it to look at her, but Beverly Neumann's a sentimental packrat.' He nodded to the large zip-lock bag nestled in the centre of the drawer, a bag full of clippings about Pneuma Inc. and Ellis in particular. 'She keeps a scrapbook at home. Can you believe it? Someone as hard-nosed as Beverly has a scrapbook. I've never actually seen it, but she always lurks like a vulture with a pair of scissors whenever there's a newspaper or magazine article about Pneuma Inc. She even saves napkins from the yearly staff appreciation party. She saves everything. Hell, half her library at home is probably filled with silly scrapbooks by now, and the woman has a huge library.'

Ellis placed the bag back in the drawer along with the newspaper, and shut it carefully. He took a deep breath and said, 'Dee, about last night ...' A moment of silence stretched between them, and just when it was beginning to get uncomfortable, they both spoke at the same time.

'Nothing like that's ever happened to me before.'

The result was a wave of nervous laughter

'Me neither.' Again they spoke at the same time.

Dee was about to say something about extenuating circumstances and about the need for comfort when Ellis said, 'You left without saying goodbye.' His voice was suddenly tight-edged, his arms stiff, fingers pressed to the top of the desk.

'You needed to rest,' Dee managed, feeling as though her breath had deserted her at the mention of last night. She hesitated for a second, then added. 'If I'd stayed ...'

'It might have happened again. I get that.' He turned to face her, the mischievous sparkle back in his eyes. 'Some things I don't mind losing sleep for, Dee. And I promise you, if I'd been anything less than dead dog tired, you'd have never gotten away without waking me up.' He offered her a crooked smile. 'I don't get sex that often, I don't have time for it, but when I do, I make it a point to stay awake for as much as I can get.'

The butterflies were back, but the breath that had deserted her still wasn't. Her pulse rate was breaking all speed records. Was Ellison Thorne telling her he was OK with what had happened last night? Was there even a hint at the possibility it might happen again? The smile on his face certainly would not exclude that possibility.

She was about to say that she personally didn't need much sleep, and that she would be happy to keep him awake again sometime, when there was a sudden harsh knock on the door and Sandra burst in.

'Damn it, Sandra, I think you're supposed to wait till I say "come in" before you ...' The words died in Ellis's throat at the sight of Sandra's tear-streaked face, and Dee's heart froze in her chest.

The secretary moved into the room as though she were sleepwalking. The sunlight from the window glistened against a single tear sliding down her thin cheek.

'What, Sandra?' Ellis breathed. They too moved like they were in a dream, moved around the desk until Ellis could lay a hand on the distressed woman's shoulder. 'Tell us.'

'Beverly's dead,' the woman blurted. Her lip quivered and she forced back a sob. 'She was with the eagles. Rope snapped. It was a freak accident. She fell from the tree and broke her neck. They couldn't get a message back because of the storm.'

Afterwards, Dee remembered holding everything in, feeling as though if she let go, she would never stop crying. She remembered Ellis holding her, holding her so tightly. Then she remembered him settling her into the chair behind Beverly's desk, giving Sandra a brief hug and fleeing. She found out from Sandra that it was Ellis who had arranged for her to sit with Beverly's closest friends at the funeral, but other than the brief words of sympathy that passed between them after the service, that was the last Dee saw of Ellison Thorne for eight weeks.

Chapter Four

As difficult as it might be, an executive assistant could be replaced. A good friend, however, could not. No one else was Beverly. She left a gaping hole in Pneuma Inc. Ellis knew he couldn't count on Wade for help. Wade's domain was research. Wade was the creative force behind Pneuma Inc., but it had always been Ellis and Beverly who marketed and sold that creativity. Without Beverly neither Ellis nor Wade could have realised their dream, and without her it was hard to see the way forward.

But Dee wasn't trying to replace his friend, Ellis reminded himself as he looked down at the previous stack of resumes she'd left with his secretary. Dee was just trying to do her job. And because Beverly had been Dee's friend too, that job couldn't be easy for her.

What he had taken as a joke only a few months ago was suddenly very serious business. Too serious, and too guilt-ridden, for comfort, so he had continually fobbed Dee off on his secretary each time she arrived with the resumes of prospective executive assistants. It wasn't that he didn't want to see her. He dreamed about her, he fantasised about her, and fuck if he didn't masturbate to thoughts of her on the floor of his lounge in his arms. But he just couldn't face her, not after everything that had happened. And now he couldn't put it off any longer. He knew, as he had from the beginning, that there was really no need to look at any of the resumes. He had made a flippant promise to Beverly before she died, but it was a promise nonetheless. Then he had gone and complicated what was already a complicated situation by having sex with Dee Henning. None of that mattered in the end, though. What mattered was that it was time to stop avoiding the inevitable and honour his promise.

On his BlackBerry, he pulled up the email Beverly had sent him from some internet café in Manaus just before she headed into the rainforest. He could picture her there among the backpackers a third her age, probably striking up conversations with them, probably getting drunk with them at the local bar in the evening, and they would have relished her company. Everyone did. They would have been star-struck, half in love with her, remembering their time with her as one of the highlights of their travels. That was the way it was with Beverly. The email was the last he'd gotten from her before she died. He read it for the millionth time.

Ellis,

Just an addendum to the conversation we had earlier about Dee Henning. Before I lose contact with all things Pneuma Inc. to bask in blissful solitude of the rainforest, I want to make it clear how I feel. I've already told you she's perfect for the position. And if you were ever going to implement the ESC, she'd be the one to do it with – that is if you've got the balls.

Dee's exactly what you need on all counts. I know you think she lacks experience, but trust me, with the right training, given half a chance, she'll be brilliant. Hire her, Ellis. Implement the ESC. Trust me, it's the perfect strategy; a secret weapon that could make Pneuma Inc. even more successful than it already is. And if anyone could do it, you could. Do this for me and I can retire and enjoy my dotage.

And in case you're planning to write this message off as a sign of dementia due to my advanced years, I plan to invite her for drinks after I get back from Brazil and feel her out about the position. Just so you know I'm serious.

Beverly

He shut the email, took off his glasses and stared for a long moment at the blurred screen. Beverly was always right, he reminded himself. Then he shoved his glasses back on, opened the manila envelope, and took out the information Beverly had left him. It was true, the list of work experiences and skills was impressive; in a couple of years, at the rate she was going, Dee would be his choice for the position, hands down. But it was too soon. She was so unprepared for what she'd be facing. How could she be otherwise under the circumstances? And she was untried. He'd be throwing her to the lions. But Beverly believed in her. He prayed she was right.

He found himself reading the personal information again, the intimate details about her that he shouldn't know, but did. He found her intriguing in quirky ways. A love child, parents never married, spending summers in Paris, defying her mother to study business at Harvard instead of pursuing a career in music. The notes were all in Beverly's hand. He wondered why she thought he should know all these things. Personal lives should be kept personal. There was no room for them in the workplace. But then, there was no room in the workplace for what he had done with Dee eight weeks ago, in spite of Beverly's Executive Sex Clause.

Maybe Dee would turn him down. There was a good possibility. And then what? He hadn't even looked at the other resumes. The only one he knew was at least halfway qualified, certainly more technically qualified than Dee, was Tally Barnes, but that was a moot point now. Ellis jumped as a crisp rap on the door broke into his silent reverie. He shoved Dee's resume back in the envelope, straightened his tie, and stood to greet her.

'Lynn? Are you in here?' Dee entered the conference room dripping wet, turning to shut the door behind her without looking up. 'Sorry I'm so wet. It's pouring out there. The garage was full, so I had to park in the drowned-dog section, or be late, and I make it a point to never be ...' She stopped in mid-sentence, frozen to the wet spot she was now making on the carpet. 'Ellis! I'm so sorry. I just assumed I'd be meeting with your secretary again.'

The classic lines of her dark blue power suit caressed her curves a little less discreetly than they might have otherwise done had it not been wet. The rain had rendered her blouse partially transparent – just enough to reveal the contours of lace beneath, and he knew from personal experience just how nice those contours were.

'Lynn told me you'd be gone,' she was saying. But he was having a hard time paying attention to her words. Rhinestone droplets of water clung to her lashes and tendrils of damp hair curled around her ears. For a second, he stood motionless, unable to take his eyes off the woman glistening in front of him. She held his gaze with a half-smile, her cheeks tinged with the slightest hint of discomfort, discomfort he was sure he could match and raise. It took another second before he realised she was waiting for him to respond. He caught his breath and spoke in a mad rush. 'I felt it was time we met in person about the executive assistant position. Can I get you a towel? I have an extra jacket if you're chilled.'

'Thanks, but I won't melt, and I'm not cold. And if you don't mind me dripping on the carpet, I have several more prospects for you to look at.'

He motioned her to follow him down the hall to his office. 'After all you've done for Pneuma Inc. in the past few years I think you've earned dripping privileges.' He felt stupid the minute he'd said it, but it was out, and it got him the smile he'd hoped for. If she were angry at him for what had happened, if she felt in any way hurt or slighted, she hid it well. In fact, she hid it a little better than he'd hoped. He'd hoped to get some idea of how she felt about him after – everything. If they were going to be working together, he needed to know if she harboured enough of a grudge to put cyanide in his coffee or set explosives off under his desk.

Clearly, she wasn't giving anything away. She sat down on the sofa in front of his desk, crossing long legs in sheer stockings, and opened her briefcase onto her lap.

He was glad for the desk between them. It kept him from shoving the briefcase aside, ripping those wet clothes off her, and licking her dry. It kept the unruly threat of his cock in his trousers under control as he tried not to think about what she'd felt like in his arms.

He took the files she offered him and sifted through them, trying to ignore the droplet of rain on her earlobe begging to be licked. God, what was the matter with him? He was offering the woman a job, not asking her to fuck him. The room seemed suddenly hot. He wondered if the air conditioner had stopped working.

'I'm afraid none of the candidates is really ideal, but these are the ones I felt were at least hopeful. If you could just give me an idea of what it is specifically you want me to look for, Ellis?'

He struggled to force his attention back to what she was saying, away from her earlobe and the fading image of mounded lace over chilled nipples he knew to be delectable.

She nodded to the files.

He gave them a cursory glance then, with a sigh, shoved them back across the desk. 'I can't put off the decision any longer, Dee. I've already waited too long.' He straightened his shoulders and forced a smile that he didn't feel. 'No one to blame but myself. Nevertheless, I need someone to fill that position.'

'Of course.' Her body language was nearly unreadable, but he had made his living catching the nuances in a person's behaviour. He was sure he saw a ripple of tension across the tops of her shoulders. She nodded to her briefcase. 'I'll double my efforts and have some more possibilities on your desk tomorrow.'

'There's no need, Dee.'

'Ellis?' This time the tension was clear.

He leaned forward over his desk, feeling like it was his first date. 'Dee, no one could have worked harder than you to help find a replacement for …' He closed his eyes and rubbed the bridge of his nose beneath his glasses, then began again. 'What I'm trying to say is as hard as you've worked, as much as you've done for Pneuma, I'm afraid I may have wasted your time.'

'Oh?'

'I've given it a lot of thought and I've come to the conclusion there's only one person right for Beverly's job. Beverly knew it for quite some time, but she was a little slow letting me in on her plan.'

He could almost sense the heat of concentration in her gaze. Her cheeks were flushed – perhaps from what she perceived as her failure to deliver. Just below her ear, at the tender side of her throat, he could see the shudder of her pulse. 'Why didn't you tell me? I'd have contacted them.'

'Oh, you don't need to contact them. I've already made the decision.'

'I see.' The flush on her cheeks spread to her temples and all expression disappeared from her face.

He scooted forward on the edge of the chair and leaned over the desk, feeling the accumulation of stress in the muscles of his neck and stomach as he thought about his promise. 'The only person who can take Beverly's job and run with it, Dee, is you.'

For a second, they sat staring at each other. The briefcase shifted and nearly fell off her lap. She righted it without looking down. 'Me?' Her lips barely moved as she spoke, and her voice was little more than a breath. She could have passed for a statue in her stillness; only in the soft spot at her throat where her pulse accelerated could he see any motion at all. Then she blinked, and moisture from the rain slid down her lashes onto the pale skin beneath her blue, blue eyes. 'You're offering me Beverly's job?'

'That's right. Not only are you my choice, but you were Beverly's choice as well, and the woman was never wrong.' He tried to reassure himself with that thought.

Dee offered him no clues as to what she might be thinking. Somehow he hadn't quite expected such a lack of response. He wondered if this were the part where she told him to fuck off, where she told him she couldn't work for a man who was unprofessional enough to have sex with her in his office, a man who fucked and ran. In his mind's eye, he had pictured her excited, smiling, pleased at the opportunity to work for him. Rather naïve, really. After all, she was an intelligent woman; if anyone would know the magnitude of what he was asking of her, she would.

The muscles of her throat tightened, then rose and fell above the pale silk of her blouse; for a second, he thought she was going to smile, but she didn't.

'Dee? Are you all right?'

31

When she spoke, her voice had thickened in an effort to disguise emotions he might not have known were there had he not been so familiar with their shared loss. 'I was Beverly's choice?'

'She told me before she went to Brazil.'

'And you've known since then?'

Suddenly he felt as though he were the one being interviewed. 'I had to be sure. After all, you have no experience in the field.'

She nodded. 'I know.'

A tight silence stretched between them, and then she asked the obvious question. 'This has nothing to do with – what happened between us?' Now the blush was evident, and she held his gaze with difficulty.

'No! Nothing.' In spite of being prepared for it, he still felt as though she had slapped him. Not that he didn't deserve it. Then he added quickly. 'That was the reason Beverly wanted you to join her for drinks after the meeting you were to have with her. She'd made up her mind.'

Chapter Five

BACK AT HOME, DEE opened her briefcase and pulled out the one remaining resume. It was hers. She had been carrying it around ever since Beverly hired her to find her replacement. She could have given it to her at any time, but she'd planned to wait until Beverly got back from Brazil.

Working with Ellison Thorne was her dream job. It had been since she first researched him and Pneuma, Inc. while studying business law at Oregon State. She'd followed the company's successes through her years at Harvard and through her time as a headhunter. All of her fantasies were of working next to Ellis, and yes, it was true, all of her fantasies, when they turned erotic, involved sex with Ellis. But never sex before she had made herself invaluable to him, to Pneuma Inc., never sex before she had proven to him that she was worthy of the position in which he'd placed her. Never comfort sex, never sex that might have been with anyone, any warm body who was sympathetic.

Apparently that was all it had been for him, or so it seemed in his office today. He treated her as he would have any other employee, and that was a good thing. That was what she wanted. She wanted the chance to prove herself without the stigma of sex between them. So why wasn't she happier about the situation?

Eight weeks he'd made no attempt to contact her and every attempt to avoid her, and now, all of a sudden, he was hiring her as his executive assistant. She had seen all the resumes that had crossed Ellis's desk. There were some really sharp people in those files, people who had much more experience than she did. She wanted to believe that she was his choice too, but she'd had sex with him, and no matter how she tried to view it, that had muddied the waters.

She changed into cut-offs and a T-shirt, all the while trying to convince herself she should be elated. This was her dream come true, but the reality of the situation made her feel she'd somehow gotten the position by cheating.

She padded barefoot into the kitchen. The rain had cleared, so the barbecue was a go. The gang would be here soon. McAllister and O'Kelly, the resident red tabbies, ignored her. They crouched on the windowsill, their full attention on the fluttering occupants of the birdbath. She poured herself a glass of iced tea then headed outside, still trying to ease the knot of self-doubt in her stomach.

She was just getting the grill started when Harris joined her on the patio with Kendra right behind. Both carried grocery bags.

Harris gave Dee a peck on the cheek, and she aimed a kiss in the general direction of his closely trimmed beard, now sun-bleached golden from time spent in his kayak.

'Thought you might like this.' He handed her his copy of *Wilderness Vanguard*. Instead of the magazine's usual photo of bear or elk or pristine mountain scenery, Ellis smiled back at her from the cover. The caption read *WV's Man of the Year: When Pneuma Inc.'s CEO deals, even the wildlife goes away happy*.

'You can keep it if you like. I've read it.' Harris was a part-time editor and photographer for the magazine. He did it for love, not for money. The magazine couldn't afford to pay him, but fortunately he did well for himself as a wildlife photographer. That he also did for love, after having given up his law practice for it. 'Thorne's pretty impressive,' Harris said, setting down the grocery bag. 'I can see why he's your hero.'

Part of *Wilderness Vanguard*'s mission was to expose corporations with bad environmental records. That Ellis had been chosen Man of the Year was no small feat.

Dee flipped to the article, which was prefaced by photos of a nature reserve Ellis's company had reclaimed on the sight of a derelict paper mill. She glanced at the accompanying caption. *In a world of corporate greed and plunder, Ellison Thorne has a refreshing penchant for win-win deals, deals that benefit both corporations and the planet. His progressive policies have made Pneuma Inc. one of the most respected companies in the US.*

Harris began unpacking a grocery bag on the table. 'Got beer, salad, chips and dip, and half a cow's worth of T-bones. Hope everyone's hungry.'

Kendra gave Dee a quick hug. 'You look a bit dazed. What's up?'

'Ellis just offered me the executive assistant position.'

'Are you serious? That's fantastic!' Harris grabbed her, and there was a round of rib-crushing bear hugs from both of her friends.

He nodded to the magazine cover. 'You've been telling us since grad school you're exactly what the man needs. Looks like he agrees.'

'You do have a bad case of Thorne on the brain, Dee. But when I see pictures of him like this –' Kendra smiled down at the photo on the cover of the magazine '– I can understand why. God, he's hot! I mean, look at those yummy brown eyes.'

'Kendra, he's going to be my boss, not my boyfriend.'

Her friend shrugged. 'Who's talking boyfriend? I'm talking hot sex here.'

Dee knew exactly what Kendra was talking about, and even eight weeks after the fact the thought of writhing on the floor beneath Ellison Thorne made her pulse do a drum roll. In spite of herself, Beverly's Executive Sex Clause flashed through Dee's head. Jesus, she hadn't even thought about that. Would they implement the Executive Sex Clause? They'd already had sex, after all. Or was that something Ellis would rather they both just forgot about?

'Don't be stupid, Kendra,' Harris called over his shoulder. 'It's not always about sex, you know, and Dee's not exactly a groupie. If anybody's the man's equal, it's Dee. I'd say he's damn smart for hiring her.'

'I didn't say he wasn't,' Kendra said. 'I'm just saying, he's hot, Dee's hot.' She elbowed Dee. 'Oh, don't look at me like that, you are hot, trust me. And you're both single. Nature'll take its course.' Kendra grabbed the magazine and studied the image on the cover. 'Normally I like my men darker, but in his case, I could make an exception and go Celtic.' She looked closer. 'How old is he, anyway?'

'Thirty-eight, I think.' Actually she knew exactly how old he was, and she knew the details of his birth, right down to the fact that he'd been born in the middle of one of the worst storms the Oregon Coast had ever had, born at home because of that.

'Have you told your mom?' Harris asked.

Dee shook her head. 'The way we communicate, I could be retired before she finds out, which is probably just as well. And Dad, he'll just want to borrow money, like always. I think we'll all be happier if they don't know, at least for the present.'

'So, if you're gonna be working for the big man, why isn't there dancing in the streets?' Harris asked.

Dee turned her attention back to the grill. 'I'm just a bit shell-shocked. I had no idea he was going to offer me the position. Besides, it's a big responsibility. Sort of scary when I actually think about it.'

'Come off it, Dee.' Harris finished unpacking groceries and leaned against the table. 'You're not scared of anything. Don't forget, we're counting on you to get rich so we can live decadent lives on your money. We're the Three Musketeers, remember?'

'All for one and one for all.' Kendra raised a baguette in salute.

Not for the first time, Dee was a little surprised that she had so completely scammed her friends as to how tough and fearless she was.

The muffled sounds of life beyond the privacy fence receded as dusk settled around Dee's back yard, shrinking the world to an island of citronella-scented light. 'What's this?' Harris reached for the book in the side pouch of Kendra's bag. '*How Deep My Heart*? By Tess Delaney? Since when do you read romance, Kendra?'

'Give me that.' She jerked the novel away and stuffed it back into her bag. 'I read what I want. Besides, Tess Delaney's burning up the charts. Plus, no one has ever seen her. Don't you find that intriguing? I had to find out what all the fuss is about.'

'And?' Harris said. Dee could see the smile threatening to reveal itself from under his beard.

'And it's entertaining, but it's just another fantasy, the way I see it. I don't believe in romance.'

'Of course you don't,' Harris said. 'How could I forget? You believe in sex.'

Dee could tell where this little chat was heading and, from behind Kendra's back, she gave him the high sign for a change of subject, but it was too late. When would he ever learn?

'That's right,' Kendra said, 'I believe in sex. Romance is something everybody wants but nobody ever really gets. But anybody can get laid.'

'Come on, Kendra. Do you really think you can have sex the way you have cereal in the morning for breakfast, and it's no big deal, no attachments, no hard feelings?' Harris grinned wickedly and fanned a wave of smoke away from his face.

Kendra began laying plates on the table. 'I don't see why not. I don't see why physical need necessarily has to have anything to do with emotion.'

Harris coughed and moved out of the line of smoke. 'It sure as hell would make life easier, wouldn't it? I mean if we could just say "excuse me, but I'm horny, and I need to have sex, would you mind?"'

Dee found herself thinking about Beverly's Sex Clause again, found herself thinking of what had happened between her and Ellis. She wasn't a big keeper of secrets. She didn't have all that many to keep, and especially not from Kendra and Harris, but she had kept sex with Ellis from them. It seemed like a betrayal to share it somehow.'

'No attachments, no regrets,' Kendra said. 'That's my motto.'

'Oh, I like attachments myself.' Dee slipped an arm around Kendra. 'My vibrator came with this neat little –'

'We're talking about real cocks here, Dee, you know – something that doesn't require batteries.'

'Hey, I think it's a great idea if you can handle it.' Harris waved the grilling tongs enthusiastically. 'But I don't know that many people who could just think of sex as physical, with no emotional strings attached.'

Dee couldn't help wondering if Ellis was one of those people.

Any attempt to sleep that night was just an exercise in futility. Dee's brain was too busy replaying the meeting at Pneuma Inc. and trying to analyse how she had ended up to be Ellis's new executive assistant.

Perhaps it was the late hour, or just the build-up of tension generated by her ruminations and the events of the day, but at last, her thoughts turned to the long-familiar fantasies. In her mind's eye, she walked the late-night corridors of the executive suites at the Pneuma Building. She could hear movement from Ellis's office, disturbing the gossamer silence. Cautiously, she approached on tiptoes, holding her breath as she peeked around the corner. There, sprawled in his chair, was Ellis, trousers open, hands occupied, cupping and stroking and rocking against himself in the privacy of his moonlit suite. Hadn't he told her he didn't have time for sex? The thought of him touching himself, the thought of him as single-minded and focused as she'd had to be, the thought of him having as little time for sex as she had, made her hot. In her fantasy she moved around the desk where she could make out the details of his exposure and his mesmerizing attentions to his erection.

In her bed in the real world, the slick rubbing and dipping of her fingers became too enjoyable to waste time rummaging in the nightstand for the vibrator. Though she couldn't keep from imagining how nice it would be to have something between her legs that – as Kendra so eloquently put it – didn't require batteries. She knew exactly what it was she wanted, and how amazing it felt. That something she imagined having between her legs belonged to Ellison Thorne.

She closed her eyes and arched against the pillow, bringing

the fantasy into focus behind her eyelids.

She eased him back in his chair, her hands taking over his efforts against his erection, freeing him to open her blouse and undo her bra. In her fantasy, his mouth quickly found its way to her throat, then to her breasts. His hands slid up under her skirt to caress the inside of her thighs, opening her with ticklish kneading. Then he stood, shoving files and correspondence, pens and paper clips off onto the floor as he guided her back on top of his desk. In her fantasy, she watched in growing arousal as he lifted her hips to remove her panties, lingering to caress her bottom as he did so. But instead of entering her, he took her with his mouth, licking and suckling her like she was ice cream melting against his tongue. When she could stand it no longer, he shoved deep inside her with a groan of pleasure, and the urgent sounds of sex hammered her imagination. She could almost feel the firm musculature of his body against hers. Her scent thickened and warmed in the sustained tension of arousal. And just before the explosion that sent her brain off-line and into the thick cotton chrysalis of sleep, she felt suddenly reassured. If both Ellis and Beverly had agreed she was the best person for the executive assistant position, then surely everything would be all right.

Chapter Six

ELLIS WOKE WITH A start, nearly falling out of his chair. In his dream, he'd been pleading with Dee Henning. Whether he was pleading for her to take the position at Pneuma Inc. or pleading for sex was disturbingly unclear, though the heavy erection pressing against his jeans indicated it was probably the latter. In the dream she was wet, just in out of the rain, and her shirt was … Well, her shirt was way more transparent than it had been in real life. Up until now his dreams had always been of falling or showing up for an important meeting only to discover he'd forgotten his clothes. The absence of sex in his life had not translated to more sex in his dreams, at least not until Dee Henning appeared on the scene. It was all he could do to keep from dwelling on the Dee in his dream, wet and dripping and … He cursed softly, rubbed gritty eyes, and felt around the desk for his glasses, staring through the bleary soft focus of sleep deprivation at the night-darkened shadows of his study.

It was nearly one in the morning. The laptop still hummed quietly, with the screen saver flashing images of planets, galaxies, and nebulae. He poured coffee from the carafe on the cart next to the desk. It was still warm enough to be drinkable.

He'd planned to finish the report for Scribal Paper tonight, along with a new proposal. Beverly had always been in charge of Scribal. She and Alan Marston had been friends, and she knew the best way to handle the cantankerous old fart.

Beverly was barely cold in her grave before Marston was allowing himself to be courted by Terrance Jamison, all anxious to sell him cheap timber from a virgin forest in Valderia, primed and ready to be clear-cut. Christ, Marston knew better. If Beverly had been here she'd have told him what an idiot he was, and he'd have listened.

Marston would be Dee's inheritance. Based on that fact alone, Ellis figured she would probably hate him before she'd been at Pneuma Inc. a month, if she didn't already. He would if he were in her shoes. And that was sad, because he really wanted her to like him.

Absently he sorted through the orderly stack of mail Harold had left on his desk. From midway down, he pulled a familiar mauve envelope. It was from New World Gallery in New York. Inside, along with the usual monthly supporter's newsletter was a handwritten note from Stacie.

Dear Ellis,

I'm so sorry to hear about Beverly's death. I know how much she meant to you. I'm sorry this note is so late in coming, but I've been away and didn't know until Garrett told me. If there's anything I can do, you only have to ask.

I'll be in Portland on a regular basis soon. I'm opening a new gallery there. My staff is liaising with a wildlife photographer named Harris Walker for our opening exhibition. Maybe you know him. His work is often in Wilderness Vanguard.

I'm looking forward to seeing more of you soon. Call me when you're in New York again, and we'll catch up. It's been too long.

Love,

Stacie

In a flood of memories, he wadded the envelope into a ball and tossed it into the garbage. Memories of Stacie and his brother announcing their marriage; memories of him turning without a word and walking out of the room; memories that used to tear at his insides like ground glass. But that was a long time ago. It was the past. Sadly, Stacie had never forgiven herself for her part in what happened at Caltech. How could she or Garrett possibly have known just how bad their timing was? He'd long since forgiven Stacie, forgiven his brother too. It was uncanny, but she and Garrett both had a way of only making matters worse the harder they tried to make it up to him. He wished they'd get it through their heads that there was nothing to make up. Their hearts were in the right place, but the best thing either of them could do for Ellis was leave him alone.

He pulled up his email and scrolled through. There was a memo from Tally Barnes railing on the secretaries in accounting. Something about inter-office emails. The memo was strident and bordered on abusive. For some reason she seemed to think that after Beverly's death every memo she sent should be cc'd to him.

He suddenly recalled his conversation with Beverly about why he shouldn't hire Tally as her replacement. He supposed he should warn Dee about her, just in case. The one thing Dee didn't need was more hassle.

And, just like that, Dee was centre stage in his mind again. And in his body. A sudden flash of Dee Henning dripping all over the floor of his office, followed by the recollection of her on the carpet with her legs wrapped around him, and his erection was back with a vengeance.

Dee and Beverly had discussed the Executive Sex Clause. She'd said so. That uncomfortable thought made him even hornier. He shouldn't even be thinking about implementing the Executive Sex Clause with Dee, yet he was. The room felt suddenly hot and Ellis squirmed in his seat, trying to get comfortable. Would Dee have been thinking of him while Beverly expounded on how much better the brain would work if the junk was well-satisfied? Would Beverly have even suggested that the two of them … That he and Dee might satisfy each other's junk. He thought of Beverly's email suggesting that he hire Dee and implement the Sex Clause. It was a joke. Dear God, surely Dee knew it was only a joke. But after what had already happened between them, how could she know? And now she had accepted the position as his executive assistant, did she think it included the Sex Clause?

Almost without realising, he opened his fly. He imagined himself helping a rain-drenched Dee out of her wet clothes as they casually discussed business. He imagined that they both agreed they'd had a stressful day, and they needed the relief the Sex Clause afforded them.

And suddenly it was too late to tuck himself back in his jeans. It had to happen, and it had to happen soon. He made the shift from chair to sofa, stroking as he went, imagining Dee allowing him access to her wet places with a towel, with his fingers, with his tongue. He imagined her forcing him back into the chair behind his desk and straddling him. He imagined himself thrusting and grinding and pressing. He imagined until his fantasy sent him over the edge into spasms of relief, spasms so hard that the chair creaked and groaned beneath his ass. Was it possible that Beverly was right, that some relief of a sexual nature might just help him deal with Marston and Jamison and the rest of the avalanche of urgency Beverly had left him with? Was it possible that an Executive Sex Clause might just be the best way of getting that relief?

Chapter Seven

TALLY BARNES WAS INTO her second or maybe third glass of expensive champagne. She couldn't remember. What she did remember was that her plans to be able to afford expensive champagne on a regular basis were down the crapper, now she had been passed over for the promotion of a lifetime. Since Beverly Neumann's death, she had allowed herself the luxury of the good stuff, certain that she'd soon be able to afford it regularly once she took over the woman's position. She'd already run up her credit cards to make sure she had a wardrobe that was up to the task. She even had an interior decorator on retainer to redo Beverly's office when she finally took over. She had been that certain. How could she have been passed over like this? Right now, she needed alcohol, and damn it, she deserved the good stuff after the shit day she'd had.

She was about to leave the bar and find a table. She had her laptop and the memory stick. She wanted to go over the files she'd downloaded from Beverly's computer back when everyone was grieving, back when she had access to the woman's office to help with the financial statements for Scribal Paper. And while she'd had access, she took full advantage and downloaded Beverly's emails, which she hadn't looked at until now. She was hoping to find something there, to figure out what happened, what Dee Henning had that she didn't. Damn it! She wasn't going down without a fight. Her mind was on the inter-office email that had announced Ellis's choice for his new executive assistance and ruined her day. She wasn't looking where she was going when she ploughed into a man who'd had the bad luck to get in her way.

Before she could tell the asshole to watch where he was going, he beat her to it, only much more pleasantly. 'Beautiful women should drink good champagne, not wear it,' he said.

Before Tally could respond, the man in Armani grabbed her gently by the shoulders and spun her back around, seating her once more at the bar before the collision that would have had her wearing the remains of her Moët and Chandon. Then he took the glass from her hand, set it on the bar, and perched lightly on the stool next to her. 'Are you all right?'

Tally was all ready to tell the man to fuck off and mind his own business, then she caught sight of his cool blue eyes and handsome face. Even in the dim light of the bar everything about him said not only business chic, but outrageously expensive business chic. He was the kind of man who filled her dreams and fantasies, and he looked really familiar, like he should be somebody famous, somebody important. But with her head slightly muzzy from the alcohol, she couldn't quite recall where she'd seen him. 'I'm sorry,' she said, allowing him to help her onto the stool. 'It's just that I've got a lot on my mind.'

He eased the computer bag off her shoulder and settled it onto the floor next to her. Then he motioned to the bartender to bring another glass of fizz for her and a Glenfiddich for him. At last he turned to face her, offering her a smile that made her feel giddy. 'Good things, I hope. On your mind, I mean.'

'Not good things. Not good at all.' She tossed back her half-empty fizz and pushed the glass aside. 'I was just overlooked for a promotion and the position was given to someone far less qualified.'

'You mean Dee Henning?'

'Yes, I mean Dee Henning. That job was mine.' Tally leaned close to him, practically hissing in his face. 'I can't believe Ellis could even consider anyone else. I've been busting my ass in accounting for five years now, and after Beverly Neumann's death, I was indispensable. Ellis barely knew which end was up without me.'

'Strange choice, Dee Henning. You're right. She's not really qualified.'

'Of course she's not qualified. She's just a headhunter and …' She stopped mid-rant. It suddenly hit her. 'How do you know about Dee Henning? Who are you anyway?'

'I had a rather unpleasant run-in with Ms Henning when she worked for Jasper and McDowell.' Her new friend waved his hand as though he were batting away a fly. 'Besides, I make it a point to know what's going on in the business world.' He offered her his hand. 'Terrance Jamison, at your service.'

She nearly fell off the stool. '*The* Terrance Jamison, of Jamison Holdings?' She thrust a hand forward.

'The same.'

'I thought I recognised you, but I was a bit distressed, you know, not thinking very straight.'

'Perfectly understandable,' he said. Just then the drinks arrived. He handed her the fizz and lifted his whiskey. 'I'd like to make a toast to new possibilities, Ms Barnes. What is it they say, a door never closes but what a window opens? Is it OK if I call you Tally?'

'You know my name?'

'Of course I know your name. How could I not know your name? From what I've heard, Pneuma Inc. would grind to a standstill without you. I think it's shocking that Thorne doesn't appreciate what a treasure he has in you.'

He barely got the words out before his iPhone rang, which gave Tally a chance to let what Jamison had just said sink in, while she did a little basking in the first good thing that had happened to her all day. She studied the man surreptitiously in his conversation. So this was the infamous Terrance Jamison. She half expected him to have horns and a tail with the reputation he had at Pneuma, Inc. – probably undeserved. Jamison was Ellis Thorne's rival and worst enemy. Everyone knew the men hated each other. She'd seen pictures of Jamison in *The Oregonian*, always looking like he was king of the world, like the kind of man you toyed with at your own peril. And he was sitting here next to her, buying her expensive champagne, reminding her of just what an asset she would be for any company. And that made him even easier to look at. In spite of the man's chivalry, he was a bit frightening with those cool eyes and pale hair. He was in his early 50s, she'd read somewhere, but oh, he was definitely one of those men who aged very well indeed.

Ellis had never been chivalrous to her. The best she'd ever gotten from Ellis, even with all her help and kindness after Beverly's death, was distant politeness. She could have been the janitor for all he noticed.

She was consorting with the enemy. It gave her a warm, squirmy feeling inside, like revenge of the very best kind, especially since Terrance Jamison knew who she was. Ellis might not appreciate her, but Ellis wasn't the only show in town now, was he? And it would serve him right to lose her.

At last Jamison hung up. 'Sorry about that, Tally.' He gave a conspiratorial smile. 'That was Alan Marston. You know Alan Marston, don't you? He certainly speaks highly of you.'

A slight blush of pleasure warmed in her chest. 'Al? Al speaks highly of me? Well, I'm delighted, of course; I mean, I've basically picked up the slack with him and the Scribal Paper account since Beverly Neumann's death, no easy task as I'm sure you can imagine.'

'Oh, I can well imagine,' he said, swirling his drink, holding her in an icy-hot gaze. 'Marston's not easy to work with, and who can really blame him. I mean the man's in a real bind, isn't he? He knows, as we all do, that anything Pneuma Inc. can offer him now would, sadly, be little more than a stop-gap. The man runs paper mills. He clearly needs trees, not environmental woo-woo.' He shrugged. 'And I can get the man what he needs at a good price.' He offered her an embarrassed grin, like he'd just been caught with his hand in the cookie jar. 'Do forgive me, Tally, it's very unprofessional of me to be speaking to you about such things. Conflict of interest and all, but I figured you would overhear enough to suspect who I was talking to, and I'm sure –' he leaned closer '– I can count on this to be our little secret. Can't I? No harm done.'

She chuckled softly and leaned forward into his gaze. 'We're not on the clock now, are we, Mr Jamison? Besides, I'll be turning Marston over to Dee Henning, so it really doesn't matter to me. I mean, I'd like to see Marston get what he needs,

47

of course I would. He's a bit of a tyrant, but ultimately he's a good man, and lots of jobs depend on the choices he makes for his paper mills, people's livelihoods, you know?' Oh, she had learned to talk the talk quite well after Beverly died; fat lot of good it had done her. 'The man's got to do what he's got to do, doesn't he?'

'Precisely, Tally, precisely. I'm glad we're on the same page here. I had heard you're noted for your practicality. No small gift in the business world, as you know, and it must be even more important, if unappreciated, when you work in the realm of such dreamers as Thorne and Crittenden.' He motioned the bartender to bring her another champagne, then leaned still closer, so close he could have almost kissed her, and she was just drunk enough to have let him. But what happened next was even better than a kiss. 'Tally, we'd both like to see Marston get what he needs, to offer him a way to protect all of those jobs, and I think we both know what Ellis has to offer isn't going to cut it, don't we?' He touched her hand very gently. 'You don't have to answer that.' His breath against her cheek smelled of expensive whiskey, which blended nicely with the scent of wealth he exuded, and her pulse somersaulted in her throat. Whatever it was he was playing at, she couldn't say she didn't like it.

'What would you say to working together, the two of us?' His lips were almost brushing her ear, his voice barely more than a whisper.

Her stomach did a dangerous flip-flop, a flip-flop that quickly migrated to her already racing pulse. She sat up straight on her stool, the fizz making her slightly dizzy, that alcohol-steeped feeling of suddenly being in a box of cotton wool leaving her in need of a reality check. 'You want me to work for you?'

He held her in a gaze that made her feel exposed – not naked. There was nothing sexual about it, but it was like he could somehow see inside her head, through the alcohol buzz threatening to escalate beyond the limits of even feigned sobriety. Just when she was feeling like the better part of wisdom might be a quick escape, he offered her a boyish smile that made him look considerably younger than he was, and considerably less threatening. 'Actually, what I had in mind was something along the lines of one of Thorne's famous win-win deals, Tally; something that would give us both exactly what we want. If you'll give me the chance, if you'll trust me and work with me, we can not only get Marston what he needs, but we can make sure when the dust settles, you are happily ensconced in that huge corner office that used to belong to Beverly Neumann.' His smile broadened and morphed until it was only slightly less than dangerous. 'Or quite possibly something even better, if you like.'

Chapter Eight

DEE'S FIRST DAY ON the job, Ellis cleared his calendar and spent the time briefing her on her new responsibilities – especially the more urgent client files she was expected to be up to speed on immediately. Thanks to the connections Dee had made while working with Jasper and McDowell she was familiar with most of the customers. Without such an advantage she was sure she would have been completely overwhelmed.

'Are you finding everything you need all right in Beverly's office –' Ellis caught himself and forced a pained smile. 'Your office. As for Beverly's jungle –' He cleared his throat and blinked. For a second, he drifted away. His eyes were dark and unreadable, half hidden behind glasses that reflected the bright sunlight bathing the room. Then his attention returned. With a controlled intake of breath, the lines of his face dissolved back into neutrality. 'We can have these plants removed whenever you like.'

She felt a tightness in her own throat, empathy mixed with her own pain of loss as she remembered the last time she had sat in the office with Beverly. She swallowed hard and squared her shoulders. 'If it's all the same to you, I'd rather keep them. They remind me of Beverly, and I like that. Sandra can show me how to take care of the more exotic plants. Besides, Beverly told me once that photosynthesis increases the oxygen content.' She nodded to the teetering mountain of files that now graced her side of the conference table. 'These days my brain can use all the oxygen it can get.'

Just then Sandra brought in sandwiches so the two could continue their efforts through lunch.

'You'll like working with Sandra,' Ellis said as they watched her leave. 'She was Beverly's secretary even before there was a Pneuma Inc. She knows the company better that I do. She must have been a psychologist in a previous life, or possibly a psychic. If you're ever in doubt about anything, ask Sandra. And –' he shuffled through the stacks of files in front of him '– she can also help you negotiate some of the more difficult personnel problems you may face.'

'Personnel problems?'

'Oh, it's nothing, really. A few people here were unhappy I hired an outsider.' He watched her as though he was sizing up an athlete for strength and endurance, and she held his gaze in spite of the clench in her stomach at one more problem she could do without. 'Nothing you can't handle after being Jasper and McDowell's only female rep. That place has a reputation for being a good ole boys' club.'

It was true, the early days at Jasper and McDowell had been challenging. But she had overcome that personnel issue by being the best in her field. Problem solved. She doubted it would be that easy at Pneuma Inc.

Aside from attending several meetings together, Dee hardly saw Ellis those first three weeks. But the growing mountain of files on her computer was proof he was always just an email away. Even when he was in, what he couldn't pass on through the miracle of IT, he sent through the secretaries. She had long since resigned herself to the fact that he had totally forgotten what had happened between the two of them in his office after Beverly went missing. He was definitely not giving her preferential treatment. He wasn't giving her any treatment at all, actually. The secretaries got way more of his attention than she did, though she seldom had time to dwell on what now seemed like the distant past.

She arrived at the office early and stayed late. The working day was only over when she fell asleep with whichever client file she had taken to bed that night. And even then the job invaded her dreams, often with Alan Marston berating her in front of all of Pneuma Inc., while Ellis stood by, shaking his head in disappointment and commenting repeatedly on how she had let Beverly down. Then she would wake up in a cold sweat, unable to go back to sleep. It was just as well. There was always plenty of work to do. She woke up groggy every morning before the alarm went off, too stressed to go back to sleep, and then the whole process started over again. It seemed like every night she got home later and slept less. She was sure she was running on adrenalin by now, but with the help of lots of caffeine and an acute fear of failure, she was managing. When panic threatened to take control, she buried herself deeper in the mountain of files and had some more caffeine, reminding herself Ellis and Beverly had faith in her, and she wasn't about to fail them.

Everything was gearing up for a big teleconference with Marston and Scribal Paper, in which Dee was to give the financial projections and a short spiel on some of the research Wade Crittenden had been doing. Wade never made public appearances, nearly hyperventilated at the very thought, so it was up to her to promote Pneuma Inc.'s latest brainchild. At best, it was a temporary fix, and an effort to convince Marston not to consider Jamison Holding's tantalizing deal of a cheap clear-cut in a part of the world no one cared about. The proposal would be a hard sell, definitely – and one complicated by the fact that, since Beverly's death, Marston was still refusing to work with anyone but Ellis. Hopefully the presentation would help ease her into Marston's good graces, of which there seemed to be precious few these days.

The problem was she hadn't received the financial information she needed from accounting. Her requests had gone unanswered and, at last, she gave up and decided to go after the file in person.

When she got off the elevator on the sixth floor, she could hear the yelling halfway down the hall. She was surprised to find the uproar was coming from Tally Barnes's office, and the door was standing wide open. It wasn't hard to hear what was going on; in fact, she figured most of accounting could hear.

'What is it, Pneuma Inc.'s new policy to hire morons? And fat ones at that. If you can't follow simple directions, maybe we can find you a job with the janitorial staff. It shouldn't take too much brain power to push a mop, and from the looks of you, the exercise would do you good.'

'But you told me to –'

'Don't tell me what I told you. I know what I told you.' Tally shoved a file at the flustered woman. 'Get out of here, and don't come back until you get it right.'

Through the open door, Dee could see a dressed-for-success blonde with shoulder-length hair and artfully done make-up seated behind the desk. She would have been attractive if not for the venom spewing past her carefully painted lips. She was in mid-rant to one of the secretarial staff Dee had met earlier. The woman, who looked to be barely out of her teens, stood red-faced, shifting from foot to foot.

Dee was about to tiptoe away quietly and come back when things were calmer, but it was too late. Tally had seen her.

'Dee Henning! What a pleasant surprise. I wondered when you were going to do us the honour.'

The secretary apologised quietly as she pushed past Dee with her head down, but Dee thought she saw tears. She tried to offer the poor thing a reassuring smile, but she was interrupted.

'Never mind her. She's just incompetent, like so many people these days. I'm Tally Barnes.' She stood to offer Dee an overly firm handshake, looking down at her from several extra inches of height. Her long acrylic nails made her grip a bit worrisome. 'Everyone at Pneuma Inc. has been talking about Dee Henning, the wonder girl. At last we meet.' She offered Dee a smile pressed tightly against impossibly white teeth.

Dee remembered Tally Barnes. Hers had been one of the resumes she'd reviewed for the executive assistant's position, one she'd found reasonably impressive. She knew the woman was more qualified for the job than she was. Perhaps she would have felt a little more guilty about the whole situation had she not just seen Tally's mistreatment of the young secretary. Was Tally one of those personnel problems Ellis had mentioned that Sandra could help her negotiate? She hoped not.

'I suppose you came for this?' Tally sat back down and nodded to the file labelled "Scribal" lying on the edge of her desk. 'I'm sorry I didn't get it up to you. It's been a madhouse down here with no end in sight. I'm sure Ellis told you that I've had to take up the slack since Beverly died. Of course, I'm more than happy to do my part, even if it means we're short-handed in other areas.'

Dee took the offered file. 'I'm hoping I'll be able to relieve some of that burden. I'll be taking over the account for Scribal soon. That should help.'

'I have to say I'm a little surprised that Ellis would want to rock the boat with Alan Marston right now.' She leaned forward over the desk as though imparting a big secret. 'I mean, Alan isn't exactly easy to work with, Dee. I'm just now getting the man to trust me a little bit. I'm more than happy to liaise with him and do my part to make your transition easier. Heaven knows you've got enough to think about without his nasty tantrums.'

'Thanks,' Dee said. 'That's very kind.'

'So tell me, are you spending another night in the Dungeon?' Tally asked. 'Oh, don't look so surprised. Gossip travels fast at Pneuma Inc., and there's been a lot of speculation as to what Ellis's new executive assistant is doing every night down in R and D.'

Dee smiled. 'Just some projections Wade's helping me with.'

Tally raised an eyebrow. 'Sounds intriguing.' Just then her phone rang. 'Damn it, Louisa, how did I end up working with someone who has the IQ of a peanut?' she yelled into the receiver.

Dee chose that moment to make her exit, waving casually at Tally, who had moved on from IQ to insulting the secretary's fashion sense. As Dee stepped into the elevator and the doors shut out the ravings in accounting, she felt pretty sure she wouldn't be soliciting any more of Tally Barnes's help than absolutely necessary, nor would she be divulging any project details.

Chapter Nine

TALLY GLARED AT DEE'S back as she left. Being nice to the little bitch felt like broken glass in the pit of her stomach. She slammed down the phone and looked at her watch. Only 15 minutes till quitting time. She began to pack up her things. Dee Henning certainly hung out in R and D a lot these days. She wondered if it had something to do with the mysterious *ESC* that kept turning up in the emails she'd downloaded from Beverly's computer.

She'd asked Wade about it, but he didn't seem to know, or wasn't paying enough attention to the question to know if he knew or not. Wade was the stereotypical absent-minded professor. She picked up the phone, and dialled his extension.

'What?' came the answer after the seventh ring. She was lucky he answered at all.

'Oh, hi Wade, it's Tally, Tally Barnes. Accounting?'

'What?' he said again. It was a good thing for Pneuma Inc. that what the man lacked in social skills he made up for in genius.

'Are you going bowling tonight?' He loved bowling, and claimed to have gotten some of his best ideas at the bowling alley.

'Nope.' She could hear him rattling around working on something, clearly not paying her much attention, which was exactly what she wanted. 'Meeting with Dee Henning about Trouvères. Running projections, numbers.'

She put on her best dumb blond voice. 'I would have thought Dee would be spending her time on Scribal rather than on some little French company.'

'Of course she's spending time on Scribal. What the hell do

you think she's spending time on? I gotta go. I'm busy.' He hung up. She didn't take offence. That was just Wade Crittenden.

All Tally knew of Trouvères came from a glance at one of Beverly's files. She had no idea what they did, or why they mattered to Scribal. Did Trouvères have anything to do with the *ESC*?

On her laptop, she pulled up the most intriguing email exchange between Beverly and Ellis and perused it for the thousandth time.

B: I've been thinking a lot about the ESC lately, Ellis, and I think it's time. When we hire my replacement, I think we need to implement the ESC.

E: lol. I can hardly put that in the requirements for Dee Henning to pass on to the lucky lottery winner, can I?

B: Of course not! It's a secret weapon. And it won't be a lottery. That's why we'll have to choose my replacement very carefully. But when we do, when we have just the right person and we implement the ESC, well, Ellis, I think you'll be taking Pneuma, Inc. to greater heights than either of us ever dreamed of.

E: Still lol! You get Dee Henning to find me just the right person for the job, and we'll do it.

B: Oh, don't you worry, Ellis. If you've got the balls for it, I'll find you just what you're looking for, and we can watch productivity soar. Won't that just sweeten my retirement package?

Beverly always was blunt. Tally had been on the receiving end of the woman's straight talk more than a few times. 'Bitch,' she whispered under her breath.

Just before she closed up shop to head home, her BlackBerry buzzed with a message from her Visa card company, thanking her for her payment. The card had been maxed and then some. What the hell was going on? A quick check online showed that the balance had been paid in full. Before she could call the card company, the soft tinkle of a bell alerted her to the arrival of a text on the new phone Terrance Jamison had given her for all their communications. She pulled it out of her bag. The text read.

A gift for a gift. I reward the deserving.

'Fuck,' she whispered, her breath steaming the screen of her phone. She had sent Jamison copies of the proposal that was to be given to Marston tomorrow. It wasn't the complete proposal, but it was as much as she could get hold of: it was enough for what Jamison needed. Had the man really just paid off her maxed-out Visa gold card?

She texted back with trembling fingers.

How did you do that?

The answer was almost immediate.

I'm rich, remember? Now go celebrate, Tally. You can afford it.

Dee spent most of the night before the teleconference with Marston cooped up in the Dungeon, as his lab in R and D was universally known. Wade had one of the best teams of scientists and engineers in the country working for him, but the Dungeon was his domain, separate from the state-of-the-art facilities where everyone else in R and D worked. It was all she could do to contain her excitement. She couldn't wait until they were ready to share their findings with Ellis. During the course of the evening there had been a couple of conference calls to Paris, a pizza delivery in the wee hours, lots of coffee, and lots of scheming. Dee had the connections from her time at Jasper and McDowell, and Wade had the technical expertise that just might be able to pull the plan together.

Back home, she read through her presentation for the teleconference one more time before she headed off to bed. It was a mid-morning meeting, so she set her alarm and settled in for what would be little more than a catnap. At least, that was her plan.

It was the sun streaming through her window that woke her. That was the first indication something was wrong. Since she'd begun work at Pneuma Inc., Dee had always caught the sunrise over the freeway just before she exited for the Pneuma Building. Somewhere in the back of her brain, a *beep, beep, beep* got louder and louder. It took a second to register that it was her alarm. She rolled over to turn it off, and her stomach turned to ice. It was almost eight o'clock! The alarm had been going off for nearly three hours. How could she not have heard it? She jumped from the bed, jamming her toe on the nightstand as she reached for her BlackBerry and punched in Ellis's number. There was no answer. She punched in a quick message, which didn't go. Then she remembered IT had had the network down all night for maintenance. Looked like they were still finishing up. She cranked the shower and stripped. The meeting was at nine. If she hurried, she just might make it.

And she probably would have had it not been for construction on I-5. Ellis still wasn't answering his phone, and neither Lynn nor Sandra seemed to be at their desks. Dee left messages at the switchboard, but could do nothing else except sit and curse the traffic. She stumbled into the executive suites at 10:03, just as Tally Barnes stepped out of Ellis's office.

Tally was the last person Dee wanted to see, but it was too late to duck behind anything. She was caught like a rabbit in the headlights.

Tally offered her a smile that was all sweetness and light. 'Thank God! Dee, you're here at last. I was worried sick that something awful had happened to you. Ellis had Lynn call me in when you didn't show up. Naturally, I dropped everything and came in to pinch-hit for you. Are you all right?'

Dee nodded, forcing herself to remain calm. 'Is Ellis in?'

'Of course.' Tally laid a solicitous hand on Dee's arm. 'I'm sorry, Dee, but he's not in a very good mood. I mean, I'm sure whatever happened, you have an excuse, and, well, Ellis is a reasonable man. Good luck. I'm sure it'll be OK.' She squeezed Dee's arm, then hurried past in a wave of some spicy perfume, her heels click-clicking on the floor as she headed for the elevator.

For a second, Dee feared she would pass out. Nothing like this had ever happened to her before, and worst of all, there was no one to blame but herself. She took two deep breaths, knocked on the door, and stepped inside.

'Sit down.' Ellis didn't look up from his laptop.

She obeyed.

He continued with his work, giving her no indication as to what he was thinking.

She sat stiff-backed, clutching her BlackBerry for dear life. Waiting.

'IT had a major glitch this morning,' he said, still not looking at her. 'The meeting was late getting started.'

'I'm sorry,' she said.

At last he pushed his chair back and looked up at her. 'Marston refused the proposal.'

'I'm sorry,' she said again.

'Not that it was a huge surprise, but I could have done without him berating me for hiring someone incompetent and irresponsible to take Beverly's place. That didn't exactly make my day. What the hell happened?'

She felt the heat rising up her spine and onto her ears. 'I overslept.' She forced the words out into the chilled room.

'You overslept?'

'Yes.' She nodded imperceptibly, feeling the scrutiny of his glare.

For a long moment, he just stared at her. She forced herself to meet his gaze and held her tongue, afraid if she tried to say anything she'd burst into tears, and she despised women who cried.

'That's it, then? You overslept.'

She nodded again, swallowing hard.

'Well, that's a relief.' He leaned forward in his chair and rose, almost as though he were going to leap over the desk and pounce. The tension in his body was palpable. 'I was afraid you were lying on the freeway somewhere in a pool of blood. I'm so relieved that it was nothing so dire, and that you simply overslept.' His voice gradually grew louder until he wasn't exactly yelling, but neither was there any way she could miss his message as each word drove her deeper into her chair until she felt as trapped as if she had been tied there.

'I'm sorry.' She forced a whisper through the block in her throat, but the stinging behind her eyes warned that a swift exit would be necessary if she were to avoid the flood.

'Sorry? You're sorry? Tally had to pick up the slack. Do

you have any idea how that looked? Just when I was starting to make progress with Marston, just when the man was beginning to listen to reason, you oversleep. You made Jamison's deal seem all the sweeter, that's what you did. Now, tell me what the hell's going on.'

'Pardon?'

He moved from behind his desk and paced the carpet in front of her like a bull ready to charge. 'You're supposed to be working to shore up the situation with Scribal. I told you up front that's your major concern at the moment, then not only do you oversleep and miss an important meeting, but I find out you've been working on something behind my back.' Before she could respond, he turned on her. 'Is Trouvères what you've been staying up half the night and missing meetings for? When I hired you, I never thought you, of all people, would neglect your responsibilities.'

'I'm not neglecting anything. If you would just –'

He interrupted her. 'Don't think just because I gave you this job, you suddenly know it all. I took a big risk hiring you.' He stopped pacing and rooted himself in front of her, close enough that she had to strain her neck to look up at him. 'You want to do something; you bring it to me first. You're not ready to make that kind of decision on your own. You don't have the experience it takes to … To … You're not Beverly.'

His words were a hard slap, felt more than heard above the roar in her ears. She wasn't sure whether the ragged breathing her brain finally registered in the chasm of silence that followed his tirade was his or her own.

The phone rang into the charged atmosphere, and Ellis jerked it from its cradle in a stranglehold. 'This had better be good, Lynn. Wade? What the hell does he want? Can't it wait? We're not finished yet. I can what?' He heaved a sigh of resignation and slammed the receiver back down. 'Wade wants to see you right now. He says I can get back to you on this, and believe me, I intend to.' He nodded toward the door. 'Well, go on; at least don't keep him waiting. Pick up the notes on the meeting from Sandra.'

She stood on trembling legs and turned to go. As she

reached for the door, he called to her. 'Dee, I strongly suggest you make no more attempts to prove Marston right about you.'

Sandra joined her in the hall. 'I have the meeting notes for you.'

'Just put them on my desk. Wade wants to see me.'

Sandra nodded. 'Yes, I know. I told him he did. And I told him to give you a few minutes in the ladies' to freshen up first.' She offered a reassuring smile and turned on her heels.

Still breathing like a freight train, Ellis watched Dee disappear, shutting the door behind her. He grabbed the phone and called his secretary. 'Lynn, hold all my calls. I don't want to be disturbed ... How long? Until I say otherwise, that's how long.' He slammed the receiver down, snapped his laptop shut, and stormed down the hall to the lounge.

He shoved his way out of his jacket and tossed it across the wing-backed chair, then practically strangled himself in his efforts to loosen his tie. From the coffee table he grabbed up the remote, and plunged the room into the wild, raucous ride of the third movement of Beethoven's *Moonlight Sonata*. Then he dropped onto the sofa struggling to breath, struggling to regain control, struggling to figure out what the hell had just happened. All through the meeting, when Dee didn't show up, he was terrified that something horrible had happened; terrified that he would lose Dee the same way he had lost Beverly. And the relief he felt at seeing her. Jesus, the relief was like nothing he'd ever felt before.

If Lynn hadn't called, if Wade hadn't demanded Dee's presence ... If Ellis had had one more second with her, he would have yanked her up from the chair and fucked her senseless right there in the middle of the day with all of Pneuma Inc. just outside his door, fucked her as though he might never get another chance, fucked her as though his life depended on it, and that's exactly how it felt. He wiped cold sweat from his forehead, struggling to breathe. If he'd lost her, Jesus! He couldn't even bear the thought.

He jerked open his fly and sucked a harsh breath as he released himself into his hand and began to tug on his cock like the world was coming to an end. Christ, he couldn't go on like this. It felt like he was always either avoiding her or jerking off thinking about her. And fuck if he wasn't thinking about her all the time; the shape of her, the feel of her, the sass of her. He'd never wanted anything so badly. And then – and then she'd fucked up so royally that all he wanted to do was punish her, to turn her over his knee for giving him such a scare, to – to … To fuck her until she couldn't walk.

The image flashed through his head, of him bending her over his desk and shoving up her skirt, of him ripping aside her panties, of him making her sorry she'd overslept, of him making her sorry she'd made him feel all those things, things he didn't want to feel, of him dropping his trousers and shoving his cock up into her very contrite, very wet slit and … That was it. Before he could reach for his handkerchief, before he could even think about making it to the bathroom, he convulsed his load onto the coffee table to the driving piano crescendo hammering into his ears and to visions of Dee Henning bent over his desk, moaning and writhing beneath him.

Chapter Ten

IT HADN'T BEEN DEE'S intention to spill her guts to Harris about the disastrous meeting. He stopped by her office to deliver a sandwich for a late dinner. He'd been in the neighbourhood, and they hadn't had much time to catch up since she started work at Pneuma Inc. She'd promised him at least 20 minutes in exchange for the sandwich. It hadn't taken him that long to figure out something wasn't right.

'I couldn't even make an excuse, Harris. There were no excuses. Marston's right. I was irresponsible.' She knocked back the last of her iced tea, wishing it were something stronger, but knowing she had way too much work to do this evening to even think about drinking anything that didn't involve high doses of caffeine.

Harris sat back in the chair and wiped his hands on the napkin. 'You look like hell, Dee. When's the last time you slept?'

'This morning! That's the problem.'

'I mean really slept. A full night, peaceful dreams, teddy bear, the whole nine yards.'

'I never thought it would be like this. I always thought I'd be so impressive, that I would somehow manage to pull everything off and come out shining. He's gonna fire me, Harris.' She quickly wiped at her eyes to stave off the threat of tears. 'He might have already done it if Sandra and Wade hadn't conspired to rescue me.' The thought made her cringe. 'It's so humiliating. I've never needed rescuing in my life. I've always pulled my own weight.'

'Yours and several other people's as well, most of the time.' Harris said. 'So then what happened?'

'Ellis said he'd get back to me, that we weren't finished, but then he got called away, so I was spared the guillotine, at least until tomorrow.'

'He's not going to fire you, Dee. Does he have any idea the hours you put in? Is he still here?'

She shook her head.

'Didn't think so. And you were here how late last night with Wade Crittenden?'

She toyed with her sandwich. 'I don't know. I think it was two when I left. We had a couple of calls to Paris, and with the time change and all …'

'And how long has this been going on?'

'It doesn't matter how long. It'll have to keep going on until I figure things out, or Ellis finally decides Tally Barnes really can do this job better than I can. She must have been looking pretty damn good to him this morning.'

'Who's Tally Barnes?'

'Someone who's a little too helpful for comfort.' Dee figured it was probably Tally who had been thoughtful enough to mention to Ellis that she'd been spending evenings with Wade, though she didn't know how Tally knew about Trouvères.

'Maybe you're right; maybe you should be prepared just in case Ellis gives you the axe.' Harris gave her a mock-serious look. 'You should probably polish up your arias. Great sopranos are hard to come by.'

She threw her napkin across the desk at him and laughed. 'True, but we mediocre ones are abundant.'

Harris caught the napkin and slam-dunked it into the trash. 'Ah! What a life it would be for you, Dee!' He stood and moved behind her desk, placing a light kiss on the top of her head. Teaching snotty-nosed kids their scales after school, auditioning for all the local musicals. Your mom would be so proud.' He looked down at his watch. 'I've gotta go. Some of us still have a life.' He shrugged. 'Well, at least Kendra does. See you later, Ms Diva.' He kissed her again and left.

Ms Diva. Harris and Kendra used to call her that all the time back when she was running here and there to music lessons and auditions, before she defied her mother and went off to study for her MBA. The memory of her day of emancipation still made her stomach churn.

'When were you going to tell me? I'm your mother, for God's sake!'

Dee remembered everything about that day like it was yesterday. Her mother had paid a surprise visit to her dorm room after one of Dee's professors had let the plan slip to her while picking up his kid from a piano lesson. The colour in her mother's cheeks always made her look like a porcelain doll when she was angry, and she had been enraged.

'There was no point.' Dee continued packing. 'I knew how you'd react.'

'Of course you knew how I'd react. How would you expect me to react when you throw your career away?' Her mother paced in front of the bed breathing like she was about to explode.

'There is no career, Mom. When are you gonna admit it? I'm not that good.'

'You are that good. You're just lazy, that's all, lazy like your father. You don't practice enough, you're not focused enough. You don't appreciate the sacrifices I've made for you to have this chance.'

Dee kept packing.

'What about *Cats*? I've talked to the producer, and he's willing to give you an audition. You're a shoo-in, Dee, you know that.'

'Of course I'm a shoo-in, Mom, it's a local production. Anyone who can carry a tune is a shoo-in.'

Her mother glared at her. 'You know that's not true. *The Oregonian* will be covering it, and that means people will see you, will hear you. That's all you need, darling. That's all you've ever needed.'

'That's all I need for what?' She slammed a stack of T-shirts into the suitcase. 'So I can sing with some minor chorus and give lessons to brats who don't practice like you do, just to pay the rent?'

Dee hadn't seen it coming. Looking back now, she should

have. The sharp impact of her mother's hand hard across her face nearly knocked her backward onto the bed. Inside her mouth, she tasted blood where her teeth had cut her cheek. For a second the world blurred in front of watery eyes, but she blinked, straightened herself, and continued to pack. She knew it always made her mother angrier when she just took the abuse, when she didn't argue or cry or get angry. That was power, something there had been precious little of in her life until then.

'I gave up my chances to be great when your father knocked me up. I didn't have to do that, you know? I gave up my life for you, to see your gifts nurtured, to see you had the chance I didn't get, and this –' She kicked over the second suitcase already packed and sitting by the bed. 'This is how you repay me?'

'It's a great opportunity, Mom, one I may never get again. And I'm good at it. I'm really good at it.' The woman had never acknowledged Dee's 4.0 grade point average nor the listing of good schools she could have easily gotten into. There was no need for any of that in her mother's eyes, not when her daughter was going to be a great soprano, or a star on Broadway. Yet somehow it had never entered her mind to wonder why none of those scholarships were music scholarships.

Her mother sniffed. 'Well, you might as well unpack, because I'm not paying for it.'

As if she even could, Dee thought. She had only managed to go to university at all because her grades were good enough for scholarships and because she always held down a part-time job or two in addition to her classes. 'It's already paid for, Mom, everything.'

Dee slung her bag over her shoulder and picked up the two suitcases, one in each hand. Her mother followed her into the hall, still ranting. 'I should have listened to your father. He said we were too young to have a baby, he said I should think of myself and my career.' Dee's ears burned as several doors along the hall opened and students stuck their heads out to see what the noise was about. They should have known it was just

Dee Henning's mother making a scene again.

'Dee?'

She started, not at all sorry to have the instant replay of her past interrupted.

Ellis stood at the door dressed in a tuxedo, and for a brief second the combination of his looks and the serene, slightly puzzled expression on his face made her wonder if she were dreaming. If so, she was pretty sure she didn't want to wake up.

'What are you still doing here?'

The memory of their encounter that morning nearly took her breath away, and she braced herself. This was it. He hadn't forgotten. He was here to fire her. Well, at least she wouldn't have to angst over it all night.

She scrambled to look a bit more business-like, tidying her jacket and running a hand through her hair. 'Ellis! I wasn't expecting you.' In spite of herself, she felt guilty for the sandwich break she'd taken earlier.

'I was at a fundraising dinner for the local Audubon Society. I have a meeting with Ab Con in the morning and didn't want to fight the traffic to come back here for the files.' He dropped into the chair across from her and held her gaze. 'Now it's your turn. Why are you still here?'

Her stomach somersaulted. So he expected her to have figured it out. He expected her to have already packed her things and vacated the premises.

Before she could reply, he stood and leaned over her desk. 'These are plans of one of Marston's plants. Wade said you had these.'

She nodded and rubbed her eyes. 'Don't worry, I'll see that he gets them back.'

'Do you have any idea what time it is?'

She shook her head.

'Jesus, Dee, do you even know what day it is?'

Before she could answer, he grabbed her computer bag from beside her desk and slapped it down in front of her. 'Enough! Put all that stuff in here, right now. That's good. All of it. And the BlackBerry. Turn it off. Now put it in your bag.'

She started to protest.

He placed a finger to his lips to silence her. 'You're no good to me if you can't function.'

Then this was definitely it. He was seeing her to the door just to make sure she figured it out. She swallowed hard, pulled the Scribal file back out of the computer bag, and laid it on her desk.

'What the hell are you doing?'

'Leaving this for Tally. I figure you'll put her in charge until you find – a replacement.'

'A replacement?' He grabbed the folder and stuffed it back in her bag. 'For what? Why would I want Tally to see this?'

'Then you're not … I mean, I thought …' Her voice cracked and she blinked back tears.

'I'm sending you home for the night – what's left of it – so you'll be worth a damn tomorrow.' He helped her on with her jacket, grabbed her computer bag, and guided her out of the office toward the elevator. 'You're not fit to drive.'

'I'm OK, really I am.'

He ignored her protests and punched a quick message into his BlackBerry as they entered the elevator. When they exited into the parking garage, she pulled her keys from her bag and turned toward her car, but he grabbed her arm, took the keys from her hand, and stuffed them in the pocket of his jacket. 'I said you're not fit to drive.' He motioned her to a waiting limo. 'Jeffries will drop you off on our way.'

'But tomorrow –'

'Jeffries will pick you up, and not one minute before eight o'clock. Are we clear?'

'We're clear.'

The driver opened the rear door for her while Ellis let himself in the other side and set her computer bag on the floor next to his leg.

'Does he know where I live?'

'He knows,' Ellis said.

'But I –'

'Dee, it's sorted.' The limo exited the pale light of the parking garage onto the darkened street. Once they were on the freeway, she reached for her computer.

'Leave it,' he ordered. 'It stays with me. It'll be in the limo waiting for you tomorrow morning. You're going home to sleep.'

She could feel his frequent glances in the dark, weighty, almost physical, like Ellis's presence filled up all the space between them and pressed up against her in the quiet interior of the limo. And she didn't know why, but she felt relieved of some burden she hadn't known she was carrying.

When, at last, he spoke again, his voice was softer, warmer than it had been since that first night in the lounge of his office. 'It never all gets done, Dee. Never. And the naïve, arrogant notion that you're going to be the first to manage it is insane. It's a hard lesson. Best learn it now and save your sanity. And mine.' Before she could reply, he continued. 'By the way, Wade tore me a new one for my mishandling of your situation today. Seems I owe you an apology.' He raised a hand to thwart her response. 'We'll talk about it tomorrow. Now get some sleep. I'll wake you when we get to your house.'

It wasn't his intention to watch her sleep. In truth, he could barely see her in the light of his BlackBerry while he attempted to answer emails, but he found himself glancing at her nonetheless. And he assured himself the glances would have sufficed had she not called his name.

'Ellis, I didn't … I couldn't … Honestly, I need to …'

It took him a second to realise that she was talking in her sleep. He held his breath, not sure what to do.

'I just need a little more time, and then …'

Before he knew it, she had unbuckled her seatbelt and reached for her computer bag, practically falling forward onto his lap as Jeffries exited off I-5.

'Dee … Dee, you're dreaming. You need to put your seatbelt back on. Dee …'

Instead of waking up, she settled back into the deep, even breathing of sleep, her head resting in his lap, way too close to his groin for polite company. His pulse went into overdrive, his trousers suddenly set uncomfortably tight across the fly. 'Dee!'

he whispered. 'Dee, wake up. You were dreaming. Dee.'

But she didn't wake up. She mumbled something unrecognisable and heaved a sigh that would have passed for a sob. Dear God, he thought, please don't let her cry. He couldn't bear it if she cried. He wouldn't know what to do, and the position they were now in was already compromising enough. He held his breath, and when she whimpered softly and thrashed, he laid a hand on her arm, as much for self-preservation as anything.

She calmed to his touch and once again he felt the warm in and out of her breath on his thigh. She'd be embarrassed if she woke up like this. She'd be even more embarrassed if he woke her, as though what she had done was something worthy of shame. It wasn't. At least not for her. He was the one who should be embarrassed. He was the one who should be ashamed. How had he missed the signs? He knew what she was up against, and a good lot of it his fault for waiting so long to make the decision to hire her. He knew how conscientious she was, and yet in his efforts to avoid her, in his efforts to keep what had happened that first night in his lounge from happening again, he hadn't noticed, he had just let her struggle through. And with Marston being such an asshole as well, Jesus, what did he expect from a woman of her calibre? It wasn't any easier for her than it was him. She had loved Beverly too. And she had been thrown in at the deep end, thanks to him. No one could have coped better under the circumstances. He'd tell her that when she woke up.

She shifted again, and mumbled something about Alan Marston. This time she settled still closer to his cock, which had most definitely noticed her nearness, though he tried not to think about how badly he wanted her, tried not to think about the Executive Sex Clause. But her lying there with her head in his lap in the dark of the limo made him feel all sorts of things, all sorts of desires that most of the time he just ignored. He mentally shook himself. How could he even think about sex when she was exhausted, and when that exhaustion was because of him? That she had called out his name in her sleep stirred him in places that weren't just his trousers. With a jolt that was much less pleasant, he reminded himself he was probably in the starring role of her nightmare. That saddened him deeply. He found he really wanted her dreams of him to be good, warm, even sexy like his were of her.

Too soon the limo pulled into Dee's driveway, and when several gentle shakes and the calling of her name didn't wake her, Ellis reached into his pocket and handed Jefferies the keys he'd take from Dee.

'One of those is her house key. Find it and unlock it for me, would you please, and let's hope she doesn't have an alarm.'

He undid his seatbelt and was able to half-coax, half-manhandle the sleeping woman out of the limo and into his arms. When he physically lifted her, she mumbled something about her computer, wrapped her arms around his neck, and nuzzled in close. Jesus, she wasn't making this easy.

By the time he'd carried her up the sidewalk, Jeffries had the door open and the hall light switched on. 'Shut the door behind me and wait in the car,' he said. 'I won't be long.'

If the driver had any thoughts on the inappropriateness of the situation, he had the good graces not to show it.

The house was large for one person, well-decorated, with clean lines and open-planned living. He reminded himself Dee could afford it. She was not living beyond her means. He carried her up the free-standing stairs to the mezzanine that was her bedroom, managing the light switch with one elbow. There he found hard wood floors and more clean lines in shades of blue and earth tones, reminding him of the colours on the coast only a short drive away. On a king-sized bed that was more like a glorified futon on a raised platform, two very large tabby cats looked up at him through drowsy eyes, blinked, then went back to sleep.

He sat Dee carefully on the edge of the bed, holding her against his body with one arm to keep her from falling, while he awkwardly pulled back the comforter. Then, with her still leaning heavily on him, he slipped off her shoes and manoeuvred her out of her jacket, feeling the press of her warmth. For a second she roused. 'Ellis?' she mumbled. 'What are you doing here?'

71

'Making sure you go to bed,' he said, not certain if she'd even heard him before she was asleep again.

He tossed her jacket aside and eased her back onto the pillow, where she nestled down and sighed contentedly. He studied her for a minute, resisting the urge to remove any more clothing to make her more comfortable. The woman was asleep. That was the main thing. He pulled the comforter up over her shoulders, then, almost as an afterthought, bent and kissed her carefully on the cheek. 'Sleep well, Dee. I'm sorry it's been so hard. It will get better. I promise.' Then he turned and left, switching off the light before he descended the stairs, fighting the overwhelming temptation to stay just a little longer and watch her sleep.

Chapter Eleven

IN THE MORNING, THERE was a message on her BlackBerry instructing her to meet Ellis in the Dungeon with Wade. She arrived to coffee and pastries from Wade's favourite bakery and a huge glass of iced tea that he'd brewed up in the coffee maker. Ellis and Wade were already settled around the Formica table that looked like it came straight from a 1950s diner. When she joined them, and everyone was settled, Ellis spoke around a mouthful of maple bar.

'Marston thinks you've been neglecting Scribal for another project, but Wade set me very straight on that little misunderstanding.'

Wade cleared his throat loudly, and Ellis glared at him. 'I'm getting there, damn it.' He turned his attention back to her. 'Dee, I apologise for my bad behaviour yesterday. Clearly I didn't understand the situation, nor did I bother to listen when you tried to tell me.' He held her gaze. 'Did you sleep?'

She found herself blushing, remembering him helping her into bed, remembering dreams in which he hadn't been such a gentleman and leaving her to sleep, dreams in which he had crawled right in next to her and ravished her, dreams that had her reaching for her vibrator to ease the tension before she hopped in the shower this morning. 'Yes, I did sleep,' she managed.

He studied her for a long moment, almost as if he didn't quite believe her, and just when she was about to get defensive, he took a deep breath and offered her a warm smile. 'Good. Now then, tell me what's so damned important about Trouvères that you'd risk my wrath and Marston's tantrums?'

She smiled back, and for the first time in three weeks she

didn't feel like she was walking on eggshells.

Wade slid the files on Trouvères and Scribal across the table to her. She thanked him, then returned her attention to Ellis. 'I'm sure you know that Trouvères specialise in paper recycling, Ellis, but what makes them so special is they've recently perfected a new technology that can take waste paper, almost any kind of waste paper, and recycle it into quality stationary.'

'We're not talking about the bumpy grey stuff you get in green shops,' Wade added. 'We're talking about the kind of stationary you could use a fountain pen on. What Trouvères has to offer could very well change the face of the paper industry.' He nodded to Dee, and she continued.

'This technology would be even better than growing Marston a new supply of trees. It would be like growing him a new forest every day. And it would stop Jamison in his tracks.'

Dee opened the file and handed him two pristine sheets of paper the size of wedding invitations. 'One of these is recycled by Trouvères. The other is virgin stock. I'm willing to bet you can't tell which is which.' She reached into her pocket and pulled out a fountain pen. 'Go ahead. Test it.' While Ellis doodled on the strips of paper, she went on, 'Trouvères is a family operation started by the Rousseau twins, Claude and Yvette. The company's always done well for itself, but with this new technology the sky's the limit. The problem is they don't have the capital for the scale up they need to make it work.'

Ellis held the two pieces of paper up to the light. 'But Marston does.'

'Exactly.' She shoved aside the doughnut box, opened the Scribal folder, and flipped through the information. 'Ah, here it is. Marston has a plant just outside Atlanta that's facing a shutdown. The resulting loss of jobs would be devastating for the community. He has another plant, possibly two, that could go the same route if something doesn't change. They're all older plants, and amazingly enough, their outdated design makes them perfect for conversion and refitting to the Trouvères technology.'

'And I'm sure we can engineer those conversions,' Wade said. 'I've designed a template for installing the Trouvères technology at the Scribal plants. It wouldn't be difficult to do, and with only a moderate capital outlay on Marston's part. Any of our engineering teams could adapt the technology for US use.'

'It would be more expensive than Jamison's slash and burn clear-cut, at least in the short term,' Dee said. 'But in the long term it would pay for itself in a few years. If Trouvères would allow Pneuma Inc. to licence the technology and Scribal to aid in its manufacture and be its sole distributor here in the States, everybody would win.

'If my projections are right, and I'm pretty sure they are, Marston would recoup his costs and start turning a hefty profit within two years of the plant's opening. Trouvères would get very nice licence fees, through us, which they would never be able to arrange on their own, with no negative impact on their home market. The trees would get a break, and Marston would get his renewable resource, plus a shining new reputation as a protector of the environment and local jobs. And Pneuma will do very well on the consulting, and licence and engineering fees.'

Ellis held her gaze for a long moment. 'You do understand that even if we close the deal with Trouvères, there's still no guarantee that Marston will talk turkey?'

'He'd be crazy not to,' Wade said.

Ellis pulled his BlackBerry from his pocket and called his secretary. 'Lynn, would you reschedule my meetings this afternoon. I'll be in the Dungeon with Dee and Wade.' He hung up. 'I've just freed up the rest of the afternoon. Dee, cancel what you need to, and let's put the full weight of Pneuma Inc. behind this project.'

Once Ellis had given his approval, the Trouvères project moved along at high speed, and the mounting excitement reminded Dee again why she'd always wanted to work for the man. Two weeks later, the numbers were in, and the following week, she and Ellis were off to Paris to meet with Trouvères.

Chapter Twelve

IN PARIS, ELLIS RESERVED a suite at a small hotel with a courtyard garden near the centre of the city. Sandra told Dee he didn't like expensive hotel chains or the people who frequented them. The place felt less like a hotel than a comfortable apartment.

Trouvères Manufacturing was in Rouen, an hour's train ride from the centre of Paris, but the company's main office was a few blocks off the Champs-Élysées on a boulevard that was a prime example of the understated elegance of 19th-century architecture. The building stood out from its marble-façaded neighbours only in a small bronze plaque set to the left side of the entryway with "Trouvères" engraved in bold, Carolinian script.

Jason Daniels, the company's chief operations officer, met them in a reception area which looked more like a Napoleonic sitting room than the vanguard of a thriving business. Ellis figured Daniels to be a few years older than he, with confidence bordering on arrogance, clearly a man used to getting what he wanted. What Ellis hadn't counted on was that Daniels very obviously wanted Dee.

The man scooped her into a bear hug that was way too familiar for Ellis's liking. 'Dee! It's good to see you again. You look fantastic.' He gave her a sloppy kiss on each cheek, and said something in French that Ellis couldn't quite make out.

Almost as an afterthought, he offered Ellis a stiff handshake. 'Thorne. Good to finally meet you.'

'You two know each other?' Ellis asked, doing his best to sound matter-of-fact.

'Didn't Dee tell you?' Daniels looked like butter wouldn't melt. 'She headhunted me for Trouvères.'

Ellis raked her with a hard glance. 'She didn't mention that.'

Daniels continued before Dee could say anything. 'I don't mind saying it created quite a stir when I joined Trouvères.' He leaned closer to Ellis, as though he were imparting a secret. 'Yvette Rousseau's not noted for being fond of Americans, that's why everyone was surprised when she hired me, and all thanks to the impressive work of Ms Henning here.'

Dee smiled, and fought back a blush. 'That was one of my finer moments at Jasper and McDowell.'

Ellis couldn't help wondering just how fine a moment it was. It was clear Daniels couldn't take his eyes off Dee, but Dee wasn't nearly so transparent.

'Though, really, it wasn't that difficult. You were perfect for Trouvères.' She turned her attention to Ellis. 'Jason was born in Metz. His mother's Parisian, so he has dual citizenship. And his reputation was irresistible to a growing company like Trouvères.'

Ellis was fine with the concept of Daniels being irresistible to Trouvères. No problems there. What he wasn't fine with was the idea that he might be irresistible to Ellis's executive assistant.

Speaking through a translator, which Dee assured Ellis they really didn't need, the Rousseau twins were politely remote. Claude talked with grandiose hand gestures and smiled a lot, but Yvette only listened. When she did speak, it was without emotion. For the most part, they both behaved exactly as Ellis would have expected, and the meeting preceded the same.

But Daniels was another matter entirely. All through the meeting, he never missed a chance to eyeball Dee, and at every break he hovered over her like a lovesick moose. Surely Ellis wasn't the only one who noticed. The bastard never let her out of his sight. He should have been suspicious when, upon their arrival, they found the sitting room of their hotel suite adorned with an arrangement of flowers the size of a small French car.

The card read *à Dee, de Jason avec l'amour*.

Ellis watched Dee for signs of mutual admiration, but she was completely unreadable. That only added to his frustration. He was more than a little relieved when the meeting broke for lunch. He grabbed Dee by the arm and whisked her away before Daniels could suggest an intimate lunch at some pretentious restaurant.

After an intense morning of meetings, a walk in the fresh air was infinitely more appealing. Along the Seine, they crossed the Pont Neuf to the Île de la Cité, and bought crêpes from a street vendor. The serpentine mirror of the river duplicated the sun as it baked its way through the heavy breath of July. Scantily clad Parisians, who had not managed to escape the heat of the city for someplace cooler, lounged on the embankment. Ellis couldn't keep from noticing that, in spite of the heat, more than a few were locked in amorous embraces. Unfortunately the heat and the lust on the embankment only reminded him of Trouvères' chief operations officer panting after Dee.

'Why didn't you tell me you headhunted Daniels for Trouvères?' The question came out sounding a lot more like an accusation than he'd intended.

'I've headhunted lots of people for lots of companies. I just didn't think about it.' Dee threw a bit of crêpe onto the sidewalk for a couple of squabbling pigeons.

'Did the two of you know each other before?'

'Never met the man before Jasper and McDowell.'

They set a leisurely pace along the river, weaving their way through eruptions of sunburnt tourists, sidestepping besotted lovers, and smiling politely at the occasional elderly Parisian walking an elderly dog.

'The interview process is very revealing, I'd imagine.'

'Pardon?'

'Daniels. I suppose you know a lot about him after the interviews. How did that work anyway, a couple of meetings over coffee?'

'A couple, yes'

'Maybe dinner at a nice restaurant?' Subterfuge in the

business world was one thing, but Ellis had always been a bit simple when it came to interpersonal relations.

'Yes, that was part of the screening. This was an important position.' Dee lifted her face to the sun, which teased out bronze highlights in her dark hair and made Ellis even more certain he didn't like Daniels panting after her.

'And did the two of you do that often?'

She stopped in her tracks, almost causing a collision. 'Ellis, what are you getting at?'

'The man just seemed a bit too familiar with you today, that's all.'

'I got him the dream job of a lifetime. Believe me, he can afford to be nice to me.'

They found themselves moving upstream through a wave of Chinese tourists following a guide with a brightly painted sign. Ellis took her arm so neither of them would get swept away in the shutter-snapping deluge.

'Nice to you, yes.' He spoke between barely parted lips. 'Nice to you's fine, but he was all over you every chance he got. Is he married?'

'Yes, with two kids.' They shoved their way through the last of the tour group and resumed a slow meander along the cobbled embankment. 'But even if he weren't, I don't date clients, surely you know that.'

He fell into step next to her. 'Well he's not your client now, is he?' He took an angry bite of his crêpe and tossed the rest to the gathering pigeons. God, he was behaving like a sulky schoolboy. He absolutely was not jealous. He wouldn't allow it! There was nothing to be jealous of. She was his employee, for chrissake!

A small group of boys whizzed by on skateboards, and he pulled her out of the way.

She caught her breath with a little yelp as he pulled her closer until they were practically nose to nose. Through her light linen suit, he could feel the rhythmic rise and fall of her breath and was suddenly aware of the shape of her insinuating itself against him, a shape his body responded to in a wave of muscle memory that nearly took his breath away. It left him feeling heavy and uncomfortable; it left him feeling desperate to rip the linen suit off and lose himself in the woman beneath.

'Ellis.' Her voice was barely more than a whisper. 'Nothing happened between Jason and me at Jasper and McDowell, and there's nothing between us now. What happened between you and me ...' Her voice drifted off, then she stepped out of his embrace. 'What happened between us never happened to me before. Ever.' Then she turned and kept walking.

Chapter Thirteen

AFTER THE FIRST DAY of meetings, things went downhill fast. The contract structure was the first of the obstacles Yvette Rousseau had in store for them. She wanted Pneuma Inc. to give Trouvères a much bigger percentage of the licence fees, and she demanded that Trouvères get a cut of engineering revenues as well. She wanted to exclude possible competitors, and she insisted that the contract be drafted under French law instead of US law. The list went on. By the end of the second day negotiations were at a deadlock, and the Paris heat was beginning to take its toll in more ways than one.

Ellis slammed the door to the hotel suite behind them and yanked off his tie. 'I know the woman doesn't like Americans, but the only one she's hurting by not accepting our offer is Trouvères. She has to see this is the only way to move things forward.'

'It's got to be some sort of bluff.' Dee threw her jacket across the couch and rotated her aching shoulders.

'Can't you talk to Daniels? Surely he can make her see reason.'

'I have talked to him. He's at his wits' end as to why she's behaving like this. Besides, he's working for her, remember?'

'True, but it's pretty clear it's you he's most concerned about pleasing.'

She slammed her computer bag down on the couch. 'I told you there's nothing between Jason and me, and I –'

Ellis interrupted. 'Look, I said up front that this deal was a long shot. Pulling it off may take a lot more time than either of us expected. Anyway, I should have known better than to get caught up in the excitement. Don't take it personally. I'm only saying you may have bitten off more than you can chew this time. You're not exactly working drive-through at McDonalds, you know?'

The pain returned to her shoulders with a vengeance. 'At first it came as a real shock, Ellis, but I figured that one out fairly early in the game.' Dee was about to excuse herself for a much-needed shower and time to cool her temper when Ellis's BlackBerry rang.

After a terse exchange, he hung up and tossed it on the desk. 'That was Yvette Rousseau's secretary. Tomorrow's meetings are cancelled. Apparently Yvette sees no reason for further negotiations.'

'Shit.' Dee turned on her heels and headed for her room. Maybe she'd have a good cry while she was in the shower. It certainly wouldn't be her first since she'd started working at Pneuma Inc.

Ellis grabbed her by the arm. 'Where are you going? We have a disaster here, Dee. We need to regroup and figure out what to do about it. Your pouting can wait.'

Anger joined frustration and became a seething boil. She jerked her arm away. 'I'm sick and tired of your snide remarks about Jason and me, and your condescension about my lack of experience. Guess what, Ellis, I know I lack experience, and you knew it when you hired me, so fucking tell me something I don't know! I'm gonna take a goddamn shower. Do you mind? Wade brainstorms in the bowling alley, I brainstorm in the shower. Then I'll fix it.'

She didn't wait for his response; she didn't care at that moment if he fired her ass. If he did, she'd jump up and down with relief, then be on the next plane to anywhere but in this room with this man. She gave her bedroom door the hardest slam she could manage, feeling her efforts wrench her biceps. She ripped at the pearl buttons of her blouse, then tossed it on the chair. As her skirt dropped around her ankles, she literally kicked it across the room. 'Goddamn it,' she cursed when it caught on her shoe and nearly tripped her before it went sailing and landed by the door. Right at Ellis's feet.

For a horrifying second they both stood staring at each

other, Ellis in white shirt and trousers and Dee in nothing but bra and panties and stockings and garter belt. He gave two fish gasps and found his voice. 'I'm sorry. I went to knock, to apologise and it just came open. I guess it didn't latch. Dee, I'm sorry. I'll just leave now, and …' He started to leave, froze like a statue for a split second, then turned back to her. 'Dee, I can't do this any more …'

Dee didn't know who started it. She didn't care, but the race to get to each other ended in a bone-crunching collision of an embrace that uprooted her completely out of her shoes as she catapulted into his arms and he lifted her off her feet, crushing her to him with a groan that sounded like agony incarnate. Then he took her mouth. Lips bruised and teeth clashed, tongues sparred, vertebrae crunched. When they came up for air, he gasped. 'Jesus, Dee, I can't take this any more. I need you now.' This time he lifted her and she wrapped her legs around him as he managed the few steps to her bed. He drove her into the mattress with the weight of his body, her clawing and shoving at his shirt. He pulled back enough to shrug it off his shoulders and undo his fly. She wriggled out of her panties, nailing him in the thigh with her heel in the process. This time he wasn't awkward with the condom. This time he was ready. He stood above her, his trousers and boxers around his knees, his eyes raking over her like hungry fire. And when his gaze came to rest on the juncture between her legs, a hand joined the exploration, fingering her open, stroking the slippery path, thumbing the hard peak of her clit until her bottom juddered against the mattress with the intensity of her need, until she gaped and pressed and ground against his fingers.

The wet scent of lust overpowered the smell of Paris summer, still heavy on their bodies. What seemed like for ever could have only been seconds. It was only the time it took for him to make her wet, which was no time at all. Even with the stress of the last few months, the very sight of him still made her wet. It was only the time it took for him to open her, lift her hips so that she gaped for him. It was only the time it took to settle himself into position, which was no time at all. And yet the eternity of it was nearly unbearable. Then he pushed into her hard, making no accommodations for her tenderness. Nor did she want him to in her impatience to sheath him, to grip him, to clamp down on him. This time he didn't wait to recover himself. He had waited four long months. That was fucking long enough. She could tolerate no more waiting. She had never wanted anything so badly in her life.

The thrusting was hard and deep, like he was fucking her whole body, not just her pussy. He cupped her ass in his hands, kneading, gripping, pulling her farther onto him until it surprised her that any of him was still left outside her.

When she came, her orgasm was hard-edged, raging, feeling as though it would break her and empty her. And Ellis; she thought Ellis would never stop coming. The look on his face was pain and pleasure and bliss and concentration. It was as though in his expression she could see what he was doing inside her body. His face, the face that was always opaque, the face that always kept everything secret, was suddenly open as she had never seen it before. When he was done coming, he shoved and pushed his way onto the bed next to her without breaking the connection, then moved slightly to one side so that his weight wasn't on her. She ran a hand down to cup his ass, and whispered against his ear, 'Apology accepted.'

The ringing of Dee's BlackBerry caused them both to start. It was on the nightstand just within her reach from where she lay beneath him. 'It's Jason,' she whispered, as she checked the screen. Then she answered, shoving Ellis off her and scrambling to the desk for a pen and paper. 'Of course we're disappointed, but that's business, isn't it?' she said calmly.

Ellis was amazed that she could stand there nearly naked, still wet from sex, and manage to sound like the queen of Wall Street. But she *was* nearly naked, and all of her curviness glistened with the sweat of their rutting. At least for him, that pretty much negated anything she was saying on the phone, until she mentioned his name.

'Ellis has been telling me from the beginning we should be offering this deal to Keller.'

He catapulted from the bed and was instantly at her side.

What the hell was she up to? Who was Keller? He didn't know any Keller. Was she crazy?

As she listened to whatever Daniels was saying on the other end of the phone, she looked up at Ellis and winked. 'Oh, you've never heard of them? English firm, actually. They're small, but they have some good ideas. Promising technology. They're very anxious to work with Ellis, as you might imagine. Yes, I'm sorry too, Jason, but maybe Yvette is right. Maybe we really can't work together.'

Ellis shoved closer in an attempt to listen in, but she elbowed him away. 'Well, I don't know. I really can't think there'd be much to discuss when it's clear Yvette's not interested.' She looked down at her watch. 'Besides, I've got a teleconference this afternoon, and I …' She listened intently and nodded. 'All right, then. If you insist. Maybe I can squeeze you in.' She scribbled an address on the hotel notepad. 'I'll meet you there in an hour.' She hung up and turned to face Ellis, her gaze lingering on places below his face.

He suddenly remembered she wasn't the only one who was nearly naked and folded his arms around himself, as if that would help. 'What the hell are you doing, Dee?'

'We have a mess. You told me to fix it. What have we got to lose?'

'Me? Nothing. You? Possibly your job.'

'Then nothing has really changed, has it?' Her eyes were wandering again, and he gave up. It was damn near impossible to sound threatening standing there in front of her with his pole at full attention. 'Does this Keller of yours even exist?'

'Oh they exist all right. Cousins of my mother. They run a small printing business in Sheffield. I'm guessing if Yvette is at all typical of the French, she may dislike Americans, but she absolutely can't abide the English. I told Jason I'd meet him in an hour. He doesn't sound so prepared to give up. Can I have my shower now?'

In 15 minutes she was ready to leave the suite, looking like she could conquer the world. 'I told him that my schedule's really busy, that I don't have much time, so I won't be there long, just long enough to feel things out.'

Ellis didn't much care for her choice of words. He held her gaze over the top of his glasses. 'An hour. That's all the time you give him, do you understand?'

She nodded, straightened her jacket and was gone.

Jason had chosen a cosy restaurant on Montmartre, just behind the Sacré-Coeur. A strange place for a meeting, Dee thought, but it was only for a drink and it was possible he wanted to make sure Yvette didn't know what he was up to. She paid the taxi driver, and he met her at the door.

'Thanks for coming, Dee.' He laid a warm kiss on her cheek, then took her by the arm and guided her inside. 'It's amazing what a man has to go through to get you away from Thorne so he can have you to himself for a few minutes.'

She ignored his attempt at humour. 'Have you talked to Yvette? Does she know you're here with me?'

'She knows. I called her right after I got off the phone with you.'

Dee ordered a glass of wine and Jason did the same, then he guided her to a table in a quiet corner of the café where they could have a little more privacy. Once they were seated, he sat his drink down in front of him and studied her as she sipped her wine. 'This is a bluff, isn't it, Dee?'

Jason was a good businessman, but he didn't frighten her. She knew she was up for anything he could dish out. 'And why would you think that?'

'Because it's you. No one else I know would be bold enough to pull something like this. Beverly Neumann might have, but I doubt Thorne would. He's innovative, but he's also gotten more conservative lately. You –well you're always full of surprises. I haven't forgotten how you manoeuvred and schemed to get Yvette to hire me. She didn't know what had hit her until it was all over. Now I'm her golden boy, her idea from the beginning, of course. And all because you were willing to take risks.'

He offered her an admiring smile that made her blush for some reason. 'I bet Thorne's wearing a hole in the carpet pacing, wondering how you'll handle this. I'm a bit surprised he didn't come with you, actually. He doesn't seem very anxious to let you out of his sight.' He leaned over the table, closer to her. 'Did you lock him in his room before you left?'

'Trouvères is not the only thing on Ellis's mind, Jason. I think he's ready to walk on this one. He's a busy man, and I'm just his assistant.'

He grunted. 'Like Beverly Neumann was?'

That he compared her to Beverly caught her by surprise. Did he really see her that way? For the past few months, if she had been compared to Beverly it was always in a negative light, to the point that she almost cringed at the mention of her friend's name. It was clear Jason meant it as a compliment, and she didn't try to fight back the resulting smile.

Jason heaved a sigh and toyed with his drink. 'Look, Dee, I don't care whether the whole thing with Keller is a bluff or not. You and I both know this alliance with Pneuma Inc. is by far the best prospect for Trouvères. And if I have my company's best interest at heart, then that's got to be what I want too, no matter how stubborn Yvette is.'

'Can you get her to change her mind?'

'I think I might be able to. But I'll need a little time to talk to her, to reason with her.'

Dee shrugged. 'I can't make any promises, but I'll speak to Ellis. He's very impressed with Keller.'

'That's all I can ask. It's clear Ellis trusts you.' Jason leaned so far over the table his nose was nearly touching hers. 'And you and I have both worked too hard to let this deal slip away.'

'Like I said, I'll talk to him, but I'm new on the job. I'm still trying to earn my keep.'

He took her hand. 'I have no doubt you've already made yourself indispensable to the man.'

She pulled away and straightened her jacket. 'No one's indispensable.' Just then her BlackBerry rang, and Ellis spoke into her ear.

'Time's up. The limo's out front.'

It hadn't been an hour, but she'd had all the time she needed. 'I'm on my way.' She shoved the BlackBerry back in her pocket and turned her attention back to Jason. 'That was

87

Ellis. I have to go.'

Jason slapped a couple of euro down on the table and stood. 'Dee ...' He was silent for a moment, lost in thought, then he squared his shoulders and tugged at his tie. 'If you think this Keller is really a threat to Trouvères' interests, I'll pass the word on to Yvette. I think she should know.'

'Please do that, Jason. We all need to know where we stand.'

Chapter Fourteen

JUST AS PROMISED, THE limo was waiting outside the restaurant. To her surprise, Ellis opened the back door and practically yanked her inside.

'That wasn't an hour.'

'It was all the time I was willing to trust you to Daniels.' He wasn't smiling.

She ignored his insinuation; in fact, she barely heard it as focused as she was on the meeting she'd just had. 'He suspects the bluff, but he knows the deal with Pneuma Inc. is exactly what Trouvères needs. He'll push for the alliance.'

'Oh, I'm sure he will.'

'What's that supposed to mean?'

'Don't be so naïve, Dee. You're the only one in Paris who can't see the man would do anything for you.'

'That's ridiculous. He's a businessman wanting what's best for his company. I'm getting really sick of your –'

He was across the seat before she knew it, pulling her to him, stopping her words with the press of his lips and a light flick of his tongue. 'The man wants you. That's all I'm saying.'

She breathed in the earthy tang of maleness just beneath the smell of soap and shampoo. In spite of her indignation, which she was having trouble maintaining, she shifted against him, closer to the scent.

He responded by altering his position just enough to make sure any space between them was filled with him. Each breath, that came a little more rapidly than the last, warmed her earlobe and the nape of her neck.

'Ellis, Jason is –'

Just then the driver braked to avoid a car that pulled

unexpectedly into his lane, and they were both thrown forward. Ellis grabbed for her before she was launched onto the floor. When the limo was moving again at normal speed, he closed the privacy window. He still held her crushed against him. His gaze was locked on hers, and his voice was a strained whisper forcing its way between efforts to breathe. 'Dee, at the moment, I don't care about Daniels. I don't care about Trouvères either.'

'But I thought –'

He kissed her again, this time with more tongue in all the right places. 'Don't think.' He spoke against her mouth. 'We'll think later. Right now we have unfinished business.'

She gave in. After all, he was the boss.

Once he'd conquered her mouth, he kissed down her jaw onto her neck, where her pulse fluttered wildly against the velvet humidity of his breath. His lips left what she was sure would be scorch marks along her throat and collarbone. He quickly dispensed with the buttons of her blouse and teased her breasts up over the cups of her bra, caressing her nipples and areolas to hard, heavy erections, empathetic to the rub and shift of the straining front of his trousers against her thigh. The delicious assault was well coordinated, far from the awkward fumbling of their earlier encounter. She lifted her bottom enough to allow him to slip the sheath of her skirt up over her hips. He caressed her thighs along the tops of her stockings and ran a thumb over the garter belt before he hooked his fingers into the waistband of her panties and shimmied them down over her ankles, easing one leg free, forcing one grey leather pump to drop to the floor in the process.

He nipped and kissed and suckled his way down over her sternum, blazing a steamy trail onto the flat plane of her belly, where progress was temporarily halted at the waistband of her skirt. She was too busy trying to breathe to tell him what she liked – though she wasn't sure that would be appropriate under the circumstances. But as he ran a hand up the inside of her thigh and insinuated warm fingers into anxious, slippery places, it was almost as though he had secretly watched her touching herself, and he knew. He knew exactly what she liked.

While she was busy appreciating his manual dexterity, he slid up the seat next to her to pay further obeisance to her breasts, watching her face while he suckled her nipples to impossible, aching buds.

'That look of pleasure; it suits you,' he said. 'You're too serious most of the time.'

'You should talk.' She arched against his face and gasped as he nipped her, an act that sent aftershocks all the way to the tips of her toes.

'I suppose we should both work on it then, shouldn't we? No time like the present.' He slid back down the seat, pausing to kiss her navel where it peeked just above her waistband, then he kissed and nibbled a ticklish trail along the sensitive flesh of her inner thigh, around the edge of her garter belt and above the tops of her stockings.

Dee's heart went into overdrive; a wave of panic shot up her spine. This was her boss, these were her fantasies, and this was intimacy she wasn't sure she was ready for. The cost for the intimacy they had shared four months ago had been high. She wasn't sure she could go through that again. 'Ellis, this is too much.' She struggled to push him away. 'I don't think I can … I don't think we should –'

He relaxed his hold on her and rose to plant a gentle kiss on her lips. 'Dee, I'll stop if you want me to.' His dark eyes held her in a gaze that was deeply earnest, and somehow moving in ways she couldn't quite figure out, especially not in her state of confused arousal. 'But I would prefer not to. I would prefer to pleasure you if you'll let me.' He kissed her again, gently, slowly, deeply, his tongue caressing her hard palate, the inside of her cheek, the edge of her teeth. For a second, she felt as though she would cry. She wasn't sure why.

He cupped her face in his hand and spoke against her lips. 'Shall I continue?'

She nodded, unable to speak, unable to quite get her mind around what was about to happen, what she was allowing to happen. Before, what they had done in the hotel room had been under stress, what they had done in his office four months ago even more so, but this … This was planned, this was deliberate. From this there could be no turning back, no pretending they hadn't overstepped the boundaries of all proper business protocol. But then he lowered his mouth to her clit where she was hard and straining with need. A long, slow circle and press of his tongue and a hard tug between pursed lips and she came, spasming and jerking, fist pressed to her mouth to hold back the guttural growl rolling up through her chest.

He gave her a little time, knowing almost instinctively how sensitive she would be, how she would need to work her way through the aftershocks. How she would need to breathe for a second. He kissed and caressed the inside of her thigh, and she could feel him shifting on the floor, shoving at his trousers and boxers. She heard the rattle of a condom wrapper. There was more shifting, then he kissed up the length of her body, positioned himself and entered her, pulling her onto him like a glove. Suddenly, the animal took control again. Several split seams and a broken zipper later, they convulsed against each other in a rush of white heat and oxygen deprivation.

Time came back into focus with a discreet knock on the glass of the privacy window, and the realisation that they were no longer moving. In a wave of panic, she grabbed for clothes.

'Shshsh.' Ellis covered her mouth with a sex-scented hand. 'Relax, we're back at the hotel.'

Her legs trembled from the gymnastics of making love in the back of a moving vehicle. She straightened and peered out the tinted glass. Ellis moved next to her and stroked her belly.

'We can't go in looking like this,' she said.

'Don't worry. We'll use the service entrance and be back in our suite before anyone notices.' He helped her on with her panties, then nuzzled each of her breasts as she settled them back into her bra. Every move he made seemed carefully calculated to keep the level of arousal just enough beneath a hard sizzle that they could function.

The fascinating sight of her boss trying to restrain his enthusiastic equipment back into rumpled business attire did little to hold the situation in check.

They didn't even solicit a suspicious glance from the

cleaning staff as they tiptoed up the back stairs. It wouldn't have taken much of a brain to figure out what they had been up to – shirts untucked; hair mussed; smelling of more than just the Paris heat. At the top of the stairs, he led her in a near jog across the polished marble floor, and unlocked the door to their suites. Inside, he pushed her up against the cool stucco of the wall and took her mouth like a starving man, the intriguing taste of herself still strong on his lips. He was pressed up tight against her, hands kneading and exploring, when his BlackBerry rang into the charged atmosphere of heavy breathing.

He cursed out loud, jerked it from his pocket, and nearly dropped it before he shot Dee a quick glance. 'It's Yvette Rousseau.' He stepped back, struggling to sound like business as usual. He barely got "hello" out before the conversation became a serious of blinks and nods on his part.

'I see ... Of course ... Of course we will.' He glanced at his watch. 'Of course we'll be ready.' He shoved the BlackBerry back in his pocket, ran a hand through the mussed spikes of his hair, and looked at Dee. 'She called me a silly man for thinking she was serious about not wanting to deal with Pneuma Inc.'

'The meeting's back on then?'

He shook his head. 'She says there's no need to meet until after the lawyers finalise the contracts, then we can get together to sign. Sounds like she's agreed to pretty much everything we proposed. She's sending a car to pick us up in an hour for a celebration. Apparently she's rented a yacht on the Seine.'

The next morning, to the unexpected praises of Yvette Rousseau, the alliance was agreed upon without a hitch, and later that afternoon, they were off to catch a plane back to Portland. They only caught a glimpse or two of the Eiffel Tower.

Chapter Fifteen

They had been in the air long enough to finish dinner. Most of the other passengers in first class were either watching the film of their choice or already sleeping. Ellis cleared his throat and loosened his tie. 'After the events of the past few days, I feel now would be a good time to remind you that you do have a clothing allowance. It's something I should have told you earlier, but it just slipped my mind. All of the executive team does, though Wade certainly never uses his. It's important you always look sharp. There's certainly nothing wrong with the way you dress. In fact, I'm impressed, but I wager you'll find what you have won't be nearly enough for the demanding schedule you'll be keeping. Then there's travel damage and – that sort of thing.'

She thought about the mounting loss of buttons and ripped zippers from their sexual encounters and could very definitely see the benefit of a clothing allowance.

'I have to say, I never would have thought we could pull off this deal so quickly,' he said. 'Things like this just don't happen. I didn't want to discourage you back before we left Portland, but I never imagined we'd close the deal on our first visit. Beverly would be proud.'

'You really think so?' Dee was surprised at the sudden tightness of her throat. She was always a bit emotional when she was tipsy. She wasn't much of a drinker, and she was halfway through her second glass of champagne.

'I know so.' He downed the contents of his champagne flute, and stroked the stem, avoiding her gaze. 'You don't suppose ...'

'Suppose what?' Suddenly it was hard to breathe.

He fidgeted in his seat, trying to get comfortable, and she

pretended not to notice. At last he spoke. 'Dee, we have to talk about what happened. You don't think what happened had … Well, you know … Anything to do with Beverly's theory.'

'You mean her Executive Sex Clause?'

He winced, glancing around to make sure no one else was in earshot. 'Yes, the Sex Clause.' He leaned closer. 'What all did she tell you about it?'

'She just said that if an executive had a reliable source of stress-free sex available when she needed it, she'd be more relaxed, more focused. More productive.'

Ellis nodded. 'She told me it could reduce sick days.'

'I'm never sick,' Dee said.

'I don't need the sick days I've got,' he agreed. 'She was also sure there'd be an increase in productivity and that an executive would be more creative if he could have sex –' he shoved the word between barely parted lips '– whenever he needed it.' He nearly dropped his glass. 'Dee, I know our situation has been ambiguous with what happened at my office back before we knew – before we knew we'd lost Beverly.' He held her in an earnest gaze. 'But the other evening in the hotel, when we were – when we were together, I hope you didn't think I'd actually…'

'That you'd implemented the Executive Sex Clause?'

He seemed relieved that she'd said it, but then his face darkened and he jerked at his tie as though it choked him. 'Because I didn't. I mean, I wouldn't.'

'No, of course I didn't think that.' She fidgeted with her own champagne flute. 'I mean, I figured if you were going to, you would have done it by now.'

For a minute, he sat staring into his empty glass. Then he spoke, avoiding her gaze. 'Do you think you could have come up with that bluff if we hadn't just – been on the bed together?'

She waited for the flight attendant to stop fussing over the passenger across from them and move back to the galley. 'I honestly don't know.'

'Something certainly happened,' he said.

There was another long silence. The tension in her stomach ached along with muscles still tender from more real sex than

95

she'd had in ages.

Ellis gave up tugging at his tie and yanked it off completely, stuffing it down in the pocket of the seat. 'You realise what we're talking about, what we did, is against every rule. It's insane. I can't believe we're even thinking about it.'

'But we are.' Her voice was little more than a whisper. 'In fact, we've done a lot more than think about it.'

He straightened his shoulders and looked up at her, eyes dark and urgent. 'I'm not superstitious, but good things seem to happen whenever we – get together. I'm less stressed, I'm more focused, and I seem more able to think outside the box. And you ... You were brilliant in Paris. Surely I'm not the only one, surely you felt it too.'

'Of course I felt it. How could I not? And ever since it first happened I can't help thinking that ...'

'That maybe Beverly was right?'

She nodded, still locked in his gaze. 'Yeah, that maybe Beverly was right.'

He leaned closer to her, then looked around again, noting everyone else in the cabin was asleep. 'No one would ever need to know except us,' he whispered.

She nodded slowly. 'Business strategy is always a secret anyway, isn't it? And if it makes us both better at our jobs ...'

'And eases the stress we're constantly under,' he added. 'Well what could be wrong with that?'

'Yeah, what could be wrong?'

'Good! Good. I'm glad we cleared that up.' The tension drained from his shoulders and his face relaxed back to neutrality.

'I'm curious. If we're really going through with this, does this clothing allowance of mine –' She sipped at her champagne. 'Does it include sexy lingerie, then?' She couldn't believe she'd been so brazen. Her cheeks felt like they'd burst into flame any second, and he looked positively crimson.

He poured them both another glass of champagne, drizzling a trail across their laps with his clumsy effort. 'Certainly. Of course. I like lingerie – on women, I mean. You should buy some ... If you'd like.'

They both laughed a little louder than intended, then quickly looked around. When they were convinced no one was listening, Dee continued. 'And what about rules?'

'Rules?' he asked.

'Yes. You know, rules you'll want me to follow for when you need sex.' They were now both doing a fine job of carrying on a stealthy conversation through barely parted lips. 'If we're really going to go through with this, then I need to know in advance what to expect so things will be a little more comfortable when it happens next time. Don't you think?'

'Yes, of course. Good point. Rules. Now let me think.' His voice sounded as though he'd swallowed a sheet of sandpaper. 'I don't like pantyhose.'

He seemed to have a hard time getting comfortable in his chair, and the sandpaper effect in his voice was not washed away by the gulp of champagne that he nearly choked on. 'Time's a luxury I don't often have. I don't want to waste it fighting my way through pantyhose.'

'No pantyhose. Right. I'm sure we'll both be happier for it.'

'I liked those suspender things you wore in Paris. Made it easier to …'

'Get to the junk?'

'The junk, yes.' He shot a sideways glance at her thighs. 'Do you always wear those?'

She nodded. 'I don't like pantyhose either. Anything else?'

He held her gaze for a long second, as though he were weighing his thoughts. The muscles along his jaw tensed and relaxed. At last he spoke. 'Actually there's something much more important than pantyhose we need to discuss. With both of us having so much time for busy social lives –' he gave her a weighted look over the top of his glasses, which slid down the bridge of his nose '– it's possible you may not be my only partner, nor do I expect to be yours. Of course, your private life is your own. But I do expect any relationship you have outside ours to be discreet and safe. I expect that of you, and you have the right to expect that of me as well. Don't you agree?'

She smiled. 'I'll try not to let the orgies interfere with my responsibilities.'

His face was suddenly serious, and he seemed to be searching for words. 'Dee, I haven't had sex in longer than I care to think about, until four months ago when we were together. That's it. There hasn't been anyone else. You know my schedule. The condom was only necessary for birth control. I want you to know.'

'Ellis –' She turned slightly to face him a little better, not able to believe she was actually discussing something like this with her boss, something she'd never discussed with anyone but Kendra. 'I've been on the pill since I was 12 to regulate my cycle, and even if I weren't, I'd never have sex without making sure I was safe from pregnancy.' She blushed hard. 'As far as sex goes, I could probably give you a run for your money on who's gone the longest without it, so condoms aren't necessary, at least with me.'

He surprised her by stroking the top of her hand and offering her a mischievous smile that made her feel tipsy in ways that had nothing to do with the champagne. 'Then I'll reserve my enormous stash of condoms just in case my inner party animal escapes on a rampage.'

They both chuckled nervously, and he heaved a sigh as though they'd just solved a pressing problem. 'Now, what about you?'

'What about me?'

'Any rules I should know about for when you need sex?'

She hadn't expected her feelings to be taken into account in the Executive Sex Clause. After all, he was the executive; she was just his assistant. The cabin suddenly seemed hot, and close. She clasped her hands tight around her glass, realising that she was trembling. 'I need to be able to say no.'

'Say no?'

She struggled with her words, trying not to sound as embarrassed as she felt. 'If I'm angry or upset or if I have PMS, I may not want to … I may not be able to …'

His gaze softened and he sat very still. 'Dee, no is always an option. I never expected it to be otherwise, but I hope it's an option you won't often be inclined to take.'

* * *

In the evening, when Dee arrived home from the airport, she barely got in the door before a delivery man rang the bell with two dozen red roses, a bottle of champagne and a note that read *Good job, Dee. Congratulations. We did it. Celebrate.*

She didn't know how he'd managed it, but the note was in Ellis's handwriting.

Chapter Sixteen

TRUE TO ITS NAME, the Boiling Point heaved with perspiring bodies all ready for the rut. Dee could swear beneath the scent of beer and sweat and too much perfume, she could smell pheromones running amuck. She and Harris were there at Kendra's recommendation. And Kendra wasn't wrong. The place was all about generating heat. It was clear to her, however, that Harris was not impressed.

'If you want to meet people, you should ask somebody to dance,' she shouted across the table to be heard over the driving bass.

'I hate the music,' Harris yelled back. For a man as techno-savvy as Harris, he avoided pop-culture like the plague. It wasn't that he was stuck in a time warp. It was just that he'd never been very tolerant of anything shallow or overly commercial. She couldn't argue too much with him on that count. She'd never really had time for it.

She patted his hand. 'Me too, but as long as you sit here with me, everyone'll think we're together and you'll never meet anyone.'

'What about you? You're not asking anyone to dance.'

'You know I'm not much for dancing, Harris. Besides, I'm jetlagged.' Ellis-lagged was more the truth.

'Jetlagged, my ass.' The small laugh lines around his eyes crinkled. His smile broadened to a chuckle. 'You're the only person I know who basks in the afterglow of a good day at the office. I never got anything close to an afterglow when I was practising law. Though I did get a rash once after a particularly stressful case. Oh, wait a minute. That was cheap laundry detergent. Never mind.'

'I told you it was a great experience. The deal we did deserves an afterglow for all parties involved and I was right there in the middle of it.'

He gave her a disapproving stare. 'You really scare me sometimes, Dee. You know that? There you were in Paris and you never went to the Eiffel Tower or the Louvre but you're hyped because of work. How about I give you the name of a really good psychologist? I still keep in touch with a few who were expert witnesses for me on a couple of cases back in the day. I'm sure one of them could help you with your problem.'

'It'd be a waste of time, Harris. I'd have to want help first. Isn't that what Alcoholics Anonymous says?'

He nodded. 'I suppose the same principles would apply to a workaholic.'

The borderline under-aged girl at the table behind them slapped the man whose throat she'd just had her tongue down, and the argument was on.

'You cock-sucking little bitch!'

She jammed her fists against her hips and glared at him. 'You'd have to rent a cock first for me to be able to suck it.'

Suddenly the loud music didn't seem so bad. Dee closed her eyes and let the after-image of the strobe assault her optic nerve. As annoying as the battle was, it distracted Harris from her afterglow.

Her mind drifted back to Paris, which now seemed almost like a dream. One minute they were arguing about the situation with Trouvères and the next she was on the bed with Ellis having a seriously angry, seriously wild fuck. And it had only gotten better with the sex in the limo. If that was a preview of the Executive Sex Clause in action, being a workaholic was exactly what Dee wanted.

'Can't we move somewhere away from that?' Harris nodded to the full-blown shouting match now going on behind them.

'We were lucky to find this table.'

'I can't believe that Kendra actually frequents these troglodyte dens,' he said.

'You know Ken. She's keen on slumming from time to

time. She likes the rough guys. Besides, you're the one who wanted to come here.'

A buxom waitress pushed and shoved her way around the overflow from the dance floor and slammed two beers down on the table. Harris paid her. She stuffed the tip into a pouch at the front of her micro miniskirt, reminding Dee of a disgruntled kangaroo. The argument behind them went up a couple more decibels.

Harris sipped his beer and made a face. 'In the city that's the microbrew capital of the world, it should be illegal to serve swill like this.'

'I'm guessing people don't come here for the beer.' Dee tried to suppress the smile that made the corners of her mouth ache in its effort to escape. 'Plenty of girls here for you, Harris, just like Kendra said.'

'Girls about covers it.' He grunted. 'Either we're getting older faster than I thought or there are a serious number of fake IDs floating around in here. The choice of men's not much better.' He squinted in the flashing lights.

'They're certainly a colourful lot.' Dee smiled over her shoulder at the man behind them, who was now using his hair-curling vocabulary to give an unflattering description of the more private parts of his girlfriend's anatomy.

'You don't seem too upset about it. In fact, you seem downright smug. Jetlag, no doubt.' Harris sniffed at the beer. 'Smells funny. Don't you think it smells funny?'

Dee sniffed. 'The waitress probably plans to drug you then have her way with you later. I could tell she was hot for you.'

'It was pretty obvious, wasn't it, the way she growled at me and all?' He sniffed again, then pushed the beer away. 'To think I turned down very expensive champagne and pizza at your house for this circus.'

'Look. That girl over there against the wall isn't too bad – the blonde in the leather slacks.'

Harris followed her gaze.

'She seems to be on her own. Why don't you ask her to dance?'

Just then the girl doubled over and threw up in the pot of an artificial palm tree, and Harris made the "I'm totally repulsed" sound at the back of his throat. 'Usually I talk to them first, then they throw up.'

'OK, never mind. She was a bit too thin for your taste anyway. Not to worry, though, there are plenty of other women here over the age of consent.' She looked around. 'Well, at least three or four.'

A woman at the next table with huge cleavage tucked in a small halter and well balanced by a backside big enough to keep her from tipping over breathed a haze of whiskey across their table.

'Hey, you two!' she yelled at the quarrelling couple behind them, who stopped in mid-rant to glare at her. 'We don't wanna hear it! Shut the fuck up!'

The girl screamed something unintelligible and made an obscene gesture. Big Tits stood, knocking over her chair in the process, and the bitch-slapping began. The disgruntled boyfriend, seeming suddenly very pleased with the situation, tossed his nearly untouched beer over the two straining women.

'Guess he didn't like the beer either,' Harris observed.

'Neither of the women seemed to notice. But even in the dim lights, it was clear the boyfriend's eyes were glued to the Halter Queen's sturdy rack, constantly in danger of a breakout.

The younger woman caught Big Tits by surprise with a head-butt to the solar plexus, which catapulted both women onto Dee and Harris's table.

Barely escaping a beer bath of her own and a rogue elbow to the face, Dee ducked and grabbed Harris by the hand. 'Come on, Harris. Let's get out of here before things get ugly.'

'What a change that would be.' Harris followed her lead as they pushed and shoved their way to the door, glancing back for one last look at the catfight just before the bouncers descended.

'I'm too old for this shit,' he said.

'You've always been too old for this shit, Harris, and so have I.'

'OK, now I know. There really are worse things in the world than slapping the monkey on Friday night.'

They had walked the mile to The Boiling Point, so neither would have to be the designated driver. Besides, the night was one of those lovely dry nights when being outside was infinitely more intoxicating than thin beer.

'Does the offer still stand to share your expensive champagne?' Harris asked.

'Can't think of anyone I'd rather share it with.' She could, actually, but Ellis had been called unexpectedly to New York. Harris was a strong second choice.

As they turned off the noisy main drag and onto a quiet residential street, Harris glanced back at The Boiling Point's flashing pink sign. 'I wonder if Kendra's actually met men who weren't Neanderthals at places like that. Or maybe she likes the odd caveman on occasion. She has eclectic tastes, or so she says.' He turned his attention back to Dee. 'You're taking it all in stride.'

Dee slipped her arm through his and felt hard muscle beneath soft cotton. 'Let's just say I came here with no expectations and I wasn't disappointed.'

'I don't know anyone as pleasant as you are when they're jetlagged. Ken's not even this cheerful after she's been laid in spades.'

'Hard work at a good job does wonders. It's the Puritan ethic, you know, the American way.'

Harris stuck his finger in his mouth and pretended to gag.

They entered the arched gateway of the park where Dee and Kendra met to run whenever Dee could manage the time. The smell of freshly mown grass sweetened the night air, and the bubbling of a fountain softened the road noise further. Several benches were occupied by young lovers, oblivious to the few late-night joggers and dog walkers.

'You sure you didn't find yourself a hot Parisian while you were there?'

'Nope. No Parisians, just a great alliance.' She tried to change the subject. 'Did you and Kendra do anything interesting last weekend?'

'You know Ken. She had a hot date. Can't remember if it was Don or Eric. Something like that. I spent my time on the lake. Got some great pictures of a great blue heron. So tell me about this great alliance, and I don't mean Puritan ethic and American way crap either.'

'Harris –'

'Wait, wait. I've got it.' He hopped on the edge of the fountain and walked carefully balanced along the concrete rim. 'Since it was an alliance with Pneuma Inc., and no French men were involved … No French women either? Just kidding.'

'Harris, I think that beer must have been stronger than you thought.'

'No, wait. Don't tell me. You're jetlagged –' he made quotation marks in the air with his fingers '– because of a Pneuma Inc. alliance. You and the big man, right? That's it, isn't it? More than one alliance going on in Paris last week, right?' He punched her arm lightly.

She punched him back. 'You got me, Harris. I can't pull the wool over your eyes. Ellis fucked me senseless.'

'I knew it.' He laughed and slapped his leg, nearly losing his balance. 'I knew that had to be it.'

She kept walking.

'You are kidding, aren't you? Dee?' He jumped off the fountain and followed her along the path. 'You're joking, right?'

Realising Harris wasn't going to give up till he got an answer, she was just about to come clean when he stepped in front of her and grabbed her firmly by both arms. 'Is that what the champagne and roses are for?'

'Fuck you, Harris.' Jerking away and stormed down the path, narrowly avoiding a couple of joggers.

'Dee!' He ran to catch up with her. 'I'm sorry, Dee. I was just kidding. It was a joke, a bad joke.'

She turned on him and he practically fell over his feet preventing a collision. 'For your information, smartass –' she forced him back another step until he nearly fell onto the bench alongside the path '– I've been busting my butt for weeks above and beyond. In fact, this alliance wouldn't have even happened without my efforts. Now you tell me, what the hell do you think the champagne and roses are for?'

Harris gave up and plopped down on the bench. 'I'm sorry. It's just I thought you were joking – about Thorne, I mean.'

She sat down next to him, feeling self-conscious after her little display. For a second, the only sound other than the whispered splash of the fountain was their own breath. Then, somewhere down the path, a dog barked. She could feel Harris's gaze in the darkness as the knot of anger in her chest unravelled, leaving embarrassment in its place, but how could she not be tetchy where her relationship with Ellis was concerned? At last, Harris stood and offered her his hand. They walked on in silence, exiting the park into Dee's neighbourhood. They were nearly at her house before Harris spoke again.

'So … Was it good? I mean, I figured it must have been the way you're jetlagged and all.'

'Oh yes. It was good all right.'

There was another stretch of silence, one Dee recognised only too well as Harris's inner lawyer choosing his words carefully.

'You know, Dee, I'm always ready to celebrate when one of us actually has sex with a real person, but are you sure this is a good idea? I mean, sex with your boss?'

She unlocked the door and they stepped inside. 'We're consenting adults, Harris. It's a mutual need satisfied – nothing more.' She wouldn't let it be anything more, considering how she suffered and angsted after their first time together. This time it was all about the Executive Sex Clause, end of story, but Harris didn't need to know that.

She took the champagne from the fridge and opened it. Still not wanting to move inside, they adjourned to the two chaise longues on the patio.

'Don't get me wrong, I can certainly understand the man's attraction to you, but after all the things I've read about him, I just expected him to be a little more ethical, that's all. I mean, shit, he's rich. It's not like he can't get it whenever he wants it.'

'Damn it, Harris, why does it always have to be a question of ethics with you?' She stood and walked onto the lawn, wriggling her bare toes in the cool grass. 'Besides, if you knew him, if you knew the schedule he keeps, his dedication, how driven he is, you'd know that he doesn't have time to get it whenever he wants. But –'

'But you're always there, working close by.'

'That's right, I'm always there. What?' She could feel his gaze where he watched her from the chair.

'Are you falling in love with him?'

'What kind of stupid question is that?'

'Dee, you've adored the man for a long time, and I don't know, I just believe love should fit into the picture somewhere, or at least there ought to be a couple of actual dates before the fucking begins.'

'That's not what it sounded like the night of the barbecue when Kendra was here. You seemed to think a fuck whenever you needed one was a pretty good idea.'

He nodded slowly, not taking his gaze off her. 'In theory, yes. But that's hardly reality, is it?'

'I don't know. It seems like Ellis and me having sex is a practical solution to a practical problem. Why shouldn't we satisfy our sexual needs calmly and rationally like we do all our other needs?'

He came to her side. 'There's nothing calm or rational about sex, Dee. That's the problem. Hey, I think it's great you getting laid and all. I just don't want you to get hurt.'

Chapter Seventeen

ELLIS HAD BEEN DREAMING of Dee when he awoke in the wee hours completely, nearly painfully, aroused. The dream was so real that he reached for her before his brain filled in the obvious fact that the woman was not right there in the bed next to him, a fact that was far more disappointing than he would have thought possible. Before he was fully in control of his thought process, he pulled up her number on his BlackBerry.

She answered after the first ring, not giving him time to reconsider what he'd done. 'Ellis? Is everything all right?'

Embarrassed, but no less aroused, especially not at the sound of her voice on the other end of the phone, he bluffed. 'Why aren't you in bed asleep, Dee?'

There was stunned silence for a few seconds, then she said, 'How do you know I wasn't? How do you know you didn't wake me up? And besides, why aren't you asleep?'

He thought he could detect a slight smile in her voice, and he, well, he was suddenly smiling into the darkness of the hotel room hard enough to split his face. 'I was asleep. I was dreaming of you.' He shifted beneath the sheets, feeling the impatient strain of his erection.

'Me?' came the response. 'Was it a good dream?'

If it were possible, his smile got even bigger and his pulse quickened. 'Why do you think I'm calling?'

'Oh.' He heard the surprised gasp of breath as she twigged. 'Oh!'

'Please tell me you're at least home and not still in the office because otherwise this could get awkward.'

'I'm home.' Her voice was breathless, and he thought he could hear a slight tremor in her words. 'In my study.'

He hadn't seen her study when he'd taken her home and tucked her in bed, but then he hadn't been interested in the house tour, only the woman in his arms. 'Dee, it's one in the morning, in Portland, and we've had this discussion before, as I recall. Get in your jammies and go to bed. Now.'

There was another second of silence, and he could hear the shuffling of papers. 'I don't sleep in jammies, Ellis.'

'Sexy nightie?'

She gave him an "as if" laugh.

'What then? T-shirt? Underwear? Anything.'

'No.' The word was emphatic.

'Jesus,' he whispered. He had to press his thumb to the head of his cock to hold back the inevitable. There was no way he wasn't going to take full advantage of Dee Henning naked between the sheets with him, even if there was a whole continent separating them. He caught his breath and spoke carefully into the BlackBerry. 'Dee, go to your room, put the BlackBerry on speakerphone, get undressed and get into bed. Now.'

It didn't take long before she said, 'OK. I'm in my room, BlackBerry on speakerphone, and now I'm getting un –'

'Wait.' He interrupted. 'What are you wearing?'

'Sweats.' Her chuckle sounded embarrassed. 'I don't wear a power suit at home, Ellis.'

He was sure she would be sexy no matter what she wore. 'Strip down to your underwear.' He shouldn't be doing this, yet hadn't they both agreed to the Executive Sex Clause? Wouldn't this help him function better and be more focused tomorrow?

'Ellis, I'm not wearing any,' she said. Then she added again, 'I'm at home,' as if that explained the lack of underwear. Whether it did or didn't, it caused a definite surge of heat beneath the sheets.

'Jesus, woman! You're gonna have me going off here before I'm ready. Take off the sweats, then, and get into bed. Mind you, it would be fun to do this with you in a more kinky place than your bed, but since you should be sleeping anyway, I'd like to make sure you're down for the count when we're finished.'

He heard the shifting of cloth against cloth, then she sighed. 'OK. I'm naked, and I'm in bed.' Her voice was thin and breathless. 'Now what do you want me to do?'

'I know how wet you get; from first-hand experience, I know. I want you that wet now. Surely you masturbate. Your libido has to be at least as high as mine and there has to be some kind of release for people like us.'

'Of course I masturbate,' she breathed. 'I've rubbed myself raw every night since Paris, and right now, if I get any more slippery I'll slide off the bed. What about you? Are you touching yourself?'

'God, you're a brazen woman, Dee Henning, asking your boss if he's jerking off?' Before she could protest, he laughed softly, a chuckle that ended in a grunt and a tug of his cock. He bit his lip to regain control. 'Of course I'm masturbating, and if you'd just woken up from the dream I was having you'd be masturbating too.'

'About me?' she whispered.

'Oh yes. About you. I barely got a taste of you in Paris before I was whisked away to New York aching for more. And Dee, you taste so fucking good.'

He heard the little whimper on the other end of the line and he held his breath, listening desperately for sounds of her arousal, sounds of her pleasure.

'I'd like to know what you taste like,' she said.

He ground his ass into the sheets and shifted against his hand, relishing the thought of Dee on her knees, Dee taking him into her mouth. 'I'll make sure that's on the calendar for when you get to New York,' he said. Then he added. 'Dee, tell me what you're doing. Tell me what you like.'

She offered an embarrassed laugh, soft and musical over the speakerphone. 'I can't believe we're having this conversation. I've stroked myself until I'm really wet. That wasn't hard, knowing what you're doing on the other end of the phone. I'm swollen, Mr Thorne, so swollen and open, and my fingers just can't seem to scratch the itch.' The sudden shift to her business voice, to the formal use of his name, had him shallow-breathing to keep from coming. She moaned and caught her

110

own breath in what was almost a sob. Then, for a long moment, he listened to her sighing and shifting, holding his breath, not wanting to miss the sound of Dee Henning all horny and needing. When she continued, her words were clipped with her efforts at what he could only imagine her hands were doing between her legs. 'And my nipples, Mr Thorne, my nipples are hard from thinking about the way your mouth felt on them when you were taking care of business in the limo.'

'Oh God,' he whispered, tightening his grip, then tugging at his cock like there was a battle to be won. With the other hand he cupped and kneaded his balls as he remembered the feel of her breasts, the rise of her nipples against his lips, the rippled press of her areolas against his tongue. He heard scrabbling noises on the other end of the line. 'Dee?'

'Just getting my vibrator,' she said. Then she laughed breathlessly. 'No need for lube tonight, Mr Thorne. I'm sopping.' She sucked in a harsh breath that ended in a whimper. When she had recovered herself, she spoke in her best naughty secretary voice. 'Now then, Mr Thorne, what's on our agenda today? What urgent business do we need to take care of?'

The surge he felt in his cock at the thought of being inside his horny executive assistant nearly sent him over the edge. He held his breath listening for the sound of the vibrator, but he could hear only her heavy breathing.

Then she said, 'I don't need to turn it on, Mr Thorne. I just need to be full, and since you're not here, the vibe will have to do. Poor substitute, really. It doesn't have your girth, nor your weight, and it's cold. '

'Jesus, Ms Henning,' he gasped. 'I can't believe I hired such a naughty girl.'

'Tell me what you were doing to me in your dream, Mr Thorne, that made you so horny you'd call me in the middle of the night. Or was it what I was doing to you, maybe?'

'It was raining outside.' He ran his hand down the length of his cock and tightened his grip. God, how many times had he had variations of this dream? 'You came into my office all wet.'

Her chuckle was rich and throaty, and he wanted to eat it, suckle it like thick, dark syrup right from between her lips. 'I recognise that dream. Did you offer me a towel?'

The corners of his mouth ached from smiling like an idiot. 'I would have, but I didn't have one.'

'I see.' Her voice was low, breathless. 'So what did you do?'

'First I helped you out of your clothes, then I licked you dry. You were really wet, but I was careful to get every drop.' He spat on his hand to lubricate himself, easing the friction from thrusting in and out of it. He wanted it wet and warm like he was inside her. Then he continued, 'It wasn't easy because you wouldn't lie still. You said you were ticklish. You said the only way you could hold still was if I fucked you.'

Her breath sounded like a windstorm coming through the speakerphone, though it was hard to tell which was hers and which was his. 'And did you, Mr Thorne?' she gasped. 'Did you fuck me?'

'I held you down on the floor, you were so open and so ready, and I could see how wet you were, and then just when I was ready to push into you, I woke up feeling like I was about to burst.'

'Oh Jesus, Mr Thorne! Oh God!' Her voice was barely a rasp against the phone, her breath harsh and quick. 'The thought of you lying there hard and heavy and full because of me drives me crazy.' It felt almost like she had pulled him into her arms and spoke against his ear.

Words stopped, except for the calling of each other's name which slipped out between gasps. "Mr Thorne …. Ms Henning … Mr Thorne … Ms Henning …" Ellis could imagine Dee lying beneath her blue comforter, one hand cupping and caressing her lovely breasts while the other shoved the vibrator in and out of her tight wetness as she thrust her whole body onto it, breasts bouncing, hips shifting. And dear God, he could imagine how she must smell, so turned on, so close to coming, sheened in the fragrant perspiration of arousal. Jesus, he wanted her. He wanted her so badly he could almost feel her, as though the speakerphone could magically turn the grunts and groans of the woman on the other end of the phone into flesh and blood here in his bed, here in his arms.

'I have to come, Mr Thorne,' she gasped. 'I can't hold back any longer.'

He heard the growl and the moan of her orgasm, and it was enough. The warm wet of his semen felt like it would turn him inside out with the sheer weight of his need. He was stunned and amazed that he could feel this way, that he could want her so damn badly.

For a few minutes, their combined efforts to breathe raged through the speakerphone. When at last he had the breath to speak again, he felt bold somehow. Maybe it was the distance between them, maybe it was simply the post-coital flood of hormones, but he asked. 'Dee, have you really been rubbing yourself raw since Paris?'

She laughed. 'You're kidding? Ellis, whatever you did to me in Paris, I think you might have created a monster. If we don't get together very soon, I'm gonna need more batteries.'

Again the face-splitting smile was back. 'Good. I'm glad it's not just me, and Sunday night can't get here fast enough. Now go to sleep, Dee. You're gonna need all your strength for New York.'

'Garrett, what are you doing here?' Ellis motioned his younger brother into the hotel suite. 'Didn't recognise you in the suit and tie. Thought maybe I forgot to tip the valet.'

Garrett Thorne stripped off his jacket and tossed it over the back of the couch. 'I'm here to meet with my editor about the next book.'

'I read your last one. It's good.'

Garrett gave him a look like he had two heads. 'You're kidding, right? I'm amazed that the great Ellison Thorne would condescend to read such drivel, but apparently there are enough die-hard fans begging for more that my employment for the foreseeable future, at least, is secured. I got a free trip to the Big Apple out of the deal too, and a room in a decent hotel. Not bad for a hack.'

'Honestly, Garrett, when are you going to stop berating

113

what you do? You're talented. Very talented, and if your editor paid to fly you to New York it's because he doesn't want to risk losing you to someone else offering you more to write for them. It doesn't take a business genius to figure that out.'

Garrett shot Ellis a bemused grin that made him look considerably younger than he actually was. 'If you weren't the filthy rich God of the business world, I'd hire you on as groupie, but then that'd ruin my reputation as Ellison Thorne's ne'er-do-well brother, wouldn't it?'

Ellis folded his arm across his chest and shook his head. 'Have it your way, Garrett, but I'm warning you, the press'll have a field day when it all blows up in your face and you're forced to come clean about who you really are.'

Garrett changed the subject, like he always did. 'The concierge thought I was you. Nearly gave me the VIP treatment.' He looked around the suite, caught his reflection in the screen of the television, and straightened his cuffs and tie.

'Surprised you didn't let him.'

Garrett bent and checked the mini-bar, then gave the door a muted slam. 'I was tempted, but then he noticed how much more handsome and debonair I am than my older brother, so I had to come clean.'

Ellis nodded. 'That's always a dead giveaway.'

Garrett was a duskier version of Ellis, with olive skin and nearly black hair that fell over his hazel eyes. He was taller, though not by much, and Ellis couldn't help noticing his brother was considerably thinner than he'd been last time they'd seen each other. Even his darker complexion couldn't hide the circles under his eyes. The symptoms were easy to recognise, and in the younger Thorne's case, they were chronic.

'I was just about to order room service. You want anything?'

'Maybe a sandwich or something.' Garrett plopped down on the sofa, found the remote for the television, and began to surf. 'It all does the same thing – peanut butter or steak.'

'Looks like you could stand to eat a little more of one or the other. Got your heart broke again, did you?'

Garrett didn't answer, but turned up the volume and slumped further down the couch. For Ellis, that was confirmation enough.

He called in the order, then sat down on the sofa near the desk. 'Have you seen Stacie?' Ellis knew Stacie was usually the first person Garrett ran to when his heart had been broken. Their strange relationship wasn't something Ellis understood, but then who knew why love drove people to do what they did?

'I talked to her this afternoon,' Garrett said. 'Told her I was coming to see you. She'd hoped you'd call. She asked if you ever look at the stars any more.'

At one time, the question would have been salt to an open wound. But wounds heal, and Ellis wasn't going to let his brother change the subject. 'Who is it this time?' he asked.

'A dancer,' Garrett said.

'A dancer? Please, Garrett. Surely you can do better than that.'

Garrett forced a smile without looking away from the television. 'Not that kind of dancer. Amy's a ballerina. She works for the New York Ballet. That's my ulterior motive for being here. She won't see me, though, so it doesn't really matter, does it?' He cranked the volume again and flipped faster. The man always had a hard time settling when he was wounded by love.

'I'm sorry,' Ellis said.

'I thought maybe the two of us could go to the ballet together. I've got an extra ticket. Afterwards we could knock back a couple brewskies, you know, for old times' sake.'

'Afraid I can't tonight.' Ellis nodded to the jumble of files on the desk next to the laptop. 'I've been swamped since Beverly died.'

Garrett flinched, almost as though Ellis had slapped him. Ellis found himself wishing he hadn't said anything.

The younger Thorne spoke above the raised volume of the television. 'Of course. I should have remembered. I'm sorry I missed the funeral. I didn't know until after.'

'It's all right. I didn't expect you.' Ellis grabbed the remote away and turned off the TV. He'd forgotten just how irritating his brother could be at times.

Without the remote in hand, Garrett fidgeted with the tassel of a throw pillow. 'I'm sorry. I know how much she meant to you.' The muscles in his throat tightened, then relaxed. 'It couldn't have been easy, losing her like that. She was there for you when ...' He clenched a fist into the soft body of the pillow.

Ellis studied his brother's profile in the dim light. He knew it wasn't Beverly he was thinking about. A broken heart always seemed to bring up past regrets. 'Yes, she was, Garrett. She was there for me, and I'll miss her.'

Thankfully, room service arrived. Ellis was relieved for the distraction, knowing the litany a morose Garrett would fall into involved a past he'd rather just forget about. He silently hoped that the two of them could get along for the duration of a short meal and not talk about the past. Surely that wasn't too much to ask. At a table by the window, they settled to club sandwiches and beer.

Garrett raised his glass in salute. 'To Beverly, a woman who made a difference.'

Ellis returned the toast.

A muffled rendition of the bar music from the original *Star Wars* erupted from Garrett's jacket on the sofa. He jumped up from the table. 'Sorry, Ellis, but it could be Amy.' He grabbed the cell phone from his pocket and disappeared into the bathroom, leaving Ellis alone with his thoughts.

For at least the millionth time, Ellis wondered how he could possibly run Pneuma Inc. without Beverly. As much potential as Dee had, she didn't know what Beverly had known, and there were things she just couldn't help with. These days it often felt as though he were stumbling around in the dark. Beverly had kept him on course when everything else in his life had been a disaster. He'd always been able to count on her for wise advice and a kick-in-the-ass reality check when he needed it. For 13 years she'd helped him guide Pneuma Inc. From his pocket, he pulled the pen she'd given him to celebrate the birth of the new company and ran his fingers along the slender barrel, remembering.

The morning he'd presented her with the proposal, he'd nearly worn a path across the Turkish carpet in front of her desk, pacing, waiting for her response. He'd come expecting her advice, but she'd given him so much more.

She came from old money, and didn't really need her professorship for financial security. Her younger brother had inherited the family business in spite of the fact that Beverly had been more suited to the task, so she chose to use her gift for business to educate young entrepreneurs.

'You're right, Ellis. Wade Crittenden's ideas for environmental clean-up are years ahead of their time, financially sound too.' She glanced up at him. 'And these designs work?'

'Wade never designs anything that doesn't.' Wade was a grad student in environmental engineering back then, and he was Ellis's good friend. He was also an inventor, and a damn good one. What he wasn't, however, was a businessman. That's where Ellis came in. He could see it all in his head; marketing, selling, manufacturing and servicing, and in three sleepless nights, he'd formulated a plan to make it all happen.

'You serious about this?' She spoke without looking up from the proposal.

He stopped pacing, stood at attention. 'Yes, ma'am. It'll work. I'm sure.'

'You do understand the commitment you'll have to put in to make it work?'

'I understand, yes.'

'And the observatory?'

He fought back panic. He hadn't expected her to bring that up. He'd hoped she'd forgotten after all this time, but why would she? He hadn't been able to. 'Professor, I already told you when I made the transfer to the business department, it was a done deal.'

'A done deal in the head and a done deal in the heart are two different things, Thorne.' She took off her glasses and studied him across the desk. 'You graduate in a few months, don't you?'

She knew he did.

'I had a very interesting conversation with Professor Morrison the other day. Gave me a fascinating tour of the observatory and the labs. Exciting news about the funding for the new telescope, Ellis, don't you think?'

'Exciting, yes.'

'He wants you, you know?'

'That's not going to happen, Professor.'

For a long moment, she scrutinised him, waiting for him to break.

He didn't.

She stood and moved around the desk next to him, glasses still in hand. 'I can get you the capital, cut through all the crap you'd normally have to deal with starting a new business, and even show you a few ways to improve the basic plan – on one condition.'

'What's that?' he asked.

'That you let me in as an equal partner.'

'Professor?'

'I'm not getting any younger, Ellis.' She stuck her glasses back on, and held him in her cast-iron gaze. 'I'm tired of teaching, and if I wait any longer, I'll be too old for the doing,'

'Earth to Ellis.' Garrett waved his hand in front of his brother.

Ellis blinked, surprised to find him sitting back at the table. 'Sorry, just taking a stroll down memory lane. Was it Amy?'

Garrett shook his head. 'Only my agent checking in. Never mind that.' He scooted his chair closer. 'Stacie tells me you've found someone to take over as your executive assistant.'

'How does Stacie know about Pneuma Inc. business?' Ellis asked.

'She's still friends with Wade.' Garrett leaned over the table and offered the same smile that usually meant trouble when they were boys. 'Stacie's heard the woman doesn't take any shit from you.'

'Wade's got a big mouth,' Ellis grumbled.

'As I remember, he calls 'em like he sees 'em, bro,' Garrett said. 'Dee Henning? Isn't that her name? Stacie hears she's hotter than hot.'

An understatement, Ellis thought. The memory of last night's phone sex was more than a little distracting, as was the knowledge that Sunday night she'd be joining him here in New York. He planned to make sure she felt very welcome. He forced his attention back to his brother.

'So, this Dee Henning, is she as much of a workaholic as you are?' Garrett asked, leaning forward over the remains of his sandwich.

'More so, I think. She definitely gets things done.' The knowing look his brother flashed made Ellis regret his choice of words.

'I know you'd never hire anybody who wasn't the best, but I'm curious; Ms Henning's job description doesn't by any chance include the Executive Sex Clause, does it?' The smile returned to Garrett's face and Ellis felt that same tension he'd always experienced as a child just before Garrett came up with a another scheme guaranteed to get them both in trouble.

'It did occur to you that the Executive Sex Clause is illegal, didn't it?'

'Of course it occurred to me. I may have been drunk the night we dreamed it up, but I wasn't that drunk.'

'You and Beverly dreamed it up, you mean. It was embarrassing the way you two went on and on about it.'

'Still, it's a great idea, you have to admit. Beverly really was ahead of her time.' Garrett gave his brother a loose-fisted punch in the arm. 'Come on, admit it. You implemented the Sex Clause, didn't you? I sure as hell would have in your shoes.'

'You're delusional, Garrett. I hired Dee Henning to be my executive assistant. That's that.'

'Right.' Garrett drew out the word until he'd reshaped its meaning to suit himself, then he rubbed his hands together with a shiver of delight. 'I can hardly wait to see what happens. You know, there might just be a novel in this.'

Ellis gave him the finger, but he only smiled, gulped the rest of his beer, and grabbed his jacket. 'I gotta go. I'll be late for the ballet. Time to win back Amy's heart. Wish me luck.'

Chapter Eighteen

IT WAS VERY LATE Thursday afternoon when Tally knocked on the door to Wade Crittenden's office. He never answered, so she stuck her head inside.

He sat behind a stack of loose-leaf binders cascading off the corner of his desk. 'What do you want?' he said without looking up from whatever it was he was doing. Her timing was bad, which was just exactly what she was hoping for.

'I brought the financial projections on the Trouvères project for Marston for you to sign off on, Wade.' She had deliberately waited until the end of the work day, knowing that if they were to go out to Marston tonight, Wade would have to Fed Ex them himself.

He did a fair equivalent of an angry bear growl. 'Put 'em there, and I'll get to 'em.' He nodded to the desk. 'Would make my life easier if the old fart would just let me email these and stop being such a damned Luddite.'

Tally gave a shrug. 'Well, he does run paper mills, after all.'

Wade glared at her like he couldn't believe she could say such a stupid thing. She changed the subject. 'Are you going bowling?'

She knew Thursday was the day Wade worked on ideas and did his trouble-shooting down at the bowling alley, and, for some reason, his favourite bowling alley was way over Mount Hood way in Sandy. No one knew why he chose one so far away, but then Wade was Wade, so no one complained. Besides, he did own a third of the company, and time spent at the bowling alley of his choice had made him and the rest of the Pneuma Inc. triumvirate very rich.

'If people would stop interrupting me with mindless drivel

so I could actually get out of this place, I would.' He nodded again to the projections. He had little patience for people who couldn't or wouldn't use technology. 'Just leave the projections and go away. I'll sign them and then Fed Ex them on my way out.'

'Tell you what,' she said with mock thoughtfulness, 'if you give them your John Hancock, I'll Fed Ex them for you. It's the least I can do.' Tally never wasted her womanly charms on Wade. She'd learned early on that it would take more than a bit of cleavage or a flutter of eyelashes to distract him. Her best bet was just to show up at the worst possible moment, when he was distracted. He'd never remember what he'd told her and what he didn't. In fact, she was pretty sure that half the time he didn't even remember she was there. Normally, she would find such behaviour highly offensive, but this was Wade.

When he was done signing the papers, he shoved them at her and grunted something that might have been "thanks" or might have been "fuck off" for all Tally could tell. 'There,' he said. 'Now go away. I'm busy.' He didn't wait for her offered smile, but headed into the lab and shut the door behind him. Just like he always did.

She was about to leave when she had an idea. She looked over her shoulder to make sure Wade wasn't watching, but she knew him well enough to know the building could collapse around him and he wouldn't notice as long as the lab was still intact. Quickly, her heart pounding in her chest, she shoved into the chair at the computer desk. The computer there was always running, but as far as she could tell seldom used. She typed in Beverly's password, keeping her fingers crossed that it still worked.

It did, and she was in. Another added bonus.

No one even realised she had the password, and it only worked from the terminals in the offices of the three executives, a system Wade had set up to keep his work secure from everyone but Beverly and Ellis. Tally figured the only reason Beverly's account was still active was that Wade couldn't bring himself to let go of that last personal connection. She knew it wouldn't last for ever. It was a stroke of luck that she'd actually got hold of the password at all. She happened to see it over Beverly's secretary's shoulder the day after Beverly died. Tally had needed access to the Scribal files and Beverly's secretary and Ellis were the only ones who knew Beverly's password. The secretary, always overly cautious, was distraught that day, and it hadn't been hard to see what keys she punched. Later that same day, Tally had found Wade's terminal up, as it always was. And *voilà*! Tally had a secret way in.

A few more keystrokes and she pulled up Dee's files on the Trouvères project. A few more and she had them downloaded on two memory sticks, one for Jamison and one for her. It only took her a few minutes, then she slipped the memory sticks into her bag along with the projections.

'What are you still doing here?'

She jumped at the sound of Wade's voice. He stood behind her, clipboard in one hand and a fist shoved into the pocket of his over-sized hoodie.

She stood, shouldered her bag, and offered him her best business as usual smile. 'Just remembered something urgent from Rosa up in accounting. I didn't think you'd mind if I sent her a quick email. I seem to have left my iPhone upstairs in my desk. I'm off now, back to the mines.'

He only glared at her over the top of his glasses, then turned on his heels and disappeared back into the lab. She heaved a sigh of relief, then quickly made sure everything was as she had found it, and left. In the elevator, she texted Jamison from the phone he had given her to use for their correspondence, then she got out in the main lobby. It wasn't that much before quitting time and no one in accounting would know how long she was with Wade.

Outside the office, she waited only a few minutes for the limo that pulled up next to the kerb. She got in, and the vehicle pulled away.

'Good afternoon, Tally. You're a little earlier than I expected. Slow day in accounting?' Terrance Jamison handed her a glass of champagne. In return, she gave over the bag with the papers in it. 'Did you have any trouble getting them?' he asked.

'It was risky,' she lied. 'Fortunately for me I have a good relationship with Crittenden, so he didn't suspect. I just told him I'd get these Fed Exed for him, just like you suggested.'

Jamison offered her a sideways glance from the paper he was already perusing. 'Well done,' he said. 'You're an amazing woman, Tally Barnes. This is very interesting. Very interesting indeed.'

'Oh, and there is one more thing you might want to see.' Digging in her bag, she pulled out one of the memory sticks.

'What's this?' he asked. 'Another surprise? Why Tally, this is almost like Christmas.'

She blushed. 'It's a copy of Dee's presentation, in case you're interested.'

Jamison flipped the memory stick over in his hand, eyeing it as though he could didn't need a computer to read the data, then he offered her an arid chuckle. 'I'll be damned, you are handy, Ms Barnes, very handy indeed. How the hell did you get your hands on Dee Henning's presentation? No, wait a minute. I don't really want to know. It's better that way.'

She lifted her champagne flute in salute. 'Then it'll be my little secret.' When she got home, she'd take a peek at Dee's presentation, then she planned to send Alan Marston an intriguing letter along with the projections, just a gentle reminder of who she was and what a valuable asset she was to Pneuma Inc.

'You are stunning, Tally Barnes.' Jamison offered her a smile that was all charm and goodwill. 'Now that I know what I'm up against, I know what to offer to make sure this little alliance doesn't happen. I get what I want, and you, my dear, are one giant step closer to getting what you want, as well.'

And then it was as though he'd completely forgotten she was in the limo with him as he scanned the papers. By the time Jamison dropped her in front of her house an hour later, Tally was more than a little tipsy after several more glasses of good champagne on an empty stomach. He had promised she'd have the papers back in time to Fed Ex them tomorrow. She had barely got the door to her flat unlocked and kicked off her shoes when a message on her phone reassured her that the last of her credit cards had been paid in full, and there was a nice little surprise waiting for her in her checking account. She smiled to herself. The alliance with Jamison was proving to be way more profitable than she had expected.

'We've got problems.'

Dee had stepped out of her office only long enough to make an iced tea run. No one else was on the tenth floor except Sandra. After nearly a week of jerking her around, Marston was finally ready to meet her over Trouvères. For some unknown reason, he still had it in his head she was neglecting Scribal. Ellis was already in New York on another project and would meet her at the hotel Sunday evening. After their earlier phone sex, she could hardly wait for their reunion, but in the meantime, Marston had to be dealt with and there was no time to dwell on the heat of midweek. In order to be prepared for Monday's round of meetings, Dee had opted to work Saturday and fly out Sunday afternoon. When the secretary chased her down in the break room, Dee knew something was up.

'Alan Marston practically tore me a new one over the phone just now. I don't know what the trouble is. He wouldn't tell me.'

Back in her office, Dee gulped tea for courage, then called Marston. When he answered the phone with a snarl, she knew it wasn't going to be pretty.

'What in God's name are you doing out there, because it sure as hell isn't your job?' Marston shouted into the phone.

Dee held the receiver at a safe distance to protect her eardrum. In a ten-minute tirade he informed her, with all the eloquence and panache of a drill sergeant, that he hadn't received the packet with the Trouvères projections he'd been promised. He was on a roll by the time he got around to assigning blame, which he laid squarely at her feet. 'This kind of negligence and incompetence had better cease, and quickly, or Scribal will take its business elsewhere. And believe you me, Jamison's offer is looking better and better all the time.' He continued to yell into her ear. 'I don't know what Thorne was drinking when he hired you, but even a rank amateur should know there's nothing to meet about until you get me those goddamned projections!'

With the beginnings of a headache clawing at the base of her skull, Dee hung up the phone, promising to make sure everything was in order for Monday's meeting. When she had calmed down enough to stop shaking, she called Sandra into her office and explained the situation.

'I don't understand. I sent everything down to accounting for a once-over. They were to deliver it all to Wade to double-check the numbers and technological facts, like you asked,' Sandra said.

They met Wade at the Dungeon. He looked like he'd spent the night there, which he often did. He wore his usual ratty lab jacket over a pair of Levis and an untucked rugby shirt – a game he'd taken a liking to on his one and only trip abroad back before he started grad school. He looked at the two women and blinked as though he'd just come out of the dark.

'Don't you ever go home?' he asked Dee.

'Probably more often than you do,' she said. In spite of his lack of people skills and his reclusive ways, both Ellis and Beverly considered him a friend and confidant. It hadn't taken her long to realise why.

'Early in the day for bowling, isn't it?' Sandra nodded to the bowling shoes on the man's feet.

He looked down as though he were surprised. 'I went yesterday. Brainstorming. I guess I forgot to take them off.' He turned his attention back to Dee. 'So that bastard, Marston, is giving you a hard time, is he?'

'Apparently with good reason,' Dee said

'Marston doesn't need a good reason. Beverly deserves sainthood for putting up with his crap. The two were close friends, though I can't imagine why.'

Neither could Dee at this point. When they explained the situation, Wade ran a hand through his eternally messy hair. 'That secretary, or whatever, you sent down Thursday night said she'd send it.'

'What secretary?' Sandra asked.

He blinked, and his brow wrinkled as though he were in deepest concentration. 'Wait a minute. It might have been the woman who works in accounting, the irritating one. What's her name?'

'Tally Barnes,' both Dee and Sandra said at the same time.

'After Beverly died, no one knew quite what to do with Scribal,' Sandra explained. 'Ellis took over most of the work, but Tally Barnes volunteered to help out. The woman's a great ass-kisser. But for some reason I can't fathom, Marston thinks she's better than chocolate. She developed quite a liking for Beverly's office. Insisted she needed access to Beverly's files if she was going to do Beverly's job. Strutted around like she owned the place. Finally Ellis told her he wanted her back in accounting.'

'I heard her bitching in the hall a couple of days ago that Dee was getting credit for all the hard work she's done on the Scribal project,' Wade added. 'What?' he said when they both looked at him. 'The woman's loud. Everyone heard her.'

'But all she's done is the projections, and she would have done those anyway.' Dee massaged the nagging pain at the back of her neck that was now working its way around to her temples.

Sandra pulled a small bottle of aspirin from her pocket and handed it to her. 'What now?' she asked. 'Should I call Ellis?'

A quick flash of Ellis reprimanding her after she'd overslept stiffened Dee's resolve. 'This is my problem. I'll solve it without bothering Ellis.' She looked down at her watch. 'At 7.30 in a Saturday morning, if I were Tally, I'd be at home in bed. I hope she's a light sleeper.' She picked up the phone and punched in the number. There was no answer. Hanging up, she turned to Sandra. 'I'm still hedging my bets that she's home in bed. Do you know where she lives?'

'I can find out.'

'Do it, and get me Jeffries. Tell him we'll need the limo.' Dee knew that if a place was in either of the great States of Oregon or Washington, the driver could find it.

She tried the number one more time to be sure, and was just

ready to hang up when a sleepy Tally answered. She listened in silence as Dee explained the situation.

'I knew I should have called you, or given Marston or someone the heads up.' Tally's voice practically oozed sympathy through the phone. 'Dee, I'm so sorry. Wade seemed distracted Thursday when I left the projections for him. I just had this feeling he hadn't really noticed what it was or how important. So on Friday, before I left, I went back on a lark and, sure enough, though everything was signed off on, they hadn't been sent. I just went ahead and Fed Exed the packet to Marston. I left Wade a note. I guess he didn't find it. Honestly, whatever it was he was working on, he barely knew I was there, and I'm sure he didn't know how late it was.'

Dee had worked with Wade closely enough to know that in spite of his absent-minded professor act, he most certainly wasn't the type to forget something so vital. She chewed on her lip and listened as Tally continued.

'I managed to get it in just before the Fed Ex place closed. Cost a little extra, but I knew how important it was. I should have called, but you've been so busy I just couldn't bring myself to bother you on a Friday night. Really, I feel terrible about this, Dee. Please don't say anything to Wade. I'm sure whatever he was working on was very important. I mean, it always is with him, and we all know that. The Fed Ex guy promised me Alan would have everything on his desk by noon today. If you'd like, I can call and try to smooth things over. For some reason Alan seems to listen to me, and I know what a bear he can be when he's upset.'

'Thanks, but that won't be necessary. I'll take care of it,' Dee assured her.

Dee was barely off the line before her BlackBerry rang. It was Marston.

'Fortunately, Ms Henning, not everyone who works for Thorne is completely incompetent. You should give that Tally Barnes a raise. She picked up on your little oversight and had the packet with the financial projections priority posted to me. It just arrived. There'll be a meeting Monday after all, no thanks to you.' He hung up.

'I'll be sure to thank her.' Dee spoke between gritted teeth into the silent phone.

Chapter Nineteen

IN SPITE OF THE late hour, there were still plenty of people milling around in front of the restaurant and in the lobby when Dee arrived at the hotel in New York. She was surprised to find Ellis was one of them. Dressed in the usual business attire, he still looked fresh enough to eat – a thought that sent warm shivers down her spine. He greeted her with a look reserved for a favourite dessert. After slipping the bellman some money to take her bag to the suite, he stood quietly at her side the few minutes it took her to check in.

As they walked to the elevator, he slid a proprietary hand to the small of her back. She was certain his massaging fingers must be scorching tight little circles all the way through her skirt to the flesh below. The presence of a couple of tourists in "I heart NYC" T-shirts tempered her urge to rip his clothes off and ride him hard all the way up to their suite. On the second floor, an elderly couple and a large party of Asian businessmen crowded in, and Ellis and Dee found themselves relegated to the back corner.

The businessmen had clearly been partying. Though Dee didn't understand the language, she could tell by the loud laughter and ribald gestures the group had imbibed enough to reach the point at which rude jokes were the order of the evening. The elderly couple smiled demurely the way people do who don't understand what's being said, but are quietly suspicious they might be the topic of conversation.

Amid the noise and laughter and jostling of sweaty bodies, Ellis and Dee were pushed ever deeper into the corner. Mantling her protectively with broad shoulders and an open jacket, Ellis slid his hands under Dee's blouse. With one deft motion, he found the clasp at the front of her bra and opened it. Acting on instinct, she leaned forward into his embrace until her breasts were completely freed into his hands.

Whatever the joke was, it had the businessmen's full attention, and the couple and the tourists were too far to the front to notice anything.

'I can't believe you just did that,' Dee whispered, applying plenty of tongue to seashell hollow of his ear and inhaling sharply as he ground himself against her, forcing her back still further into the corner.

'If the damned elevator doesn't hurry up, I'm gonna do a whole lot more than that.' He took time out from his kneadings to guide her hand into his pocket, then shifted just enough to impress on her the urgency of the situation.

'My God, Mr Thorne, I'm amazed you can even walk.'

'Actually, I was hoping for a ride, Ms Henning.' He guided her hand to mirror and intensify the tight, almost undetectable rocking of his hips.

Oblivious to their actions, the businessman produced a bottle of something volatile and passed it around while singing a version of *Yesterday* that would have brought tears to Lennon and McCartney's eyes. Once assured Dee knew her way around the inside of his pocket, Ellis retraced the route to the closest breast. His other hand snaked up under the front of her skirt and, with a slight tilting of her hips to open a path, he manoeuvred into her panties. In the subtle but intense rubbing and stroking that ensued, she nearly forgot where they were until the door opened and disgorged everyone but themselves and the elderly couple. Ellis quickly pulled his hand from beneath her skirt and licked wet fingers, the way a chef might test his favourite recipe. In a vain attempt to look respectable, they rode the last two floors straightening clothing and breathing heavily, finally making a quick escape to their suite.

By the time they got inside, Ellis's shirt was undone and he was working on his belt. Dee yanked down the zipper of her skirt and stepped out of it.

Standing with his trousers around his ankles, Ellis shoved her blouse and the unhooked bra out of the way, and reintroduced her nipples to his enthusiastic tongue. 'Come on,' he gasped, when he finally pulled away and kicked aside his trousers. 'My bed's in here.' Hooking a finger into the waistband of her thong he pulled her at a fast trot through the sitting room.

At the door to his bedroom, she grabbed his boxers from behind, nearly tripping him as she tugged them down, freeing his erection, and giving herself a mouth-watering view of his ass.

Struggling to regain his balance, he turned on her. 'So, that's how you want to play, is it?'

'This is how I want to play.' She pushed him against the wall and dropped to her knees in front of him before he could take the initiative. Then she dragged the boxers down still further so she could cup the weight of his balls in one hand while the other closed around his erection.

'Dee.' His voice was tight, edgy. 'Dee, what are you doing?' He ran a hand down to cup her chin and lifted it until she met his gaze.

'I told you I wanted to taste you. You said you'd put it on the calendar. You didn't forget, did you? Of course not. Ellison Thorne would never forget such an important meeting.' She took him into her mouth, afraid if she waited she might lose courage, she might remember who she really was in this relationship and not be able to do what she so badly wanted to.

'Jesus, Dee.' He sucked breath between his teeth and grunted. 'I won't be able to hold off long with you doing that. Are you sure?'

'Positive.' She pulled away from him just enough to speak, running her fisted hand down the length of him, slickened and shiny with her saliva. 'I want to taste you. I want to see *your* pleasure.'

He was thick and heavy, more than she could take into her mouth. She wrapped her fingers tightly around the base of his erection, where it rose from the soft mass of pubic curls. She sheathed him with her lips hard-pressed around his girth, her tongue stroking and caressing the underside of his penis, taking in the shape of him, the rounded tip, the tight slit, the path of veins coursing beneath the skin. His flesh was warm and the scent of was slightly yeasty, like bread baking. It was a scent that made her hungry in parts of her that had nothing to do with her belly. His large hand cupped the back of her head and controlled her movements, and she let him, yielding and opening more to him with each controlled thrust of his hips. All of him was hard, like he was one giant muscle waiting to flex, waiting to explode with power. And she felt all of his need as though it were her own, building between her legs where she gaped hungry and begging and wet.

'Are you sure?' he asked again, his voice forced up the back of his throat with an effort she felt at the base of his spine, where she now rested an open palm. 'Because I can't … Because I won't be able to …'

She murmured and tried to nod, intensifying her efforts to match the crescendo of his need, tightening her grip until her cheeks ached, until her tongue thrust, until her eyes watered with her efforts to breathe around his assault on her mouth, the assault she had encouraged, the assault she had demanded.

His control slipped. She gagged, then placed a hand against his hip and forced herself to relax as his fingers curled in her hair, as his breath caught in his throat, as his control slipped again then vanished. He shuddered his orgasm into her mouth in a strangled cry that could have been pain as easily as pleasure. At first he tried to push her away, but she clung to him, taking his semen, all of it, taking the taste of him, the rich, thick taste of him onto her tongue, into her throat, swallowing back the heat and the tension and the power of the man she admired most in the world until she was weak and giddy from the act, until she was euphoric and drunk from the feel of him. Then he slid down the wall onto the floor next to her, taking her into his arms.

'Now you know how I taste.' He took her mouth like he wanted to possess it, like he wanted to devour it. When he pulled away, he forced a laugh that tightened his abdominal muscles beneath her open palm. 'And now *I* know how I taste.'

Then he shifted and rearranged himself until her back rested against his front, his penis pressed, still wet and still at half-mast, against the side of her spine. 'You need to come now, Dee. It's your turn.' He kissed her nape, then wrapped both arms around her, one hand kneading and caressing her breasts, the other moving down over her belly, down to cup her pubis. And as she arched into his palm, his middle finger found its way first to circle the sheened pearl of her clit, then to push into the slick, swollen folds of her. 'God, woman,' he whispered against her neck, 'how can anyone feel so damn good?' He slipped a second finger into her and began to thrust and stroke while his thumb circled and pressed her clitoris. 'Just a quickie to make you feel better, then I'll be ready for round two.' As if to demonstrate, he thrust his already burgeoning erection playfully against her back. One last hard stroke of his thumb sent her over the edge, nearly knocking him in the chin with the top of her head as she spasmed against him.

'There. That's better, isn't it?' He kissed her ear. 'And now that we've cleared the calendar and taken care of the more urgent business, we can play.' He helped her to her feet, turned her to face him, then lifted her onto his erection. He pushed in deep, filling her to capacity. She wrapped her legs around him. For the first several thrusts, she ached from the grudging stretch to accommodate, then she forgot about the ache and felt only the building friction and the promise of more pleasure to come as he carried her, fully impaled, to his bed. There, he rode her deep into expensive linens, putting the mattress to the test. It soon became evident that he was up for the long run.

It was much later when he collapsed on top of her, both of them spent and glistening from their efforts. When he could manage enough breath to speak, he whispered against her ear between not-quite-painful nips. 'I think I'm starting to understand just why we need the Executive Sex Clause.

She nipped him back. 'I'm amazed we got anything done without it.'

Curled against each other, they drifted in the place between sleep and wakefulness, surrounded by the smells of sex and body heat. He rolled to one side to ease his weight from her, but he was still nestled inside her, almost as hard as he had been before he came the last time. The lingering physical connection was reassuring in its intimacy. His breath slowed to the deep, even rhythms of sleep, but she found herself waking up and wondering whether she should stay or sneak off to her own bed. The idea of severing the connection wasn't appealing, but she reminded herself he was her boss, and sex was now just a part of her job. Sex with Ellis was not a complication, she told herself. It was simple, really, a part of their working arrangement that would make them both better at their jobs. Like exercise, she told herself. Still, she could never remember her workouts at the gym with Kendra or their Sunday morning runs in the park being anywhere nearly this exciting, nor had thinking about them ever given her butterflies down low in her belly.

Ellis roused from the dream world like a great cat, stretching the full length of the bed, breaking the physical connection in a warm flood of moisture against the inside of her thigh. Kissing her ear, he slid out of bed. 'I've gotta pee. Don't go away. I'll be right back.'

In a few minutes, he returned with a towel, crawling back in next to her. 'What is it, Dee? Something's on your mind. I can tell.' His efforts to clean her with the towel made her squirm with ticklish pleasure, made it hard to focus on what she wanted to say.

'Just wondering if you want your bed back now that we've … Now that it's … Should I probably go?'

He tossed the towel and scooped her into a spoon position. 'I want you right where you are. If I hadn't, I would have finished the job in the sitting room.' His words vibrated soporifically against the nape of her neck. 'Besides, what if I need you again before morning?'

'It's already morning,' she said.

'And so it is.' He ran a hand down over her belly and fingered her clit, causing her to jump and gasp and rearrange herself just enough for him to push into her from behind. 'It's a good thing you stayed then, isn't it?' The serpentine shifting of his hips, combined with the stroking of his thumb, had her full attention, and suddenly it wasn't really complicated at all, suddenly it was all about two people helping each other come. Again! As she reached back to grasp his hip, to pull him still deeper into her, she couldn't keep from smiling. Even her fantasies hadn't been this good.

Chapter Twenty

DEE'S FIRST DAY AT Scribal was a circus, and she was performing without a net. Alan Marston hadn't even bothered to be present for the meeting. The reps he'd sent in his stead were nothing more than Scribal cheerleaders unwilling and unable to progress the negotiations without Marston at the helm. They all listened enthusiastically, but Dee knew for all the good she was doing, she could have been standing in front of a class of third-graders.

When the session ended with still no sign of Marston, Dee made an unannounced pilgrimage to his office on the 25th floor of the Scribal Tower. His secretary phoned him while Dee waited quietly. It really wasn't necessary to pass on what Marston said. She, along with half the office personnel on the floor, could hear every colourful word he yelled into the poor secretary's ear, especially the parts about Dee being an incompetent, irresponsible pain in the ass. Just when Dee was seriously considering a quick escape, the woman hung up red-faced, and forced a smile.

'He'll see you now.'

Dee took a deep breath, squared her shoulders, and stepped into the lion's den.

In an office bigger than her house, Alan Marston sat in a burgundy leather chair, burgeoning belly keeping him a safe distance from the formidable mahogany desk that kept her a safe distance from him. He didn't bother to get up, nor did he offer her his hand. In fact, he didn't even speak. He just glared at her.

'You weren't at the meeting.' She felt stupid the minute she said it, and Marston didn't miss her fumble.

He folded pudgy hands on the blotter, which was the only thing on his desk other than the phone and a very expensive pen. 'If you came to tell me what I already know, Ms Henning, don't waste my time.'

She forced herself to speak around the desert her mouth had become. 'If we're planning to negotiate this alliance to everyone's benefit, I'm going to need a little input from you.'

He chuckled. '*You* need input from *me*?'

'That's right.'

With an effort that made the chair groan and creak, he stood and adjusted his belt. 'Ms Henning, I just heard a rumour that your boss is in town. Seems a bit strange to me that he'd not head up these negotiations himself, since they're so important. Thorne and I go way back. That's no way to treat a friend.' Marston hailed from Atlanta and no amount of Ivy League schooling could completely rid the man of his southern twang. But then a man of Marston's wealth could intimidate inferiors in whatever dialect he chose.

'I assure you, Ellis values that friendship very much.' Although at the moment she couldn't for the life of her understand why. 'He wants the best for both of our companies, and so do I.'

Marston laughed in the dismissive way men do when they think women can't possibly understand the intricate complexities of the masculine world. 'His opinion of you's that high, is it?'

Her dislike of the man was growing exponentially every time he opened his mouth. 'Opinion has nothing to do with it.' She spoke between gritted teeth. 'Since I've taken on Beverly Neumann's responsibilities, I'm the one who's most familiar with your needs, and I'm anxious to see these negotiations through to the benefit of both our companies.' Her face hurt from her efforts to force a sincere smile. She squared her shoulders, trying to project more confidence than she felt. 'Let's not play games here. Pneuma Inc. is offering you a win-win deal, and you know it. I can show you how to make Scribal a lot of money, and I can show you ways into markets you never dreamed of.'

He gave her a look normally reserved for something found stuck to the bottom of a shoe. 'If I believed for one minute that you were the one who was most familiar with my needs, I'd have been at your goddamned meeting with bells on.

'You're absolutely right. What Pneuma Inc. is offering is a brilliant proposal, if it works. An offer that Scribal Paper will give serious consideration. In fact, I'm just fucking intrigued to death by the whole damn thing.' He leaned forward, breathing stale coffee into her face. 'And I might even be tempted to jump for fucking joy if I thought as much of the work was yours as you're getting credit for.'

'Excuse me?'

He towered over her, forcing her back against the desk, his expansive belly diminishing the space between them. The smell of too much Hugo Boss made her eyes water. 'What I want to know is why the hell you're here instead of Tally Barnes?'

'Tally Barnes? What does she have to do with this?'

He offered her a sour chuckle. 'That's rich. Covering your butt to the end, are you? I tell you what, Ms Henning –' he made the word "Ms" sound like an obscenity '– from the way things look on this end, Tally Barnes has pulled your ass out of the fire so many times her poor fingers must be burnt to cinders, yet she's not even here as a part of the team. Why's that?'

'Because she's *not* a part of the team.' Dee fought back the growing sense of alarm and bit her tongue, knowing it would only make her look worse if she told him Tally had caused the problems to begin with.

'Your arrogance astounds me.' Marston shook a thick finger at her. 'In my day, Ms Henning, people had to earn their keep. Thorne has a reputation for making smart business decisions –' he raked her with a scorching gaze '– so I can only conclude that the man was temporarily insane when he hired you.' He turned on heavy heels and marched back behind his desk, plopping down hard in his chair. 'If someone else has to do your work, then someone else should get the credit, I say.' He nodded to the door. 'Now, if Ellis wants me to attend this meeting he's so keen on and hear what Pneuma Inc. has to say, and if he can't send the person doing the work to talk to me about it, then he'd damned well better come himself or, as far as I'm concerned, we have nothing else to say.'

Chapter Twenty-one

BACK AT THE HOTEL, Dee dropped her computer in the suite and then went down to the lounge, where she was to meet Ellis. Still reeling from her meeting with Marston, she settled in at the bar for a much-needed glass of wine. A small band played a Latin set designed to pick up drooping after-work spirits, and she definitely needed all the help she could get. She knew Tally Barnes was a troublemaker, but she never dreamed the woman would be so devious. The problem was; Dee didn't know what to do about it. She couldn't bring this information to Marston. He'd only think she was doing exactly what Tally had done, stepping on other people's backs to get what she wanted. No doubt Tally knew that.

She'd have to tell Ellis about the situation. Certainly, she didn't want him hearing it from Marston. It bothered her less that Tally was getting credit for her work than it did that Marston was accusing her of stealing that credit. Her faced burned with shame just thinking about it. She was contemplating the crap day she'd had and how best to prove her innocence when someone elbowed in next to her at the bar.

'Dee? Dee Henning?'

With a start, she found herself looking at a man who could have almost, but not quite, passed as Ellis's twin.

'I've heard so much about you. I've been dying to meet you in person.' He offered her a slight bow, which caused his dark hair to fall rakishly over one eye. 'Forgive my interruption, but I'm Garrett, Garrett Thorne.'

'You're Ellis's brother?'

'In the flesh.' He bent over her hand and laid a warm kiss across her knuckles, all the while holding her in a quicksilver gaze. 'Rumour has it you're rapidly becoming indispensable.' Before she could do more than gape, he continued. 'Are you all right? You look like you could use some cheering up.'

Dee forced a smile. 'It's not really been a stellar day.'

He patted her hand sympathetically. 'Well, there you go, then. Just consider me a fast-acting happy pill you don't have to swallow.'

'Fast-acting and extra strength, I hope.'

'I'll do my best,' he said. Unlike Ellis, Garrett needed a haircut, yet he had that look about him that Dee knew other men would imitate, and women would pant after. Never having being much of a panter herself, she was unimpressed. But, when he smiled, the lines of his face echoed those of his brother, and that softened her considerably toward him.

Garrett ordered a glass of wine for himself and another for her, then leaned closer. 'So tell me, do you really enjoy working with that twit? I hear you're as much of a workaholic as he is.'

She looked into eyes that seemed to be searching for the punchline to the universal joke that was existence. 'He said that?'

'Who knows, maybe it's like math.' Garrett shrugged. 'Two workaholics cancel each other out and become carefree and fun-loving.'

'It's a plausible theory, I suppose.'

The bartender brought their drinks, and Garrett studied her unabashedly over the top of his glass. 'I know my brother well enough to be certain he'd never hire anyone who wasn't the best, so I can only say he got an incredible bonus when he hired someone who's also witty and beautiful.' He heaved a sigh, then dazzled her with a thousand-watt smile. 'The providence of the universe is a wonderful thing, isn't it?'

Her own smile felt a bit forced. 'I'm curious, Garrett, how did you know I was Dee Henning and not some other witty, beautiful woman who just dropped in for a drink after work?'

'I'm psychic.'

'Of course you are. And does the Thorne charm run in the family?'

'Only the younger son. It skipped Ellis completely.'

'Oh?'

'Yep. Genetic defect, I'm afraid. Sad, really.'

'Yes, very sad.'

'Good evening, Dee. I see you've already met my little brother.' Ellis slipped between them, took her hand, and pulled her up from the stool. Then he turned his attention to his brother. 'You've monopolised the poor woman long enough, Garrett. Make yourself useful. Order us a bottle of wine or something.'

Before Dee realised what was happening, she was on the dance floor with Ellis. Her pulse went into overdrive, and nerves jangled down through her chest and into the pit of her stomach. This was her boss, this was the man who, only last night … Her knees suddenly felt like water, and there were little tingles down low in her abdomen. 'I don't dance, Ellis. Really, I don't.'

'I'm surprised Garrett didn't already have you on the dance floor. Normally I wouldn't trust him with any respectable woman, but the man's in love at the moment – a ballerina – so he's fairly harmless, if a bit annoying. Besides, you're doing fine.'

'No, really. I had a single dance lesson back when I was in college. There weren't enough guys, so I had to learn the men's part.'

He offered her a wicked smile. 'Oh? Would you like to lead?'

She shook her head stiffly. 'I kept stepping on my partner's toes.'

'I'm not worried about my toes, Dee.'

'You're a brave man.'

Ellis pulled her closer. His voice was a pleasant vibration as he deliberately brushed his lips against her earlobe. 'Just relax and let me worry about the rest. It'll be OK. I promise.' His breath made gooseflesh along the nape of her neck and down over the tops of her breasts beneath the linen suit.

'What if your brother's watching? What will he think?' she whispered, making a futile attempt to pull away.

'He's not watching. His ballerina just arrived. Trust me, my brother's full attention is now on her.' He offered her a wicked chuckle. 'You could fuck me right here on the dance floor and he wouldn't even notice. Not a bad idea, really.'

'He might not notice, but other people would.' Again she tried to put a little more respectable distance between them, but he was unyielding.

'Just relax, Dee. It'll be all right.' And, really, how could she do otherwise. How could she doubt him? She was with Ellison Thorne, and his full attention was on her, and it was way too easy to forget that she worked for him, that he was her boss. Ellis moved with the same grace with which he did everything else, and Dee let the experience settled around her like a gossamer fog seeping into muscle and marrow as she gave herself to the ebb and flow of his lead.

'You see. It's not so hard.' He pulled her still closer. The music stopped, and another tune started. They kept dancing. 'It's good to get out once in a while, and do something that doesn't involve Pneuma Inc. You've been under a tremendous amount of pressure these past few weeks, Dee. I'm sorry for that, but I'm afraid there's not much to be done about it.'

The gossamer fog dissipated with the mention of work, and a cold knot tightened in her stomach as she recalled the disaster at Scribal. 'I didn't expect it to be any other way, Ellis. It's just that with Scribal … Well, Marston seems to think that I –'

'I don't care what Marston thinks, at least not tonight.'

She pulled away enough to look into his eyes. 'But, Ellis, I –'

'Don't worry about Marston. He may be a lot of things but he's not stupid. He'll come around.'

'It's just that he thinks I –'

It came as a complete shock when, right there in front of everyone, he stopped her words with a brush of his mouth, lips parted just enough for her to taste his breath and sense a feather flick of his tongue. But it was enough to shut down the speech centre of her brain and speed her pulse rate to a drum-roll.

'Dee, I don't want to talk business. I want to dance. There'll be plenty of time for business tomorrow.'

Three songs later, Garrett joined them on the dance floor with a willowy brunette, who Dee later learned was his ballerina, Amy.

It was one of those evenings when it was more of an effort to go out than it was to stay put, so the four danced, shared wine and dinner, and never left the comfort of the hotel. It was nearly midnight when Garrett and Amy left for her place, and Dee and Ellis took the elevator to the 19th floor.

In the suite, Ellis switched on the lamp next to the sofa. Dee kicked off her shoes and threw her jacket across the back of a chair. 'I suppose it'll make for a long day tomorrow, but it was fun tonight.' She wriggled her toes in the thick carpet and stretched, aware he was watching her, surprised by how much she liked it when he did.

'We both needed a break,' he said. 'You definitely deserved the chance to get your mind off Marston for a while.'

And it had worked. She'd actually been able to forget about Marston's accusations for a few hours. But the problem wasn't going away. The press of the small pool of light in which they stood suddenly felt claustrophobic. She forced her voice around the tension in her throat. 'Ellis, we need to talk about Marston. He's got this idea that I –'

'Not tonight, Dee.' He took her hand and pulled her to him. 'You're already grossly negligent of your need for rest, something you've been reprimanded for more than once, and something that, shame-facedly, I've enabled the last two nights.' With his free hand, he switched off the lamp, and the room dissolved back into the monochrome hues of night. Then he lifted her into his arms, causing her to gasp and throw her arms around his neck as he carried her to his room.

The bed was turned down, and he deposited her gently onto the crisp white sheets. 'We've done this before, Dee, though you probably don't remember much of it.' Both hands went to work carefully, deliberately unbuttoning her blouse. Then he lifted her to him just enough to ease the blouse off over her shoulders, unhook her bra, and toss both onto the chair by the bed. 'After all, you were unconscious with exhaustion.' He eased her back onto the pillow and settled a kiss onto her sternum, between her breasts. 'I've always been the good Thorne brother, but seeing you there in your bed, so vulnerable, helping you out of your jacket and your shoes while you slept and dreamed secret things I couldn't see, made me rethink my strategy.' He cupped each of her breasts in turn, tracing a finger around the tight puckering of her areolas, running a thumb over pearled nipples, causing her to arch up into his touch. Then he lowered a kiss onto each nipple, pursing his lips enough for her to feel the pressure of his nursing before he crushed their straining peaks with the hard lavings of his tongue, making her whimper.

He unzipped her skirt and she lifted her bottom so he could slip it off, hooking his thumbs in her panties and dragging them down too, so that she lay exposed, with only the stockings sheathing her legs, held in place by a pale blue garter belt. 'I wanted to share your bed so badly that night.' With careful deliberateness, he undid the garter belt from her stockings and rolled them down one at a time, lifting each leg in turn so that she was open, so that she was vulnerable and tender, so that, if he chose to, he could see the rise and fall of her, every plane, every fold, every moist crevice of her inner landscape. 'I wanted to be inside you, not just your body, but inside your dreams too.' He sighed, kissing the curve of her ankle. 'Though I can't imagine your dreams of me would have been very pleasant ones after what I'd put you through that day.'

'Ellis, I –'

He bit the inside of her thigh just above her knee and she gasped and squirmed down into the soft bedding. 'Shhh!' She felt the hiss of his breath against her splayed sex, and she moaned. 'Don't talk, Dee. This is on my calendar. Remember, the calendar with all the important meetings I never forget? This is what I want you to feel before you fall asleep.' He rose and unhooked the garter belt from behind her waist and tossed it aside, and when she reached to unbutton his shirt, he slapped her hands away. 'Tonight I want your dreams of me to be good ones.'

'Ellis,' she protested, 'don't you want to …? Shouldn't you let me –'

He stopped her words with a kiss. 'Shh! Dee, don't talk. Just feel.' He kissed his way down over her belly, lingering to nibble and lap at her navel while his fingers stroked and caressed her pubic curls. Then he scooted down, lifted her butt into his palms, and spread her swollen landscape with his thumbs, making her feel as though he really could look right up inside her, as though he really might be able to see her dreams, her hopes, her fears. But before she unnerved herself with thoughts of her vulnerability, his mouth filled the void, warm and humid, way stronger than she would have thought lips and tongue could be, supple and dextrous, intuitive and relentless. He probed and laved and nibbled until he found the secret places, the tight, wet, tender places that were swollen and waiting to burst like soft fruit beneath the press of his lips and the nip of his teeth. And she came, kicking and writhing and clawing to get him closer to her.

She mumbled something about wanting to satisfy him, but she was asleep by the time he pulled the comforter up. Later – it could have been hours, it could have been minutes – he slid under the covers next to her and pulled her against him. She remembered he was naked. She remembered he was hard, but when she reached for him in some strange state somewhere between dreaming and waking, he pushed her hand away. 'When you're rested, Dee, then you can take care of me.' He kissed her ear. 'And then I plan to be very, very demanding.'

Chapter Twenty-two

'YOU'VE BEEN A VERY sneaky girl, Tally Barnes.'

Tally jumped and slopped her Moët and Chandon onto the bar as Terrance Jamison slid onto the stool next to her. 'Mr Jamison, I wasn't expecting you.' She dabbed at the spill with a cocktail napkin.

He ordered his usual Glenfiddich from the bartender, then turned his attention back to her. He gave her a once-over that was disconcerting but not sexual, maybe more disconcerting because it wasn't sexual. 'New suit?'

She straightened her jacket and opened her arms so he could see. 'Christian Dior. Do you like it?'

'Very nice,' he said. 'And it goes really well with the necklace. Is that new too?'

'It is, yes. They were just too perfect together for me not to have both.'

He scooted closer, too close for comfort. He hooked a well-manicured finger beneath the braid of gold chain around her neck and pulled her so close that she would have thought he might kiss her, except the curl of his lips had nothing to do with passion, and his eyes were cold, icy cold. 'You have exquisite taste, Tally. Expensive, but exquisite.'

He held her there, heart hammering, cheeks burning as he lowered his eyes and examined the chain. Then the bartender brought his drink, and he released her. For a long moment he said nothing, only swirled the whiskey absently around his glass without tasting it, studying her as if she were something he had never seen before. Then he heaved a sigh and sat the glass down untouched. 'As I said, you're a sneaky girl, Tally Barnes.'

'How am I sneaky?' she asked when she could manage to find her voice and make sure it wasn't trembling.

'I talked to Alan Marston yesterday, teleconference. Made him a counter-offer to the Pneuma Trouvères offer. Seems for some reason, he's refusing to meet with Dee Henning.'

'Oh?'

He lifted his drink again and looked down into the whirlpool he created. 'He doesn't like the woman. He thinks she's a bumbling idiot with a penchant for stepping on other people's backs to get what she wants. '

'Well, Alan's a good judge of character.'

He turned on her so quickly that she nearly fell off the stool, but he hooked his finger in the gold chain again and held her in his poisonous gaze. 'I know Dee Henning. I don't like the bitch. But that's personal and, I assure you, it doesn't cloud my mind to the fact that she is neither bumbling nor an idiot, and she's way too bright to need to step on anyone to get where she wants to go.' He tugged the chain until it bit into the back of Tally's neck, until her forehead was almost pressed to his. 'So I can only assume his opinion is coloured by his interaction with you.' He twisted his finger in the chain until it tightened around her neck just enough to feel threatening. 'What did you do, Tally?'

'I only sent him a letter,' she breathed. 'It was nothing, really.' She tried to shake her head but thought better of it as the chain bit into her nape. 'It's just that I've done so much work on the project, work I'm not getting credit for. I just mentioned how I wished I could be on the team to be presenting our project, Pneuma's project, to him. I only thought it would help,' she said, her voice little more than a scratch at the back of her throat.

'And tell me, Tally, just what do you know about the Pneuma Trouvères project? I assume you've been in on it from the beginning? Hmmm? I sincerely wish you'd told me that up front. Why, you wouldn't have had to bother with copying Dee Henning's presentation, would you? You could have explained it to me personally.' He twisted the chain once more, and it bit into her throat. 'Well?'

She fought back panic, wishing like hell she hadn't been too drunk to study Dee's presentation when she'd gotten home the other night. In fact, she had only barely looked at it, just enough to find a few key words to draft her letter to Marston. She meant to read it. She really did. In fact, she was planning to read it this evening.

The look in Jamison's eyes was cold and unreadable. What was most frightening was that he didn't really seem upset sitting there at a bar in public, choking a woman with her own necklace. For all the emotional cues he gave, they could have been talking about the weather. Then, as if nothing out of the ordinary had happened, he released the necklace and smoothed it gently against her collarbone. 'Tally, Tally, Tally, you're thinking small. Dee Henning's in the inner circle now, and she's bright and good-looking and everyone loves her. Don't you understand that Marston will only believe you until he talks to Thorne or Crittenden or even Dee's secretary? What do you hope to gain but to make yourself look bad, to possibly lose your job?'

With a shaky hand, she downed the champagne she now really needed. The other hand rested protectively at her throat. 'Do you really think that bitch will talk to Marston?'

He grunted a laugh that left little doubt as to his thought of her idea. 'Dee isn't your problem, Tally, don't you get it? Dee is way too ethical to play the tattle-tale, so you'd better hope that things blow over with Marston.'

'I don't understand,' she said, watching him order her another glass of champagne.

'It's simple, really.' He returned to swirling his glass. 'Dee is as good as people say she is, Tally. Maybe better.'

'But you said –'

He raised a hand to stop her protest. 'What I said is that she lacked experience. Technically, I could see the logic behind hiring you to the position as a safe option. But hiring Dee Henning was typical of Neumann and Thorne. They hired her because the woman has potential off the scale.' He sounded like he admired the bitch!

He continued. 'If you want Beverly's job, proving Dee

Henning's incompetence isn't going to happen. Keep pulling stunts like this and eventually you'll get caught, and Thorne will fire you without batting an eye. You can't do this alone. You have to let me help. I have the power.' He stroked the necklace against her collar bone with cool fingers. 'And the money to make things happen, to make sure we both get what we want, and that can only happen if we work together against Thorne. Trust me, Tally; I've locked horns with the man before. I know his weaknesses, I know how to get to him, and thanks to you and the projections you got for me, I've made Marston a counter-offer that will cost Pneuma Inc. one of their biggest, most loyal customers. I couldn't have done it without you, Ms Barnes. Believe me, I'm very aware of that fact, and very grateful for all of your hard work.' He lifted his glass in a toast, and she released a tight breath she didn't know she'd been holding.

'What about Marston? What about the letter?'

'Don't worry, Tally. It'll all blow over. At this point it doesn't matter anyway. Marston would be a fool not to take my offer. And Marston is no fool. So you taking credit for a deal that isn't going to happen is a moot point. But in the future,' he said, smoothing the collar of her jacket and running a hand over the expensive fabric, 'I would suggest you keep your head low, and your eyes open, and don't act without discussing it with me first. Are we clear?'

'Very,' she said.

'Good.' He looked down at his watch. 'Now I have to go. I have a meeting across Portland in an hour.' He leaned forward and brushed cool lips against her cheek. 'Oh, one more thing, Tally. If you check your account this evening, you'll find a little something, a token of my appreciation for all you've done, and all I hope you will do in the future. And don't worry. You'll get Beverly Neumann's office soon enough. Just trust me, and do as I say.' He left without touching his drink.

Chapter Twenty-three

'THAT WAS MARSTON. DEE, why didn't you tell me he was refusing to work with you?' Ellis stood framed in the doorway, with his BlackBerry clutched in a suicide grip. The hard set of his jaw and the tense square of his shoulders were a flashing beacon indicating the mood he wasn't trying to hide.

Dee was already packing up her computer bag for a meeting with Jason Daniels. She had waited for Ellis to finish the early conference call he had with clients in Spain especially so she could tell him about Marston. It was literally the first chance she'd had without shaking him awake in the middle of the night, something she couldn't have done if she'd wanted to because, in spite of everything that had happened the day before, she slept like a baby after Ellis's tender ministrations. 'That's why I'm still here,' she said. 'I never dreamed he'd call you at 7.30 in the morning.'

Ellis came into the room and stood near the sofa, arms stiff at his side, still clenching his BlackBerry. His gaze bore into her, riveting her to the spot where she stood in front of him. 'Marston says if I want him to negotiate with you then I'll need to make Tally Barnes a part of the team. Why didn't you tell me?' Though his face betrayed nothing, she heard disappointment in his voice, which brought on a wave of guilt, making her feel like she was 13 again, and in trouble for not practising hard enough. She forced back anger. She had nothing to feel guilty about. But before she could respond, he continued, the disappointment giving way to something a little more tetchy. 'Do you have any idea how it felt hearing such a thing from Marston? I couldn't even say you'd already told me. Dee, do you know how that looks?'

Her legs were suddenly not very cooperative, and she dropped into the chair by the desk before her knees gave. 'I tried to tell you last night, but you –'

He wasn't listening. 'Marston believes a good bit of the scheming and planning behind this deal has actually been Tally Barnes's work.'

The room tilted around her. She pressed her feet hard against the floor to lessen the shakes. 'You know that's not true.' Her voice sounded thin and tinny in her ears.

'It doesn't matter what I know. Can't you see the situation you've put me in?'

She forced herself to stand and meet his anger face to face. 'It matters to me, Ellis. You're my boss. Believe me, if Tally had helped with this deal, if the ideas had been hers, I'd have been right behind her, cheering her on.'

'I know that, Dee. But Marston doesn't.' He turned away from her and paced in front of the sofa. 'Marston won't negotiate with you until Tally's a part of the team. He seems to think she's been somehow slighted, and –'

'She's that little personnel problem you mentioned on my first day, isn't she?' She followed him. 'I saw her resume too, Ellis, remember? I recommended it to both you and Beverly. She has a right to be upset. Look, I don't know why you didn't hire her. That choice was yours to make, but she's clearly gone out of her way to humiliate me in front of Marston, running the risk of sabotaging a huge deal, and you're upset at me for not telling you about my run-in with Marston?'

He stopped pacing and turned to face her. 'I'm sorry, Dee. I knew Tally was unhappy about you getting the position, but I never imagined she'd pull such a stunt.'

'Well, she did.' She grabbed her bag, shoved her way past him, and headed for the door.

He grabbed her by the arms and forced her to face him. 'Look, I'm trying to make sense out this mess, Dee. If I'd known before, if you'd told me what was going on –'

She jerked free of his hold and stomped her foot. 'I tried to tell you. I tried, but you wouldn't listen to …' She let the sentence trail off, afraid she'd make a fool of herself by crying in front of him if she continued. Her mother had always used tears as a last resort when rage didn't work. She promised herself she'd never stoop to such behaviour.

'Look –' Ellis fidgeted. 'This deal is yours. You know it way better than I do, and you need to be the one presenting it. I don't see how I have any choice but to placate Marston and put Tally Barnes on the team.' He raised his hand to stop her protests. 'Besides, you said yourself Tally does have experience you lack. It might be a real benefit to you to have her.'

'Because she's been so damned helpful up till now.'

'I'm sorry, Dee, but at the moment, that's the only thing I know to do. Maybe I should have done that from the beginning. I know it's my fault, but there's nothing for it now.'

She bit her lip and forced back her anger. 'You're the boss. What? What is it you're not telling me?'

He looked down at his feet, avoiding her gaze. 'It's about Marston's birthday party tonight. He's pretty upset with you and, well, under the circumstances –'

'You don't want me to go to his party.'

'Of course I want you to go.' He looked down at the BlackBerry still gripped in his fist. 'But Marston doesn't.'

She avoided his gaze and fidgeted with the strap on her bag, hoping he wouldn't notice the burn in her cheeks. She knew Marston didn't want her at the party. He'd hinted rather strongly, but that he'd broached the subject with Ellis made her feel even more like a misbehaving child. She caught her breath, trying to sound calmer than she felt. 'It's all right. He made sure I got the message. Don't worry.'

He moved next to her and laid a hand on her shoulder. 'If it weren't for you, there would be no deal on the table, but it might be better if you let me unravel this mess alone. Then, after the party, once the dust has settled and Tally is on board, you can take back over. You've had a heavy load on your shoulders, Dee, and so early in the game. You're not –'

She pulled away. 'I'm not Beverly. Yes, I know. You've already told me that. Don't worry, I get it.'

He followed her. 'That's not what I was about to say – Dee?

Where are you going?'

'I have meetings with Trouvères this morning. As far as I know, Marston has no say on who works with them yet.' She grabbed her jacket and left without saying goodbye.

When Ellis returned to the hotel to get ready for the party, which he wasn't thrilled about going to without Dee, he found the suite empty. He was even less thrilled at the thought that she might very well still be with Daniels. He was less thrilled still with the thought that she might actually be commiserating with Daniels. If anyone should be comforting her, if anyone should be making her feel better, agreeing with her about what a bastard Marston was being, it should be him. He'd fire Tally Barnes right this second, over the phone, in person, if the situation wasn't so complicated. He was completely sure Marston would come around and realise that Dee was the brains behind the sweet deal he was being offered. Marston was not stupid, and he had a hell of a lot at stake. And when that happened, when Marston came around, he would see that Tally Barnes got what she deserved, whatever it was. One thing he was already certain of was that she didn't deserve to be his executive assistant. Beverly had been right about Dee. But then the woman was never wrong, he reminded himself. Still, he wished he'd had a chance to tell Dee that before she'd left this morning feeling angry and betrayed.

As he slipped into the jacket of his tux and inspected himself in the mirror, he ached to have Dee on his arm. That's how he'd fantasised about the evening; having Dee alongside him, basking in the limelight of her first major triumph, a triumph she so richly deserved. And he felt responsible that she was being deprived of it.

A chill passed down his spine. Was he getting too close to her? Last night, when she'd tried to tell him what had happened, he had behaved like his brother, insisting on a business-free evening, and Dee had suffered for it. This whole situation wouldn't be nearly so painful if he'd kept a safe distance between them from the beginning. The thought crossed his mind that maybe he shouldn't asked her to his bed again. When she was sleeping in his arms, in his bed, it seemed like something altogether different from the Executive Sex Clause, and that was a thought that scared the hell out of him.

Dee was thankful for the breakfast meeting she'd scheduled with Jason Daniels, who was more than happy to accommodate. It had kept her mind off the disaster with Marston and the knot in her stomach at wondering what Tally Barnes would pull next. Fortunately, there were no meetings planned with Marston, and though he hadn't attended the meeting she'd led, the man wasn't stupid either. She was sure he would have gotten detailed notes from every person in the room. She didn't know how serious the negotiations were with Terrance Jamison, but she was pretty sure his short-term fix would be looking good to Marston with plant shut-downs looming.

Until Jason had asked her to accompany him to the party, she had managed to keep the whole nasty situation between her and Marston quiet. It was immediately clear Jason didn't believe her excuse of a headache – not very original, but the best she could come up with under the circumstances. After she'd left Jason, she found a nice corner in a coffee shop to do a little research of her own.

She was careful not to return to the suite until she was sure Ellis had left for Marston's party. Then she ordered room service and continued her research. She was ensconced in the middle of her bed with the laptop in front of her and a huge glass of iced tea on the nightstand when the room phone rang.

'Ms Henning, there's a Mr Daniels here to see you,' the concierge said

Dee looked down at her watch. He should be at Marston's party. She couldn't imagine why he was here. Before she could dwell on it, there was a soft knock on the door and Jason, dressed in a black tux that made him look a bit like James Bond, stepped inside, shoving a long garment bag in her direction. 'Dee, I need your help. We all need your help.'

She stood staring at the bag. 'What's going on? What's this?'

He was already pulling her toward the bathroom. 'It's a gown. Please don't talk. Just listen – preferably while you're putting on the gown. We're late for Marston's party.' Before she could respond, he continued, 'I know about all his bullshit, and so does Yvette. She's insisting that you be at the party.'

'What? She can't be serious. Marston will have a fit.'

'You didn't take credit for someone else's work. It's absurd to even entertain such an idea. Yvette's not sure she wants to work with such a stupid man, and she told Marston that. Things aren't going well. Now get dressed, please.' He pushed her toward the bathroom. 'I'll fill you in while you're getting ready. We've worked too hard on this deal to let it all collapse because Yvette's pigheaded and Marston's an ass.'

Dee stopped mid-stride between the sofa and the door. 'You don't understand. Marston specifically requested I not be there.' Her face burned in spite of her effort to pretend it didn't matter. 'I'm not welcome, Jason. There has to be another way to work this out.' She felt the threat of tears again, and turned her back.

Before she knew what was happening, he took her in his arms, then lifted her chin, forcing her to look at him. 'Dee, Marston needs this deal, and he needs you.' He ran a finger along her cheekbone. 'We all need you.'

She pulled away and picked up her BlackBerry. 'I'll call Ellis, tell him what's going on.'

'Yvette's probably already called him by now.'

She hesitated. 'You're sure about this?'

'Of course I'm sure. You're the one who's put this deal together. Ellis'll understand.'

Through the bathroom door, Jason filled her in on Yvette's little scene with Marston while she dressed. The dark blue sheath showed just a hint of cleavage, but made up for it by exposing a large expanse of back. In spite of herself, she couldn't help imagining what Ellis's reaction would be when he saw her in something so sexy. The matching kitten heels that looked slightly vintage and very romantic made her wonder how Jason had managed to size her perfectly for both.

As she stepped out of the bathroom, Jason, who had been

talking to Yvette, nearly dropped his iPhone as he stowed it back in his pocket. 'Wow!' His voice was breathless, and his gaze felt a little too much like a caress for comfort. 'You look incredible, Dee. Perfect, in fact.' He bent to kiss her hand, then offered her his arm. 'I'll be the envy of the party with you by my side.'

Chapter Twenty-four

AT THE DOOR TO Marston's penthouse, Jason took her hand. 'You're absolutely stunning, Dee. If this weren't so important, I'd skip the party and keep you all to myself.'

She pulled away. 'I'm still not sure this is a good idea. Yvette did talk this over with Ellis, didn't she?'

'Would you stop worrying? Now that you're here everything'll be all right'

'Just answer my question. Has Yvette talked to Ellis?'

'Yeah, of course.' He straightened his cuffs with a shrug. 'Probably she did.'

She took a step back. 'What do you mean, probably? This is my job we're talking about, as well a deal that all of our companies need.' She snapped open her handbag and pulled out her BlackBerry.

'What are you doing?'

'I'm not going in there until I'm sure Ellis has had the heads up.'

Before she could call, Jason pushed the doorbell, and almost at once a steward in full livery answered, looking as though he had just stepped out of a Victorian novel.

'Damn it, Jason!' She elbowed him beneath the ribs, still trying to maintain as much dignity as possible in front of the steward as she shoved the phone back in her bag. 'This is no joke.'

Jason caught the offending arm and folded it over his, whispering close to her nape. 'Just relax, Dee. I'll protect you from Ellis, and Marston.' The brush of his lips across her earlobe barely registered above the storm of nerves in her stomach as the steward announced their arrival.

Marston's soirees tended toward extravagance, according to Ellis, and Dee could tell immediately this little gathering was no exception. A large alcove held a small band, which played a Glenn Miller set. The main reception room, which had been turned into a dance floor, opened onto the large terrace decorated with fairy lights and citronella torches.

'Daniels! It's about time.' Receding hairline moist and brow furrowed, Marston greeted Jason with a handshake. 'Ms Rousseau was beginning to get a little worried about you. I see you've solved our little problem.' He offered Dee a curt nod, and mopped his high forehead with a neatly folded handkerchief.

Dee didn't care much for being referred to in the third person as "the little problem"; however, it was worth it to see the man sweat.

Marston had barely gotten greetings out when Ellis approached. The look on his face told Dee Yvette hadn't informed him of the change in party plans. Just as he was about to speak, Jason tugged her toward the dance floor. 'I've been waiting all evening to dance with you.' He gave her an admiring look. 'And well worth the wait, I'd say.' He slid an arm around her to pull her close. 'Sorry, Thorne. You left her at home alone. Now she's mine.'

As Jason lapsed into French, which he knew Ellis didn't understand, Dee figured it was probably a good thing that looks couldn't kill.

'Cantankerous lot, the French.' Marston shook his head and watched as the two began to dance. 'She's got the whole damn Trouvères contingent eating out of her hand; I'll say that for her.'

'Did you ever stop to think it might be for good reason, Al?' Ellis spoke to Marston, but he couldn't take his eyes off Dee as she moved on the dance floor. Daniels led Dee with considerably more grace than Ellis would have liked. Ellis was not in the mood to be toyed with. If the bastard tried anything, Trouvères deal or not, he'd wish he hadn't. With his mind on Dee and Daniels, Ellis missed the rest of Marston's babble about the foibles of the French and something about Yvette insisting that Dee be at the party. It was only when Stacie appeared at Marston's side that his attention was catapulted front and centre.

'Oh Ellis, it's so good to see you. It's been ages. I hear congratulations are in order.' She offered him a smile that could melt a heart of stone. 'Nothing unusual in that for the Win-Win Guru, is there?' Before Ellis could respond, she gave him a kiss on the mouth and a hug that, in his opinion, was a bit too close for polite company, but then that was Stacie.

He pushed her away.

'I guess I don't need to introduce my date, do I?' Marston gave Stacie's hand a squeeze. 'Sorry I've been so distracted tonight, my dear. Business, I'm afraid. The French always have to complicate things, you know? I promise I'll make it up to you.' He kissed her cheek, then turned back to Ellis. 'The last time Stacie and I partied together we were celebrating a coup she'd made with an impressionist exhibition from Russia. The woman has serious clout in the art world, you know?'

She batted impossibly long lashes and offered Ellis a pout that at one time he would have happily lapped off her face. 'Sadly, Alan, Ellis doesn't have time for the finer things in life.'

'Damn shame, Thorne.' Marston handed them each a glass of champagne from the tray of a passing waiter. 'We all need a little culture from time to time. I hear Stacie's bringing some your direction too, with the new gallery in Portland.' As he spoke, his wandering gaze fell on Yvette across the room, where she dominated the small knot of people with whom she was in conversation. Her short silver hair complimented the black sheath that hugged her tall, athletic frame. She was probably Marston's age, and still a beautiful woman in her late 50s, but Ellis knew Marston's tastes ran toward much younger, much more agreeable women. He wondered what the hell the man was doing with Stacie. Marston lost his smile and nodded in Yvette's direction. 'If you'll excuse me, must mingle. Don't want 'em finding another excuse to ruin the party.'

For a second, Ellis and Stacie stood watching the dance

floor in silence. Ellis had learned from experience that being paranoid where Stacie was concerned was actually just self-preservation. Though he had no doubt her efforts to make up for past transgressions were well intended, somehow, just like Garrett, they both ended up making matters worse rather than better and, in this case, matters were bad enough without her help. Dealing with Stacie was one more complication he really didn't need this evening.

Stacie nodded toward the dancers. 'The one in blue with the Trouvères hunk – she's Beverly's replacement?'

He shot her a quick glance. 'How'd you know?'

'Because you've been ogling her ever since the man whisked her away.' She offered him a wicked smile. 'Oh, don't look so surprised. A woman can figure these things out, and you always did have exquisite taste in women.'

'She's my executive assistant, Stacie, not my woman.'

She ignored his comment. 'Besides, Garrett did tell me that she was lovely. He certainly had nothing but good to report about her, and all I can say is it's about time. I'm dying to meet her.' She leaned in and brushed impossibly warm lips against his earlobe. 'I hear she's very good at her job.'

She'd barely gotten the words out when the music stopped. He noticed Dee say something to Daniels, then move through the milling guests toward them. 'Excuse me.' Ellis left Stacie alone and went to meet Dee. Taking her by the arm, he spoke between barely parted lips. 'What the hell are you doing here, besides the obvious?' He nodded to where Daniels now stood next to Yvette Rousseau and Marston.

She followed his gaze, then turned her attention back to him. 'Yvette was supposed to call you. It appears I was shanghaied to prevent a possible disaster. Either that or I was duped. Not sure which.'

'What disaster? What the hell's going on? This better be good.' He slipped an arm around her waist and guided her toward the balcony.

Before he could get her to a more private place, Stacie intercepted them and took his other arm. 'Ellis, aren't you going to introduce us?'

He forced a smile and ignored the gnawing in the pit of his stomach that intensified as the two women eyed each other from either side of him. 'Dee, I'd like you to meet Stacie Emerson. She's an old schoolmate of mine.'

Stacie took Dee's hand in an enthusiastic grip. 'I'm his ex-fiancée, actually, but that was a long time ago. I've been dying to meet the famous Dee Henning Garrett's told me all about. Honestly, I feel like I'm meeting a celebrity, and I'm so happy for Ellis that he's finally found someone. For his executive assistant, I mean.'

Dee showed no sign of surprise at Stacie's little bomb. She simply accepted the handshake and offered that smile that could almost make Ellis forget he was mad at her. 'If I'm the best you can do for excitement, I'm guessing you don't get out much.'

As the band began to play *String of Pearls*, Marston approached the trio, his eyes on Stacie, but as he reached for her, she sidestepped and took Ellis's arm. 'At last, you finally find the woman of the hour without that Casanova from Trouvères hanging all over her. Now's your chance to dance with the belle of the ball.' She offered him an innocent smile. 'Come on, Al, I know the two of you must have so much to talk about.'

Marston looked like he'd just swallowed a toad. 'Ms Henning. If you would.' He offered her his arm and led her stiffly toward the dance floor, leaving Ellis feeling stranded in dangerous territory.

Before he could confront Stacie, Daniels pushed his way through a small knot of people, his hand extended. 'I've been talking to your executive assistant, Thorne.'

Ellis returned the handshake grudgingly. 'So I saw.'

'I hope Marston's thanking her for coming to the rescue. Yvette is just unpredictable enough that she might have done something stupid.' He nodded to where Dee and Marston were dancing, both looking like they'd rather be anywhere else.

Ellis had no idea what Daniels was talking about. Whatever it was, this was not the kind of conversation he wanted Stacie to overhear. But Daniels continued, 'I can confidently speak for Trouvères when I say I'd love to steal her away from you. After what the poor woman's been forced to put up with in the past few days, I wouldn't blame her if she were looking elsewhere.'

If the man were any more smug, he'd have to have a bigger face to put his smirk on. But before Ellis could do more than just bristle, one of the reps from Scribal asked Daniels to dance, leaving Stacie and Ellis standing alone near the open terrace.

'Oooh, he's hot for her, Ellis. Don't listen to him, though. Garrett says Dee's exactly what you need, and I'm sure the Trouvères hunk won't have any trouble finding someone when he looks like that.' Stacie slipped her arm through his. 'Hell, with a juicy package like that around, I'd follow him off to Paris.'

'I'm sure you would, Stacie.'

She sat her glass on a nearby credenza and pulled him by the hand. 'Come on, let's dance. It's been ages.'

Over Stacie's shoulder, Ellis empathetically watched Dee with Marston. His own position was no less uncomfortable as Stacie did her best to pump him for information about Dee, and to be heard over the music, that meant pressing her well-displayed cleavage a little too close for comfort. 'Anyway,' she was saying, 'when Garrett told me the news about you and Dee, I had to see for myself, and since Alan and I go way back, I figured I could wrangle an invitation from him. He may not look like much, but the man's a lot of fun at a party normally. He seems a bit stressed tonight. That's too bad. I mean, it is his birthday.' Ellis kept pulling away in hopes Dee wouldn't notice how close they were.

Stacie moved in again for the full frontal rub-up. 'God, Ellis, Garrett's right. You really do have it bad for her, don't you? You can't keep her eyes off her.' She leaned in still closer, her lips brushing his ear. 'Garrett thinks you've initiated the ESC with her.'

Ellis stiffened, feeling the words like a tight fist in his gut. He couldn't believe his brother would blab to Stacie of all people about the Executive Sex Clause. Why not just broadcast it on Facebook and Twitter, for fuck sake? 'I suppose Garrett neglected to tell you that he was drunk when he and Beverly schemed the ESC for my benefit.'

'No. He told me that, but still, a woman doesn't miss that look. And the way you look at her, Ellis, wow! I never thought I'd see the day. I can't tell you how excited I am for you.'

The knot in his stomach tightened. The one thing he didn't need was Stacie and Garrett being excited for him. The one thing neither he nor Dee needed was Stacie and Garrett trying to play match-maker. 'Listen, Stacie,' he began, forced to pull her close so she could hear him, hoping Dee wasn't watching. 'I don't know what Garrett told you, but I really don't need either of you to –'

Before he could finish, Marston tapped him on the shoulder. 'If you don't mind, Thorne, I'd like to cut the rug with Stacie now.' He offered Dee's hand to Ellis. 'I've been a good host, now for my reward.' He gave Stacie a cheek and jowl smile.

Ellis and Dee watched as Marston and Stacie waltzed off, both well into each other's personal space. Then Ellis pulled Dee close, as though she were a child needing his protection. 'Are you OK?'

She smiled. 'Me? Marston's the one you should be concerned about. I seriously considered stomping on the man's foot with a nice pointy heel. He escaped just in time.'

The band began *Moonlight Serenade*, and Ellis stood looking dumbly at her, wondering how he could be both angry and enchanted with her at the same time. Finally, he willed his feet to respond to the music. Dee quickly caught his rhythm and they moved as a unit, like they always did, he thought.

'I don't know what's going on with you and the Trouvères team, but you should have warned me,' he said. 'I don't like finding out these things second hand.'

'Believe me, I intended to. It all happened so fast. Jason showed up at the hotel in a panic and rushed me off to Marston's. He promised me Yvette had informed you.'

'Well, she didn't. Daniels was out of line. Bringing you back in should have been my job.'

'So where were you, then?'

He pulled her close, feeling her ribcage expand against his. 'This isn't funny, Dee. You made me look like I don't know what's going on with my own people. Again.'

She pushed him away. 'And you made me look like the unethical person Marston believes me to be.'

'That was never my intention, and you know it.' His voice came out a harsh whisper against a backdrop of big band music.

'Would you rather risk losing the deal? I'm supposed to be doing Beverly's job, Ellis. You'd never rein her in for doing what needed to be done.'

'Beverly had 30 years of experience on you, Dee.'

She stopped dancing, and glared at him. 'And my lack of experience gives you the right to treat me like a naughty child?'

He pulled her back into the dance, holding her closer. 'I wouldn't have to treat you like a naughty child if you didn't act like one.'

'You started it.'

'I didn't start it. Daniels started it.'

'He kept the evening and possibly the whole alliance from ending in disaster.'

'Did he really? I'm inclined to believe he manipulated the situation just to get you to himself.' Daniels had deserted the Scribal rep and stood once again on the edge of the dance floor with Yvette Rousseau, his full attention on Dee.

'If he doesn't quit staring at you,' Ellis growled, 'I'm going to break his arm.'

Dee gave a glance in the direction of the Trouvères contingent. 'So now you're mad at him for looking at me? I haven't heard, Ellis, has Marston declared that a crime as well?'

'Don't be naïve, Dee. Where you're concerned, this whole mess was just the opportunity Daniels has been waiting for.' In a flood of possessiveness, Ellis pulled her close, forcing a startled rush of oxygen from her lungs. She made no attempt to re-establish proper dance posture as the anger between them dissipated to something much more intriguing.

He was just about to apologise, make his excuses to Marston and whisk Dee away to somewhere quiet and intimate, when the music stopped, the band took a break, and Dee was pulled away by several of the Scribal party. He was about to follow when his BlackBerry rang. It was Wade, calling from Portland. Sometimes days went by with Ellis not hearing from Wade, but the one thing the man didn't have was a sense of timing, so if he thought he had something to say, he'd call anytime, day or night, and when he did, it was usually important. Ellis exited to the balcony for a little privacy. Twenty minutes later, he returned to the party.

'You're looking for Dee, right?' A breathless Stacie met him at the French doors. She grabbed Ellis's hand and led him toward the marble staircase.

'You know where she is?'

'Of course. Come on. I've been trying to get a minute with her since the last set. Alan got pulled away for an important phone call in his study and I couldn't seem to pry her away from the French contingent. Oh Ellis, I'm just dying to get to know her a little better.' She pulled him up the wide, spiralling steps, taking them two at a time. She's just gone up to the ladies' room up here and I thought maybe –' Stacie missed the last step, turned her ankle and, with a loud yelp, practically fell on top of Ellis, who would have gone over backward if he hadn't been holding on to the rail.

'Ouch! Oh damn it! I knew I shouldn't have worn these shoes,' She crumpled against Ellis and he half carried, half dragged her to a furnished alcove directly across from the closed door of the bathroom. The hall was dimly lit, and the alcove even more so.

'Jesus, Stacie, when are you gonna learn to be careful? You know you can't walk and chew gum at the same time. How many times have I had to cart you off to the emergency room?'

'I'm sorry! I'm sorry, Ellis. It's just that I'm so excited.' She sucked a harsh breath between her teeth. 'Oh shit, that hurts.'

He seated her on the small love seat and knelt to ease off her shoe. 'OK, let me look at it. What did you do?'

She lifted her skirt. 'Ellis, I think I sprained my ankle. It really hurts.'

'Here, let me see it. Just relax.' He knelt in front of her and eased the shoe off. 'It looks like it's already swelling. Damn it, Stacie, if I hadn't been there to catch you, you could have broken your neck. God, it's black and blue clear up your shin. I hope you didn't break it.'

Stacie gasped and shifted in the chair. Her eyes watered from the pain. 'Oh! Oh Ellis, oh God. Ah!'

And that was how Dee found him when she came out of the bathroom, on his knees between the hiked skirt and open legs of his ex-fiancée, who was moaning and writhing on the loveseat in front of him.

Ellis had no doubt as to what it looked like to Dee. For a brief moment, their eyes met. The whole débacle lasted seconds, but to Ellis it seemed as though he were freeze-framed on perpetual display – a reluctant participant in Stacie's eternal clumsiness. As long as he'd known her, Stacie had been an accident waiting to happen. He'd have preferred an unpleasant scene with scorching reprimands to what happened next. In fact, he would have preferred almost anything to what happened next. Dee let him off the hook. She simply turned and hurried noiselessly past and down the steps.

He sat stunned, half nauseated, remembering again why he avoided Stacie.

'Oh God, Ellis,' Stacie whimpered. 'Oh God, I'm so sorry. I know how that must have looked. If you just let me talk to her, I'm sure I can sort everything out.' She tried to stand, then winced and crumpled in agony.

'Jesus, Stacie, you've done enough already. Just leave Dee alone, all right? And you need to stay off that ankle. I think I saw Marston's doctor downstairs. They play golf together. I'll get the maid to send him up.' He lifted her from the chair and found an empty guest room. When he had her settled on the bed with the already swollen ankle elevated on a pillow, he asked one of Marston's staff to fetch the doctor, then he headed downstairs to find Dee.

'There you are. Marston's been looking for you.' Daniels

came to his side. 'He's just called Dee and Yvette and me into his study. You're the only missing lamb. He didn't look happy.'

'So what else is new?' Ellis said, falling into step with Daniels, skirting the dance floor where the guests were now doing a disco set.

Daniels looked down at his watch. 'I hope whatever it is doesn't take long. I know this lovely place I was planning to take Dee to listen to French poetry and drink expensive wine as soon as I can drag her away from Marston.' He continued as though he was oblivious to deadly look Ellis unabashedly levelled at him. 'I'm not much on French poetry, personally, but the company would be exquisite, and who says we have to listen?'

'I'm curious how your wife would feel about that?' Ellis said.

Daniels shot him a quick glance. 'Oh, Lydia and I are separated. The divorce'll be final soon.'

Daniels was getting a divorce. How convenient. Ellis wondered why Dee hadn't told him this. He'd given her ample opportunity while they were dancing. Surely she didn't return the bastard's feelings? But then, Ellis reminded himself, they had both agreed they were free to see other people if they wanted to. Had he just missed the clues? Dee was always so adamant that she wasn't interested in Daniels. Ellis's fist ached from his sudden desire to bury it in the man's smug face, and after what had already happened this evening, the veneer of civility was wearing very thin.

In Marston's study, they were all seated on two heavy sofas of burgundy leather on either side of a large coffee table, drinks in hand. Marston's ample backside was overflowing the seat of a ladder-backed chair at one end. When everyone was present and the double doors were closed behind them, he shifted nervously in the chair and unbuttoned the jacket of his tux.

He took a deep breath and said, 'Terrance Jamison just offered me a birthday present I'm afraid I can't refuse.' The room was deadly silent. He tossed back the whiskey he had switched to at some point in the evening and ran a thick thumb around the top of the glass. 'It appears there's considerably more forest in that tract in Valderia than what he first offered me, and the increased acreage means a lower price.'

'Clear-cut,' Ellis said. 'Al, you can't be considering clear-cutting virgin forest, surely?'

Marston drew his lips tight around his teeth and nodded. 'Yes, clear-cut, Ellis. It's not ideal but I have a lot of people whose jobs depend on my choices, and five years will buy me the time to maybe consider something innovative with Trouvères here. By then maybe you'll have ironed out your personnel problems –' he nodded to Dee '– and you'll have someone who knows what they're doing to present me with the facts.'

Dee's back stiffened, and Ellis's stiffened in sympathy. He didn't know if Marston knew French or not, but he knew enough himself to know what Yvette said under her breath was not complimentary. She laid a supportive hand on Dee's arm.

He was just about to launch into Marston when Dee said, way more calmly than he was sure he could have managed in the circumstances, 'May I have your napkin, Mr Marston?'

He handed it to her, too surprised by her request to question. Maybe he though she was going to tear up and cry. He got that one way wrong, Ellis thought. He was about to intervene, then changed his mind. Damn it, the woman deserved her say. She took a pen from her bag and began to write furiously on the napkin. For a long second no one said anything. They just sat there and watched Dee scribble. Then Marston shifted uncomfortably in his seat. 'Really, Ms Henning, I think you'd just –'

She held her hand up, and he fell silent. For another endless second she continued to write. Ellis, who found himself unconsciously leaning over her shoulder, could see that it was mostly figures.

'Ms Henning, what in the hell are you doing?'

'Let her finish,' Ellis said. 'You owe her that much.'

She filled the napkin, grabbed a second from Yvette, and filled that too. At last she spoke. 'Mr Marston, you wouldn't talk to me, wouldn't listen to me, wouldn't give me a chance to prove to you that this project would mean way more to you than five years of destroying virgin forest. You've abused me, you've insulted me, you've done everything in your power to make my life miserable, you've treated me like I was some unethical gold-digger, but I've put up with your bullshit because I believe in this project, because I know it's good for your company, and because Beverly believed in you. Beverly considered you a worthy and loyal friend.' She slapped down the pen and shoved both napkins in his direction. 'And up until now, I believed Beverly was never wrong.'

She stood and walked out the door as calmly as if she'd just left the dinner table.

Ellis grabbed the napkins and scanned them, then let out low whistle. 'Jesus Christ,' he whispered.

'*Mon Dieu*!' Yvette leaned over Ellis's shoulder. 'Did you know this? Does Monsieur Crittenden know this?'

He shook his head. 'Wade might. I certainly didn't.'

'What the hell is it?' Marston said.

'Dee's just written out the 10 – no, wait a minute –' he strained his eyes at the corner of the napkin, 'make that 15-year projections of how an alliance between Scribal, Trouvères, and Pneuma would benefit Scribal, taking into account improvements in technology over time, money spent for upgrading as needed and inflation at 2 per cent.'

'And the benefits for Trouvères as well,' Yvette said. She clucked her tongue. 'Oh Monsieur Marston, you are a very foolish man. A very foolish man indeed.'

Ellis shoved the napkins at Marston and stood. 'Happy Birthday, Al.' At the door he turned back. 'Two things you need to know. I'll fight you tooth and nail if you go through with this deal to clear-cut virgin forest. If there's a way to stop you, I will find it, and I'll make damn sure that Trouvères benefits in the extreme for their alliance with Pneuma Inc. And second, if you'd bothered to ask, I would have told you that Beverly hand-picked Dee as my executive assistant before she went off to Brazil.'

He left without closing the door, pushing his way past the

dance floor and past the doorman, his heart racing in his chest. He had to catch Dee.

Chapter Twenty-five

THE TAXI WAS JUST pulling away with Dee in it when Ellis got outside Marston's building. He caught the next one. Immediately he called his lawyers and turned up the fire under their asses to find out anything and everything they could about loopholes, laws, regulations, whatever might thwart Jamison. It didn't take him long. He talked, they listened, assured him they were on it and hung up. And then, all the rest of the way to the hotel, he replayed, in his head, everything that had just happened in the past few hours. Dee was brilliant! She was bloody brilliant! He knew she was good, but he was completely stunned at just how good. Beverly had known, though. Beverly truly *was* never wrong.

And in spite of everything that had just happened, in spite of the pending disaster with Marston, and with the forest in Valderia, by the time Ellis paid the taxi in front of the hotel, the only thing on his mind was Dee. The day had been a nightmare on all counts until her brilliance had put everything in perspective. Their work was cut out for them, but right now, this moment, it was her he needed, and he wanted her with an ache that was almost physical. He wanted to apologise, he wanted her to forgive him, he wanted to tell her that she was amazing. But, most of all, he just wanted her.

When he opened the door to their suite, he found her on her BlackBerry, pacing the sitting room floor, still dressed in that outrageously sexy gown, still wearing those shoes he wanted to fuck right off her. And the sight of her made him want her even more. He motioned to her to hang up. When she saw him, she nodded her greeting, said her goodbyes and disconnected. 'Ellis, that was –'

He crossed the room in two strides, took the device from her hand, and tossed it on the over-stuffed chair. Then he took her mouth in a hard, brutal kiss, feeling her teeth against his tongue, biting her lip and tasting the sweet flavour of her breath. When he finally pulled away, gasping, she said, 'You're angry.'

'Hell yes, I'm angry. Aren't you?'

'Of course I am. Furious, but –'

'I want you, Dee,' he said, feeling her chest expand against him, forcing her breasts more tightly to him. 'I want you so damned bad I can't stand it.'

Struggling to breathe, she pressed a hand to his sternum, putting distance between them that he didn't want, distance that deepened the ache which now felt like it would split him in two. 'Ellis.' She spoke his name carefully, as though she were afraid she might damage it somehow. She studied him for what felt like an eternity, and if he hadn't wanted the rest of her so badly, he could have gotten lost in the depths of those eyes. 'Ellis.' Her voice was barely more than a breath. 'Are you sure?'

'Jesus, Dee –' He pulled her hand to his lips and kissed her knuckles. 'I've never been more sure of anything in my life. You have to know what happened between Stacie and me, what you saw, it wasn't what it looked like.'

She shook her head and closed her eyes. 'I don't need to know, Ellis. I just need to know you're sure that this … That the Sex Clause …' She suddenly seemed at a loss for words.

'I'm sure, Dee.' He kissed her and worried her bottom lip between the tug of his teeth and tongue. 'I promise you, I'm sure.' Then he took matters into his own hands. He didn't want a discussion; he just wanted Dee, here and now.

She let out a little whimper of surprise as he turned her bodily and bent her over the bare top of the cherry wood desk. He moved in close behind her so his aching cock pressed through his trousers against the silk-sheathed crevice between her buttocks. Then he rested splayed hands on each of her shoulders and ran them along the sides of her spine, his tongue and lips and teeth taking the middle route along the vertebrae, causing her to shiver and gooseflesh as he worked his way down. 'I had no idea it was possible for a woman to have such an outrageously arousing back,' he said between kisses and nibbles. 'Jesus, Dee, you had me hard all through the damned party, I wanted to touch this back so badly.' He pressed a kiss to the base of her spine where the gown barely covered the intimation of the cleft of her ass. She groaned, and her hips rocked forward then back to press her bottom against his chest.

'Lift your skirt for me, now,' he ordered. 'I know what you have under there and I want it.'

She was already obliging before the words were out of his mouth. He made quick work of his fly and shoved his trousers and boxers down over his hips. 'Jesus, Dee, you're not wearing underwear?'

'There wasn't any room under the dress,' she hissed. 'Besides, I was in a hurry.'

'Fuck! If I'd known there was nothing between the dress and you, I'd have completely embarrassed both of us right there on the dance floor. I never know what to expect with …' His words trailed off. In fact, he pretty much forgot how to speak as she eased the skirt up over the rounded pillows of her butt, and slowly, tortuously, revealed the soft, moist press of her slit, little more than a swollen suggestion peeking from between the demure clench of her thighs below the deep cleft of her buttocks and the dark knot of her anus. He eased her thighs apart with one hand, and suddenly he couldn't breathe at the sight of the slick, tender pout of her. The rocking of her hips had grown more insistent, and he could smell her arousal, reminding him of the sea in the heat of summer. He slid two fingers down over her perineum, in between her heavy lips, and she gripped him with a little sigh that nearly sent him over the edge.

She sucked breath, then whispered, 'Do it, Ellis. I need you to fuck me. Please don't keep me waiting.' With one hand on her left buttock, she pulled herself open to further emphasise her need, which only inflamed Ellis more.

He rested a palm on the small of her back, just above the tangle of silk, and with the other he guided the leaden reach of his erection to part her, entering her slowly, feeling her yield grudgingly, deliciously. Jesus, she felt better than anything! Then he thrust hard, running his hands over her spine, kneading her, palming her, shoving up against the ridges of her vertebrae with the heel of his hand, feeling her give and shift and undulate beneath him, all supple and soft and hard at the same time.

She reached behind her neck and undid the hooks that secured the top of her dress in place. With a serpentine arch of her body it fell away, and she grabbed his hands and guided them around to cup the sway and bounce of her heavy-nippled breasts.

'Dee, I can't hold out much longer.' He spoke in harsh gasps against her ear.

'Me neither,' she whispered.

Then it had to happen. He slipped one hand down over her belly and gave her clit a hard stroke with his thumb just as he thrust. She growled and bucked back against him, her orgasm tightening her already exquisite grip around his cock still further, and he gave in, convulsing in wave after wave inside her, feeling a visceral sense of release that, if he'd had the wit left to think about, he would have suspected might be far more than just the relief of sexual tension.

Suddenly, in what felt like serious déjà vu, Dee's BlackBerry rang. She shoved him off her and scrambled for it.

He cursed at the jarring sense of disconnection. 'What is it with that damn thing and coitus interruptus.'

'It wasn't interruptus,' she said, struggling to catch her breath. 'Besides, this is an important call from my Uncle Gustavo.'

She answered it in French.

'You're talking to your uncle? That's it. I'm gonna toss the fucking BlackBerry out the window,' he growled under his breath. He yanked off his bowtie, and was giving some serious contemplation to the demise of the offending device when Dee switched to English. 'OK, I'm putting you on speakerphone now, Uncle Gustavo. I know Ellis will want to hear this. Give me a second.' She turned to Ellis and nodded for him to pull up his trousers.

'Why would I want to talk to your uncle?' he said, jerking his boxers up.

'Because he's the undersecretary for the Valderian Department of Natural Resources.'

Before Ellis had time to do more than make a couple of shocked fish-gasps, Dee was introducing him to Gustavo Rojas.

'Mr Thorne, my niece has made me aware of your situation,' came the greeting in perfect English. 'I don't have much time, but for Deirdre, I'd do anything, she knows that.' Before Ellis could mumble even a thank you or a greeting, the man, clearly used to the no-nonsense approach, continued. 'Though the sale and management of mineral and timber rights are not my jurisdiction, I am able to throw my weight around a little, so to speak. I can make sure there's a bit more red tape involved. That's not unusual when certain hands think they haven't yet been greased adequately, if you get my meaning. I'll do my best to generate a few delays to slow Terrance Jamison's progress and perhaps buy you a little more time. Sadly, the contracts have already been signed. All that remains are formalities, I'm very sorry to say. If that were not the case, I might have been able to be of more help to you.'

'Of course I understand that, sir.' Ellis sat on the sofa next to Dee. 'How much time are we looking at?'

'Perhaps a week, maybe two if I'm lucky. But sooner or later, you must understand, the right hands will be greased and the situation will be beyond anything I can do. I am sorry.'

Ellis glanced at Dee and found her watching him. He held her gaze. 'Then we'll have to work fast, won't we?'

'If there's anything else I find out or anything else I can do, I'll be in touch. And please don't hesitate to call me. And Deirdre, darling, it's lovely to hear you. But next time, perhaps you will call for something less distressing and we may have a proper chat.'

Dee blushed that lovely blush that Ellis took way more pleasure in than he had realised until just now. 'Thanks, uncle. The next time I call, I promise I'll bore you with way more information than you'll ever want to hear.'

'You could never bore me, my darling. But now I must go. I'm late for a meeting. I wish both of you the best of luck.'

Dee reached across the coffee table and disconnected the BlackBerry.

Ellis sat stunned, open-flied, shirt untucked, staring at his executive assistant. 'Your uncle is the undersecretary for the Valderian Department of Natural Resources?'

Dee sat holding the top of her dress over her breasts, still staring thoughtfully at her BlackBerry. 'Well, he's not really my uncle. He's my father's sometime lover.'

'Your father's gay?'

She offered him a warm smile. 'My father's versatile, and he and Uncle Gustavo are kindred spirits. They had to keep their relationship pretty low-key, of course, but back then Uncle Gustavo was only a low-ranking civil servant, and no one paid much attention. It was easier for them then.' Ellis watched while she booted her laptop, absently clasping the halter of the dress back behind her neck. 'My visits to Paris to see my father were always best when Uncle Gustavo was there. I never had a real uncle. Both my parents are only children.'

There were so many questions he wanted to ask her, so much he wanted to know about the mysterious young Deirdre running around Paris with her opera-singing father and his secret diplomatic lover. Suddenly he found himself wishing Beverly had gathered more information about Dee, so much more. She sat down next to him and plopped the computer on the coffee table where they both could see it. 'I've been doing some research.'

He zipped his fly and scooted closer so he could see the monitor, struggling to concentrate on something other than the scent of their blended sex which was all over her. 'Good,' he said. 'I've got my lawyers on it, and I think we should give Wade a call, meet with him as soon as we get home. You OK to take an earlier flight?'

'I've already made reservations for the first flight out.'

He raised an eyebrow. 'For both of us?'

'I figured you'd think this was important enough to merit a

quick return home. Besides you, only stayed on to placate Marston.'

He ran a hand through his hair and shook his head. 'Jesus, Dee, where have you been all my life?' He leaned over and kissed her hard on the mouth, pulling away far more quickly than he wanted to, but knowing if he didn't he'd have her again right there on the sofa, and that would have to wait. 'OK, we've got a week, maybe two, to prevent a disaster. Let's use it wisely. I'll have room service bring up sandwiches and coffee. Lots of coffee.'

'And some iced tea.' She was already pulling up maps of the Valderian forest slated to be clear-cut.

Several hours and a lively conference call with Wade in Portland later, Ellis took off his glasses and laid them on the coffee table. Then he raised his arms over his head and stretched, arching upward over the back of the sofa until his navel peeked from beneath his untucked shirt and the waistband of his trousers. At the sight of him doing something so ordinary, so unassuming, Dee's stomach did the little clench it always did when she had been totally pulled in by the man's genius only to be pulled back out again by the his animal physicality. They were still in their worse-for-the-wear party clothes, him rumpled and only partially buttoned, her barely concealed in silk that crinkled and clung and smelled of sex.

'There's not much more we can do here, Dee. Wade will have more for us in the possible techno-bribery department when we get back to Portland.' He palmed her laptop shut, and his dark gaze was suddenly locked on her. 'I need a shower, a long, hot, steamy one. Would you care to join me?'

Everything in her felt somehow softened and warmed as he offered her his hand and helped her up from the sofa. When she stood, she felt the heated wetness of his semen from their earlier lovemaking against the inside of her thigh, and the smell of him aroused, him angry, him impatient, him brilliant hugged her like a second skin. She wasn't so anxious to wash away that scent, but she was pretty sure washing wasn't really what he had in mind, and that made her own scent thicken with anticipation. He led her to his bathroom, where he stripped out of his shirt and regulated the water in the big sandstone shower. She stood watching, still struggling to get her head around the idea that Ellison Thorne, *the* Ellison Thorne, who she had admired, practically worshipped from afar for so long, was flesh and blood and lust and passion and all of those things her fantasies were made of. All of those things had moved her, inspired her long before she knew him personally, but when he was like he was tonight, irritable, vulnerable, needy, human, smelling of their sex and about to shower in her arms, he moved her most of all.

He interrupted her ruminations by wiping his wet hand on the leg of his trousers, then turning to her, unhooking the halter top of her dress and cupping her breasts as it fell away. He settled a kiss on the press of each of her nipples before he eased the ruined silk down over her hips, lingering to cup the flare of her hips, the swell of her bottom. Finally, he knelt in front of her and carefully helped her out of the shoes she had forgotten to take off. So unlike her, she reflected, and he kissed her instep and moved to suckle her toes, causing her to squirm with ticklish pleasure and place a hand on his back to keep from losing her balance.

When she was completely naked, he stood to inspect her, while absently opening his fly and sliding off his trousers and boxers to release the erection she knew would be waiting there. They laughed as he struggled with his own shoes, hands made clumsy by lust. When they were both naked, he scooped her into his arms and pulled her under the heavy pulse of the warm water. Then he knelt in front of her and began soaping her, beginning with her calves, then moving up her thighs. 'First I'm going to wash you very thoroughly,' he said, moving up to soap her pubic curls and working his way over her belly as though he'd never had a task that demanded quite so much of his attention. 'Then, once you're all clean and pink and shiny –' he stood and held her gaze '– I'm going to get you all dirty and messy again.'

He kissed her in a long, lingering tongue kiss, giving her time to contemplate his plans for her, then he carefully soaped her breasts, cupping and kneading and thumbing the nipples he wasn't quite able to hide beneath the lather. Finally, he moved a hand around to soap and palm her ass cheeks, easing a thick finger in along the crevice between. He held her close while he lathered her butt, caressing and lingering and trailing fingers over the sensitive knot of her anus. In his embrace, the soap from her body slicked his chest and his erection, fat and heavily pressed against her belly. He pulled her still closer until she could feel the rapid rise and fall of his chest pressed to hers, then he slid a solicitous tongue into her mouth in unison with the soapy finger he eased, almost stealthily up into her tight back hole. And she sucked breath, nearly biting his tongue at the startling invasion that felt too personal to be shared, yet, as her anus relented to his insinuation, the rest of her responded in heavy, swollen ripples of need as he probed.

He nipped her earlobe. 'I want to explore all of you, Dee.' He turned her into the spray and washed off her front, still probing her back hole with a middle finger, then once again he went down on his knees and pulled her to him, kissing down her belly, then working two fingers up into her slit to move in tandem against the one in her anus. Dee didn't realise it at first, but his relentless stretch and pull and stroke in untried places had compelled her into a shallow squat, hands resting on Ellis's shoulders, hips rotating around the efforts of his beautifully dextrous fingers, fucking them, riding them, squatting to get them deeper inside her. The pressure was such that with the rake of a sudden insistent thumb over her hardened clit, he catapulted her into her first orgasm. He didn't wait for the aftershocks to ease, but instead he stood, pulled her to her feet, and lifted her onto him.

She was heavy and wet and ready for him as he slid home, cupping her butt while she wrapped her legs around him and buried her face against his neck as she strained and clenched. And the orgasm she thought was ending built on itself instead with each deepening thrust of his cock.

She hung on for dear life as he battered her, tightening the grip of her thighs around his waist with each shove and push. As he grew closer and closer to his release, he felt more and more like the hard sandstone on the walls of the shower, every muscle tense, every sinew stretched. Breathing became a distant memory as they thrashed and hammered against each other; the sounds coming from their throat became primal, instinctive, far removed from language and thought. When at last they came, the world exploded and Dee was certain she would die from the cataclysmic collision of so much powerful need. How had she not known that this part of her existed? How had she ever kept it quietly tucked away inside her? Had it really take Ellison Thorne to rouse the animal in her, to awaken parts of her even more powerful than her driven nature? There were no real thoughts, just urges and half-formed queries inside her overheated brain. As they collapsed onto the shower floor in the warm wet, engulfed in a cloud of steam, she wondered if maybe some of what she felt, some of the not quite formed thoughts, were Ellis's, overflowing into the mix of chaos and lust and so many other feelings she hadn't the brain left to dwell on.

Chapter Twenty-six

THERE WAS ONLY TIME to clean up, dress, and pack before they had to leave for JFK. Dee's mind was abuzz with all of their planning and scheming of possible ways to thwart Jamison's efforts. She made it a point not to think about the amazing sex that had happened between her and Ellis. Thinking about it took her mind in places it shouldn't go, places she was sure weren't included in the Executive Sex Clause. Yet when she and Ellis settled into their seats on the plane, she was asleep before their flight took off.

As soon as they were in the air, Ellis undid his seatbelt and leaned over Dee, effectively blocking her in her seat. 'You're a slut, Dee Henning, fucking me to get what you want, a regular filthy slut. Everyone knows it. Marston knows it, Wade knows it, Stacie knows it. Tell me, did you fuck Jason Daniels to get the Trouvères deal? I bet you did.'

Several of the other passengers were eavesdropping, covering their mouths in shock, scandalised at what they were overhearing. Even the flight attendants stopped what they were doing and listened, arms folded across their crisp tailored jackets, shaking their heads in disgust.

He ran his hand up under her skirt and, though she tried to push him away, he shoved fingers into her panties, then tisk-tisked. 'Always wet and ready, aren't you?'

To her horror, she was wet, and she couldn't keep herself from moving against the probing of his fingers. To make matters worse, she found herself suddenly cupping and tugging at her breast through the silk of her blouse.

'What a slut,' she heard one of the passengers whisper to another.

'But I'm not! I didn't! You're the only one,' she gasped, trying desperately to calm herself, to push him away, but no matter how hard she tried, she just kept riding his fingers harder and harder.

'Of course you are,' he said. 'And a slut who'll fuck her boss will fuck anything if it'll get her what she wants.' He undid his trousers and released his cock. 'You'll do anything for a promotion, won't you, Dee?' He pulled her roughly to the edge of the seat and shoved her skirt up. 'Oh, I'll take it if you're offering, who wouldn't? And I am a busy man, after all.' He pushed into her and began to thrust.

'Of course he will,' another passenger agreed. 'Who wouldn't if it's offered? I would, wouldn't you?'

'Sure, if the slut's offering,' someone else said.

Ellis finished and shoved off her. 'I'm done with her,' he said, zipping himself back into his trousers. 'Anyone else wants a go, help yourself. I've got business to take care of. I have to find a new executive assistant, someone who's more interested in work than spreading her legs.'

'What about the Executive Sex Clause?' Dee gasped.

Ellis gave her a sour chuckle. 'Oh Dee, are you really so naïve that you couldn't figure out the Executive Sex Clause was just a joke?'

Dee awoke with a start, shoving her way up from under the airline blanket. Her heart felt like it would burst her chest and a cold sweat bathed her forehead. She covered her mouth to hold back the whimper of relief. A dream. Damn it, it was just a dream.'

Next to her, Ellis slept with his glasses slipping down the bridge of his nose and his laptop screensaver showing off the wonders of the universe. It was only a dream, she reassured herself again. Nobody knew like she did just how neurotic she was, and her dreams often reflected it, taking her into bizarre, uncomfortable places. Still, it wasn't a nice dream, and she really didn't want to go back to sleep and risk part two. She booted her laptop and summoned the attendant, who brought her some iced tea. One of the pleasures of first class was that she could actually get someone to brew her real iced tea. There was plenty of work to do, and for the briefest moment she felt guilty for the time she and Ellis had spent making love. Making love; could she really even call it that when it was only a part of her job? Ellis said nothing had happened between him and Stacie, but so what if it had? It was none of her business. It was his private life, and whatever he did in his private life was private. It was a hard thing to think about, so she buried herself in the files her uncle had emailed her. It was mostly basic information on natural resources and environmental law, or the total lack thereof in Valderia. The world of business, no matter how messy and fucked-up, was always a much safer place to be than inside her neurotic, runaway train of a mind.

Back in Portland, the two went straight to the Pneuma Building. After an hour of catch-up with their secretaries, Ellis and Dee headed to the Dungeon where Wade was waiting for them. In his Boudoir, as they all called his inner sanctum. With a couple clicks of a keyboard, he had figures, maps, lists of ecologically sensitive species, and just about every factoid imaginable on Valderia, including all of the information Dee had uploaded to him from her uncle. At his touch, it could be pulled up onto a flat screen of almost cinema dimensions. All they lacked to complete the viewing experience was popcorn.

Wade gave Dee half a hug and a hard slap on the back that nearly knocked her off her feet. That was about as sentimental and affectionate as he ever got. 'I hear you tore Marston a new one.' His eyes shone with enthusiasm and he seemed suddenly more like a college student than one of the most brilliant minds in the US. 'That would have almost been worth putting on a tux to see. Ellis.' He gave his friend a nod, then motioned them to sit. Dee was still amazed at just how fast news travelled through the Pneuma grapevine. But then again, Wade had eyes on the world that would have shocked most people if they'd known. Plus, his best friend was the CEO of Pneuma Inc. Even though they worked in the same building, they didn't see each other often, but they talked and texted. She'd read an article once, back in her hero-worship days, that had compared Thorne, Crittenden, and Neumann to three parts of the same brain working to make Pneuma Inc. the progressively stunning organisation it was. She wondered if she could ever hope to function as that third part of the Pneuma brain. So far, her track record was spotty at best.

One of the possible strategies Wade had been looking into concerning the Valderian crisis was technology and information swaps that could serve as bribes or at least deal-sweeteners to prolong the red tape and extend the time before the first tree was cut. There was no such thing as a real done deal when working with the natural resources of a country with such an unstable government. Anything could be nationalised and any foreign entity could be kicked out at the drop of a hat no matter how much they had paid. It was a testament to how desperate Marston was that he was willing to risk it. And Jamison was the king of third-world, underhanded deals. Though Valderia was open for foreign business, as it were, the risk was still there. It happened all the time. There was no doubt that Jamison had done more than his fair share of bribing and hand-greasing to make the deal as secure as possible, and he had very deep pockets. Jamison Holdings was about money changing hands to make more money. It didn't create. It didn't invent. That was what Pneuma had over it in spades, though Pneuma was technically a much smaller company.

'The money for the forestry rights will only pad the bank accounts of people in high places,' Wade said, as if they needed reminding. He flipped through images of some of the amazing Pneuma technology that might interest the Valderians. There was everything from state-of-the-art low-impact farming technology, not yet even marketed in the States, to water purification systems, to eco-friendly desalination plants. It would have made for fascinating viewing under different circumstances.

'I'm sorry to say it, but it's really very unlikely the powers-that-be in Valderia are going to scrap serious cash in their bank accounts for technology that could actually help the Valderian people,' Wade said.

'Didn't think they would,' Ellis replied. 'I just want all the facts in front of me so I'll know what I've got to work with.'

'They're not hiring Valderians to do the clear-cut,' Dee said. 'I'd pretty much bet on that. It's the way Jamison operates. Valderia is poor, but its neighbours are poorer, several having survived recent civil wars. He'll hire the cheapest labour he can find. Then he'll have them shipped in to live in tents and squalor on location, and there won't be anything anyone can do about it.'

Ellis and Wade nodded their agreement, but seemed surprised she would know such information. 'The man was trying to hire someone to round up a cheap labour force in some other shady deal when I had my run-in with him at Jasper and McDowell,' she clarified. Then she added, 'Does Marston know this?'

'I doubt it,' Ellis said. 'I would imagine he's salving his guilt by telling himself the clear-cut will generate jobs for the locals in Valderia.'

Ellis stood and paced. 'There has to be another way. You're right, Wade. None of what we have is enough. But there has to be something we're missing.'

'What about our lawyers?' Wade asked.

'They're on it, but it takes time, like everything, time we don't have.'

Dee's BlackBerry rang into the tense atmosphere and both men stared at her expectantly. Her uncle had been in touch several times since they'd landed in Portland, always with tidbits that were helpful but not enough to sway the situation. But this time it wasn't her uncle.

'Ms Henning. Alan Marston here.'

'Yes?' It was all Dee could manage through her shock. Marston was the last person she expected to hear from.

'Ms Henning, your secretary told me I'd find you in the Dungeon with Wade and Ellis, which suits me down to a tee, since I want them to hear what I have to say, as well as you. That is if you will be so kind as to put me on speakerphone and not just hang up on me like I so richly deserve.'

She looked up at Ellis and Wade. 'It's Alan Marston,' she finally managed. 'He wants to speak to all of us.' Then she put him on speakerphone.

'Al,' Ellis said. Wade didn't say anything.

'Ellis, Wade. I wanted all three of you present when I eat crow and apologise to Ms Henning.'

Dee felt her way to a wing-backed chair that looked like it belonged in Wade's grandmother's sitting room rather than his office, and dropped into it.

'Ms Henning? Are you still there?'

She nodded, then remembered he couldn't see her, only hear her. 'I'm here.'

'I owe you a very big apology, ma'am. I was wrong. And I have always prided myself in being able to admit when I've made a mistake and do my best to rectify it, and, well, this one was a doozy. It should have been good enough for me that Ellis felt you worthy to be his executive assistant. I've known him long enough to know he only chooses the best. He told me Beverly played no small role in his choice of you for the position, something I'd have seen for myself if I hadn't been such a stubborn old jackass. I've gone over everything. Not just the artwork with which you decorated my cocktail napkins, but everything, like I should have from the beginning. I was swayed by Jamison's offer before I even gave you the benefit of the doubt. Well, Ms Henning, I'm giving it to you now. I'm ready to talk turkey if you haven't offered that fine deal to someone else.'

'You're not going through with the deal with Jamison Holdings?' Ellis asked.

'No. The man was pretty bent out of shape about that. Said he'd ruin me. I told him I'd like to see him try.'

'I'm sorry, Al,' Ellis said. 'I'm glad you're back on board with Pneuma, but I'm sorry you ended up on Jamison's bad side. Not a good place to be.'

There was a moment of silence, and they could hear Marston shifting and settling on the other end of the phone. 'He'll find someone else who will take the deal, you know. I've not solved your problem, Ellis. I've only made myself a better deal; a deal my conscience could live with.'

'Don't you worry, Al,' Ellis said. 'We'll take care of Jamison.'

Marston chuckled softly. 'Figured if anyone could you could, Ellis. Now, Ms Henning – seems a bit formal to call you Ms Henning. Don't think I was ever that formal with Beverly. Is it all right if I call you Dee? After all, the two of us'll be working closely together from now on.'

'Of course, Mr Marston.'

'It's Al. Just Al. If we're gonna work together as a team like Beverly and I did, then it's just Al.'

'Al.'

'Dee, I want to move on the alliance with Trouvères ASAP. Time's wasting and if I have to fight that bastard, Jamison, I'd prefer it were from a position of strength and with good allies.'

'Of course, Al. I'll get right on it.'

'Good. That's good. I know ya'll are busy, so I'll let you get back to it. I've made some notes and a few observations, Dee, that you might find helpful for the next time we meet. In the meantime, Ellis, Wade, good luck.' He hung up.

Dee sat, too stunned to move. Ellis reached over and turned off the speakerphone on her BlackBerry, then he stood and offered her his hand. 'Congratulations, Ms Henning. When you deal, you don't mess around.' He pulled her up from the chair and gave her a bear hug, lifting her off her feet.

Wade followed suit in an unaccustomed show of enthusiasm. 'It feels like old times again,' he said. 'I'll order a celebratory pizza with everything, then we can figure how to kick Jamison's ass and save some trees.'

After lunch, Ellis and Dee both returned to their offices to business as usual. Dee was already in New York in her mind. Ellis had never known anyone as focused as she was. She said she could be ready for a quick turnaround. The Rousseaus were sending Daniels to finalise the deal. Ellis wasn't pleased about that, but it couldn't be helped. Daniels couldn't get away from other business until next week, so there was at least a few days of respite.

Maybe Ellis would be able to join her for part of the closings. But she really didn't need him there. And maybe she'd think he didn't trust her. Maybe she'd think he thought her not capable of closing such a big deal alone. None of that was true. It was Daniels he didn't trust, and he wasn't keen on the two of them being together on the other side of the country, especially not since Daniels had made his intentions very clear. Still, he reminded himself, it had been his arms Dee had spent the night in after Marston's disastrous party, not Daniels, even when she'd had every reason to run to him. That thought gave him a cold shiver. It didn't bear thinking about, her running to Daniels. She was with him now, and they were a team. That was what mattered. And he had no intention of ever giving her a reason to want an alliance with anyone else.

They'd been unable to connect for the rest of the day. She got called away to a meeting across town with a client she hadn't met with since Beverly's death. It was mostly a meet and greet, but it was important. It was essential to establish relationships. Ellis insisted she go home after the meeting. He knew she was running on adrenaline and in need of a good sleep. He still felt pangs whenever he thought of how close to exhaustion she had driven herself earlier and how he could have prevented it if he'd been paying attention. She was a little bit crazy that way, but then he supposed it took one to know one. He had insisted she go home. By herself. To rest. And he had done the same. However, he'd found he didn't rest nearly as well without her in his arms. Had he really gotten used to having her in his bed that easily?

He was always in the office early, but he was a little earlier than usual the next morning because he knew Dee would be there. He also knew there would be no one else at Pneuma Inc., and try though he might, he couldn't convince himself to stay away from her.

It was only a little past seven when he knocked softly on her office door. She was already busy at her laptop, but she offered him a warm smile and motioned him in.

'Meeting go well with Frazier?' he asked.

'Great, yes. I think we'll get along just fine.'

'Good. That's good. No surprise. Good people over at Frazier. Easy to work with.' He forced a laugh. 'A real change

189

from Marston.'

She smiled. 'A real change, yes. Any progress with the Valderian situation?'

'Nothing new,' he said. He felt suddenly nervous and giddy in front of her. Well, he couldn't actually say what was on his mind, could he? He couldn't tell her that he couldn't begin his day without seeing her, that he'd hoped ... Jesus, he didn't dare even admit to himself what he actually hoped. This was work, for chrissake! This was her office! It was one thing in a hotel room, or in a limo, for him to take her like a horny water buffalo, or even in his lounge after hours when they were both under stress, but this was working hours – well, almost. It was the Executive Sex Clause, a small voice in the back of his head reminded him. She had agreed to it. She certainly seemed to enjoy it. And they were in the executive suites. Instead of just asking for it, he said, 'Did you rest well?'

She shrugged. 'It was hard to settle after last week. I couldn't shut my mind down, you know?'

'I know. Me neither,' he said. He couldn't tell her that he'd been unable to sleep because she wasn't in bed next to him. He couldn't tell her he'd had to rub one out while thinking about her in order to get any sleep at all. 'Then I guess it's pretty much business as usual, isn't it?'

She nodded. 'Business as usual, yep.'

'I thought we might need a little debriefing session after the change of landscape with Marston and all, and we really didn't get a chance to discuss it yesterday.'

'Of course. I've taken a few notes.'

Even with his internal dialogue running amok in filthy ways, he was still unprepared for his reaction when she bent over her desk to drop several files in the drawer. Suddenly he found himself fighting back a visceral urge to lift her skirt and take her from behind right where she stood. He made an effort to breathe deeply, struggling to keep his brain in control of his cock.

It wasn't about sex this morning, he tried to convince himself. He needed her to know that she had his support where Marston was concerned, and that he completely trusted her to handle the alliance with Trouvères. But when she turned to reach for her jacket, the early morning light shining through the window rendered her blouse transparent enough for him to make out the contour of her breasts caressed in the lace that held her fullness. His hands ached with muscle memory as he recalled the way he had held her the first time, the way he had cupped her and kneaded her with hands made awkward by desire. In a vivid flash of memory, he was with her again in Paris, and there was no Marston, no Jamison, no pending disaster, just the two of them. Suddenly it was no use; his brain lost the battle for control.

'Don't,' he whispered, moving into the room and closing the door behind him. 'Don't put that on.'

She let the jacket slide onto the back of the chair, her eyes questioning.

'I can't think when you're like this.'

'Like what, Ellis?' She followed his gaze to her breasts and blushed. 'Maybe the jacket would be better.'

'No.' He crossed the space between them and reached out to brush an anxious nipple with the pad of his thumb at the same time his mouth brushed hers.

She caught his wrist and held it just beyond the reach of her breast. 'Ellis … Here?' Her voice was a whisper millimetres from his lips. He could hear the tremor in it.

He raised her hand to his mouth, kissing her knuckles where they encircled his wrist. 'Yes, Dee. Here and now. I need you. We need each other if we're going to get through this.'

She held his gaze as though she were searching out his secrets, but relaxed her grip on him and laid his hand against her breast. He felt the slight arching of her back as she pressed herself into the cup of his palm. From under the computer desk in the corner, he pulled an armless chair and seated himself in front of her. She stood looking down at him from beneath a flutter of lashes and half-closed lids. 'Unbutton it.' He nodded to her blouse. As she did so, he slid the skirt up over her hips, running a finger along the tops of her stockings, planting a kiss on the silken mound of her panties while he watched the uncovering of cleavage and marvelled at the distortion of lace stretched over taut nipples.

The tensing of muscles low in her belly and hips brought silk and body heat closer to tongue and teeth, making his mouth water as he tugged and nuzzled his way past fabric to flesh. Just when he could almost taste the salty-sweetness of her, she placed a restraining hand on his head and pushed him away.

'Unzip them.' She nodded to his trousers. For a second his attention was focused on releasing himself, a task that suddenly seemed more difficult than usual. She watched almost dispassionately until his erection was free, then she stepped out of her panties and positioned herself on his lap, and for the first time since they'd been in the shower together in New York, he felt like himself again.

An hour later, they made it to his office, freshly dressed and ready to work. At least, Dee seemed ready. Ellis had only thought to have a quickie, but he could never get enough of her. He'd always known he had a high libido, and he'd channelled it nicely into his work after what had happened at Caltech, but from the first time he touched Dee it was as though the dam had burst and there was no stopping the flood of need. They should talk about it. Surely they should talk about it, maybe discuss how the Sex Clause had worked so far. That would be a short discussion. It had been bloody genius so far. At least, that's what he thought. He hoped Dee thought the same. He was about to force the issue when the phone rang.

'Ellis, it's Stacie. Please don't hang up. I'm so sorry about what happened the other night at Al's. I called to apologise. You did tell Dee it was all a misunderstanding, didn't you? Everything is OK between the two of you, isn't it?'

Even over the phone, and with the drumming of his pulse in his ears, her contrition was palpable. Stacie lived from her emotions, just as his brother did. But neither of them had ever been very good at keeping their emotions to themselves, or out of other people's lives. 'I can't talk. I'm in a meeting.' He glanced up at Dee, who sat at the conference table looking over her notes.

'Is Dee with you?'

He didn't answer.

'Ellis, just listen for a minute. I'll be in Portland this weekend. I've got a business meeting. In fact, I'll be travelling back and forth a lot in the near future. I'd really like to see you.'

He hoped Dee wouldn't notice the heat in his face as he thought once again about the disaster at Marston's party. 'Is this Garrett's idea?'

'It has nothing to do with Garrett. I haven't even talked to Garrett. I just want to apologise for what happened. Ellis? Are you still there?'

'I accept your apology, so there's no need for you to see me.'

'Ellis, wait –'

He hung up. He wanted that to be the end of it, but the sinking feeling in the pit of his stomach warned him that it probably wasn't.

Just then, there was a knock on the door. His secretary arrived with the morning mail. The day began in earnest, and running Pneuma Inc. once again took priority.

Chapter Twenty-seven

THE MINUTE TALLY GOT into the limo, she could tell Jamison was not in the best of moods. She had had been careful not to wear anything from her growing new wardrobe to their meeting, just in case. She didn't want to anger him further.

He spoke without a greeting, his voice cold and brittle. 'Marston's turned downed the offer.'

Tally felt like the bottom of her stomach had fallen away. 'I don't understand. You said it was a done deal.'

'That's right, Ms Barnes, it should have been. It should have been.' He didn't raise his voice, but the near hiss of a response was a lot more threatening than if he had.

She wanted to ask what happened, but a cold clutch of fear tightened in her chest. She was alone with the man. He was clearly livid, and he was Terrance Jamison. He could do whatever he wanted. She sat quietly, shoulders stiff, stomach knotted, eyes locked on the white-knuckled clench of his fist in the seat next to her. Other than the little incident with the necklace he'd never touched her. Surely he wouldn't ... Still, she kept her mouth shut and waited.

She waited, but he said nothing. The limo pulled into rush-hour traffic. There was no offer of champagne, no discussion of strategy, just Jamison, fists clenched, staring straight in front of him as though she weren't even there.

The longer the silence continued, the tighter the knot in her stomach became. She tried to breathe deeply, fearing she might be sick. The realisation that she was too scared to speak was like a hard slap. She had never in her life been too scared to speak. But this time it was different. She had done her homework, later rather than sooner, silently kicking herself for being too lazy to do what she should have done right up front. And she hoped against hope that it wasn't too late. She didn't have to dig too deeply to understand why Jamison was enemy number one for Pneuma Inc. And she didn't have to Google much to find out that Pneuma Inc. was not the only company which saw Jamison in that light. If she were honest with herself, she would say the man deserved their hate. But that didn't help her any. That didn't make her situation any easier. So she sat in silence, cold sweat beading against the back of her Ralph Lauren silk blouse.

At last he spoke. Instantly, she wished he hadn't. 'You're no good to me if you can't give me information.'

'I have given you information. I gave you exactly what you asked for, more than you could have ever gotten any other way. It's not my fault that it didn't work out.' For a horrifying second, she thought he was going to hit her, but he squared his shoulders and glared at her, the muscles along his jaw looking as though they could crush iron.

Then his face broke into a smile and the soft chuckle that followed was stunning. 'Of course you have, Tally. I couldn't have asked for more from anyone. And –' he ran a hand over the linen skirt covering her thigh '– you've been very well rewarded for your efforts, I'd say.'

'I've given you company secrets that could land me in jail. Well rewarded seems pretty relative to me.'

Suddenly the large hand resting on her thigh became a claw, digging deep into the muscle beneath the skirt. Pain shot through her leg and she cried out, unable to keep back the tears that filled her eyes. Then, as quickly as it happened, it passed. He smoothed the fabric of the skirt and folded his hands serenely in his lap as though he were about to say a prayer.

Tally frantically blinked back the tears. Her heart hammered. Nausea clenched her stomach; she struggled to breathe it away. She wanted desperately to rub her bruised thigh, but she was too frightened to move.

For a long, painful moment, Jamison held her in a curious gaze, as though she were an experiment and he wanted to understand what would happen if he hurt her. Then, once again, the bright smile broke across his face. 'Of course I can't place a monetary value on having eyes and ears inside Pneuma Inc. You're right. I apologise for being so badly behaved, Tally. I'm afraid I'm a rather sore loser.' He shrugged inside his jacket and chuckled softly. 'Never mind. Marston isn't the only fish in the sea, and there are always other ways to skin a cat.'

The limo stopped and, with a start, Tally realised they were in front of her house. But before she could open the door and make a quick escape, Jamison grabbed her arm, this time more gently than he had her thigh. 'I've been monitoring your credit cards, Ms Barnes. They're being paid off monthly, and will continue to be so, in spite of your very expensive tastes, as long as I find you useful to me. I've made another little deposit in your checking account as well. After all, as you say, it's not your fault that the deal with Marston didn't happen, and what you're doing could, indeed, land you in jail.' He leaned close. 'However, be warned, the minute, the very minute, I find you no longer of use to me, I'll cut you off, and you'll have to learn to survive on your Pneuma Inc. salary again.' He raised an amused eyebrow. 'Which is a fairly substantial amount from what I can tell, but then Thorne has a reputation for paying his employees well, doesn't he?' He released her arm and nodded to the door. 'Good day, Ms Barnes. It's been a pleasure, as always.'

In addition to the Trouvères/Scribal project, and liaising with her uncle, and Ellis and Wade about the situation in Valderia, Dee spent a chunk of her week reconnecting with several local companies that had been Beverly's responsibility. Ellis made two trips to Seattle and another to Salem. Most of the time, their respective secretaries were the go-betweens that kept them connected and informed on each other's progress. Even when they did see each other, it was only in passing and for both of them, no matter how hungry they might be for each other, there were only so many hours in the day. For the first time, Dee wasn't sorry for the buffer. The fantastic, if all too confusing, sex of Monday morning had done little to ease the discomfort brought on by the nightmare on the plane, so the busy schedule eased the stress and kept her mind from wandering where she didn't want it going.

It was late Friday when Ellis and Dee found time to meet again. Wade had gone bowling and the rest of the Pneuma Building was deserted. After a number of long conversations with Daniels and Marston and plenty of research on her own, Dee was ready to roll on the first of the Trouvères/Scribal projects as soon as the deal was closed. Since Marston had eaten crow, as he called it, he couldn't have been more helpful or more cordial. She could see now why Beverly had considered the man a friend. He might be stubborn and pigheaded, but then who wasn't? It certainly had stood him well all these years. Scribal was a powerhouse to be contended with, even in times of serious recession.

She and Ellis stood shoulder to shoulder, leaning over a small conference table where the files were spread. The slice of sunlight through the window near Ellis's desk had taken on the mauve and melon tones of evening. The room smelled faintly of coffee, and of Ellis's own scent, but Dee was sure she was the only one who knew that scent intimately enough to be aware of it.

'I'll be joining Marston and Jason in New York on Monday,' she informed him. 'Sandra has taken care of the reservations.'

He sat down on the edge of the table, dangling one leg over. 'I'm not sure I should send you off alone.'

'Are you still obsessing over Jason?'

'Trust me. I know animal lust when I see it.' He raked her with a look that was nearly physical, and suddenly Scribal and Trouvères were the last things on her mind. He traced the contour of her cheekbone and slid his hand down to stroke the nape of her neck.

'Familiar with it, are you?' She turned her head and nipped the tip of his thumb with her front teeth.

'Not only am I familiar with it, but I have a pretty good idea what to do about it.' He spoke the last words against her mouth, his tongue nestling in between her lips, making itself at home. Curious hands went exploring. Amid the rising friction of body heat through power suits, the sound of their breathing grew heavier against the silent approach of evening.

Ellis had just slipped his hand under her skirt and was navigating garter belt and panties when the door burst open and Stacie blew in, dressed in a sage green power suit and matching stilettos. 'Ellis, I just couldn't wait for you to get in touch with me. I had to see you now, so we could ...' She stopped mid-stride in the middle of the office floor, words dying in her throat.

The two jumped apart as though they were rocket propelled. 'What the hell are you doing here, Stacie? Can't you see I'm in the middle of a meeting? How did you even get in?'

'Oh God, oh shit! I am so, so sorry, Ellis! If I'd known you were ... I mean, I thought you'd be ... And I was afraid you didn't get my email with the name of my hotel on it, so Garrett gave me his code to get into Pneuma, and I thought that ... Well, I know you've been busy and I ... God, I'm so sorry I interrupted you.' She took a card from her bag and grabbed a pen from his desk. 'Look I'm really sorry. I'll leave now, but here are my details. I'm at the Airport Hilton at the moment, and we need to talk. I'm sorry for the interruption.'

She gave him an awkward hug, nodded to Dee, then hurried out, closing the door behind her.

Ellis straightened his tie, and shoved his glasses up the bridge of his nose with such force that Dee feared he'd break them. 'Jesus, Dee, I'm so sorry. I had no idea she would show up like this.' He waved a hand toward the door and caught his breath.

Dee moved to gather her belongings before things could heat up again. She wasn't sure she could handle sex with Ellis knowing she was only the appetiser before the main course waiting for him at the Hilton. Maybe what had happened at Marston's party between him and Stacie had been nothing to him, but it certainly didn't seem as if Stacie felt the same way. She shivered as she thought of her nightmare again. Sex was a part of her job. Suddenly the thought felt sharp-edged and painful, and she forced it away to concentrate on what was immediate, what she did have some control over. 'I really don't think there's much else,' she said in her "business as usual" voice, willing herself to stay calm and focused. 'As I said, Sandra is already taking care of travel arrangements, and with any luck I'll come home with lots of plans and new ideas from both Trouvères and Scribal.'

'That's good, that's great.' He moved back behind his desk and dropped into his chair. Taking off his glasses, he scrubbed a hand over his face. 'Dee, I'm really sorry about Stacie.'

'Nothing to apologise for. These things happen.' She hadn't meant to sound cold, but it was hard not to, with thoughts of Ellis and his very sexy ex ordering room service, and having each other for dessert. Damn it! She had no right to be jealous. Sex with Ellis was a part of her job, nothing more. How many times would she have to remind herself before it finally sunk in?

An hour later, Ellis stopped by Dee's office, but she was out. Her things were still there, so he knew she hadn't gone home yet. Then he remembered that after Wade got back from bowling, she had a meeting with him and the head of the engineering team for the Trouvères/Scribal project. He had hoped to apologise properly, but it would have to wait until next week. Cursing Stacie, he returned to his office, gathered his things and headed home.

Chapter Twenty-eight

ELLIS TOOK THE ELEVATOR from the tenth floor, all the while fighting the urge to go back and wait for Dee so they could finish what they started. It would only take a minute for him to clear up the misunderstanding, that's all. He should have known Stacie couldn't leave well enough alone. Her intentions were good, but the road to hell was paved with them, wasn't it? One minute Dee had been in his arms, open and vulnerable, and the next she had been the stone maiden with all deflector shields up. Under the circumstances, how could he expect anything else? She was his executive assistant, and she behaved as such. Once again, he wished she wasn't quite so good at playing the game.

When he was out on the freeway, Ellis headed home without bothering to call Stacie. In truth, he hadn't even looked at the card she'd given him. Surely she didn't really expect him to come to her in her hotel room? He had no intention of meeting her. He didn't owe her an explanation. He didn't owe her anything. And he couldn't imagine what she might have to say to him that was important enough for her to ruin his weekend. He'd planned to ask Dee home with him for dinner and a quiet evening. He didn't like the tension between them, and he'd hoped tonight they'd be able to straighten things out. Now, thanks to Stacie, he'd be alone – not a first for him by a long shot, but he found it much more difficult when he knew Dee would also be alone.

He stared out the windshield at the lights from thinning traffic and wondered if Dee would spend the evening cooped up with the Scribal files. He should have talked to her. But how could he explain Stacie without digging up a chunk of the past he'd rather not be reminded of, and about which he certainly preferred Dee knew nothing. He wondered what she did in the evenings. Did she play piano? Did she sing? Maybe she had a lover he knew nothing about. The thought made him queasy as he pictured the conversation in his head.

"So how was it at the office today, honey? Your boss did you on his desk? How unoriginal is that?"

Surely it was ridiculous to even consider. He couldn't imagine her agreeing to the Sex Clause if she were in love with someone else. She wasn't that kind of woman. And certainly no man who was lucky enough to merit Dee's heart would want to share her with anyone. Then there was Daniels. She always brushed any mention of the man aside, but he was persistent, and he knew exactly what he wanted. Ellis knew exactly what he wanted too, and that's what worried him.

At home, Harold met him at the door and took his computer bag. 'Anything I need to know about?' Ellis asked.

'Only that your brother arrived an hour ago,' the butler said.

Just what he didn't need right now; both Stacie and Garrett in the same state with him. He swallowed back his frustration. 'Garrett's here?'

Harold fell into step beside him. 'Not at the moment, no. He went into town. But I think he plans to stay a while. I had his things delivered to the guest suite.'

Concern replaced the surge of anger Ellis felt at his brother's part in the mess with Stacie. Garrett hadn't been to visit in three years. 'Is he all right?'

'He's thin, and he looks tired.' Harold gave a knowing nod. 'Love problems again, I assume.'

'Isn't it always?' Ellis undid his tie and slid out of his jacket, both of which Harold gathered from him. 'I thought he and Amy had worked out all their problems. But things change fast in the world of love.'

'True.' The butler draped the jacket and tie neatly over his arm. 'Dinner at 9.00?'

Ellis looked down at his watch. 'Make it 9.30. I want to swim a few laps to work out the kinks.' He rotated his shoulders and stretched his neck. 'Then I'll take a peek at the sky.'

'Ah yes, the Perseids. I hear it'll be good viewing this year.'

'Oh, and Harold, if Garrett comes back before too late, let me know. Maybe we'll watch together.'

Ellis headed to the pool. For him, time was always tight, and he'd given up almost everything that wasn't Pneuma Inc., but the swimming he held on to.

He had the Perseids to look forward to tonight. It was usually one of the best meteor showers of the year. He might not be able to avail himself as regularly as he had in the past to the wonders of the universe, but he still knew the cycles like he knew his own heartbeat. These days, when he indulged in the beauty of the night sky, it was a solitary affair. It had taken years of encouragement from Beverly before he could even face that without the pain of the past and the shame that went with it.

Beverly had told him repeatedly that it wasn't his shame, but he still felt it, and he had never, in all the years since he left Caltech, shared his passion with anyone else. He had hoped to share it with Dee tonight. Perhaps there would be another time.

Once changed, he did a few brisk warm-up stretches at the end of the pool and executed a perfect racing dive into an easy crawl stroke. By the third lap, he relaxed into his pace. His mind was clear of all else but the movement of his body slicing endlessly through the water. By the fifth lap, his brain had settled and cleared itself so he was focused. He'd call Dee when he was finished swimming. No law said he couldn't. If she was busy, she was busy, but if she wasn't he'd send Jeffries for her, whether she was at the office or at home, and he'd have her here within an hour. Better yet, he'd go get her himself in the Jeep and he'd drive her up on the back side of Mount Hood. He'd have Galina pack a couple of sandwiches and a couple of warm blankets. That would be a far better place to watch the Perseids, and then … He smiled as he imagined watching the spectacular meteor shower under a clear sky, wrapped around Dee, keeping her warm with his body while he gave her a tour of the night sky. And when he had shown her as much as they could see with the naked eye, when she had been dazzled and amazed by the fireworks display of the Perseids, he'd see if the two of them could generate a few fireworks of their own.

'Why aren't you with Dee?' He looked up to see Stacie barefoot at the edge of the pool. He had been so focused on his plans for Dee that he hadn't seen her come in.

'It's not really your business how I spend my evening, Stacie.' He continued swimming, hoping she'd go away, but knowing she wouldn't.

After the last lap, he pulled himself up to the edge of the pool next to her, but didn't get out.

Stacie wore a blue sundress that buttoned down the front and belted at the waist. Her hair was gathered in a loose ponytail. With one bare foot, she kicked at the water splashing him playfully, then giggled. 'I hate you, Ellis Thorne. You're the only man I know who looks great in a Speedo without gyms, or personal trainers. Me, I have to spend a fortune on both.'

He moved back slightly, out of splashing range. 'How did you get in here? Harold knows better than to let strangers wander through the house.'

'I'm hardly a stranger, Ellis, and just because Harold left me to wait in the sitting room doesn't mean I'll wait. You know how tenacious I am. If I want to see you bad enough I'll figure out a way.'

Just then, as though he had heard his name, Harold appeared at poolside. 'I'm sorry, I left Ms Emerson –'

Ellis raised a hand. 'It's all right, Harold, there are some things even you have no control over.'

'Right.' The butler's eyes might have sparkled, but the rest of the face remained completely neutral as he turned on his heels and left.

With a feline stretch of her neck, Stacie looked around the pool area. 'So I'll ask you again, Ellis, why the hell isn't Dee here with you? She can swim, can't she? And even if she can't, there are other things you could do together in a pool.'

When he didn't give her an immediate answer, her face softened to something nearing empathy. 'She wouldn't come with you? Because of me? Oh Ellis, I knew I should have stayed and made things right.'

The alarm bells always went off in his head when Stacie or Garrett suddenly had the overwhelming desire to make things right for him. 'It's none of my business what my executive assistant does on Friday night, Stacie. When she's not on Pneuma time, she does as she pleases.' And he wanted her to do what she pleased with him, but he sure as hell didn't want Stacie to know that.

Stacie nodded as though she completely understood now. 'She thinks you're with me.'

'No! Maybe. I don't know, I didn't ask her.'

'Well why not, Ellis? Why didn't you make sure she knew? Why didn't you just tell her that I wish you both the best? I'm absolutely elated that you found someone as brilliant as she is who's hot and sexy and interesting enough for you to implement the Executive Sex Clause. Garrett and I have been saying all along that this is exactly what needed to happen; for you to find someone and get off your abstinence kick.'

Ellis bristled. 'Who said anything about abstinence?'

She shrugged. 'Well not now, obviously, but pre-Dee Henning, you were much sought after and totally unavailable. Some of my friends even thought you were gay. I set them straight on that, of course. And speaking of abstinence, you did hear that Garrett's little ballerina cut him off, didn't you?'

'No, I hadn't heard. Harold said he showed up here earlier this evening. But he decided to go into town. I haven't seen him yet.'

She scooted closer to the edge of the pool. Ellis knew this was the bit where Stacie imparted the latest gossip, and since she had a better relationship with Garrett than he did, he moved closer and listened. 'I phoned him a little while ago. Apparently she feels he's interfering with her dancing – no time for both love and career. It's the tragedy of the modern world, as you and Dee well know.' She clucked her tongue. 'Too bad he wasn't able to work out some sort of Executive Sex Clause with her.'

'I'm sorry to hear that,' Ellis said. 'I liked Amy, and Garrett seemed happy.'

'Mmmm, me too. I liked her.'

'I'm glad you could be there for him, Stacie.'

'You know I'm always happy to do what I can for the Thorne brothers,' she said. Then she changed the subject in the usual abrupt Stacie Emerson way. 'Garrett says you're in love with Dee.' She leaned close to him, and nearly lost her balance. 'And I think he might be right.'

He grabbed her arm and righted her before she could topple over the edge. 'That's ridiculous.'

'Right.' She shook her head and looked down at him like he was a naughty child. 'Now are you going to call her and make things right, or shall I?' She pulled her iPhone out of the pocket of her dress.

'You have her number?' Ellis felt panic rise in his chest. He grabbed for her phone, but she jerked her hand out of reach.

'Of course I have her number. It wasn't that hard to get, not when I was surrounded by the Trouvères reps at Marston's party and they all worship her.' She began to punch the keypad.

'Stacie, don't. Stacie, I'm warning you …' He grabbed for her wrist but, she when she pulled away, the iPhone flew from her hand and went skittering along the tiles of the pool. Stacie lunged to retrieve it, caught her foot in the hem of her dress, and toppled over the edge. With a wild splash and a yelp of surprise, she landed in Ellis's arms.

Chapter Twenty-nine

FIXING STACIE'S AFTERNOON FLUB-up in Ellis's office hadn't been in Garrett's plans for the evening, but it was something to keep him busy, and keep his mind off Amy. And maybe with him and Stacie scheming together, at least one of the Thorne brothers could have a nice, romantic weekend.

He had Ellis's limo driver take him to the Pneuma Building when he'd gotten Stacie's call. He was in the neighbourhood anyway. He was Ellis's brother, and technically he worked for Pneuma, Inc. Though it was just a part of his ne'er-do-well cover-up, it would still get him into the building and into an empty office that Ellis had reserved for him, not without lots of complaining and nagging at him to stop the masquerade and come clean. But Garrett wasn't ready to do that just yet. Having nothing expected of him made for interesting observations of people who did have things expected of them, and it was their lives that inspired most of what he wrote. In the back of his mind, he was already imagining how he could turn Dee and Ellis's story into fiction without his brother recognising either of them as characters and promptly committing siblicide. But if Ellis hadn't murdered him by now, he figured he was pretty safe. Besides, he was a good writer. Neither Dee nor Ellis would recognise themselves when he finished with them.

Garrett wasn't sure how long he stood at the open door of Dee's office, but it was long enough for him to observe her unnoticed, long enough for him to be convinced that she was definitely the perfect heroine for his next novel. Her face was sculpted in concentration and haloed in the incandescent lighting that staved off the night rapidly encroaching through the window behind her desk. She sat head and shoulders above heaped open files and three-ring binders, chewing on the end of a pen and twisting a strand of hair around her finger.

No doubt she was every bit the professional his brother bragged about, but after spending time with her at the bar in New York, he was certain those skills, no matter how savvy, were only the surface of a deep wellspring. There was an unpretentiousness about her that finally urged him across the threshold, as he knocked on the jamb of the open door to announce his presence.

The smile she offered was transparent, playful, and though for a moment he desperately wished it might be otherwise, clearly not intended for him. She realised her mistake with a startled intake of breath and a subtle shifting of boundaries in the expressive angles of her face, a distancing he felt as physically as if she had pushed him away with her hand. 'Garrett! For a second I thought you were Ellis.' She came from behind her desk and gave him an enthusiastic hug. He was relieved Dee's boundaries were semi-permeable, and warmth won out over reserve. Even if she were only being kind to him because he was Ellis's brother, these days he'd take what he could get.

He returned her embrace with his own enthusiasm, born more out of need than politeness. Before he could make too big a fool of himself, he stepped back, straightened his denim jacket, and lied. 'Sorry to bother you, Dee, but I'm looking for Ellis.'

'He's gone for the day.' Her mouth softened with concern, and he could tell by the darkening of her eyes she wouldn't be fooled into thinking all was rosy in paradise. Ellis was the one who kept his feelings hidden away. Garrett, for the most part, never really tried. 'Is there anything I can do for you?'

He dragged up a sigh from the gaping abyss he felt beneath his sternum and leaned against the wall, feeling suddenly as if he hadn't enough energy to stand. 'I should have known better than to come without calling.' Oh, he was good, he thought, really good. Maybe he should have been an actor rather than a writer. Then again, he wasn't really acting, was he? 'Did he say where he'd be?'

'I think he's meeting someone at the Hilton.'

Just then his iPhone chimed a text. It was from Stacie.

Ellis is at hoooooo, it said. He knew Stacie wasn't the best with technology, but it wasn't hard to figure what it meant. It was exactly what they expected, and that being the case, he knew what he had to do.

He quickly recalculated the situation, and bluffed. 'Stacie said she was meeting him. I thought she was kidding.'

Her relaxed smile didn't change at the mention of Stacie's name. She motioned him to the chair in front of her desk. 'I take it you know her too.'

'Oh, I know her all right.' He flashed a wicked smile. 'Stacie's always kind of capricious. You never know what to expect from her. But she's great fun at a party.'

'So I gathered.'

Garrett was glad he didn't have to face Dee across the negotiating table. Still, a little probing might be fun, though he was already dead sure what it would reveal.

'She and Ellis and I, we go way back. I'm talking junior high way back. We used to be close friends, the three of us.'

'Oh really?'

He offered her his best confidential smile. 'Of course as the younger brother, half the time Ellis and Stacie viewed me as a pest. Things got a little better when I got older.' He held her in a weighty gaze. 'Then they got a whole lot worse.'

'Should I be hearing this?' God, she reminded him for a minute of Ellis, always the stickler for private lives remaining private.

'Oh, it's no big secret. We all went off to university together, and while Ellis wasn't looking, I married her.'

'You married Stacie?'

It did him good to see the surprise on her face. She was no more immune to surprises of the heart than his brother. 'You probably guessed by now it wasn't exactly happy ever after. It was a very short marriage, and certainly not good for any of us.'

'For any of you?'

'Stacie would be the first to tell you she never could decide which of the Thorne brothers to choose. When she was engaged to Ellis, she wanted me. When she was married to me, she wanted Ellis. Me, I'm a pushover. Me, she could have whenever she wanted. Ellis, however ... Well, Ellis wasn't quite so easy.'

'Apparently they must have worked that out.' She said it like she had just told him the weather forecast – maybe a little too much like the weather forecast.

He leaned forward in his chair. 'Does that bother you?'

She leaned forward, mirroring his posture. 'Should it?'

With a keen-edged stab of memory, he recalled why he was in Portland in the first place. His effort at a laugh felt bruising. 'Well, don't worry. Now that she knows Amy's not seeing me any more, Stacie'll be sure to make plenty of time for me in her busy schedule.'

'God, Garrett, you broke up with Amy?' Her gaze turned stormy, and the voice that had been so neutral up until now was weighted with tenderness.

'Seems I'm not a good career move for her. She's got the opportunity to dance as a principal dancer, and doesn't have time for a love life.'

'Garrett, I'm so sorry.'

The lump in his throat surprised him. Dee didn't play by his brother's rules. His brother would have listened to his sad story and, not knowing what else to do, would have been embarrassed by Garrett's display of pain. But Dee didn't seem the least bit uncomfortable. He hadn't expected someone who was so skilled at negotiating deals to be equally skilled in the fine art of empathy. He stood and paced the floor in front of her desk. 'I knew it was coming; in fact, I was in New York hoping we could make everything right again. I thought we were going to make it, Dee. I really did.'

'She seemed like such a nice person.'

He stopped pacing and plopped back into the chair. 'Oh, she is. She's a wonderful person, but she dances. That's her passion. She says she's got a few good years at best. It's now or never. There'll never be another chance.'

Dee closed the file in front of her and, with a few deft movements, prevented the threatening landslide of the rest. Then she stood and came to sit in the chair by his side. 'I'm sorry, Garrett, but I understand how she feels.'

'I understand too. That makes it harder. I can't even claim she's a jerk and let it go at that. I respect the woman and her choices too much.'

She touched his hand. 'It's hard these days. It's hard for all of us. I'm sorry you missed Ellis.'

'I'm not. He's not nearly as nice to talk to as you are.' He closed his hand around the warmth of her palm and ran his index finger over her knuckles. 'Not very nice of my dear brother to leave you chained to the desk on a Friday night. I'll have to talk to him about that.'

She extricated her hand and sat back. 'Well, actually, I just lost track of time. If you'd like to talk to Ellis, I can give you his cell phone number.'

'I have it, but I wouldn't dream of interrupting.'

She made no response to his hints at what might be going on between his brother and Stacie. She definitely was good. He could almost believe she really didn't care. But he was the romantic in the family, and something in his gut told him that wasn't the case.

'I'll see him soon enough anyway. I've decided to stay at Ellis's a while. He doesn't know it yet, but I dropped my things off there before I came back into town. Great guest suite.' He raked her with a suggestive grin. 'One thing I can say about my brother, he's got good taste.'

She met his gaze with a hint of a smile and not a trace of a blush. 'Yes, your brother does have good taste.'

It was then he remembered the reason Stacie had sent him there. The best way he knew to get Dee to Ellis's house was to ask her to join him for a meteor shower. She didn't have to know where he was taking her. 'What could be more fun on a Friday night than a little morose brooding under a cascade of meteors?' he asked.

'Sounds intriguing. You're in luck. I have an opening in my social calendar.' She gathered her belongings and the two of them left the now deserted building and headed for the parking garage.

'I hope you don't mind driving,' Garrett said. 'I had Ellis's limo driver drop me off thinking I'd just ride back with him.' Jeffries was actually on stand-by, but a discreet text while Dee gathered her things had sorted that. Garrett buckled himself into the passenger side of her Audi and sat back against the sigh of leather seats. 'Nice car. Payments must be a bitch, though.'

'It's paid for.'

'Graduation gift? Inheritance? Don't tell me you won the lottery?'

'I bought it for myself with the bonus money from my last year at Jasper and McDowell.'

He let out a low whistle. 'You do all right for yourself, Ms Henning.'

'Yes, I do, Mr Thorne.'

In the darkness he could just make out the sparkle in the corner of her eyes. The rest of her face was bathed in shadow, but the woman didn't have to be seen to be appreciated, and Garrett was a man who lived through his senses. He sensed the brush of expensive clothing pressed between the leather of the seat and the pliant curve of soft flesh. At the end of the day, deodorant and soap had acquiesced to female scent that was just barely a scent, almost a taste at the back of his throat, a hint of something rich and fine and sensual that made him understand completely why his brother was so enthralled.

He fiddled with the radio until he found a jazz station where a suggestive saxophone purred music that was positively copulatory. 'Tell me, Dee, just how much of your leisure time do you spend at Pneuma Inc. anyway?'

'Not enough, probably.'

'Wow, Ellis wasn't kidding when he said the two of you had a lot in common.'

She shot him a quick glance as they merged on to the freeway. 'He said that?'

'I have my doubts if the man knows the difference between leisure time and work, and it doesn't look like you do either.'

'That's how you get things done in this world. You can't let yourself be distracted.'

'You sound just like Amy.'

'I'm sorry, Garrett, I didn't mean to bring up bad memories.' Compassion melted the edges of neutrality, and he would be the first to admit he was enjoying the warming trend.

'It's OK. Stacie always said that I was in love with being in love, and Ellis …' He shot her a surreptitious glance, now that his eyes were beginning to adjust to the darkness. 'She said Ellis was incapable of love.'

Her face remained unreadable in the slow pulse of headlights on the freeway, and when she spoke, her voice had once again cooled to neutral. 'Sounds like the three of you have quite a mottled history.'

'You could say that.' He waited, giving her every opportunity to ask any of a plethora of questions he knew she must be dying to ask. And he – unlike his brother – would be more than willing to answer in detail. The saxophone made seductive suggestions in the darkness. Garrett sat poised to shock and titillate with the lurid tale of two brothers, but Dee simply didn't ask.

When she finally did speak, it was not to question. 'As far as Amy's concerned, Garrett, I can't imagine any job demanding more of a person's time and energy than being a ballerina.'

'Except maybe yours?'

'Except maybe mine.'

'If you were in Amy's shoes, would you do what she did? Would you give up love for your career, or would you throw caution to the wind and go for it?'

In the soft glow of the dashboard he could see her mouth soften into a cautious smile. 'I can't really answer that question, Garrett. It's been a long time since I've had anything even remotely resembling a relationship.'

'Get off at this next exit.' He switched off the radio, leaving the car awash in silence. 'What about Ellis?'

'What about him?'

'The two of you certainly seemed to be doting on each other

last week at the hotel, and I haven't seen my brother dance in years.'

'It was probably temporary insanity on both our parts.'

'That simple?'

'That simple. Where are we heading anyway?'

'To Ellis's place.'

Though her recovery was quick, it wasn't quite quick enough. Garrett didn't miss the flash of alarm in her eyes at the revelation of their destination. He was certain of it now. The lady was smitten. Just how smitten remained to be seen. But he hoped, for his brother's sake, very.

He motioned her down a narrow gravel drive flanked by woodland on either side. At the end of it was a huge house with simple lines that fit the landscape as though it were a giant bird settled into just the perfect nest. 'Ellis didn't buy this place because it was fabulous and opulent, and green,' he said. 'Of course, it is all those things, but my brother's so single-minded he'd have happily lived in a cardboard box if Beverly hadn't intervened. Beverly picked this place out for him, actually. The two things Ellis wanted, it had. He wanted a pool because he swims, and he especially liked this place because there's almost no light pollution on the back bit of the property. Perfect for sky watching. He bought up all of the acreage behind to make sure it stayed that way. I guess you could say Ellis has his own private wildlife reserve, which doubles as an observatory at night.'

Within minutes they were lying on a stretch of open countryside left to grow up wild behind Ellis's house. The night smelled of ripening grasses, summer heat, and newly mown hay from the fields nearby. The dome of the sky coalesced with a light show of meteors. Garrett had polished off one turkey sandwich the cook had provided for an impromptu picnic and had started on a second, but Dee only lay next to him and watched the sky.

'I've never seen anything like this. It's amazing.' Dee nodded to the domed housing of a telescope not far from where they were lying. 'The telescope. Was it here when Ellis bought the house?'

Garrett followed her gaze. 'That, he built himself – well, at least the telescope part. The housing he hired someone to build, but Wade told me that he actually took time off from Pneuma Inc. to supervise and make sure it was just right.

'You seem to know a lot about astronomy,' Dee said.

'Just a fan of the night sky. Have been for years. I studied astronomy briefly at Caltech, but then I got a good contract with my publisher and had too much on my mind to stick with it. Ellis, on the other hand, he was passionate about it. He probably doesn't have much time for it any more. His loss.'

'I never would have imagined Ellis as a stargazer. He always seems so firmly rooted on the ground.'

'My brother's actually a very interesting person despite his capitalist ways.'

They lay quietly for a few minutes, watching nature's pyrotechnics. 'Ellis is the one who got me interested in astronomy, actually; me and Stacie. He even discovered his own asteroid. Bet you didn't know that, did you?'

'Wow! Astronomy's a far cry from running a cutting-edge company. What made him decide on business?'

When Dee finally did ask a real question, it happened to be the most devastating one, the answer to which had shredded all their lives 17 years ago. Garrett's heart hammered his ribs, as though it were still trying to escape the truth. But he wasn't one to keep secrets, not any more. He took a deep breath and tried to sound matter-of-fact. 'I eloped with his fiancée and he got expelled from the astrophysics program at Caltech for cheating.'

She came up on one elbow as though she were spring-loaded. 'That's ridiculous! Ellis would never cheat. He wouldn't need to.'

Garrett could feel the heat of her anger pressing against him. It wasn't hero worship he sensed in her. She believed in Ellis, and she believed in him from a place of knowing. With startling clarity, he realised he had never been in that place with another human being, and he envied her the experience.

'Of course he didn't do it. He and Daren Jamison were up for a position at the observatory in Hawaii. It was a summer programme and it was a position based on merit. Ellis was a shoo-in for the post, but Daren was Terrance Jamison's favourite nephew, and suddenly there was all this evidence that Ellis had cheated on his last two exams, manufactured, of course. He never got a chance to prove his innocence, never got a fair hearing of his side of the story. He was just expelled.' Garrett drew a shaky breath. 'It all happened the same day Stacie and I announced that we were married.'

'Jesus,' Dee whispered.

'Yeah,' Garrett agreed. 'We didn't know. We marched right in, hand in hand, told him we were married, and all the while he's standing there with his walking papers in his hand. He didn't say anything. He just turned around and left. I mean, we expected him to be upset, and we were prepared for that. We didn't find out until the next day that we were just the final straw.

He could hear Dee's ragged breathing. Clearly she was struggling to take in what he had just said. He continued, 'Do you have any idea how much time and energy is involved in the study of astrophysics? It's not a degree you could whip through using Cliff Notes.' He could feel Dee glaring at him in the darkness as he hurried on. 'You know the old adage "no time for romance"? Well, that was Ellis. It didn't mean he didn't love Stacie. He adored her, actually. It just meant she wasn't the only thing in his heart, and that was the problem.'

He lay back in the grass with his arms folded behind his head, still feeling the burn of Dee's gaze. 'I was just beginning my freshman year when I got lucky and sold my first novel. It was probably a fluke. I mean, I was young, but it was the kind of pulp fiction testosterone stuff that sells. That's what I wrote back then. It wasn't long till I got a contract for more of the same.

'When I got my big break, Ellis was at the observatory, so Stacie celebrated with me, and before the night was over the celebration took a turn for the personal.'

'Even though she was engaged to your brother?'

'It just happened. God knows neither of us intended it, and I swear we didn't see it coming. But by the time it did, there was no turning back. After the first time, we couldn't get enough of each other. I skipped classes during the day to write, and at night we made love into the wee hours. Finally one weekend, on a wild hair, we eloped. We had no way of knowing that while we were tying the knot, fucking each other's brains out, my brother was being sold up the creek.'

Dee sat up, hugging her knees to her chest. 'Ellis must have been devastated.' Her voice was anguished, and for the first time Garrett wished he'd kept his mouth shut and let her think he was really not a bad guy, just the typical younger brother. It was too late for that now. Besides, he reminded himself, it didn't matter what she thought of him. What mattered was how she felt about Ellis.

'Not pretty, our little story, is it?' Garrett sat up next to her and chafed his arms.

'Surely Ellis's name was cleared?'

'Of course it was, but not until after he was already enrolled in the Business Department at Portland State. Beverly had the situation investigated – without Ellis knowing about it, of course. And she found out about Jamison's involvement. Jamison's nephew isn't the sleaze his uncle is, and he confessed to everything, making sure to cover his uncle's ass, of course. Though I'm sure he was well rewarded for that.'

Dee plucked a handful of grass and tossed it into the darkness. 'But surely once Ellis's name was cleared, they would have accepted him back into the programme? Surely once everything was made right...'

'Everything couldn't be made right, Dee. Don't you understand?' His head suddenly ached and there was the sharp pain beneath his ribs he always felt when he talked about that night, and the horrible time that followed. He deserved the pain. He took a deep breath and continued. 'Ellis applied at Portland State, like I said. His best friend was there, studying engineering. He knew the head of the Business Department.'

'Beverly.'

'That's right. Based on Wade's recommendations, she pulled strings to get him into her programme in spite of the blight on his academic record.'

'I knew Ellis and Wade went to Portland State together and Beverly had been Ellis's professor. I didn't know – the rest.'

'Of course you didn't. Beverly went out of her way to make sure that information was well covered up, mostly because she knew how it tore Ellis up, even after the fact. If Ellis hadn't been expelled from Caltech, there would have never been a Pneuma Inc.,' Garrett said. 'I often try to salve my conscience with that fact.'

'His being expelled wasn't your fault,' Dee said.

Garrett didn't respond. Somehow, it always felt like his fault. 'Once the truth came out, Ellis was cleared, but he didn't go back to the astrophysics programme. Too many painful memories, I suspect.

'Stacie and I aren't proud of what happened. I know we've both wished a million times we could go back and undo the damage. We were young and stupid, and I would have done anything for Stacie. I was in love with her. She was engaged to him. Ellis was left to pick up the pieces.'

An uncomfortable silence thickened like fog around them. He could tell she was looking at him and not the sky, studying him in the darkness, probably wondering what kind of a monster would do something so terrible to his brother. He tore up the uneaten piece of sandwich he no longer had appetite for and threw the bits onto the grass for the birds to find in the morning. 'Oh, he's forgiven me, which I'm not sure I could have done if the tables had been turned.'

'I can't really picture Ellis being the kind to hold a grudge.' Her voice was now soft. The disappointment and anger had vanished into the silence.

'He's not. I'm just neurotic, that's all.'

He could still sense the press of her gaze, which he felt woefully inadequate to return. 'Why did you tell me this, Garrett?'

'You asked.'

'You trapped me.'

His laughter rang hollow in his ears and stung the back of his throat. 'Yes, I suppose I did, didn't I?'

'I'm not your confessor, Garrett. Ellis's past – well, it's his past. We all have one. And I'm an only child. I don't know anything about sibling rivalry.'

'But you know my brother – maybe better than anyone else right now.'

She forced a laugh. 'I doubt that very much.'

He inhaled the scent of summer grass and settled back on the ground. 'Ellis would be appalled. At the best of times I'm not very good at keeping my mouth shut. And this past week hardly qualifies as the best of times. Anyway, if Ellis has told me once, he's told me a hundred times, personal lives should be private – not that he has much of one any more.'

Dee scrunched her knees up under the edge of her skirt and pulled her jacket tighter around her. 'Your brother who has no personal life is at the Hilton with Stacie ordering in. Sounds pretty personal to me.'

'Why, Dee Henning, if I didn't know better, I'd think you were jealous.'

She tugged at the tail of her skirt. 'That's ridiculous. I'm just stating a fact.'

'Then why are you trembling?'

'I'm cold.' She chafed her arms. 'That's all. I'm just cold.'

'Right, cold.' He slid out of his jacket and spread it across her shoulders, relieved for the change of subject. 'Anyway, trust me, there's nothing of any consequence between my brother and Stacie.'

'And you would know this because she's your ex?'

'I would know this because I know my brother, better than he thinks I do, actually.' He looked over at her; and though he couldn't see her expression in the darkness, he could feel everything inside her stretched tight beneath the controlling reins of neutrality. 'Ellis wouldn't fuck Stacie, Dee. That was over a long time ago. If either of the Thorne brothers would be fucking Stacie, it would be me, because Stacie has always been the one I run to when I need comfort. I don't have Pneuma Inc. and saving the world to keep my mind off things.'

'I don't think I need to be hearing this,' Dee said. 'I agree with your brother, private lives should be private.'

'Look, look!' Slipping an arm around her, he pointed to a

particularly brilliant display in the sky. They both watched, awestruck.

'It's really too bad Ellis missed this.' Her voice was breathless, punctuated by the heavy beat of her heart.

And suddenly he felt the core of her laid bare, and he knew exactly what was at the centre, just as he had suspected. 'You're in love with him, aren't you?'

She pushed his arm away with such force that his jacket fell from her shoulders. 'Of course I'm not in love with him. Don't be stupid.'

'I'm very observant, Dee – the way you say his name, the way your eyes sparkle when you mention him, or when I mention him, the way you hang on every word when I'm talking about him. Oh, it's all right. He's in love with you too. It's just neither of you have figured it out yet, that's all.'

'You may pride yourself on being very observant, Garrett, but you're wrong.'

He slid the jacket back around her shoulders. 'I suppose it's possible. But not very likely. I make my living observing, remember?' He could feel her trembling against him. They both watched another spattering of meteors. He waited. She didn't speak. He figured she had decided on silence being the better part of wisdom. But now was too late. He knew it, and she no doubt did too.

He dropped the bomb. 'Dee, I know he's having sex with you.' Before she could do more than utter a startled gasp, he continued, 'I know about the Sex Clause, and I know that's a part of your job.'

'He told you?' Her voice was a strangled whisper, and the storm of emotions she'd until now kept hidden flared brighter than the meteors.

'Let's just say I figured it out. It was a theory Beverly and I cooked up one evening over too much wine and too little sleep.' He forced a laugh he no longer felt. 'I never dreamed he'd try to implement it.'

'Tell me, Garrett, how many other people has he discussed this little experiment with?' She threw off his jacket and tried to stand.

He pulled her back down. 'Take it easy, Dee. It's not like that. It's not what you're thinking.'

'What I'm thinking is that Monday your brother can find himself another lab rat. And I'm just the daytime entertainment. He has to have Stacie too? Well, at least I get paid for it.' She fought back a sob.

'Dee, will you listen to me? I only know because I know my brother. I saw the way he looked at you and I knew. I told you I'm pretty perceptive. He would never tell anyone. He would never betray you, and he certainly doesn't view you as the paid entertainment.' He took her hand, which was now icy and rigid. 'Far from it. He can't stop talking about you. Like I said, he's in love with you.'

She jerked her hand back. 'And that's why he's off with Stacie at the Hilton, and I can't believe we're even having this conversation.'

Before he could speak, she raised her hands. 'I don't want to talk about any of this any more, Garrett. Ellis's private life is none of my business –'

He covered her mouth with his hand. 'If he's with Stacie, it's because he's afraid of his feelings for you. He's just afraid. Just like you are.'

She shoved his hand away from her mouth. 'I don't want to hear any more, and don't assume you know me and what I feel because you don't.'

'Dee, Ellis and Stacie –'

'I think it's time to go home, Garrett. I've had enough revelations for one night.' This time she bolted and was halfway to the house before he could catch up with her.

Chapter Thirty

ELLIS HALF DRAGGED, HALF shoved Stacie out of the pool. She sat on the edge making fish gasps and trying not to laugh. Ellis had to admit she looked laugh-worthy. 'You're the clumsiest woman on the planet, Stacie. Next time you visit, I'll be sure to have an ambulance and a lifeguard standing by. Come on.' He climbed out of the pool and offered her his hand. 'There's a spare robe in the cabana. I'll get Galina to dry your dress, and set an extra plate for dinner.'

She stared at him. 'You want me to stay?'

'Well I can't very easily send you out like that, now can I? It won't take long to dry your clothes, then I'll send you home before you kill yourself or me.' He slipped into his own robe and nodded to the dressing room in the cabana. 'Leave your clothes. Galina will get them.'

'What about Dee?'

He gave her a sharp look. 'Dee's none of your business, Stacie.'

It didn't take her long, and when she stepped out of the dressing room barefoot and nearly swimming in a robe that was clearly meant for him, he frowned. 'Sorry it's so big. I don't have many visitors. You get what you get. Now come on, I've already had Galina wait dinner once so I could swim. I don't want to keep the woman waiting again.'

Ellis rounded the corner into the hall with Stacie right on his heels and collided head-on with Dee. Before she completely lost her balance, he closed his arms around her and steadied her. 'Dee, what are you doing here?'

With a little gasp of surprise, she shoved him away and stepped back just as Stacie ran into him and Garrett came charging down the hall behind Dee, stopping short before ramming into all three of them. For a long moment, no one said anything; everyone stood frozen to the spot. Dee's gaze moved from Ellis to Stacie and back again. With them standing in matching robes that had guilty-as-charged written all over them, Ellis found himself caught in another other one of those horrible déjà vu moments. Then Stacie broke the silence with a breathy little laugh. 'Oh God, Dee, this isn't how it looks. I fell in the pool and Ellis let me borrow a robe and, well, it was supposed to be –'

'Shut up, Stacie,' both Thornes ordered in unison.

She covered her mouth with a delicate hand.

'Garrett, Harold told me you were here. He didn't tell me you were entertaining out back.' Ellis struggled to keep his voice civil. He spoke to his brother, but he couldn't take his eyes off Dee, who stood rigid in a palpable halo of anger, her gaze now slicing laser-edged through the charged space between them.

'We were watching the Perseids.' Garrett ran a hand through his hair, dislodging several blades of grass as he did. 'Honestly, Ellis, I thought that's where you would be. I didn't know you were going to take Stacie for a swim.'

Ellis ignored his brother and reached for Dee's hand. 'I think we need to talk –'

'I've got to go.' She stepped back, blistering him with an incinerating glare. Her tone was icy, lethal – a warning to be ignored at one's own risk.

As she turned down the hall, Garrett risked life and limb and grabbed her hand. 'Thanks for commiserating with me, Dee. I'm sorry I was such an ass.'

'Forget it.' She jerked away without stopping and fled down the hall like a brewing storm, leaving Ellis alone with his brother and Stacie, both standing in front of him repentant and subdued.

Ellis cast a rigid shadow down the dimly lit hallway, for the moment at least ignoring Stacie, his hard gaze boring into his brother. 'Leave her alone.' His voice was soft and deadly.

'Ellis, I –'

'You heard me.' He raked Garrett with a serrated glare. 'I said leave Dee alone.'

Garrett forced back an amused smile, brushing several more blades of grass off his shoulders. 'I was surprised to find Stacie here. What's going on?'

Before Stacie could reply, Ellis raised a hand to silence her. 'Nothing's going on.'

Garrett moved a step closer, as though attempting to intercept juicy gossip. 'Did you two fuck?'

Stacie shook her head wildly. Ellis practically growled. 'No! I didn't fuck her, and stop changing the subject. What the hell you were doing with Dee?'

'We were watching the Perseids, like I said. Honestly, I was trying to get her here for you. I figured you'd be out watching the stars and we'd join you, then I'd discreetly leave; you know, let nature take its course. I'd forgotten that you swim in the evenings when you have time.' His demeanour was that of a choirboy, disturbed only by a roguish half-smile. 'It was all perfectly innocent.'

Ellis took a menacing step closer to his brother. 'Then why did she storm out of here like she was going off to war?'

Garrett sidestepped and bent casually to admire a vase of flowers arranged on a pedestal table in the alcove near the stairs. 'Oh, it's no big deal, really. I'm sure once she's had time to cool down she'll consider –'

'What's no big deal, Garrett?'

Garrett plucked a daisy from the arrangement and sniffed it, avoiding his brother's shrivelling glare. 'I sort of let it slip that I knew about her working arrangements with you – you know, the Sex Clause?'

Ellis was in his face in a heartbeat, knocking the daisy from his hand and vice-gripping his arm. 'You did what? What the hell were you thinking?'

Garrett jerked free and squared his stance, hands hanging loosely at his side. 'I wasn't thinking anything; it just slipped out. We were talking about – stuff, and one thing led to another. I'm sorry.'

Ellis surged forward. and the two stood nose to nose in the

soft glow of a Victorian wall sconce. 'You're sorry! What a fucking lot of good that does. Can't you ever just leave anything alone? Jesus, you're not even here one night and –'

'She deserves more, Ellis. More than the Executive Sex Clause. And so do you.'

Ellis crowded Garrett until he could see the fine pores along the bridge of his nose and the bristled stubble that shadowed his jaw. 'I'm sorry about you and Amy, really I am, but my relationship with Dee is none of your business. Stay away from her.'

Garrett forced a strangled laugh and stepped back, nearly knocking the vase of flowers off the table behind him. 'I don't see what the big deal is, Ellis. What does it matter if Dee sees me or someone else, as long as she fulfils her business obligations to you and meets your –'

Ellis lunged at his brother, grabbing him by the lapels of his shirt and nearly lifting him off his feet. Stacie let out a little yelp of surprise and stepped back just as the vase behind them went over with a loud crash, spraying flowers, water, and glass across the hardwood floor. Ellis's voice was knife-edged in the expanding silence that he could barely hear over the roar of his blood in his ears. 'What happened with you and Stacie was a long time ago. We were all young. I wish the two of you would get the fuck over it and stop interfering. But I promise you, Garrett, if you even think about touching Dee, this time I won't roll over and play dead.' He let go of the lapels and shoved Garrett hard, then stormed up the stairs, taking them two at a time, and leaving Garrett and Stacie staring at each other in the hallway.

Chapter Thirty-one

HARRIS FOUND DEE STRUGGLING to unlock the door, with a carpet-covered scratching post balanced against one hip and two heavily laden plastic bags suicide-gripped in the opposite hand. When she was upset, she shopped for McAllister and O'Kelly. She was extravagant where the cats were concerned. The bottom shelf of her pantry was full of expensive toys and treats which had failed to pass the discerning feline test.

He kissed her cheek, and took the scratching post from her hip just as the key turned in the lock. 'You've been to the 24-hour Pet Smart. Bad day?'

'I've had better.' She gave the door a hard shove, and he followed her inside. 'What are you doing here?'

'Thought I'd take a chance I might catch you home and awake. After all, you seem to have sacrificed sleep to the God of business since you started working for Thorne. I just finished up at the law library, doing a little research on international environmental stuff for an article in *Wilderness Vanguard*. In fact, Pneuma's enemy number one figures pretty heavily.'

'Jamison?' She shot him a glance over her shoulder.

'Yep, the same.' He set the scratching post down just inside the living room. 'What's that on your skirt, a grass stain?'

She shot him a peevish look that left no doubt as to her present mood, and he abandoned the direct approach for the time being.

She kicked off her shoes and dropped onto the living room floor. The tabbies came to investigate the sound of rattling shopping bags, which they usually enjoyed more than the toys and treats that came out of them.

Harris tossed his jacket over the back of the couch, then stepped over the growing pile of cat toys to search out strong drink in the kitchen. He returned with a bottle of Cabernet and two glasses, and sat down next to her.

He scooted closer. 'You want to tell me about it? Is it Ellis?' When she offered only a half-committed shrug, he figured that was answer enough. 'I was afraid sex with your boss could only end in grief.'

For a long second, she watched the cats in silence. The pungent sent of liver treats and red wine permeated the air. When she finally spoke, her voice sounded as though it belonged to someone else, as though she were keeping it at arm's length. Harris knew that voice, and he braced himself. 'Sex with my boss is a part of the job, Harris.'

He listened tight-lipped while she told him about the Executive Sex Clause. He tried to keep the emotion from his voice when he finally spoke. 'Dee, it's illegal, what he's doing.'

'It's not like that, Harris. My job's not contingent on it. It all started out as some ridiculous idea of Beverly's – a joke, really. Then things just sort of happened …'

'Some joke.'

By the time Dee had finished telling Harris about what had happened on the plane home from Paris and all the events that led to the night's misadventure, both cats were curled up asleep in the two shopping bags.

Harris, who had listened to the whole story with minimal comment, tossed back the last of his wine and refilled the glass. 'Do you think Garrett's telling the truth – I mean about just figuring things out?'

'Probably. I can't believe Ellis would deliberately betray that trust. And really we did dance the night away with Garrett and Amy in New York. We weren't subtle. I can see, if Garrett knew about the Sex Clause anyway, how he could have figured it out.'

With some effort, Harris refrained from interjecting his opinion of Thorne, which was severely lowered by the fact the man's kid brother should have reason to suspect what was going on between him and Dee. 'So what will you do?'

'I'll talk to Ellis when I get back from New York, I guess. At first I thought I'd just turn in my resignation, but I love the job, and I love working for Ellis. I know Garrett was in a bad place tonight.' Dee started to refill her glass, then thought better of it. 'I need iced tea.' She heaved herself to her feet, and headed for the kitchen.

Harris followed her.

On impulse, she turned and slid her arms around his neck. 'Thanks, Harris, for listening, for just being here for me like you always are.'

'That's what friends are for.' He folded her close.

'Yeah. That's what friends are for.'

From the living room, Dee's BlackBerry rang, and she broke away and made a run for it. Harris cursed out loud. No doubt she expected it to be Thorne. He grabbed the huge plastic travel mug that Dee always drank her iced tea from, and went about the business of pouring her a tall one, all the while trying to catch her side of the conversation, which didn't sound at all like a lover's spat. Her voice was excited, energised. When he'd finished fixing her tea, he found her cross-legged in the middle of the living room floor, frantically pulling up files on her laptop.

'What's going on?' He handed her the drink and sat down next to her, looking over her shoulder at satellite maps.

'That was Wade,' she said. Before he could ask details she continued, 'Harris, the research you were doing, does any of it have to do with forests in Valderia slated for clear-cut?'

'Yeah. That's a part of why I stopped by. I knew that after what you'd told me when you got back from New York, you'd be interested. Why?'

There was a knock on the door and they both jumped. 'That'll be Jeffries coming for me,' she said. 'Harris, I have to go meet Wade and Ellis. I think we might just have found a way to stop Jamison.' She palmed her laptop shut, and Harris went to get the door, her still calling after him. 'I need you to come with me. I need you to tell me what you found out, to tell us all what you found out. This could be big, and if we do this, we may be able to –'

Dee was still talking, but Harris stopped listening. He opened the door and found himself face to face with Ellison Thorne, standing on the threshold dressed in jeans and a Portland State T-shirt.

Dee rounded the corner into the hall behind him, heading for the stairs, still clutching her oversized tea mug. 'Tell Jefferies to give me five minutes to change clothes and grab my –' For a long moment she stood rooted to the floor in the hallway, staring over Harris's shoulder at Thorne.

Until Dee appeared, Harris was pretty sure if looks could have killed, he and Thorne would have cancelled each other out. But the change was transformative when the man's gaze locked on Dee. Jesus, Harris thought, of course Garrett could figure out something was going on. A person would have to be blind, deaf, and stupid not to feel the power surge between the two.

If Dee missed a beat, it was only a very small one. 'Ellis, this is my friend, Harris Walker,' she said. 'He'll be coming with us over to Pneuma.' She took another swig of tea and bounded up the stairs, calling over her shoulder, 'Just give me two seconds to change and get my computer bag and I'll be ready to go.'

Dee in work mode, Harris thought. God, the woman was amazing. Suddenly she sounded like it was business as usual, like she hadn't just survived the evening from hell – and all because of the bastard standing at the door.

Thorne held Harris's gaze in a stare-down, and Harris grudgingly stepped aside for him to come in. 'Fill me in, Mr Walker, why are you coming with us?'

'Dee thinks what I know may be helpful,' Harris said.

'Wait a minute, Harris Walker. From *Wilderness Vanguard*? That Harris Walker?'

'That would be me.' As much as he wanted to hate the man, Harris was surprised that Thorne knew who he was. He folded his arms across his chest. 'More importantly, I'm also Dee's best friend.' He took a step closer to Thorne. 'And just so you know, I'll rip your throat out if you hurt her.'

If Thorne was surprised by Harris's statement, he didn't show it, but before he could respond, Dee charged back down the stairs, now wearing jeans and the Eddie Bauer pullover Harris had bought her for her birthday two years ago. Her BlackBerry was glued to her ear, and she was talking to someone named Keith. She disappeared into the living room and returned almost immediately with her computer bag thrown over her shoulder, still talking to Keith. She motioned them both out the door, locked it behind them, then spoke to Harris. 'Get what you need from your car, and we'll go.'

Once in the limo, Thorne pulled Dee down next to him and motioned Harris into the seat across from them, glaring at him expectantly.

'Harris is a lawyer,' Dee said. 'Environmental law.'

'I have a law degree that sometimes come in handy,' Harris corrected. 'I don't practise any more. I can do more good with the camera.'

'Tell us what you found out,' Dee said.

There was no traffic that late on Friday night, so the trip into the Pneuma Building didn't take long. Most of what Harris had discovered didn't seem like much of a surprise to either Dee or Ellis, but when he started talking about access to the land slated to be clear-cut, they shot each other a knowing glance and listened even more intently. Before Harris could finish, they'd arrived at the Pneuma Building, where, to his surprise, Wade Crittenden personally ushered them through the state-of-the-art laboratory that was his domain. Being more than a bit of a nerd himself, Harris would have loved to linger and fondle, but he followed Dee in silence.

To Harris, Wade's office looked like a nerd's wet dream come true, but before he had time to really take it in, Wade spoke. 'You're right, Ellis, it's all about access. That's the key. Who are you?' He turned his attention briefly to Harris, who introduced himself.

'Oh, the one from *Wilderness Vanguard*,' he said, without further niceties. Harris couldn't help but be pleased that a genius like Wade Crittenden knew who he was. Wade motioned everyone to be seated and, on an enormous flat-screen monitor, he pulled up a map of the area around and including the forest slated to be clear-cut, then he nodded to Ellis.

Ellis stood and took a laser pointer from a desk buried under computer parts and other techie-looking detritus, some of which Harris recognised, some he didn't.

'We can't do anything about the forestry rights that Jamison's already bought,' he said, pointing to an area on the map that was highlighted in pink. 'But what we can do is cut off his access.'

Dee was sitting on the edge of her chair. Harris could practically see the excitement coursing through her body, and he had to say he was feeling a fair bit of it himself.

'Jamison has to be able to get his work force in and his timber out,' Ellis said. 'Interestingly enough, he seems to have taken for granted that wouldn't be a problem.'

Looking at the geography of the map, Harris could see exactly what Ellis had in mind, and his grudging respect went up still another notch.

'Jamison bought the forestry rights,' Ellis continued. 'The access land all belongs to the Valderian government, which means it's up for grabs too, but it doesn't have anything on it Jamison wants. However, it happens to have exactly what we want.'

'We'd have to sweeten the deal technologically, of course,' Wade said.

'What about sweetening it economically?' Dee added. 'What about ecotourism and extreme sports?' Suddenly all eyes were on her again. 'I've just been on the phone with Keith Harker. He's the CEO over at Sportwide Extreme Adventure. I found SEA several key players when I was working with Jasper and McDowell. Keith owes me big time. Plus, this is just the kind of thing his company would drool to get in on.'

For the next few hours, Harris found himself enthralled by the schemings of the three executives of Pneuma Inc. The sun was coming up when a plan was set into motion. Wade had just had breakfast delivered from his favourite all-night diner, and Ellis had just joined them after pacing in the outer office with several phone calls. As he settled in next to Dee, he spoke. 'I have the jet on stand-by. I'll take off at noon. No one·is to know where I am until I get home.'

'You're going to Valderia?' Harris asked.

'That's right.'

'I should go with you,' Dee said. 'It's my uncle you've been liaising with.'

'No. I'll need you in New York to close the deal with Scribal,' he said.

'But –'

'We'll discuss this later, Dee.'

Harris recognised the tightening of Dee's shoulders and the look of determination on her face that said she wasn't pleased with Ellis's decision, but she said nothing.

After they'd all eaten, Ellis looked down at his watch. 'Right. Email the plans I'll need, Wade. Harker's been up all night with his people. They're ready to run with the deal if I can negotiate something on the Valderian side. I think we could all use a little rest. 'He extended his hand to Harris. 'Thanks for your help, Walker. When the dust settles, I'll see that you have one helluva story for the magazine.'

Then he turned his attention back to Dee. 'There are a few more things you and I need to discuss. At my place.'

Harris bristled and Ellis gave him a warning glance, then addressed Dee again. 'There's important business we need to take care of, things you need to know, before I leave you in charge.'

Dee blinked, squared her shoulders, and nodded, and Harris found himself reeling at what had just happened. Did the two always communicate on so many levels or was he just reading more into it than was there?

When they were all tucked in the limo, Ellis spoke to Harris. 'I need you to go with me, Walker.'

'What!' Dee and Harris both said in unison.

'The photographer I usually use in these situations is down with the flu, and I know you're no stranger to remote shoots. I saw the photos you took for *Wilderness Vanguard* in Papua New Guinea. It's important that we document as much of what will happen next week as possible. A picture *is* worth a thousand words, and I need the best, and I need someone who understands what the hell we're up against. If we're going to turn this around and shut Jamison out, I want all of the bases covered.'

Harris ran a hand through his hair, took a deep breath, and nodded. 'I have several shoots this week, but I can reschedule them.'

'Email my secretary and I'll make sure she takes care of it.' Ellis said. 'Dee'll give me your address and I'll have the limo pick you up around 11.'

Harris only nodded. He couldn't believe any of this was happening. Dee reached across the seat and squeezed his hand. 'Be careful.'

When they arrived back at Dee's place, they all got out of the limo. Harris took Dee in his arms and hugged her tight, lifting her off her feet. 'Take care of yourself, Ms Diva. I'll see you soon.' Then, for good measure, he shot Ellis a warning look that was returned in spades.

Chapter Thirty-two

THEY WATCHED HARRIS LEAVE. Dee waved as he turned out of her driveway, and he waved back. She watched him until his car disappeared at the end of the street, not really ready to face whatever might come next and hanging on to the last view of her friend for courage. When she turned to Ellis, his gaze was locked on her.

'You told him.'

Her insides knotted and she found herself blushing furiously. 'He came over to tell me what he'd learned at the law library. He knew something was wrong. He doesn't give up easily.'

'I got that,' Ellis said.

'And he isn't exactly known for keeping his opinions to himself.'

'I got that too. He told me he'd rip my throat out if I hurt you.'

'He's pretty protective of me,' Dee said.

He lifted her chin, forcing her to meet his gaze. 'I was damn near tempted to let him.'

She tried to look away, but he held her.

'We don't have to go back to my place if you're more comfortable here, Dee, but I'm not leaving until we've talked.'

'Here's better,' she said, feeling like her pulse would hammer a hole in her throat. She'd rather have this discussion in her territory this time. At least there'd be no running into prying brothers and on-again-off-again former fiancées.

Ellis nodded. 'OK. Let's talk here then.'

Inside, the two cats were still curled up in the shopping bags and the floor was still littered with cat toys. The open bottle of wine and the two glasses still sat on the floor where she and Harris had left them, and her tea mug was still on the table by the door. The insulated lining had kept a bit of the ice from melting. She grabbed it and took a sip for courage as she closed the door behind them.

'Ellis, I –'

'Shh!' He placed a finger to her lips, and sat the mug on the table. 'Don't talk, just listen. Stacie's a clumsy oaf. She really did fall in my pool. Tripped on her own dress. I didn't invite her. She just showed up. Stacie's like that.'

'Ellis, this is none of my –'

'Shh! I'm not finished. My brother's a jerk sometimes, but he means well. I didn't tell him about the Executive Sex Clause, about us. Though it is my fault that he figured out what's going on. I wasn't exactly discreet about my desire for you when we were in New York, and Garrett's not stupid. Dee, I would never tell anyone. I would never do anything to hurt you. You have to know that.'

'Ellis, I –'

This time, he stopped her words with his mouth. She was shocked at the power of her own response, practically eating his face off in the explosion of need that tore through her. He crushed her against him, then his hands moved up to stroke her face, rake through her hair, caress the nape of her neck, and he groaned. 'I don't want to leave without knowing things are OK between us, Dee. Hell, I don't want to leave without making love to you until neither of us can walk. I wanted you in my office yesterday evening. I wanted you every second of every day all week long. Don't make me wait any longer.' He held her until she relaxed into him, until she settled her head against his shoulder. Then he lifted her into his arms, and she offered a yelp of surprise as he carried her up the stairs like she weighed nothing. 'I know my way to your room, Dee, and I've taken you to bed there before. But this time I won't be taking you there to sleep.' He settled her onto the comforter and sat down next to her.

Then he lifted his T-shirt off over his head, helped her out of hers, and lay down beside her, easing one thigh between her

234

legs and positioning it to rub intriguingly against her crotch. She closed her thighs around it and shifted her hips, her breath catching as the friction of denim against denim translated to heat on the bare skin underneath. He kissed along each of her bra straps and worked them off her shoulders, then he nuzzled his way into her cleavage, forcing a lace cup down with the nip of his teeth. The shove and press of his cheek and chin were stubbled and rough after the all-night session with Wade and Harris. The rake and scratch worked delicious counterpoint to the velvet humidity of his tongue and lips and the sharp tug of his teeth at first contact with the tetchy swell of her nipple. She arched up and held him to her, fingers scrabbling in his short hair.

Her nipple became engorged and leaden, sensitive to the point that even the slightest flick of his tongue sent aftershocks down between her legs to the empathetic engorgement of her clit. When he finished with one nipple, he nuzzled aside the other cup and repeated the pleasure. This time when she arched up to him, he slid a hand down over her belly and undid her jeans. Everything between her legs clenched in anticipation as he scrunched her panties aside and rested the cup of his palm on her mound. 'Dee.' He breathed her name against her nipple. 'I can't get enough of you. I can't even come close.'

He slid two fingers down either side of her clit and stroked. She moaned and shuddered. He lifted his face from his attention to her breast and looked up into her eyes. 'I want to watch your pleasure, Dee. I want to see it on your face. You can't imagine how stunning you are when you're turned on.' He slipped a finger between her swollen folds and she thrust her hips up to meet his touch. 'And when I'm the source of your pleasure, Dee, I feel like the best, most powerful man on earth – that I can give you what you need, that I can make you come.' He slipped a second finger into her to press and stroke her G-spot, and she felt the rush of her juices against his touch. He felt it too, and the catch of his breath, the dilation of his pupils, told her the effect it was having on him.

He guided her hand down onto the strain of his cock against his fly and held it there. 'You see what you do to me, Dee

Henning. All the time. Every time I think about you. And I think about you a lot.'

She curled her fingers around the shape of him through his jeans. His eyelids fluttered and his chest expanded with his gulp for air. He frantically fumbled to release himself into her hand, slapping away her clumsy efforts to help.

'I want to see you, Ellis,' she breathed. 'I want to see how much you want me.' With efforts made awkward by need, they both shifted on the bed. He lifted his butt and shoved at his jeans and boxers with his free hand, not missing a beat with the press and stroke of fingers that slickened her, eased her open in anticipation, made her swell and pout and hunger.

Once his cock was free, she raised herself up on one elbow, which not only gave her a good view of his erection, resting heavy and full against his thigh, but also gave her more leverage with which to bear down against his hand. She took hold of him, feeling the silken softness that sheathed iron, feeling the surge of his penis and the tensing of his balls beneath her touch. 'There, now.' He shuddered and rested his hand on hers. 'You see how badly I want you.'

She pushed away from him and slipped out of her jeans and panties. While she was at it, she lost the bra. Then she straddled him, taking her time to touch herself and rake her clit, fingering herself open so he could see the whole of her, so she could hear his groan of appreciation, so she could feel his gaze taking in the height of her arousal almost as physically as his fingers did. Then she positioned herself and slowly settled onto him. He lay still, holding his breath, hands cupping the swell of her hips as she eased down the length of him, feeling the head of his cock opening her relentlessly until he was deeply and fully sheathed in her tight grip.

He sucked breath between his teeth. 'Fuck, Dee! You feel better than anything.' He kicked and bucked his own jeans and boxers off. He would have unseated her had he not held her hips firmly. Then she began to rock and shift against him and he mirrored her movements from below, raking against her clit with each upward undulation.

He cupped her breasts, gliding his thumbs over the hard

peaks of her nipples, then he pulled her forward against the rise and fall of his chest, her knees bent so that her thighs pressed in tight on either side of his ribs. His hands moved down to cup her bottom, to knead and clench and spread her open, the act of which made her anus tighten and grip at its sudden unexpected exposure. He teased around and over it with the press of his middle finger, making her squirm, making her grip and anticipate anything, everything Ellison Thorne might do to her.

He clasped her to him and rolled with her until she was beneath him. His angle of penetration was steep enough that her bottom and her hips were off the bed. She grunted at the sudden shift of positions, an act which caused her to clench at his probing finger, and he chose that moment to push it home. She bit her lip to maintain control, and tightened her grip on his cock.

His breathing was laboured; his eyes were dark with need. All the while the angle of his penetration grew steeper and steeper until each thrust forced him up onto his knees. Each thrust felt deeper than the one before, deeper than she'd ever thought possible, until it felt as though he were thrusting up into the very heart of her. Her world was reduced to Ellis Thorne. He filled her head as well as her body, as though he had penetrated every cell of her, every breath of her. The bed shook beneath them and she rose up to meet each thrust, feeling suspended between the fullness in her slit and the press of his finger in her anus, feeling lost in the man whose world she had only begun to understand. And there was nothing else.

And Ellis. He spoke her name over and over again, like a mantra, like the in and out of his breath, like he'd somehow come to possess her, heart and soul. And if she hadn't been frantic, on the edge of orgasm, she might have run away in terror at the bright glimpse into the heart of the man, but even that she could have stayed for. It was the revelation of her own heart laid bare that would have terrified her. But then Ellis slipped another finger into her anus at the very second he plunged into her deep and hard. She gripped him in a clench that felt fatal and they tumbled over the edge together, into a release that threatened to shred both of them.

'Let me go with you,' she whispered against his chest. They lay curled around each other in her bed, with time quickly becoming their enemy.

'I need you in New York,' he said, kissing the top of her head. 'What you're doing is every bit as important as what I'm doing. You know that. We can't give Jamison any way out.'

She raised herself on one elbow and looked down at him. 'Why are you going, Ellis. I know you don't have to. You're Ellison Thorne. You have people who can do this for you. I know you do.'

'Dee,' he said, brushing the pad of his thumb over her lips and holding her gaze. 'I have to go because I have to. What I do, what we do at Pneuma Inc., is what it is because I understand, because I go and see for myself. Then I tell Wade, and he understands. He understands differently than I do, and things happen, good things. If I send someone else – well, people are too willing to tell me what they think I want to hear, and their opinions are coloured by so many variables. That's just the way it is. But I have to know what needs to be done, and I need to be sure that I never get complacent, that Pneuma Inc. never gets complacent. You have to understand that. It's the most important thing of all.'

She fought back the lump in her throat she hadn't expected and nodded, afraid of what might happen if she spoke, then she nestled down against his chest, next to the powerful, steady beat of his heart. His heart. Did anyone have any idea of the depth and the tenderness of that heart? She suspected Beverly did, and suddenly she missed the woman terribly. She wished Beverly could tell her what was going on in her own heart.

When the limo came for him, Jeffries discreetly waited in the car while they said their goodbyes. 'I'll have satellite link-up at least some of the time, Dee, and I'll keep in touch as best I can. Word's out that I had to make an emergency trip to Spain. My connections there will make sure the cover story holds. Probably it won't be necessary, but I've learned from experience it's wise not to take chances where Jamison's concerned.' He lifted her chin, and brushed a kiss across her

238

lips.

'Good luck in New York – and Dee, be careful with Daniels.' Before she could protest, he raised a hand. 'I know you think I'm being paranoid, but trust me on this, I know what the man wants.'

He ran a finger along her cheekbone and looked down at her over the top of his glasses. 'You're in charge of Pneuma Inc. until I get back, Dee. That being the case, I know the ship's in good hands.'

This time when he kissed her, it was more than just a brush of his lips. He lifted her off her feet and his mouth ravaged hers, bruising and hungry in its efforts. When he pulled away, breathless, he held her in his dark gaze. 'That's just to remind you that I'll be pretty tetchy when I get back. I'll need a debriefing in the worst way. You'll want to make sure that's in your calendar. It's already in mine.'

Chapter Thirty-three

KENDRA OFTEN HOUSE-SAT for Dee when she was away on business. Since Kendra had sold her PR firm in Los Angeles and returned to Portland, she'd been living in a small studio apartment until she could find just the perfect place, so for her to stay in a real house was a treat. And Dee was happy to have someone to look after the cats and just be there. Since Dee's flight to New York was an early one, Kendra came over the evening before so they could have some much-needed girl time. They'd managed a run together on Mount Tabor, then they ordered Chinese and sat on the living room floor eating kung pao chicken and dumplings. Afterward they adjourned to Dee's bedroom so Dee could pack.

Well into her glass of wine, Kendra watched Dee place lingerie into the bag for New York. 'Wow! Nice stuff you've got there, kiddo. I see you've had an upgrade in the lingerie department as well as the career department.' She nodded to the leopard print French-cut panties and matching bra Dee pulled from the drawer. 'Too bad the oh-so-hot Mr Thorne won't be there with you. I'm sure he'd appreciate a quick peek at that juicy little combo. Is he a tit man?'

'If he is, I missed the memo.' Ellis's admiration for her breasts hardly needed a memo, she thought.

'I suppose most guys are, aren't they?' Kendra said, taking a look down the front of her T-shirt at her own braless rack.

'Yep,' Dee agreed. 'In the same way most women like cock.' Just as Dee turned to put several pairs of stockings into the bag, McAllister did a twisty turn around her ankles and she pulled up short to keep from kicking him, showering Kendra in stockings.

Both women laughed, which McAllister found highly offensive. He scurried out of the room while the two bent to pick up stockings.

'Whoa! What have we here?' Kendra came up from fishing under the edge of the bed with a pair of men's boxers hung over one finger. Ellis's boxers. They'd not been able to find them when he left on Saturday and he'd had to fly off to Valderia commando, a thought which made Dee all moist and tingly. Fantasy fodder for sure.

Dee reached for them, but Kendra pulled them away, lips curving in a filthy smile. 'Mmm, expensive boxers too.' She twirled them casually around her finger. 'I can only think of two men in your life, Ms Diva. Harris, I figure, is more of a tighty-whitey sort of guy, and neither of you would ever consider fucking your friends, which I find quite sad, really, but there you go.' She looked back at the dark blue silk hanging from her finger. 'So unless you're doing the mail man and he's got a second income to afford silky little numbers like these, that just leaves Mr Ellison Thorne, with whom you spend an enormous amount of time and who is outrageously sexy and who, I'm sure, must have exquisite taste in women. Therefore, who else can it possibly be?' She grabbed Dee's hand and pulled her down on the bed next to her, giving her the evil parent look. 'Come on! Come clean. You know I won't give up until you tell me.'

Dee heaved a sigh and reached for her own glass of wine. This time Kendra didn't pull away when Dee took the boxers from her and quickly stuffed them into the top drawer of her nightstand. OK, she was dying to tell Kendra. She needed to tell her, actually. Harris already knew, and both her friends would be racked and tortured and take her secret to the grave with them before they would tell. And with everything that had been happening, she needed their support. The nod she offered in response was only half a nod before Kendra smothered her in a bear hug, threatening a wine bath for both of them.

'Fuck me!' she squealed. 'I'm all a-flutter.' She fanned herself with an open palm. 'You and Ellison Thorne!' She gave Dee another bone-crunching hug, ignoring the spill of wine on her pale lilac yoga pants. 'I suspected all along the man had exquisite taste in women, and that's why he was waiting for you.' She scooted back enough to look into Dee's eyes. 'Details, babes, I want all the juicy details. Does Harris know?'

'Yep. He knows.'

Kendra offered her a little pout. 'You told him before you told me?'

'It wasn't like I had much choice,' Dee said. 'There are no secrets from either of you. You know that.'

'I always hoped you'd fuck him,' Kendra said. 'You and Harris are far more picky than I am. I like to get laid, but I'm not into anyone, don't want to be, but you two, well, you're different.' She sniggered into her hand. 'Harris told me about your mishap at The Boiling Point.' She raised a hand to stop any comments. 'My fault. I should have known better than to suggest the place to you and Harris. And here you were fucking Ellison Thorne all the time. That's good. You two fit each other. You're right for each other.'

Dee felt a knot tighten below her ribcage, remembering her nightmare on the flight home and the uncomfortable fact that Garrett knew what was going on. 'It's just sex, Kendra. That's all. I mean, we're both free to see other people if we want.'

'Bullshit,' Kendra said. 'It's never just sex with you, Dee Henning. That's why you keep a steady supply of batteries handy for your vibrator. You don't do *just sex*.'

Dee stood and continued with her packing, not quite sure how much to tell her friend. But Kendra was often more insightful than Dee and Harris gave her credit for, and it was almost always when they would have preferred her not to be. 'So what is it you're not telling me, Dee?'

'It's just that he's my boss, Kendra. I have a very difficult job with huge responsibilities, and sex –'

'Sex complicates things. Yes, I know, sweetie. But sex always complicates things. You're into him, aren't you? Well, I mean, obviously you are.'

'He's my boss.'

'And you're into your boss. I got that. And he's into you?' She raised a dismissive hand. 'Well, of course he is. He'd be a

242

fool not to be, and Ellison Thorne is no fool. His expensive boxers covered in hot male sweat under the edge of your bed – that speaks volumes, sweetie.'

This was definitely not a topic Dee wanted to discuss further, but it was too late to get squeamish now. Kendra was in pitbull mode.

'You know, Dee, Ellis Thorne didn't get where he is by being stupid. Seems to me he's pretty smart having sex with you. I mean, I know you don't have time for sex, and I can't imagine him having any more.' She shrugged. 'Oh, I'm sure there's a bevy of expensively groomed socialites and a long list of perspective trophy wives who'd jump at the chance to be seen on his arm, but then he doesn't seem the type.'

'He's not!' Dee said. 'He's not the type. And you're right. With sex as a part of our working relationship, we both get it, and our work benefits.'

'Hold it, hold it!' Kendra gulped back the last of her wine. 'Sex is a part of your working relationship? Did I just hear you right?' She refilled their glasses and pulled Dee back down next to her. 'OK, whole story! I want it now, and no hedging. Come clean, Ms Diva. Now.' Dee sat down next to Kendra, took a deep breath, and told her about the Executive Sex Clause.

'Can you see? Can you see it?' Ellis moved in close to where Dee stood gazing into the telescope, and rested his chin on her shoulder.

She gasped. 'My God! It's beautiful!'

And it was. He'd never seen the night sky so clear, or the stars so brilliant. He felt a swell of pride, as though he had laid it all out himself especially for her benefit. 'That's the Andromeda Galaxy, our nearest neighbour. The way you're seeing it now is the way it looked two and a half million years ago. That's how long it takes light from there to get to here.'

'It's like seeing eternity.' Her voice was barely more than a whisper pressing against the luminous darkness.

He slid his arms around her waist, and moved still closer. 'It's on a collision course with our Milky Way.'

He felt her ribcage expand against him as her sense of wonder spread upward with her breath and found release in her voice. 'Imagine the fireworks.'

'Yeah, imagine.' They both looked up with a start as the sky effervesced in a cascade of meteors. Then she turned in his arms and whispered against his ear. 'You betrayed me, Ellis. Everyone knows about the Executive Sex Clause, and it's all your fault. I can't stay with you. I can't stay with a man I can't trust.'

'No Dee, I didn't betray you! I wouldn't. I promise I wouldn't ...'

But she wasn't listening. She stepped out of his arms, shaking her head. He reached for her, but she pulled away. Then she turned and walked into the woods at the edge of the field.

He stood for a stunned second and watched her, then he called after her. 'Dee, wait. Don't go. I don't want to lose you. I can't lose you.' And suddenly he was running after her through dense woodland hung with moss, ferns slapping at his legs, roots threatening to send him sprawling. He ran. But she was always just ahead of him, just out of his reach. 'Dee, I can't lose you. Please stay. Please let me explain.' But she grew farther and farther away with each step, with each desperate breath, until he caught one last glimpse of her through the trees, and she was gone. All around him the forest was silent, unmoving, too dark for the night sky to penetrate the canopy. 'Dee!'

He woke with a start, drenched in sweat, gasping for air that was close and humid, thick with the smell of humans in a small space. It took him a second to recall where he was. The tent was tight and hot and next to him the two other men still slept, oblivious to his distress. One of them was Harris Walker. God, he hoped Walker hadn't heard him cry out, because it was Dee's name he called. And if any of the other details of the dream bled through to the waking world – well, he'd rather it not be Harris Walker who caught the gory details. He fumbled for the flashlight at the side of his sleeping bag, then he slipped out from under the mosquito netting and quietly unzipped the tent. He had to have some air. He had to think. He had to feel what was real again.

Outside the air was no less thick, but it was less fetid. It smelled of fecund earth and damp heat. Not wanting to use the flashlight unless he had to, he felt his way to a tree at the left of their tent and leaned up against it, feeling the hard ripple of the thick bark pressing through his T-shirt. He couldn't see the stars for the canopy, just like in his dream. The oppressive darkness brought back the ache beneath his sternum that he'd felt in his dream, that he'd felt when he thought he'd lost Dee. Suddenly he was desperate to call her, but the place they were tonight was in the deepest part of the Valderi forest. There would be no contact from where they were.

It was just a dream, he told himself. He was tired and it had been an exhausting forced march to get here. He wasn't at his best. When he'd left, things had been good between them. She had welcomed him to her bed. She had wanted to come with him, and God, he'd wanted her to. But it was an unnecessary risk and he would never put her in harm's way. Besides, she was the only one who could close the deal with Scribal and Trouvères. And it was hers to close. She deserved all the credit. He could imagine her now in New York, in the big bed in the hotel room all alone. Was she missing him? He looked at his watch. It was just about time for her to get up and start her day. He hoped she hadn't stayed up too late working. He hoped she had rested. If he'd been there he'd have made sure she did – after they'd made love, of course. His cock stirred in his shorts at the thought of being in her space, in her bed, in her body.

How could he miss her so badly? They'd only been away from each other three days. But at the moment every part of him ached for her. It was crazy. She was his executive assistant, he reminded himself. No doubt she would have the common sense to keep her personal life from interfering with work. No doubt she would be level-headed enough to remember the Executive Sex Clause was a part of their working relationship. Neither of them needed, nor had time for, the complications of anything else, and what they had now worked so well for both of them.

He tried not to think of Garrett knowing about the Executive Sex Clause, and even more distressing, the fact that now Stacie knew, or at least strongly suspected. Dear God, surely they wouldn't do anything to sabotage what he had with Dee. Surely it would all be all right, since they both liked her, since they both were pleased with his choice of her. He mentally kicked himself. It wasn't like he was bringing his girlfriend home to meet the family, the embarrassing family, but it sure as hell felt that way. He wiped sweat from his forehead and swatted away an insect which buzzed around his face in the darkness. Sometimes he had strange dreams when he was tired. He hadn't had the really bad ones since that first year after Caltech. But even they hadn't disturbed him like this one did.

'You all right, Thorne?'

Ellis could barely make out the shape of the man in the inky black of the night, but he recognised Harris Walker's voice coming from the dark shadow now standing beside him.

'Heard you thrashing about. You OK?'

Ellis gritted his teeth. 'Fine. I'm fine. Just a dream. Probably the strange place and not enough sleep.'

Harris came to his side. 'And missing Dee. You called her name.'

'Probably dreaming about work,' Ellis lied, and did his best to sound matter-of-fact. 'I do that a lot.'

'Who doesn't?' Harris said. 'I had nightmares all the time when I was practising law. Not so much any more, now I'm not. But I never called out my legal assistant's name and told her I couldn't lose her.'

Ellis felt the muscles in his shoulders knot. 'I told you it was just a dream.' He shifted against the tree, sensing the presence of the man rather than seeing him, and knowing full well that even though Walker couldn't see any better than he could, he was still studying him.

'I talked to Dee before we left,' Harris said. 'She said the two of you were good.'

Ellis didn't say anything. He wanted to tell him it was none of his fucking business, but, at the same time, he was pleased that Dee had such a loyal friend. If the shoe were on the other foot, Ellis might have already resorted to violence if he'd been Dee's best friend and she had returned home from the stupid comedy of errors she'd had to deal with at his house.

Harris continued, 'You didn't ask for my opinion, but as long as I'm Dee's best friend and you're both playing at this stupid Sex Clause thing, you get it anyway. You're both in over your heads. The sooner you figure it out, the sooner you face what's really going on, the less painful it'll be when the shit hits the fan. And you can't possibly think that it won't happen when you're playing with the kind of fire you two are playing with.'

Ellis bristled and pressed up away from the tree, nearly bashing heads with Harris. 'You're not the only one who want what's best for Dee, Walker.'

'Of course I'm not. I'm just the only one with a clear head at the moment,' he said. Silence fell between the two of them, and the night sounds of a strange place flooded around them, feeling close and ominous. At last Harris heaved a sigh. 'I'm betting if you make it right with Dee, Thorne, the dreams will stop.' Then he turned and went back into the tent, leaving Ellis alone with his thoughts.

Chapter Thirty-four

TROUVÈRES HAD NO OFFICES in New York, so the planning for
the first of the joint project between Trouvères and Scribal was
done at the Scribal building. Marston had been doing his best
to arrange a trip to Atlanta before Jason headed back to Paris so
he and Dee could see the plant that was to be fitted with
Trouvères technology. So far, the trip had been cancelled three
times due to interruptions on all fronts, including heavy rains
that had caused flooding of the roads into the plant. In the
meantime there was plenty to do, and Dee was happy to
immerse herself in the work and the scheduling of future
projects. She was finally beginning to understand why Beverly
had liked Marston. In spite of his cantankerous ways, the man
was forward-thinking and enthusiastic about the new
technology and about what it would mean for the future of the
industry.

There were business dinners almost every night. When there
weren't, Dee had made excuses to avoid Jason's constant offers
of attention. He had offered to take an afternoon off and show
her around New York City. He had asked her to join him for
dinner. He had offered to see her back to her hotel when one of
the dinners with the Scribal contingent had run long. With each
new offer, Dee became more convinced Ellis might be right
after all.

In all honesty, there had been a few fantasies about Jason
when she was headhunting him for Trouvères, but he was
married, and he was her client, so they had never been more
than that. And now there was little room for thoughts of any
man who wasn't Ellison Thorne. But the week would be over
soon, and she'd be back in Portland and so would Ellis. At the

moment, when she had time for fantasies, they all pretty much headed in that direction.

Marston had just left for a charity dinner, and Dee was packing up for the evening, hoping to order room service and have a nice long bath before she settled in to write her report on the week's negotiations. She wished the trip to the paper mill had happened. She really wanted to see for herself what would be taking place, but there was no help for it. The Scribal building was nearly empty; she could hear the cleaners vacuuming a conference room down the hall. Jason knocked on the door of the little office Dee had sequestered. 'You're gonna kill me,' he said, offering a sheepish smile.

'Why would I do that, Jason?' she asked, checking her BlackBerry before she shoved it into her bag.

'Because I left the flash drive with the template for the training manuals on the table in my apartment. I'm sorry, Dee, I took it out of the bag to get to the adapter plug and forgot to put it back.' Though Trouvères didn't have an office in New York, Jason maintained a flat there after the move to Paris, since he made frequent trips back.

He looked down at his watch. 'I know you have an early flight tomorrow. Look, the apartment's not far from your hotel. Why don't we share a taxi there? I'll get you the flash drive, then you can go on. What do you think?'

There wasn't much choice now, she thought. She packed the last of her belongings and shut the door behind her, falling into step next to him.

'I finished looking over those projections a few minutes ago,' he said when they stepped into the elevator. 'They sound too good to be true.'

'I know, but actually, they're rather modest.' She hefted her bag onto her shoulder. 'That's the beauty of this project. It takes all three of our companies to do what none of us could manage on our own. And one of the results will be amazing profits.'

He offered her an amused smile. 'I see Thorne has instilled in you his philosophy for win-win deals.'

'That philosophy's what attracted me to the company in the

first place.'

His smile became suggestive. 'You sure it was the philosophy and not the company's dashing CEO?'

She bristled slightly at the remark, but Jason didn't notice. 'Dashing men are easy to come by,' she replied. 'Good philosophies aren't.' Her BlackBerry rang into the quiet elevator and they both jumped. 'It's Ellis,' she said. She wished like hell she was alone. She hadn't heard from him in three days. The butterflies in her stomach felt like a raging stampede.

She moved as far away from Jason as she could get and spoke softly. 'You all right? How's it going?'

'I'm fine Dee. I can't talk,' he said. 'I knew you'd want to know we just closed the deal. Harris got lots of pictures and as soon as I'm at a place where I can, I'll call and tell you all about it.' His voice was suddenly soft, warm. 'You OK?

'Better now,' she said, hoping Jason didn't notice the flush in her cheeks, the acceleration of her pulse.

'Good. I'm looking forward to our debriefing. I think we'll have lots to celebrate. See you soon, Dee.'

It took her a second to realise Jason was staring at her. 'Everything all right?' he asked.

'Fine. Yes, fine. Things are coming along in Spain.' She shoved her BlackBerry back into her bag just as the elevator opened on to the ground floor.

Jason hailed a taxi in front of the building and they settled in for the ride. For a minute they rode in less than comfortable silence, then Dee spoke. 'Marston thinks the trip to Atlanta may happen after all. If so, I'll know before my flight leaves in the morning. He'll have his secretary take care of it. Will you be able to come?'

'Sadly not this time,' he said. 'The timing is bad. But I'll be back as soon as I can and then I'll fly straight to Atlanta. Tomorrow, it's back to Paris for me.'

'You must be anxious to get home to your family,' Dee said.

He shifted awkwardly next to her and adjusted his safety belt. 'I guess you haven't heard the news.'

'News?'

'I'm surprised Yvette didn't tell you, actually. I figured for sure Thorne would. Dee, I'm separated. The divorce is final in three weeks.'

She caught her breath, feeling more uncomfortable at being alone with him in the taxi. 'I'm really sorry, Jason. I didn't know.'

He gave her hand an unsolicited squeeze. 'Don't be. I'm not. But I should have let you know the situation first hand.' He paused, as though he weren't sure where to begin. 'Things have been rough between Lydia and me for a long time, and now that the girls will both be in college this fall, it felt like the right time to do something about it. That, and the fact neither Lydia nor the girls wanted to live in France.' He set his jaw and looked away from her. 'Though they don't seem to mind the nice increase in salary working for Trouvères means.'

'Jason.' She extricated her hand. 'You don't have to tell me any of this.'

'No, really, it's all right. Honestly, I want you to know.' He spoke without looking at her. 'I was living in a flat in Paris and commuting back to New York. Finally, we both decided it was enough. With me in Paris and Lydia in New York, we were already separated. When we started talking about a divorce, the position at Trouvères was still new and demanded my full attention. I'm only just now beginning to feel like I might actually be in control and have a little time for a personal life.'

Dee felt her insides tense. This was the part she was pretty sure she didn't want to talk about. Not now, anyway, not after so much had changed.

He looked up at her. 'Dee, you were always there at the back of my mind, and I always wondered what might have happened if I'd been free.' He touched her hand tentatively, then drew back, fidgeting with the collar of his shirt. 'Anyway, when you called me the first time from Pneuma Inc., I felt like someone had turned the lights back on.' He heaved a sigh, and stroked her fingers cautiously. 'Now that the divorce is almost final, now that we see a fair amount of each other anyway – well, I'm hopeful.'

She pulled her hand away, feeling a wave of panic rising in the pit of her stomach. Ellis's warnings flashed in her mind, the ones she'd always brushed aside. 'That was almost two years ago, Jason, and life's gone on since then. There's so little spare time for me right now that I can't really imagine having time for –'

Before she could say anything else, he leaned across the seat and kissed her, one hand at the nape of her neck, the other snaking in at the middle of her back. It wasn't a lingering kiss, but there was no doubt as to its intent. When he pulled away, he held her in a tight gaze, his warm breath brushing her ear. 'Now that we're free to pursue it, Dee, don't you want to find out?' The man's charm would have won her over in a heartbeat if Ellis hadn't already stormed the castle and taken over every bit of space within.

Before she had time to do more than catch her breath, the taxi arrived at his flat. They took the lift in silence to the sixth floor, and when he unlocked the door and ushered her inside, he turned to face her. 'Stay for a drink, Dee.' He held her gaze. 'Just one, and we can talk.' He ran a hand through his dark hair, and offered her a flustered smile. 'Best we talk, don't you think? We both make our living negotiating good deals, and I ... Well, I consider you a friend as well as a colleague. Dee, just let me say what I need to say.' His smile became boyish and charming. 'Just one drink, then you can go back to your hotel.'

When she nodded her consent, he opened a bottle of wine and went in search of glasses. While she waited, she looked out the window onto the city below, feeling strangely like a teenager breaking curfew. Since Ellis had come into the picture, she had forgotten all about her passing attraction to Jason. Ellis wasn't really in the picture, she reminded herself again. Sex was only a part of her job. But it didn't feel that way. At least, not for her it didn't. She didn't know what he felt, and what did feelings have to do with it anyway? It was the Executive Sex Clause. It was their secret weapon. Had he ever given her any indication it was more than that? Hadn't he said right up front they were free to see other people?

Maybe they should see other people. Maybe it would be better to mix things up a bit, to back off a bit so every little thing that happened didn't make her feel like a giddy teenager stuck somewhere between ecstasy and despair. Christ, it had already been such a rollercoaster ride. And maybe what Jason was actually doing was offering her a way to pull back just a little bit, just enough for her own self-preservation.

And Jason was a good man, an interesting man, a man any woman would be happy to be with. It wasn't like she was spoiled for choice, she reminded herself. A man who was a workaholic was a catch, a good provider. A woman who was a workaholic, on the other hand, was someone to be avoided at all cost. No time to cook, no time to clean, no time to pop out the babies and sit in front of the television and unwind in the evenings. The thought made her feel a little queasy.

'Dee, you are amazing.'

She turned to find Jason looking at her from the kitchen doorway. 'I just want to stand here and take you in. You have no idea how long I've dreamed about having you with me.'

He sat the glasses on the table and came to her side, slipping his arms around her. Then he stepped back and ran his fingers down the lapel of her jacket. 'Let's lose this. No need to look so business-like. You're not on Pneuma Inc. time now.'

He helped her out of her jacket, taking time for his eyes to admire the woman beneath, and she reminded herself that he was right. She wasn't on Pneuma Inc. time. Being here with him was OK. Maybe she should make an effort to be a little more like Kendra. Maybe this was the way to remind herself that sex with Ellis, no matter how amazing, was just a part of her job. In spite of her efforts to convince herself, she would have bolted if Jason hadn't engaged her mouth again. This time the kiss was neither quick nor ambiguous, with the insinuating dart and press of his tongue.

She felt the rush of his breath as he pulled her closer, felt the press of his groin as he shifted against her. The shape of him beneath the trousers became more evident with each shifting of his body. His touch felt awkward compared to Ellis's, and somehow his mouth didn't fit hers quite as well.

Mentally she reprimanded herself for making comparisons, trying to relax into the kiss. Jason's scent was different, uncomfortable at the back of her throat, like being in someone's house without permission.

He tightened his embrace and his mouth became more insistent, making it hard for her to breathe. The smell, the feel, the taste; nothing was right about them together, and the room seemed to be getting tighter around her by the second.

Fighting panic, she pushed him away, opening a space between them, amazed and slightly frightened by how strong he was. He released her and stepped back, panting. 'What is it, Dee? What's wrong?'

'This is just too fast, Jason, I can't –'

The phone rang. He let it ring and spoke over it. 'I'm sorry, Dee.' He caught his breath. 'I know I said we'd just talk. I'm sorry I got carried away and –'

The answering machine interrupted and, in the trained reflex to technology, they both paused to listen.

'Jason, are you there? Pick up … It's Lydia …'

He cursed softly and tugged at his tie.

The message continued. 'Annette's down at the police station. We need to go get her. She and some of her friends have been drinking and … Damn it, Jason, you're never here when we need you –'

His face reddened, and he jerked the receiver from its cradle, trying to breathe normally. 'I'm here, Lydia. What happened?'

Dee took advantage of the time to slip back into her jacket and gather her things. When she finished, he had hung up the phone. 'I'm sorry, Dee, it's my youngest. I don't think it's anything serious, just being 18, but Lydia doesn't deal with this sort of thing very well, and I need to go. I'll drop by your hotel room when I'm finished.' He tried to kiss her, but she pulled away.

'No, Jason, don't.'

'Dee?'

'You asked me if I wanted to find out if there could be something between us and, well, I just found out.'

'Dee, these things happen. It's just a part of being a parent. Don't worry about it. We can get through it.' He reached for her again, but she stepped back.

'I don't want to get through it, Jason. I have enough baggage of my own. I don't need what you bring along from a broken marriage and two kids. I'm sorry. It's not something I can deal with at the moment. And anyway, it's not just that. It's everything. Pneuma Inc. makes huge demands on my time right now, and I'm happy to give it, but that doesn't leave me much to spare. I like you, Jason, I respect you, but I don't want to run the risk of more.'

'Dee, sometimes you have to throw caution to the wind and go for it.'

'That's true, but right now, I'm not willing to do that.'

As she left with the flash drive tucked safely in her bag, she couldn't keep from feeling like she'd just had a very narrow escape, and the urge to be home with Ellis was nearly overwhelming.

Inside the taxi, she was still struggling to get her head round what had just happened when her BlackBerry rang.

Dee, Al here.'

She tried to hide her disappointment She really could use a call from Ellis about now.

'You still at Jason's place? He said he was inviting you over for a drink. Did Ellis get hold of you? I told him you were there.'

Her stomach somersaulted and she nearly dropped the phone. 'No. What's going on?'

'Oh nothing, really. I just called to see how things had gone in Spain. He said he couldn't talk, was about to board a plane home, but gave me the two thumbs up. The man's got balls the size of boulders, I'll give him that. He didn't sound very happy, though. Just jetlagged, I reckon.'

Dee's clench on the phone was nearly painful.

Marston chuckled. 'I hate international travel these days. Not enough comforts in the world to make jetlag easy at my age. Never mind that. Just wanted to let you know my driver'll pick you up in the morning at seven and take you to the jet. I'll meet you there and shuttle you on down to my neck of the woods to see the plant. You up for it, Ms Henning?' He always called her Ms Henning when he was joking or being chivalrous, which, much to her surprise, he quite often was.

'I'll be ready'

When she hung up there was a text from Ellis.

Al says you were with Daniels. We'll talk in Portland.

That was it. In spite of her efforts not to read anything into it, she felt unsettled and wished desperately she could hear his voice. But that would have to wait. She wouldn't be home until Sunday, and no doubt he was in the air by now.

Chapter Thirty-five

'DO YOU THINK ELLIS really isn't here or do you think he's avoiding us?'

'His secretary says he's away in Spain, but he's supposed to be home tomorrow sometime.'

'For fuck sake, Garrett, you're his brother, and you're even staying at his house. How can you not know if he's out of the country?'

Garrett? Garrett Thorne? Tally was suddenly at full attention. The booth she sat in was separated from the couple talking by only a thin trellis. She couldn't believe her luck. If it hadn't been covered with climbing foliage of some sort, the trellis would have reminded her of the confessional she used to go to every Friday night when she was a child. There she'd mumbled all of her sins across the wooden screen into the listening ears of the bored priest. She quietly scooted closer to the trellis and held her breath. Who knew, a confessional might turn out to be exactly what it was.

Through the trellis she could see Thorne handing a coffee to a woman she couldn't get a good view of. Tally was stunned at how much he resembled his older brother. He spoke. 'Well, he hasn't been too interested in talking to me since Friday night's disaster with Dee, has he?'

The woman giggled wickedly. 'I actually thought he was going to hit you. In fact, I thought Dee was going to hit both of you.'

'That's not funny, Stacie. Ellis and I were just starting to get along again. Up until New York, every time I was in the same state with him, he remembered something he has to do in some third-world country.'

Stacie? Where had Tally heard that name before?

'There, you see? Massive improvement. The man's only gone to Spain this time.'

'I was trying to be helpful,' Garrett said. 'I was trying to make sure my brother and Dee had a good weekend.'

The laugh again. 'I think egging him on about the Executive Sex Clause wasn't the best way forward if you were trying to be helpful. And telling Dee you knew about it didn't win you her undying love either.'

The Executive Sex Clause? Tally sipped absently at her champagne. Wait a minute, she thought. Could it be? ESC? The Executive Sex Clause. Had to be. Still, what the hell was it?

Tally frantically pulled up the ESC files on her lap top.

Hire her, Ellis, then implement the ESC and you'll have the best of both worlds.

That's what Beverly's email said. She wanted Ellis to implement the Executive Sex Clause. But how could a sex clause be a secret weapon?

Tally racked her brain. Almost as an afterthought, she pulled out her iPhone, set it to audio record and carefully placed it as near to the partition separating the tables as possible. This was too good to miss.

Garrett drummed his fingers on the table. 'I can cope with her being pissed off at me. That I wouldn't mind so much if she hadn't decided to take it out on Ellis.'

'Well, what the fuck did you think she'd do?' Stacie retorted. 'Did you think she'd be thrilled that his kid brother knows?'

Garrett growled. 'I don't think she was overly happy to find Ellis's ex following him down the hall all wrapped up snug-like in his bath robe either, was she?'

Tally's pulse accelerated. Stacie was Ellis's ex? And she'd been caught in his bath robe? It just kept getting better and better.

'Stop changing the subject, Garrett. My presence could have been easily explained away if you hadn't made such an ass of yourself. What about Dee? Is she in?'

'She's in New York,' Garrett said. 'No chance of talking to her either.'

'Wish I'd known that,' Stacie said. 'I might have caught her before I flew back to Portland.'

'I'd at least feel better if I knew the two of them had talked it through and made up,' Garrett said.

'Me too,' Stacie agreed 'But I wouldn't count on it. She was furious, and rightly so. What woman wants her work denigrated by the fact that she's sleeping with the boss? Especially not when she's as brilliant as Dee.'

Jesus. Tally could hardly believe it. Dee was sleeping with Ellis? She'd have thought Ms MBA too much of a tight-assed stickler to the rules for that.

'I wasn't denigrating her work, Stacie. I know she's brilliant or Ellis wouldn't have hired her. I was just trying to prove my point that even two people as focused on work as she and Ellis are can't fight their hearts.'

'Well announcing you know that sex is a part of her job probably wasn't the best way to go about proving that point, Garrett.'

'Sh!' Garrett hissed. 'Why don't you just broadcast it to everyone?'

Suddenly Tally couldn't breathe. She felt like the sun had just come out, and her luck was changing right before her eyes. She held her breath and listened carefully, as the two lowered their voices.

'Oh for heaven sake, Garrett, we're the only ones in here,' Stacie said. Then she leaned across the table 'So, do you think it worked? Do you think sex on demand has improved their productivity?'

'With those two, it's hard to tell,' Garrett said. 'And Ellis sure as hell isn't going to put it in the monthly progress report, is he? Still, I can't think they'd have implemented it if they didn't think it would work. I know Beverly thought it would, but you know how Beverly was. I just doubt they expected the side-effects from the chemistry between the two of them.'

So the Executive Sex Clause was really just Ellis paying Dee to have sex with him. That was it? That was the secret strategy? Quickly, with trembling fingers, Tally scrolled back through the email exchanges between Ellis and Beverly before Beverly had gone to Brazil, and read the final email.

Dee's exactly what you need on all counts. I know you think she lacks experience, but trust me, with the right training, given half a chance, she'll be brilliant. Hire her, Ellis. Implement the ESC. Trust me; it's the perfect strategy, a secret weapon that could make Pneuma Inc. even more successful than it already is. And if anyone could do it, you could. Do this for me and I can retire and enjoy my dotage.

Beverly

So Dee Henning got the executive assistant position because she was willing to spread her legs. Tally knew there had to be some reason Ellis chose the bitch over her. At last the truth was out, and Thorne's secret weapon was just about to become her secret weapon.

'What's going on?'

Tally jumped at the sound of Jamison's voice.

'I've had the limo circling the block for ten minutes, and I find you here in the bar drinking –'

She placed a finger to her lips and silently shushed him. But it was too late; the couple across the trellis suddenly began to speak in whispers.

'Don't shush me, Tally. I've not had a good day and you keeping me waiting's done nothing to make it better. Now come on. Let's go.'

She stuffed her laptop into the bag, and grabbed up her purse and her iPhone as he hauled her out of the booth and escorted her out the door.

Garrett craned his neck at the couple just leaving. The guy had practically manhandled the woman from the booth next to theirs. They hadn't even known she'd been there. 'That's Terrance Jamison, isn't it?' he said, nodding after the couple.

Stacie followed his gaze. 'Sure looks like it to me. He's got a lot of nerve, showing his face here in Pneuma territory.'

Garrett nodded his agreement. 'He didn't look too happy either. And it looked like that Tally chick from accounting with him. I wouldn't want to be her about now. I don't think he's planning to wine her and dine her if that glare is any indication.'

'Bastard,' Stacie said watching as the two cleared the door and disappeared into the parking lot.

Once outside, Jamison hurried Tally into the waiting limo and the driver took off. Tally didn't wait for him to ask what was going on, and she sure as hell didn't want to endure his bad mood.

'I have the secret weapon,' she said. 'The ESC? I know what it is, and it's just about to become our secret weapon too.'

Jamison handed her a glass of champagne and sat back to listen while she pulled up the ESC emails between Ellis and Beverly and told him about her unexpected encounter with Ellis's brother and his ex. The longer she talked, the more Jamison smiled.

Chapter Thirty-six

WHEN DEE ARRIVED AT PDX, the last rays of sun were sinking to the west of the city. Instead of the Pneuma Inc. limo she was expecting, Ellis was waiting for her in the Jeep. She knew something was wrong when his greeting was barely more than a grunt. Without a word, he took her bag and put it in the back. She buckled into the passenger seat. In an ideal world, she would have shrugged off his mood and dozed until he was ready to talk about it. But this wasn't an ideal world. It felt like a slap in the face after she had been so delighted to see him, after she had been looking forward to their reunion ever since he left. This was not what she was hoping for. The tiredness she felt dissipated with the clenching of her stomach and the tightening of her shoulders as she racked her brain, trying to think what she might have done to upset him.

When it was clear he wasn't going to break the ice, she braced herself and smiled, acting as though she hadn't noticed his mood. 'I want to hear all about Valderia.'

He offered an enormous shrug, as if he couldn't be bothered to reply. The muscles in her shoulders felt like they'd snap from the tension. 'Jamison won't be tempting anyone else with Valderian virgin timber,' he said, not taking his eyes off the road.

'Good. That's good. Then everything went according to plan?'

'According to plan,' came his clipped reply. It was then that she realised they were heading out along the Columbia River Gorge at break-neck speed.

Ellis turned off I-84, away from the river, and took a series of steep roads upward into the wooded hills. At last, he exited onto a winding gravel road.

'Where are we going?' she asked, and the tension went up another notch.

'Scenic route,' he answered. 'Hang on. It's not for the faint of heart.'

She shot him a withering glance, which was swallowed up in the growing dusk. 'Do you see any faint of heart in this vehicle? Now, you want to tell me what the hell's going on?'

He glanced at her, then downshifted as he turned onto a dirt road that was barely more than a trail. It rose steeply until it twisted into a series of sharp hairpin turns. It was deeply rutted and strewn with rocks, an obstacle course that rattled teeth and bruised anything that wasn't buckled to the seat.

'Did you know about Daniels's divorce?'

'What? I just found out Friday night. Why?'

'And as soon as you found out you went running to his apartment.'

'What?' Dee grabbed for the edge of the seat and stiff-legged the floorboard to brace against the bone-jarring ride. 'What the hell's that supposed to mean? I went to his apartment to get the flash drive he forgot to bring to Scribal.' She slammed the palm of her hand against the dashboard just as Ellis hit a large rut and the Jeep rocked dangerously.

'The Sex Clause doesn't include Jason Daniels, Dee.'

For a heartbeat, everything stopped. For an instant, his words left her speechless. They felt like a gut-punch and hurt a hell of a lot more. Then anger filled the gap and the world swung back into real time. 'Fuck you, Ellis! I work for you. I don't have to take abuse from you. Let me out. Right now! Let me out!' She undid her seatbelt just as they hit another deep rut that nearly sent her flying out of the Jeep.

'What the hell are you doing?' Ellis grabbed her arm and slammed on the brakes. Then he turned off the engine with her slapping and shoving at him.

'Let go of me, Ellis, goddamn it! How dare you, how fucking dare you?' She shoved open the door and was halfway out before he could scramble over the gear shift and haul her bodily back in, kicking and struggling. She pushed him hard, and he held tight. But when she jerked back against him, he overcompensated and unbalanced both of them, catapulting them out the open door onto the ground beside the Jeep with a hard, breathless thud. Dee was still punching and kicking like a wild woman. 'How could you even think that of me? How could you even think it?'

'Dee, I'm sorry.' He took a knee to the upper inside of one thigh, dangerously close to his cock, before he finally rolled with her and subdued dangerous arms and legs beneath the weight of his body. 'Christ, Dee,' he gasped. 'This is not the way I planned our reunion to be.'

'Is that what you think of me, that because I fuck you, I'll fuck anybody? You might as well have called me a whore, goddamn it.' She bucked beneath him, nearly unseating him in her rage, but he held her.

'Dee I didn't mean it, I would never call you … I fucked up. I'm sorry. I was … I was jealous, OK. I was so damned jealous. I know how badly he wants you, and I couldn't stand the thought that you might want him back.'

For a brittle moment, he sat astraddle her, both of them freeze-framed against the gloom, both struggling to catch their breath.

'I didn't fuck Jason,' she breathed. 'How the hell could I fuck Jason when I couldn't get you out of my head?' Suddenly, she was ripping at his fly like it was on fire, and he was hard enough that he was certain he could have burst the zipper without her help. He caught his breath at the none-too-gentle raking of her nails along the sides of his hips as she yanked at his boxers and jeans. She slapped his hands away from his efforts at her clothes. Then she wriggled and shifted until she'd shoved her skirt up and tore the crotch of her panties aside. 'I fuck you, Ellis. You and nobody else. Surely you can't be too stupid to figure that out.'

And Jesus, it was like she'd given his life back. The outrageous relief of it translated into raw animal need. He pushed and shoved his way inside her. Even in her rage she was slick; she yielded to him grudgingly, sheathing him in a grip that felt tighter than his own skin. He was furious at himself that he'd driven her to this, yet she was stunning in her anger. He didn't have much time to contemplate before she rolled on top of him, ripped open his shirt, and bit him hard just above his left nipple. And fuck, it nearly made him come. When she bit him again on the soft pulse point of his neck, his brain engaged enough for him to realise that this was shaping up to be a very dangerous fuck.

He caught the driving force of her hips pressing him back against the ground, forcing his tender ass cheeks into an abrasive mix of grass and pebbles at the edge of the road, forcing the oxygen from his lungs in a startled gasp, which she swallowed back hungrily in a hard kiss. She savaged his mouth, the tension in her body tightening her like a fist around his cock, making him sure he would either die or come, or maybe both. He fought to focus on the fire of her anger, anger which he fully deserved, even wanted; anger so thoroughly infused with passion that it sizzled between them like heat lightning. Dee Henning making him pay, Dee Henning devouring him in her rage, Dee Henning inflicting punishment this exquisite was well worth dying for.

'What I've given to you, do you really think I'd give to anyone else? The Sex Clause puts my career on the line. It's bad enough that it's not just between you and me. And then there's your fiancée back in the picture.'

'Ex-fiancée.' He cried out as she rode him until bones jarred and joints wrenched. 'And she's not back in the picture.'

'I didn't sign on for a part in a damned soap opera, Ellis! And I didn't sign on to be abused.' He was certain if she were any closer, she'd be inside his pelvic girdle. 'If you ever, ever pull that stunt again, I'm gone. Do you understand? Gone!'

'Dee.' He choked the words out from under another fierce, driving thrust. 'I was jealous. I was stupid. I'm sorry …Oh my God!' He was sure by now there must be gravel embedded in his ass, but it didn't matter; he couldn't get enough and he thrust up into her hard.

'Sorry? You're sorry?' She gripped his shoulders hard enough to bruise, and her whole anatomy clenched. He held his breath – what little he had left to hold. 'People will nudge you in the hall and pat you on the back for coming up with the Sex Clause.'

'Dee –' That was as far as he got before her tongue lapped up the rest of his words and emptied his head of all rational thought with another kiss that was delectably near fatal.

Then she pulled away, fists clenching tight at the open lapels of his shirt, her breath coming fast and furious. 'But me, they'll say I'm a slut.' Her words were humid against his mouth. She bit his lip, then tongued his hard palate, making him squirm in the vice of her anger. 'All the hours of sweat and research and hard work when I wasn't fucking you.' She thrust again, driving the breath from his lungs. 'The hours that are already making Pneuma Inc. richer – they won't give a second thought to.' She fought back a sob. 'All they'll say is I fucked the boss and my career's over.'

'Dee, Dee! That's not going to happen.' He pulled her down to him and held her close, taking back as much control as physical strength would allow. For a second, he caught his breath and found himself moved by the glisten of tears on her cheeks.

'I'm sorry about Garrett and Stacie, and I'm really sorry I've ruined our reunion by being such an asshole, but you have to believe me, I would never betray you, Dee, and no one could ever doubt your reputation.' He took her face in his hands, and forced her to meet his gaze. 'And if I'm jealous of you with Daniels, how can you really blame me for that? No one knows better than I do why he wants you so badly. And I don't want him to have that, Dee. I don't want him to have what you give to me. I want it. I want you all to myself.'

This time he took *her* mouth and she let him. It wasn't a gentle kiss. There was too much passion between them for gentleness, but he felt her anger dissipate, and her body softened and conformed to the contours of his own as she moved, riding the tenuous edge between arousal and release. The next time she stiffened it was in orgasm, tightening and rocking against him until the friction and the tension sent him over the edge and he came too.

When they could breathe again, they found a more comfortable place not far off the rutted jeep trail, where the moss was soft and their view of the night sky was unobscured. There, they sat side by side. Ellis slipped his arm around her, and pulled her down onto the moss, cradling her head in the crook of his shoulder. 'I was planning to invite *you* home to watch the Perseids with me when Stacie so rudely interrupted us, but we don't need meteors to enjoy the view.' He kissed the top of her ear and pulled her closer. 'In fact, I'd say the view is breathtaking.'

For a long time, they watched the sky, silently clinging to each other with the smell of evergreens and wild flowers adding a rich background to the scent of pheromones and sex. Eventually, she became aware of his gaze. 'Are you OK?' he asked.

She nestled in closer. 'I'm better than I was.'

'That's a start, at least.' He slid an arm down to stroke her hip. 'Garrett told you about Stacie, about the three of us?'

'He told me, yes. And about Jamison.'

'Everything?'

'Pretty much.' She rose on one elbow, looked down into his eyes. 'Are you all right?'

His breath shuddered in a deep groan and he covered his face with his forearm. 'All the things I didn't want you to know about me, all the tender spots, all the ugly bits.'

'Doesn't matter,' she said. 'I like you anyway.'

He threw his arm aside with a burst of laughter, and pulled her on top of him. 'You have no idea how glad I am to hear that.'

Resting against the warmth of his chest, she studied him in the darkness.

'What is it, Dee?' He eased a hand up under her shirt to stroke the small of her back. 'What's on your mind?'

'I can't keep from wondering, Ellis, after everything that's happened, all you've been through because of the two of them, why are you seeing Stacie again?'

He closed his eyes. For a long time he was silent, and she

267

wondered if maybe she shouldn't have asked. But at last she felt his chest expand against her in a deep sigh, and he spoke.

'After everything that's happened between Garrett and Stacie and me, the bond runs pretty deep. We've known each other for a long time, and in spite of all the pain that's passed between us, there's still some weird sense of loyalty. Whenever Garrett's between relationships, if Stacie's free, they get together.'

'So now you're between relationships, and she's in town.' Dee tried to pull away, not wanting him to sense how difficult this was for her, and not sure she could hide it. But he held her close and lifted her chin, forcing her to look him in the eye.

'I'm not between relationships, Dee. I'm never in a relationship; I haven't been in ages. And before Marston's party, I hadn't spoken to Stacie in three years.'

'So, it was a reunion, then.' She forced her voice to remain calm.

'Nothing happened.'

'Ellis, I'm sorry, this is none of my business.' She tried again to pull away, but he held her.

'Nothing happened, Dee. I meant it when I said things weren't how they looked at Marston's party. I didn't fuck her – not Friday night and not at Marston's. I know how it looked, but I swear to you, I didn't. I didn't want to be with her. I wanted to be with you.' The moist heat of his breath brushed her throat, then her ear. 'To be with you is all I ever seem to want these days and it scares the hell out of me.'

In spite of the late-night nature romp with Ellis, Dee was at Pneuma Inc. by seven. They had a breakfast meeting with Wade in the Dungeon. Harris was already in Wade's boudoir, setting up to show some of his Valderian photos on Wade's big scream. He swept Dee off her feet into a bear hug. 'You got a little sun,' she said, touching his face as he sat her down.

'And you didn't.' he said, kissing her cheek.

'My jungle was concrete and air conditioned,' she said, stealing a glance at the new supply of freckles across Ellis's cheeks from his time in Valderia. They made him look outdoorsy and even more Celtic. She fought back a wave of desire. Those sexy freckles had been pressed up tight between her legs just a few hours ago. The thought made her giddy and weak-kneed.

Against a backdrop of Harris's stunning rainforest scenes, many of which included Ellis looking as relaxed in khakis and hiking boots as he did in Armani, Ellis's debriefing sounded more like an adventure story. The Valderian people would benefit from the technology for new eco-friendly desalination plants to deal with water shortages. Pneuma Inc. would send engineering teams to work with their own engineers in the construction of the plants. In addition, the chance to develop the lucrative eco-tourism industry at someone else's expense had sweetened the government toward Ellis and Pneuma Inc. even further, and at the end of the day, the sale of all of the access territory surrounding Jamison's forest was a done deal, closed, sealed and delivered before Ellis and Harris landed on the tarmac at PDX. By 8.30, Dee had filled Ellis in on the details of the New York trip, and by 9 she settled in to her office to go over her Trouvères presentation one last time.

She was finishing up when Ellis rang and summoned her to his office. She grabbed up her BlackBerry and a note pad, wondering what it was that they hadn't already discussed.

As she entered his office, he gave her a distracted nod from behind his laptop. 'Lock the door, please.'

She did as he asked, feeling a frisson of excitement low in her belly, but when she started to sit down in front of his desk he looked up and shook his head. 'No, not there. Come here, and you won't need those.' He nodded to her BlackBerry and the pad. She sat them on the chair and came around the edge of his desk. Standing beside him looking down at him felt awkward until he took off his glasses and smiled up at her. 'You know, I've been trying to set up a meeting with Blankenship over at Defoe for almost a year, and he can see me this afternoon. I've got to go. I'd hoped to be there for the Trouvères kick-off meeting, but I won't be back in time. I'm sorry.'

'Don't worry. The Trouvères meeting will practically run

itself. We all did our homework in New York, you know. I'll fill you in when you get back.'

'Thanks, Dee. I'd hoped it wouldn't be so hectic, but then it always is, isn't it?' He palmed his laptop shut and pushed it to one side. Then he took her hand and pulled her toward him, rolling his chair back until she stood between his legs with her upper thighs pressed tight against his desk. 'Maybe this weekend you can come out to my place for dinner, and then we'll have some time.'

'I'd like that, Ellis.' She curled her fingers around his.

'Good.' He lifted her hand to his lips and pressed a warm kiss to her knuckles, but his eyes were locked on hers. 'In the meantime, I've been admiring that skirt you've got on. It's my favourite shade of blue.' He scooted closer until she was trapped between the spread of his legs and the desk. He made no attempt to hide the hard-on beneath his trousers; in fact, it was pretty obvious he wanted her to see it. Then he ran his hands up the outside of her thighs, stroking the fabric, easing it up with each caress. 'It's soft too. I thought it might be. I've been wondering what one wears beneath a skirt just that shade of blue.'

'Shall I show you?' She placed the flat of her hand low against her belly, then curled her fingers, scrunching the fabric until the tops of her stockings, caught up in the crème lace of the garter belt, peeked from beneath the skirt. With her hand splayed low across her mons, she scrunched until he sighed his approval at the sight.

'Leopard print,' he breathed. 'Yes, I think that's a perfect match.' He looked up at her, his eyes bright with humour and something more. 'I seem to recall you saying once that you liked animals.' Before she could respond, he pushed in close with his chair, forcing her to sit back on his desk with a little gasp of surprise. 'I don't know about leopards,' he said, shoving her skirt up further until her bottom rested fully on the cool, smooth oak of his desk, 'but I bet your McAlister and O'Kelly mark their territory by rubbing their faces against what belongs to them.' He rubbed his cheek against the inside of her knee in a very feline gesture that ended with the press of his lips and a soft flick of his tongue. 'They probably mark your sofa.' He moved up the inside of her thigh and repeated the gesture, this time with a little nip of his front teeth. 'And maybe your bed too.' He did the same to the other thigh, lingering to rub his cheek and the soft ruff of his hair before he nipped her just above where her stocking was attached to the garter belt. The heat of his breath brushed the crotch of her panties and she squirmed with the sheer tactile pleasure of it. 'And no doubt your leg.' He cupped her bottom and brought her mons against his cheek, nuzzling and sniffing and nipping until the blissed-out sounds coming from her throat weren't unlike those she'd heard McAlister and O'Kelly make. 'Right now, I feel the need to mark my territory, Dee, one animal to another.'

She couldn't hold back the little whimper of pleasure as he kissed and nipped down to the apex of her, where she could feel her clit pushing tight and tetchy against the leopard print. There, he inhaled deeply and began to press and lick and circle with his tongue until she would have bucked and wriggled off the desk if he hadn't held her firmly.

He worked his way lower, lapping and nibbling and kissing through the fabric, tugging at the swell of her labia, no doubt now fully displayed through the combined wet of his saliva and her arousal. He pressed his tongue up from her perineum along the full length of her slit until he found her hole, gripping hungrily. He thrust his tongue into her, pressing the leopard print crotch up into the yield and clench, yield and clench. Then he settled to suckle her still clothed clit, as though he were a nursing infant. And she flooded herself in the pleasure of it, causing him to gasp and suckle all the harder. The room smelled of her damp heat and the scent of Ellison Thorne aroused, the animal in rut, woodland damp and desert heat slicked with his sweat, and his insatiable need. It was the best smell ever; she breathed it into herself in great, heaving gulps, lifting her feet, still in their dove-grey stilettos, onto the arms of his chair and bearing down to press closer to him.

She heard the zip of his fly and the rustle of his trousers. Then he shoved aside the ruined strip of leopard print and pulled her onto the deliciously familiar length of him with a grunt. He held her there, impaled, while he ran a hand over his glistening face. 'Look, Dee, you marked me too.' Then, holding her gaze, he unbuttoned the top several buttons of his shirt and wiped her juices down his sternum.

'You can't go to Blankenship smelling like my cunt,' she said, both embarrassed and moved at the same time.

'I'll take a shower before I go, Dee, but I'll still go wearing your mark. I've worn your mark since the day I saw you. That can't be washed away.' Then he pulled her to him, guided her to wrap her legs around him, and began to thrust, filling her in ways that were tight and frightening and stunning, that had nothing whatsoever to do with his penis inside her.

Chapter Thirty-seven

'WHAT DO YOU WANT?'

Dee assumed Sandra must have stepped away from her desk because the secretary knew Tally Barnes was not welcome anywhere near Dee's office. But here she was, closing the door behind her, marching in as though she owned the place. Clutched between her mauve lacquered fingernails, she held a battered manila envelope. She maintained the pretence of politeness.

'How was New York? I understand it was mostly wrap-up stuff, wasn't it?'

'Mostly wrap-up, yes. Now, what are you here for? Have you come to offer more invaluable ideas on the alliance?' Dee looked down at her watch. 'Because now's a little late. The meeting's about to begin.'

'Don't worry. This won't take long, Dee. I just have something I thought you might like to see before the big kick-off meeting.' Tally sat down in the chair in front of Dee's desk without being invited, and slid the envelope across to her. 'I've been puzzling over this secret weapon, this ESC, ever since Beverly's death. Have you heard of it? Of course you have.'

Though summer was in full bloom outside, the room suddenly felt cold as Dee flipped slowly through the stack of emails, which now wavered in and out of focus in front of her eyes. 'Where did you get these?'

Tally's mouth curved upward in a smirk. 'Well, right here, of course.' She crossed her legs and leaned back in the chair, making herself comfortable. 'I mean, I did have access to Beverly's files when I volunteered to help Ellis out with Scribal. With everything being in such chaos after the big woman's death, it just seemed easier for me to work here – at least I thought so.'

'And Ellis approved?'

'Oh come on, Dee. Ellis was worthless those first few days, surely you know that. I could have practically taken over *his* office and he wouldn't have noticed.' She heaved a sigh. 'But suddenly here you are in the office that should have been mine, and here's me racking my brain trying to figure out why Ellis would hire a headhunter, a woman with no real experience, for such an important position. Well –' she offered Dee a confidential smile. 'Now I know.'

Ignoring the warning prickle up her spine, Dee bluffed. 'Now you know what?'

The sneer on Tally Barnes's face made her perfectly painted mouth, with its halo of dark lip liner, look like an angry gash. She leaned forward in the chair as though she were about to impart a secret. 'Don't get me wrong, I certainly would have taken the man up on the offer if he'd asked me. I mean, he's Ellison Thorne, who wouldn't?'

'All I see is some cryptic messages between Beverly and Ellis. No doubt there are plenty of things in those files only the two of them would understand, Tally. Now if you'll excuse me, I've got a meeting to prepare for.'

'Oh, you have to see this one before you go. This one's my personal favourite.' She shoved a tattered piece of paper at Dee.

Ellis,

Just an addendum to the conversation we had earlier about Dee Henning. Before I head off to Brazil ...

The text wavered before Dee's eyes.

... if you were ever going to implement the ESC, she'd be the one to do it with – that is if you've got the balls.

Dee struggled to breathe deeply, struggled to overcome the fluttering in her ears that felt like the wings of a flock of very large birds.

Dee's exactly what you need on all counts. I know you think she lacks experience ... Hire her, Ellis. Implement the ESC ... If anyone could do it, you could.

Dee fought hard to stay focused, to stay calm. It surely met nothing. After all, Beverly had joked with both her and Ellis about the Sex Clause.

Tally spoke up. 'You'd think I'd have figured it out, as close as you two seem to be, and then when he didn't fire you after missing that teleconference like you did ... But I missed it entirely until a couple of days ago when I had the pleasure of meeting Ellis's ex fiancée and his brother downstairs in the bar. They were both waiting to see Ellis.' She chuckled suggestively. 'For different reasons, I have no doubt. She's lovely, by the way, his ex. I'm sure he was very happy to see her. Anyway, they confirmed what extra services you provide for Ellis and suddenly it was all clear to me why you got the job that should have been mine.'

There it was at last; the source of the betrayal. Dee felt it like a knife to the heart. With Tally's little revelation, everything Dee had worked for in the past few months, everything she had believed about Ellison Thorne and the business he had created, slipped away. It wasn't so much that Tally knew about the Sex Clause, rather the source of Tally's information that was the true betrayal, and after the promises Ellis had made her.

Tally continued, 'Oh, I do understand. Ellis is a busy man, and you are, shall we say, extremely convenient. I mean, that was the point, wasn't it?'

Dee carefully placed the accusing memos back in their envelope, amazed that her hands were still so steady.

'Pity, really. All this time you've been busting your ass when all that was really required of you was to spread your legs. Surely someone else would have picked up the slack. However, I think Human Resources will find all of this very interesting indeed.' Tally stood and reached for the envelope, but Dee stuffed it in the top drawer of her desk and locked it.

'It doesn't matter,' Tally gloated. 'Keep them. I have copies.' She turned to go.

'Oh, by the way, Tally.' Dee grabbed her briefcase and bag. 'You'll be running the kick-off meeting today, which should be no problem since the whole Trouvères/Scribal alliance was your idea anyway.'

Tally spun to face her, and the colour drained from face. 'What are you talking about? Where are you going?'

Dee didn't answer. 'As for the office you seem so fond of, it's all yours. Knock yourself out.' She left, shutting the door behind her with Tally still inside.

In the hall, Sandra was waiting for her. 'Is that Tally Barnes in there? Dee, I'm sorry. I only stepped away to take some files to Lynn. Dee? What's going on?'

'I quit, Sandra. I quit.' She handed the secretary the key to the top drawer of her desk. 'Give this to Ellis when he gets back.'

Sandra fell into step next to her, struggling to keep up as she headed toward the bank of elevators. 'But what about the meeting?'

'Not my problem any more. I'm sure Tally can handle it.'

'What shall I tell Ellis?'

'You can tell him …' The sense of betrayal made her feel like her chest would explode. 'I don't care what you tell him, Sandra, just give him the damned key.'

'Dee?'

'Thanks for all your help. It's been a pleasure working with you.' She left the secretary standing in the hallway in front of the elevators.

Chapter Thirty-eight

WHEN SANDRA CALLED WITH news of Dee's departure, Ellis was heading back from Defoe, congratulating himself on the short but productive meeting and looking forward to telling Dee about it. He'd made up his mind not to wait, but to invite her home this evening. It was supposed to be a clear night. They could do a little stargazing and enjoy a quiet dinner together. But Sandra's news had shattered his daydream. Desperate to make things right, he had broken the speed limit and more than a few traffic rules getting to Dee's place. He had asked Sandra to check what Dee had left in her desk drawer that had caused her to quit the job she so clearly enjoyed and was so good at. When she told him about the emails and Tally Barnes's presence at the time of Dee's departure, he tromped harder on the gas, thinking of nothing but making things right with Dee.

He went straight to her house, but no one was home. Dear God, he only hoped she hadn't caught the first plane out to who knew where. But there hadn't been enough time, he reassured himself. She was probably driving off some anger. He did that. He hoped she did too. In the meantime he headed back to Pneuma Inc. to find out as much as he could about what had happened.

His first stop was Dee's office. In spite of the jungle, the room felt desolate. Her desk was bare except for the Christmas cactus and a few neatly stacked files. The faint scent of her still lingered in the room like a subliminal footprint, stirring memory and inflicting pain with the knowledge of her absence. There was no note, no hint as to where she might have gone. He resisted the urge to search her desk. Sandra had already found the damnable emails, and it was still Dee's desk. However, Sandra hadn't relocked the middle drawer and something was wedged in it, preventing it from closing. When he tried to unstick it, he pulled it completely out, scattering the contents across the floor. He swallowed back a curse and his throat tightened at the sight of the zip-lock plastic bag in which Beverly had kept the articles on him and Pneuma Inc. she had collected for her scrap book. The clear plastic of the bag bulged with clippings and photos. As he lifted them to put them back in the drawer, he saw that the top one was dated just this morning. There was an interview with him in *Le Monde*. It had been a phone interview he'd done with Dee sitting by his side just before he went off to Valderia. She had been there to translate for him, though it hadn't been necessary since the reporter spoke perfect English. The photo was one of him shaking hands with Yvette Rousseau, smiling like the king of the universe, and that's how he'd felt. Only a few hours before, he'd been in the limo making love to Dee. The ache low in his chest was deep and serrated. Nearly half the clippings in the bag had been added since Dee had begun working at Pneuma Inc. He'd had no idea. He laid them carefully back in the drawer, promising himself he'd buy her a scrap book to put them in when everything was settled. And it would be settled. He was not about to let her go that easily.

Sandra met him in his office with the emails and the transcribed notes from the Trouvères/Scribal alliance meeting. He handed them back to her. 'Not now, Sandra, not until we can get to the bottom of what happened here.'

She refused them. 'I think you really need to see these, Ellis. The meeting was a disaster. Tally Barnes led it, and she clearly had no clue what was going on or what she was doing.'

Ellis took the transcript from her, scanning the notes. 'This is what happened?'

'Yes, sir, it is. My shorthand is flawless, if I do say so myself. That's exactly what was said. Quite enlightening, isn't it? Looks like Dee gave her just enough rope to hang herself. You should see the way she's slinking around this afternoon. I think she might be updating her resume.'

Another glance at the transcript knotted his insides. 'I don't think she'll need a resume to flip burgers.' Over the top of his glasses, he held the secretary's gaze. 'And when I'm finished, that'll be the only kind of work she'll be able to get. Did Dee mention anything about where she might go?'

'Only that she was going home. Wasn't she there?'

'No. She wasn't.'

'She was very upset.'

'With good reason.' He took off his glasses, and the words on the transcript slipped out of focus. 'You don't think she'd go to Paris, do you? The Rousseaus would snatch her away in a heartbeat if they could.'

'You can't let that happen, Ellis. You can't lose her. She's the best thing that ever happened to you.' The secretary's face reddened and she fidgeted in her seat. He'd seldom seen her agitated, and never without a damn good reason. 'I mean ... That is to say, Ms Henning is the best thing that ever happened to Pneuma Inc.'

He put his glasses back on and pushed the transcript aside. 'Sandra? How long have you known?'

For a second, she studied him in stiff silence, then the hard line of her jaw softened and she relaxed back into the chair. 'That you love her? From the beginning, Ellis.'

Her words were a searing revelation of the obvious that he'd somehow managed to miss. It was ironic that someone so good at reading other people's feelings had to have a secretary translate his own. How could he have missed it? The signs had been there all along. 'I was that transparent?'

'Of course not.' She reached out to touch his hand, thought better of it, and straightened the pens and pencils in the holder on the corner of his desk instead. 'It's just that you've been so happy. I've known you for a long time now, Ellis, longer than anyone else here, and this is the first time in all these years I've ever seen you really happy.'

She left him alone with the monumental task of finding Dee. He doubted she'd go to her mother in Salem. This wasn't the kind of thing one shared with a parent, especially not one who was guaranteed to say "I told you so". He prayed she wouldn't go off to Paris. He was sure Daniels would be waiting there with open arms to comfort her, and that was a thought he couldn't bear.

From the middle drawer of his desk, he pulled the copy of Dee's resume, and looked down at the photo. The ache he felt became ravenous. He shoved the resume aside and grabbed the phone. Twice he dropped the receiver before managing to punch in Dee's cell number, but there was still no answer.

He closed his eyes and tried to breathe around the growing tightness in his chest. How could he have been so stupid to think they could simply incorporate sex into their working relationship and keep it impersonal when it had already been personal long before he'd ever touched her?

He couldn't function like this. Certainly there'd be no concentrating on business when the only thing on his mind was Dee. There had to be some way of finding her, some way of making things right. He left instructions for the secretaries to call if they heard from Dee. Just before he left the office, the phone rang. It was Wade Crittenden with more enlightening news, and it was followed almost at once by a call from Garrett with still more enlightening news.

On the ninth floor, Tally Barnes waited for the elevator, still kicking herself that she had forced the issue with Dee before the meeting. She never dreamed the woman would call her bluff. The meeting had been a complete disaster, with her looking like a total fool. And that damned little secretary just kept taking down every stinking word. How could she have possibly foreseen this? She tried to calm herself. It didn't matter, not really. Jamison's plan was foolproof and once word had been leaked to the press, she could have any job at Pneuma Inc. she wanted. He'd promised her, and she'd done her part. More than her part.

She was thinking of how best to approach Jamison with the news of what had happened when the elevator arrived. She stepped inside and pushed the button before she realised Ellis was standing next to her, flanked by two security guards. A sudden wave of nausea clawed at her insides and her hands felt clammy against the files she clutched to her chest. She tried to smile at him.

He reached over and hit the stop button on the elevator, and her heart jumped. It wasn't anger she saw in his face, but a coldness she'd never seen before. And when he spoke, she felt the chill in her bones. 'What are you still doing here?'

'Ellis, I'm sorry about the meeting. I mean, I haven't had a chance to get up to speed on what's been …' Her gut clenched and her efforts to speak became breathless. 'I'm sorry about this afternoon.' She glanced nervously at the two guards. 'It was all a big mistake, I should have never –'

He ignored her. 'I had a phone call from Wade a little while ago. Seems you've been using his computer.'

For a second, it felt like the elevator floor would fall away. For a second, she wished to God it would. 'Ellis, I can explain.'

He took a step closer. 'You don't work here any more, Ms Barnes.' He held her in an arctic glare. 'What did you think would happen when Wade found out about your little game? And surely you should have known he would. Stealing documents from my executive assistant's office using Beverly's old password, that's bad enough, but sharing them with Terrance Jamison? Did you really think you could get away with it?'

Her knees gave. She grabbed for the elevator railing.

He moved still closer and, for a horrifying second, she feared she might throw up on him, but she clenched her jaw and swallowed hard, trying to focus on his words over the buzzing in her ears. 'These gentlemen will go with you while you clear out your office. They they'll escort you out. Go with them and I won't press charges. You don't, Ms Barnes, and I promise you'll be looking at serious jail time, and if you think for one second Jamison will come to your rescue under the circumstances, then you're a very stupid woman. Understood?'

She nodded.

He pushed the start button again. When the elevator opened on to the sixth floor she nearly fell out, pushing her way blindly through the people waiting at the door.

Escorted by the two security guards, she stumbled back to

her office, dug the phone Jamison had given her from her bag, and pulled up his number. He would make it all right. Surely he had a plan. Surely he could handle Ellis. Oh, he'd be angry at her, but he'd been angry since Ellis had trumped him in Valderia. She'd just have to buck up and take it, then he'd make everything all right. He still needed her. Surely he did. She waited. And waited. Then her insides froze. A mechanical voice on the other end informed her that the number she had reached was no longer in service.

Chapter Thirty-nine

AT HOME, MCALLISTER AND O'Kelly watched as Dee pulled a suitcase onto the bed and randomly tossed clothes into it. She didn't know where she was going, but there probably wasn't any place far enough away from here to ease her humiliation. She'd just go to the airport and pick a flight. Any flight would do at this point. She left a message with Kendra to ask if she could stay in the house and watch the cats again. She wasn't sure how long, but she'd give her the details when she had them. She was glad Kendra hadn't answered. The woman was tenacious when it came to figuring out what was going on, and Dee really didn't want to try to explain the situation right now.

The sense of betrayal and loss ached deep in her chest. Was it really just a few hours ago Ellis had talked of inviting her to his home? She had to admit that, more than anything, she'd miss the closeness they'd come to share. Well, she'd have to get over it. After all, it was just a part of the job, and it wasn't her job any more.

'You're prostituting yourself for the almighty dollar, that's all you're doing,' her mother had screamed at her when she started working for Jasper and McDowell. She could only imagine what her mother would say about her situation now. She was glad she hadn't told her.

It didn't take her long to pack. Ignoring the ringing of her BlackBerry, she threw the bag in the Audi and headed for PDX. She'd call Harris once she knew where she was going and have him pick up the car and take it back home from short-term parking.

At least her healthy finances meant she had options. When she was ready to return to the work force, she was pretty sure she could get Yvette to hire her in the mailroom, if nothing else. Living in Paris would certainly be a plus, though it would be hard to leave her friends. And she wasn't sure she was up for working with Jason.

In the meantime, she'd not been to Vienna to see her father since he moved. Seeing him would cost her, like always. He knew how to have a great time and would, no doubt, do his best to take her mind off things – as long as she paid. And she'd gladly pay if his efforts would work. Since she knew they wouldn't, she'd have to decide if she wanted to be miserable in an exotic place with a father she barely knew, or miserable in the comfort of her own home with friends who would never say "I told you so", no matter how much they might be thinking it.

Of course that would mean showing her face in public, all the while wondering if people were talking behind her back. She couldn't picture Tally Barnes keeping quiet about the Sex Clause. What an ego she had to think she mattered that much in the scheme of things. At worst, it would all blow over in a few weeks and no one would even remember who the hell Dee Henning was. Somehow that wasn't much comfort either.

She fought the traffic into the short-term parking garage at PDX still not entirely sure whether she'd go somewhere exotic or just get back on the freeway and drive. There were lots of gorgeous places in Oregon she could hole up until she felt able to face the world again, and they wouldn't involve her sitting for hours on an airplane, trying to hold herself together until she could get somewhere she could fall apart in private.

There was a red Jeep in the space next to hers. It reminded her of the last time she'd been in Ellis's Jeep. How could she ever have expected to keep something like the Executive Sex Clause a secret? If she were honest, she never really wanted to keep what was going on between her and Ellis a secret. In fact, the Executive Sex Clause seemed only a minor part of what the two of them had shared the past few months. She had never had such challenges and never shared the experience with such a worthy partner. It was all like a brilliant dream, and now it was time to wake up.

The waking world felt desolate without the challenges of Pneuma Inc. and the camaraderie of its CEO. Certainly she'd find no one who could understand and sympathise with her loss in Paris or Vienna. Ellis had betrayed her, she reminded herself. She should be furious. Instead, she felt a deluge of pain.

She sat for a long moment, the vision of the packed parking garage in front of her wavering in and out of focus as she fought back tears. Finally, she stopped fighting and let them come, let the pain of loss crash against her in waves, each one feeling as though it would pull her under and drown her. How could anything hurt so bad when she'd known Ellis such a short time?

She cried until there were no tears left to cry. Then she sat feeling dry and desolate until the world around her came back into focus and her mind was made up. There would be no going to Vienna, or to Paris. Her life, and the mess she'd made of it, was here, and that's where she'd face it. It wouldn't be easy, or pleasant, but at least here at home she wouldn't face it alone. She'd call Harris and see if she could use the lake house for a while. It would be good to get out of the city and into the countryside.

Harris answered after one ring. 'Dee, thank God! Are you all right? Where are you? Jesus, you had us worried stiff.'

'I'm all right. I'm at the airport.' Before she could say more he spoke again.

'Dee, you're not bringing sexual harassment charges against Ellis, are you?'

Her stomach dropped to her feet. 'What? Of course I'm not. I'd never do that. What the hell's going on?'

She could hear a heavy sigh on the other end of the line. 'Well, rumour's somehow gotten to the press that you're going to. Ellis is nowhere to be found. He's off looking for you, and Pneuma Inc. is crawling with press.'

'Jesus, Harris, does he think I would do such a thing?'

'I don't know what the hell he thinks, Dee. I've been here with Wade all day, working on the photos and putting together the article for *Wilderness Vanguard*. When you walked out, the shit really hit the fan. You've not been answering your phone, he's not been answering. I don't know what he thinks.'

Dee wiped a hand over her face, then squared her shoulders. 'Put Wade on the line, will you?'

Before the man could do more than say hi, she spoke. 'Wade I need you to get Sandra to call a press conference. If the press wants a statement, I'll give them one. I can be back to Pneuma in an hour at the most. I'm betting this is Jamison's doing, and if Ellis won't defend himself I will. I'll be there as soon as I can.'

She hung up without saying goodbye, then punched in Ellis's number, her throat clenching tight when he picked up almost before the phone could ring.

'Dee. Dear God, where are you? I've looked all over. We have to talk.'

'I'm heading back to Pneuma Inc., Ellis. I've asked Sandra to call a press conference right away, and you need to be there.'

For a second, there was silence, and Dee wondered if she'd lost the signal, then he said, 'I'm on my way.' The phone went dead.

It was only when Dee relaxed the suicide grip on the phone that she noticed there were a dozen text and at least that many missed calls from Ellis. There were several from Kendra and Harris and even a couple from Garrett. She'd have to listen to them later. Right now, she needed to get to the Pneuma Building and end this. Even if she could no longer work for Ellis, even if he had broken her confidence, it still wasn't sexual harassment, and no matter what had happened between them, the man didn't deserve this. She'd make it clear to the press that Ellis had done nothing out of line, then, once the press conference was out of the way, she'd call Harris and Kendra. They were her friends. In spite of their warnings about the Sex Clause, in spite of the mess she'd made of things, they would understand and love her anyway.

Chapter Forty

ELLIS TURNED OFF HIS BlackBerry, stunned. For a horrible moment it felt as though all the oxygen had vanished and he'd never be able to breathe again. Even when the moments of panic passed and the next breath was no longer in doubt, the part that felt most horrible still remained. So Dee really was going to bring him up on charges, then? He felt an icy chill inside that had nothing to do with the legal implications for himself or Pneuma. That his reputation would be damaged mattered far less than the implication that what had happened between Dee and him had meant so little to her. That she had really believed he could have broken her confidence felt like a knife in his chest. He would take whatever she dished out to him. He had, after all, started it all in Paris when he couldn't keep his hands off her. He deserved it, he supposed. It didn't matter. It didn't change how he felt.

So he would take it, settle out of court, give her whatever she wanted and move on. Though, at the moment, it was hard to imagine there'd ever be anything worth moving on to again. But he would still have the balls to be there to face his accuser. He wanted to look her in the eyes. He wanted to see her face when she accused him, when she said what happened was just an unethical wealthy bastard taking advantage. The thought caused bile to rise in his throat. Everything he hated, everything that repulsed him, everything that he'd worked so hard not to be a part of that involved money and power misused – he would now stand silently before the woman he loved while she accused him of just those things. He supposed he should call his lawyers, but he just couldn't bring himself to do it. He drove back into Portland feeling like the world had somehow opened beneath him and swallowed up his life and everything in it that mattered.

He would have been back to Pneuma Inc. in 20 minutes if not for the construction on I-5.

Dee would have rather skipped the trip to the Dungeon and hid out in her office until time to face the press, but Wade had made her promise to stop by as soon as she got to the Pneuma Building. She figured it was more so he and Harris could make sure she was fit to face the press, but she could certainly understand their concern after the way she'd cut and run. Best get it over with.

The din of raised voices and what sounded like something hitting the wall with a splat assured Dee, even before she entered the Dungeon, that Kendra was in the building. She felt a sudden surge of sympathy for Wade, having to referee the warring sides, but that was no longer her problem, and Stacie and Garrett would just have to fend for themselves against the other two-thirds of the Three Musketeers. She wasn't very sympathetic.

Inside there was a huge splash of what she figured must be Diet Coke running down the wall above Wade's ratty leather sofa, which was covered with ice and a smashed soft drink cup. Kendra stood with her arms folded across her chest, looking like lightning ready to strike. Garrett stood beside Stacie next to the ruined sofa, looking as though he'd like to make a run for it.

Before she could completely take in the war zone, Harris scooped her into his arms in a bear hug that was nearly bone-breaking. Kendra ploughed in next to him, practically smothering her in the effort.

'Are you all right?' Harris spoke fiercely against her ear, 'Jesus, Dee, don't ever do that to us again! You had us so worried.'

'God Dee, I'm so, so sorry.' Garrett seemed willing to risk life and limb by stepping forward. 'You can't really believe Ellis would ever deliberately hurt you. He –'

Before he could finish, Kendra whirled so quickly that no

one saw it coming, and slapped him with a smack that sounded like the crack of a whip. He recoiled and cursed.

'You shut up!' she yelled. 'You don't have the right to talk to her, not after what you've done.'

He straightened and wiped a hand across his watering eyes. But before he could respond, Stacie said, 'I think it's best to keep your mouth shut, Garrett.'

Then Kendra turned on her. 'Oh, and look who the fuck is talking? That's really rich, one big mouth telling another to be quiet.'

Stacie bristled. 'Oh right, and you come marching in here like you know something, like you know what you're talking about.'

Dee was sure Stacie was about to receive some of what Garrett had gotten, but Harris grabbed Kendra by the arm and pulled her back. 'Stop it, Ken. Leave it.' His voice was soft, dangerously soft.

'Finally, level heads prevail,' Stacie said. 'If you'd just listen, just let us explain –'

Harris cut her off at the pass. 'Kendra's a lightweight compared to me, lady, so don't push it.'

The Dungeon erupted in chaos, with everyone yelling at once and accusations flying fast and furious until a loud, shrill whistle cut through the noise. They all turned to find Wade standing with a referee whistle in his hand. 'Shut the fuck up, all of you. Now!'

The room fell silent. Harris and Kendra moved to flank Dee. Garrett and Stacie stood behind Wade's raised arm like they were waiting for a traffic cop to give the all clear for crossing a busy street.

'Dee, we never meant to hurt you, either of you. That's the last thing we wanted,' Garrett managed before Wade placed a brusque finger to his lips.

When he was satisfied with the resulting silence, Wade turned his attention back to Dee.

'You all right?'

She was sure he knew the answer to that, but she squared her shoulders and nodded. 'I'll manage.'

'You'd better go, then,' he said. 'Sandra's waiting for you, and the press is gathering in the atrium.' He glanced around the room at the angry factions glaring at each other. 'I'll keep the peace.'

Dee started to leave, then turned back and threw her arms around Wade. 'It's been a real pleasure working with you,' she said, struggling to keep her voice neutral, to keep emotion as far away as she could for as long as she could, at least until after the press conference, then she could safely fall to pieces. Before he managed more than an awkward pat on her back, she turned and left.

Back in her office, Dee paced the floor. Ellis was stuck in traffic. He'd called his secretary, not her. It had hurt that he'd done that, and it made her angry that it hurt. What did she expect him to do? What did she want him to do? The damage had been done. There could be no going back to how it was. Now the whole world knew, or at least strongly suspected. But she still wouldn't let that bastard Jamison destroy a man who was a hundred times the man he'd ever be.

The place had been like a madhouse since she'd returned to Pneuma. Sandra had informed her that Tally Barnes had been fired for selling information to Terrance Jamison. It came as no real surprise, after all the woman had put her through.

It was still a struggle to get her head round the fact that she didn't work for Pneuma Inc. any more. She'd find a graceful way to exit without the press knowing as soon as they could stop Jamison in his tracks. It was about damage control now, she told herself. That was all. And still she ached with an emptiness she'd not known before. How could this place, and the man who created it, matter so much to her in such a short time?

There was a gentle knock on her door. Sandra stuck her head inside. 'You've got to go down, Dee. You've kept them waiting long enough. Ellis will be here when he gets here. Even the press will understand construction work on I-5.'

The words were encouraging, but Dee knew they weren't true. Without Ellis by her side, the press would only assume his lawyers were keeping them in separate rooms and that she was being paid off to keep her mouth shut. Without him by her side, she wasn't sure she could get them off the fresh blood scent of sensationalism, and that's exactly what it would be: Ellis's name splashed all over the papers, caught in a sex scandal, a sex scandal that never happened. But that wouldn't matter to the press, would it? They didn't care.

'Dee?' Sandra said quietly.

Dee forced a smile and prepared to leave the room. 'All right, Sandra, time to face the music.' The secretary flanked her, feeling almost like a bodyguard, and Dee was sure she couldn't have had a better one.

In the hall, Lynn gave them a nod. 'He'll be there as soon as he can and he'll go straight to the atrium.'

For a sick second, Dee wondered if she could possibly distract them for a few minutes with a ballad from *Cats*. Her mother would be pleased if she finally got the chance to use her musical talents.

In the elevator, she checked her appearance one last time. She looked every bit the professional she was. But at the moment she felt anything but. She felt like she wanted to crawl into a corner and cry for the next few weeks or so. That would have to wait. The elevator opened. A part of the main atrium had been quickly set up for the press conference and her stomach did a little clench when she saw just how full the space was.

She barely had time for a quick breath before the first reporter caught sight of her, the first camera flashed, a murmur passed through the crowded room. She took a deep breath, squared her shoulders, and made her way up to the podium, through the flash of cameras and the whispers of the reporters. None of that mattered. All that mattered at the moment was that she do all she could to make sure Ellis's reputation remained undamaged by everything that had happened.

For a long second, she looked out over the sea of expectant faces. A camera flashed, and then silence fell. All eyes were on her. Now was the time to do what Dee Henning had earned a reputation for over at Jasper and McDowell: building bridges, making connections, and earning people's trust. She offered what she was certain passed for a relaxed smile.

Ellis froze at the elevator door, just out of sight of the reporters and cameras, his eyes locked on Dee as she mounted the podium, took in her audience with a calm smile, and addressed them with the sure, quiet confidence he'd come to expect from her. In spite of what he was anticipating, he felt proud.

For a brief second, she looked around her audience, almost as though she were making eye contact with every single person there, almost as though she spoke to each one personally. A camera flashed. She paused for another fraction of a breath and Ellis could see the whole audience pressing forward toward her as she began to speak.

'The opportunity to work for Pneuma Inc. under the tutelage of Ellison Thorne is every MBA student, every aspiring executive's dream. I was no exception. And when I was given the opportunity, of course I jumped at the chance. But I wasn't prepared.'

The knot in Ellis's chest felt like it would choke him. He stood paralysed, unable to move, waiting for the accusation. He should move now. He should move to face her, to stand next to her while she told the world about the Executive Sex Clause. But he couldn't move, he couldn't breathe. He felt the press of Wade, who, out of nowhere, now flanked him on his right. Lynn stood to the left policing his brother and Stacie and Harris Walker and some other woman he'd never met. Probably another one of Dee's friends waiting to tear him a new one once Walker got through with him. It didn't matter; none of it mattered any more. Even surviving the next moment seemed questionable as he braced himself.

Dee took a deep breath and continued. 'How could I have been prepared to step into the shoes of another one of my heroes, and a dear friend, Beverly Neumann, after her tragic death? And yet, Ellis Thorne took me on board, unprepared as I was. And the experience has been way beyond anything I could put into words.'

'Ms Henning,' one brash reporter in the front row

interrupted, his arms folded defiantly across an ill-fitting sports jacket. 'Did Ellison Thorne sexually harass you?'

There was a murmur among the crowd. Ellis would have flattened the man if Wade hadn't grabbed him by the elbow. But then Dee always could take care of herself.

'Mr Pittman – that is your name, isn't it?' she said.

The man nodded. He seemed surprised that she knew who he was.

'Please let me finish?' Before the man could do more than offer a couple of fish gasps, Dee continued, 'Ellison Thorne most certainly did not harass me sexually, or any other way, and I find the idea that anyone could even think such a thing totally absurd. Every one of you in this room has covered the man and his company extensively at one time or another. Surely you knew better. All of you.'

Again there was a murmur among the crowd. And for a second Ellis heard nothing else, felt as though he'd just been saved from certain death. There was air in his lungs, and it was sweet. There was light pouring in through the atrium's large windows, and it was suddenly brilliant. It wasn't that she hadn't accused him so much as it was she had defended him. Dee Henning had defended him.

'Then where is he, if he's as morally upright as you say?' The rude reporter up front said again. 'And why are you here alone?'

And suddenly Ellis came back to himself. 'She's not here alone,' he said, feeling all eyes suddenly on him. 'I was delayed by construction on I-5.' There was a nod of understanding as he moved up between the reporters to the podium, his eyes locked on Dee. Her eyes locked on him. The flash of cameras was suddenly nothing but a minor peripheral irritation.

For a second, the two stood gazing in each other's eyes, surrounded by the expectant silence of the reporters, and Ellis wished like hell everyone would go away. There was so much he needed to say to Dee, so much he wanted to make right, and every second he had to wait to do that seemed like an eternity.

But the abrasive Mr Pittman would not be put off. 'Mr

Thorne, did you sleep with Ms Henning?'

For a second, Ellis ignored him, not wanting to take his eyes off Dee. Then he turned to face the sea of reporters all splashed with sunlight from the atrium's skylight and brushed with the shadows of fronds and leaves and flowers that softened the space of glass and steel, fronds and leaves and flowers that Beverly had insisted upon. He looked out over the space he and Beverly and Wade had created together, and it seemed more beautiful than he ever remembered it being. He took one more quick glance at Dee, who shone brighter than anything else in the room, then addressed Mr Pittman and everyone else in the room, and everyone else in the world. 'Yes, I slept with Dee Henning.'

Dee gave a little gasp of surprise and grabbed on to the podium for support, and the crowd erupted in chaos. Once again, cameras flashed like lightning. Ellis moved closer to Dee, gave her arm a reassuring squeeze, then raised a hand, and the room fell silent. 'I've slept with her more than once, and I hope to do it again soon.' He leaned forward over the podium. The crowd was deathly silent. 'First of all, if you've done your homework –' his gaze came to rest on the pale face of Mr Pittman '– you'll already know Ms Henning's credentials are impeccable. Her talents, her enthusiasm for the company's unique philosophy, mean that Pneuma Inc. was damn lucky to get her before someone else snapped her up. In the short time she's been here she's already become indispensable. She's making this a richer, more well-rounded company. Just so you know. Secondly, as far as I know there's no law against a man sleeping with the woman he loves.'

Dee gave a little sob of surprise, and clutched at the podium with both hands. Cautiously, he slipped an arm around her waist for support and, blessedly, she didn't push him away. He addressed the press again. 'Most of you know I believe private lives should be private, and I've always attempted to keep mine that way.' He gave them a hard stare. 'Yes, I'm aware of all the speculation; everything from me being gay to me being a closet dom who runs a secret dungeon. So now I'm going to tell you the truth. And the truth is that some things weren't meant to be kept secret. I handled the situation poorly.'

He shot Dee a sideways glance. He could see her pulse hammering wildly in the tender spot of her neck, the part he loved to kiss, the part he loved to feel flutter against his lips, against his tongue. 'Though it seems I may have been the last one to figure it out, I did finally figure it out, and now that I have, the fact I love Dee Henning is not a secret. Nor do I want it to be.'

With a hand he was sure the ill-mannered Mr Pittman would note was none too steady, he reach out to cup Dee's cheek. Her eyes fluttered. Her breath hitched, and his heart pounded like it was desperate to get closer to her. The cameras went crazy, but still Dee Henning didn't pull away from him. Feeling giddy with the nearness of her, with the fact that she had stood up for him, he took a risk, leaned in and brushed a kiss across her lips. And still she didn't pull away.

'Now,' he said, still holding her gaze, 'if there are no further questions ...' He turned to look out over the sea of faces daring any of them to question him further when all he wanted to do was have Dee to himself. Even the tenacious Mr Pittman was silent. 'If you'll excuse us, we have a business to run.'

The silence was stunning as the press parted like the Red Sea to let Ellis and Dee through.

She didn't protest, his arm around her waist gently guiding her. She wasn't sure she could have walked without it, and certainly she would have never made a scene. But he did. She was reeling at the scene he'd just made. Ellison Thorne, *the* Ellison Thorne, had just told a roomful of reporters, equipped with cameras and hungry for a scandal, that not only had he slept with her but he loved her. It was a dream. Surely it had to be a dream. When they reached the bank of elevators, even her friends and Garrett and Stacie moved aside for them.

They rode the elevator in silence to the tenth floor and the Executive Suites, which they had completely to themselves with the secretaries downstairs, no doubt still dealing with the reporters.

Inside his office, Ellis closed and locked the door behind them and guided her to the sofa in the lounge. Dee could never remember the coffee table in front not being buried in a constantly changing array of books, none of which had anything to do with business. She suspected Ellis had spent more than a few nights on that sofa.

When he reached for her, she stepped back. 'Did you mean what you said out there?'

He blinked hard, as though he couldn't believe she'd just asked that. The hurt on his face almost made her wish she hadn't. 'Of course I meant it.' He held her gaze over the top of his glasses. 'Every word.'

Before she could respond, he pulled her to him and kissed her hard. When he released her, reeling from the feel of him, the feel she thought she'd never have again, she dropped onto the sofa, weak-kneed and unable to stand. He sat down next to her, gripping her hand between his as though he were afraid she might bolt. 'I didn't betray you, Dee. I would never ever do that to the woman I love. Tally Barnes, I fired. Garrett and Stacie – well, they've both got big mouths, and they try way too hard. I can't do anything about that. But they were right. I shouldn't be keeping a secret of how I feel about you.' He cupped her face. 'I was keeping it a secret from myself too, but not any more. I can't lose you, Dee. I can't.'

She stopped trying to blink back the tears and viewed him through a shimmering mist. 'But what about the Sex Clause?'

'I don't want the Sex Clause, Dee. I never wanted the Sex Clause. What I want is something a hell of a lot more comprehensive than that, something legally binding.' His eyes were feverish, pupils dilated in the sunlight now bronzing with the approach of evening. 'It was only when I thought I was losing you that I realised the sex was good because I love you, Dee, and not because there were no strings attached. I've loved you almost from the start, from the very first time we made love on the floor here by the sofa. You had my heart, even then. I just didn't understand. But I do understand now, and I don't want to be without you, Dee, not ever. I want to come home with you in the evenings and wake up with you in the morning.' Laughing softly, he kissed her knuckles. 'And still have sex in the elevator and in the Jeep. Married people can do that, can't they?'

The beat of her heart suddenly felt like the pounding of a huge drum. She was almost certain now that she was dreaming. These were not the kind of negotiations she was used to, and her calm neutrality had gone out the window when Ellis dropped the bomb at the press conference. She spoke around a hiccup of a sob. 'This is a proposal, then?'

'Of course it's a proposal. It's what I've wanted all along. I hope desperately that it's what you want too.'

She snuffled back tears, and tried to laugh, but it came out more like the sound of a startled bird. 'Let's hope you still feel that way after 50 or 60 years.'

He did his own imitation of a startled bird. His voice was tight against his throat, laced with emotion he no longer made any attempt to hide. 'Does that mean you're accepting my proposal?'

'Oh, I'm accepting it, all right. I'm a businesswoman, remember? I know a good deal when I see one.'

His gaze moved over her, suddenly warm and hungry, making her feel heat that didn't come from the sun filtering through the huge windows. Then he pushed her back on the sofa, wriggling and manoeuvring until the two lay nestled tightly in the small space, and he pulled her still closer, knocking his glasses askew in the process.

She removed them for him and shoved them onto the coffee table, surprised and touched to find his eyes were misty too; not that he gave her much time to think about it. Not that he gave her much time to think at all as his mouth found hers and his embrace tightened. For her part, she was definitely ready to move forward with this win-win deal. And after experiencing life full-on with Pneuma Inc. and its amazing CEO for the last few months, she was very much looking forward to enjoying a level of intimacy that went way beyond the Executive Sex Clause.